Mickey Spillane
on Screen

Mickey Spillane on Screen

A Complete Study of the Television and Film Adaptations

MAX ALLAN COLLINS and
JAMES L. TRAYLOR

McFarland & Company, Inc., Publishers
Jefferson, North Carolina, and London

Library of Congress Cataloguing-in-Publication Data

Collins, Max Allan.
Mickey Spillane on screen : a complete study of the television and film adaptations / Max Allan Collins and James L. Traylor.
p. cm.
Includes bibliographical references and index.

ISBN 978-0-7864-6578-1
softcover : acid free paper ∞

1. Spillane, Mickey, 1918–2006—Film adaptations.
2. Spillane, Mickey, 1918–2006—Television adaptations.
3. Detective and mystery stories, American—Film adaptations.
4. Detective and mystery stories, American—Television adaptations.
5. Film adaptations—History and criticism. 6. Television adaptations—History and criticism. 7. Detective and mystery films—History and critisism.
8. Detective and mystery television programs—history and criticism.
I. Traylor, James L. II. Title.
PS3537.P652Z59 2012 794.43'6556—dc23 2012015541

British Library cataloguing data are available

On the cover: Mickey Spillane gets tough in a staged still promoting the film *Ring of Fear* (other actor unknown) (1954 Wayne-Fellows Production, distributed by Warner Bros.); background image © 2012 Shutterstock

Manufactured in the United States of America

McFarland & Company, Inc., Publishers
Box 611, Jefferson, North Carolina 28640
www.mcfarlandpub.com

For our favorite screen Mike Hammers—
Biff Elliot
Ralph Meeker
Darren McGavin
Armand Assante
Stacy Keach
and
Mickey Spillane

Table of Contents

Appendices

Acknowledgments: A Tip of the Porkpie Hat

Since the publication of our initial book on Mickey Spillane, *One Lonely Knight: Mickey Spillane's Mike Hammer* (1984), the authors have continued to closely follow the writer's life and career, examining his body of work extensively.

Co-author Collins collaborated with Spillane on various projects, including the *Mike Danger* comic book and numerous anthologies, and is currently working to arrange and sometimes finish the wealth of uncompleted material in the late author's files.

These uncompleted works included the non-series crime novel *Dead Street* (2008) and the long-delayed sequel to *The Delta Factor* (1967), *The Consummata* (2011), and perhaps most significantly, the six unfinished Mike Hammer novels entrusted to Collins shortly before Spillane's death. Also, Collins' 1999 documentary, *Mike Hammer's Mickey Spillane*, has been screened at film festivals internationally and was recently revised and updated for inclusion on the Criterion Collection's DVD/Blu-ray release of "Kiss Me Deadly."

Co-author Traylor has continued to write about Mickey Spillane in various articles, reviews and biographical entries (sometimes alone, sometimes with co-author Collins), including but not limited to *The St. James Guide to Crime & Mystery Writers*. The authors have written about Spillane in such magazines as *Mystery Fancier*, *Armchair Detective*, *Mystery Scene*, *Journal of Popular Culture*, *Videoscope*, *Video Watchdog*, and *Psychotronic Video*.

Together and separately, we interviewed Mike Hammer's creator on several occasions. Mickey Spillane inspired us both in many ways: our love of mystery novels and the hard-boiled PI, our appreciation of a style of writing that has come to be called "*noir*" (by way of French film critics), and of course our high regard for the talent and artistry that this giant in multi-media possessed. At every opportunity, Mickey encouraged our best efforts, all the while sharing his humanity and down-to-earth nature. This book reflects not just our love for his work, but his encouragement and friendship.

The first challenge of writing about the translation of prose fiction to film and television is obtaining copies of the movies and television shows. With Spillane, this was occasionally problematic. Fully half of the material has never been officially released to the public. "I, the Jury" (1953), "The Long Wait" (1954), "The Delta Factor" (1970), the one-hour episodes of the CBS-TV series "Mickey Spillane's Mike Hammer" (1984–85), CBS-TV's "The New Mike Hammer" (1986–87), and the telefilms "The Return of Mickey Spillane's Mike Hammer" (April 18, 1986), "Murder Take All" (May 21, 1989), and "Come Die with Me" (December 6, 1994) are not, and have never been, commercially available.

"Margin for Murder" (1981) and "I, the Jury" (1982) saw home-video release only on

VHS. "The Girl Hunters" (1963) has been sporadically available since the dawn of home video, but not in a wide-screen edition until Castle Hill's March 2000 release. Other material became accessible only relatively recently. "Ring of Fear" (1954) was released in 2005 in a DVD boxed set with three other John Wayne–produced features. "My Gun Is Quick" (1957) became available on demand from MGM's limited edition collection in 2011, as did the syndicated TV series "Mickey Spillane's Mike Hammer" (1958–59), a multiple-disc boxed set from A & E. The 1997–1998 syndicated "Mickey Spillane's Mike Hammer, Private Eye" is available from Tango Entertainment in a handsome package with an informative booklet.

Other material was accessed via "gray market" Internet sources. Our friend (and Spillane scholar) Lynn Myers tracked down the elusive Brian Keith Hammer pilot, which now is included on co-author Collins' DVD boxed set "The Black Box: Shades of Neo-Noir" (2005) from Troma (with the earlier, longer cut of the documentary "Mike Hammer's Mickey Spillane"). "I, the Jury" and "The Long Wait" came from the collection of co-author Collins, video-taped off a PBS station in the 1970s.

The authors have corresponded with and/or interviewed an array of individuals notably associated with Spillane. These include Spillane's youngest daughter, Caroline; Ruth Boyer, his classmate at Kansas State Teacher's College, Manhattan, Kansas; Jon Gerrity, son of writer Dave Gerrity, Spillane's longtime friend from Newburgh, New York; George Wilson, Spillane's "buddy" dating to the days of the Army Air Corps in Greenwood, Mississippi; Don Watts, who became Spillane's friend after the writer moved to South Carolina in the early 1950s; Shirley Eaton, Spillane's co-star in the film "The Girl Hunters"; actress Lee Meredith, "the Doll," who shared wonderful stories of her long association with Mickey as a Miller Lite All Star; the late TV producer Jay Bernstein, Mickey's friend and collaborator; Stacy Keach, the definitive Hammer of several generations; and Jane Spillane, Mickey's gracious widow.

Early mainstream criticism and reviews of both the Spillane novels and movies and TV shows were not kind. For example, "I, the Jury" received a two-star evaluation in Steven H. Scheuer's *TV Key Movie Reviews & Ratings* (1961): "Film version of Mickey Spillane story lacks violence, sex and excitement." Eight years later, Leonard Maltin echoed that rating in his famous *Movie Guide*. Scheuer's assessment of "The Long Wait" was similar: "Spillane adventure about amnesiac victim falsely accused of murder. Even Spillane fans will be disappointed." *TV Key* did not even bother to review "My Gun Is Quick."

In addition to Scheuer and Maltin, other standard sources were consulted: Tim Brooks and Earle Marsh's *The Complete Directory to Prime Time Network and Cable TV Shows: 1946-Present*; Richard Meyers' *TV Detectives*; *The Rough Guide to Cult Movies*; Barry Forshaw's *The Rough Guide to Crime Fiction*; and Leslie Halliwell's *The Filmgoer's Companion*. A special thank you goes to Kristi Finefield, reference librarian, Prints and Photographs Division, Library of Congress, who helped co-author Traylor through its maze of material.

Elliot Lavine and Bob Stephens' article "Dark Voyage: A Passage through 25 Years of Film Noir" in *The Perfect Vision*, Fall 1992, provides insights on "Kiss Me Deadly." Also helpful was J. Hoberman's article "The Thriller of Tomorrow," included in the Criterion booklet accompanying "Kiss Me Deadly."

Two directors of Spillane films have autobiographies, which are quoted in these pages: *Evergreen: Victor Saville in His Own Words* and *Light Your Torches and Pull Up Your Tights* by Tay Garnett with Fredda Dudley Balling.

Several film noir historians and devotees have offered help and advice. These include Shadow pulp expert Will Murray, who provided additional clues about the mysterious "Frank

Morris" who—in the waning years of the pulp magazines—contributed stories that were either written by Spillane or in imitation of him. Pulp historian Stephen Mertz, who knows as much about Spillane's idol Carroll John Daly as anyone, was especially insightful.

The wonders of the Internet, including YouTube, Facebook, and a myriad of helpful web sites, proved a lively source of information. For example, several actors who portrayed Mike Hammer—the late Darren McGavin, Stacy Keach and Biff Elliot—have web sites. Some sites, such as IMDB (the Internet Movie Database) and Turner Classic Movies, are more trustworthy than others, but all supply leads and hints toward the discovery of elusive facts. For instance, Spillane's old high school Erasmus Hall has a wonderful site with information about its famous alumnus. Similarly, Kansas State College's site also provided valuable information.

Finally, the authors acknowledge their own work, *One Lonely Knight: Mickey Spillane's Mike Hammer,* where we first discussed these films, telefilms and TV series in much less detail. We have drawn upon material from that out-of-print work, but have extensively rewritten, expanded and (frankly) re-thought our views, revisiting virtually every film and TV show discussed there and here. We have substantially changed a number of our opinions—for example, "The Long Wait" and the McGavin TV series have both risen in our shared view, while "The Girl Hunters" has perhaps dropped a notch. Only the discussion of "I, the Jury" (1982) draws directly from that source, however, and we hope this work indicates the fluid nature of the study of popular culture.

For clarity, in a work that frequently discusses a novel and a film of the same title, we use italics for novels and quotes for films, TV series and episodes.

Our format is generally to begin with historical background and critical commentary on a film, telefilm or TV series, followed by a synopsis interwoven with more commentary, and then a few final thoughts. Where the films are concerned, there are no "spoiler" warnings (other than this one). In the case of TV episodes and most of the telefilms, we have avoided revealing the identity of the bad guy or gal, unless the telefilm has made no secret of it.

All photographs are either studio publicity material or behind-the-scenes shots provided by (and with the permission of) Mickey Spillane Publishing, LLC.

Introduction

Mickey Spillane on the set of "I, the Jury" (1953), seated by a Stereovision 3-D camera.

While the name Mickey Spillane continues to resonate through popular culture, explaining to anyone born after 1970 the enormous impact of this king of the hardboiled mystery writers is next to impossible.

Recent generations know Spillane chiefly from his astonishing eighteen-year run as a spokesman for Miller Lite Beer—in a trenchcoated persona spoofing both himself and his fiction—and the various Stacy Keach-starring "Mike Hammer" telefilms and television series of the '80s and '90s.

For those of you who came in late....

Mickey Spillane was the most popular—and reviled—mystery writer of the immediate postwar era, his reign extending into the 1970s despite a sporadic output. As a former comic book scripter and World War II fighter pilot, the burly wordsmith tapped into the psyche of his fellow veterans, giving them action-packed, sex-drenched novels that reflected the kind of books he himself would have liked to read, had anyone else been writing them.

Though the shocking violence and steamy sexuality of the Hammer novels caught the attention of an adoring public and condemning critics, Spillane the writer (never "author," a term he despised) is characterized by a rough-hewn surrealism and a thematic bent for vengeance.

Spillane crafted a seemingly tossed-off tough guy first-person prose that was both accessible and idiosyncratic, and most of his novels—*I, the Jury* (1947), *My Gun Is Quick* (1950), *Vengeance Is Mine!* (1951)—run on engines fueled by personal retribution. Blue-collar, unpretentious Spillane opened the floodgates for franker, more violent popular fiction, and set a pattern for vigilante heroes followed by Dirty Harry, James Bond, John Shaft, Billy Jack, Jack Bauer, and just about every vengeful movie/novel/TV loner you can think of. The James Bond film "The World Is Not Enough" (1999), in which the secret agent kills his murderous lover, takes a page—specifically, the *last* page—out of Spillane's seminal novel, *I, the Jury* (1947).

Movies of Spillane's bestsellers—the first '50s spate produced by expatriate Britisher Victor Saville—were popular but perhaps not to the expected degree of wild enthusiasm (witness "Gone with the Wind" and the Harry Potter films). Certainly the Spillane pictures were not embraced by Mike Hammer's creator. "I, the Jury," (1953) and "Kiss Me Deadly" (1955, minus Spillane's characteristic direct-address comma) did prove modestly successful at the box office. But "I, the Jury" a rare 3-D noir with considerable attributes—including superb cinematography from the esteemed John Alton, and a haunting score from the great composer Franz Waxman—remains little seen in recent years and unfairly dismissed. And it has taken decades for that definitive film *noir* "Kiss Me Deadly" to achieve a status of high critical regard, at least in America—the French knew immediately it was a masterpiece.

Victor Saville had not anticipated two key problems that stood in the way of filming these stories: Spillane's violence and sex were strong medicine for the era, *too* strong; and the first-person nature of the Mike Hammer character (described by his creator as "a state of mind") made the private eye's satisfactory translation to the screen difficult if not impossible.

The television Mike Hammers—Darren McGavin in the '50s, Keach in the '80s and '90s—were effective if not definitive, with McGavin's very tough Hammer appearing with neither the private eye's trademark .45 automatic nor lovely secretary/partner, Velda. Keach was strong in a campy updating that made Mike Hammer a fedora-sporting, politically incorrect anachronism in the "modern" 1980s. Both television versions benefit from the skill the two actors bring the voiceover narration that does indeed suggest the first-person style of the novels.

Arguably the best screen Hammer—Ralph Meeker in "Kiss Me Deadly"—represented the anti–Spillane vision of director Aldrich and screenwriter A. I. Bezzerides, liberals who deplored the conservative mystery writer's "fascist" fantasies. Almost by accident, Aldrich and Bezzerides achieved a kind of paperback perfection, conveying the surrealism and underlying nihilism of Hammer's world, and capturing the feel and mood of the novels more completely than a faithful acolyte ever could.

Even such acceptable screen Hammers as Biff Elliot and Armand Assante in the two versions (1953 and 1982) of "I, the Jury" were subject to (unfairly) withering reviews largely because the actors could not live up to the disparate mental visions of the character Spillane's prose had conjured, a character the writer had never described, to encourage reader identification.

Spillane tried to take a hand in the casting of the Victor Saville-produced films, rather typically reaching out to a good friend, ex-cop Jack Stang, a towering, Palance-pussed brute. The writer claimed Stang was his ideal Hammer, pitching him unsuccessfully to producer Saville, even filming, writing and directing (around 1954) a short, unfortunately lost sixteen-millimeter test film starring Stang as Hammer.

The test led to Stang appearing as a Hammer-style detective in the oddball Batjac production, "Ring of Fear" (1954). The circus-themed thriller stars Clyde Beatty and his circus, with Pat O'Brien and other real actors joining amateurs Stang as Hammer and Spillane as himself in a psycho-on-the-loose-under-the-big top tale ghost-revised by Spillane, at producer John Wayne's request.

Stang—who also appeared in a small role in "I, the Jury"—was towering but not charismatic, and "Ring of Fear" director James Edward Grant (a frequent Wayne collaborator) tossed much of the detective work and dialogue to Spillane, who comes across as natural and Mike Hammer-ish himself, right down to a final confrontation scene with the villain.

After "Ring of Fear," Spillane increased an already displayed tendency to pose with guns in Hammer-appropriate attire in publicity and book-jacket photos (including publicity photos from the circus thriller), the blurring of creator and character further achieved by self-spoofing TV appearances with the likes of Milton Berle and Johnny Carson. An early 1960s Lifebuoy soap commercial foreshadowed the long-running Miller Lite campaign to come.

So perhaps it was inevitable that Spillane—disgusted with Hollywood's attempts—would script, produce and star as Hammer himself in a film of one of his novels. Just how strange and wonderful this is can only be addressed by a series of rhetorical questions ... can we imagine Conan Doyle portraying Sherlock Holmes on screen? Edgar Rice Burroughs wearing Tarzan's loincloth? Probably not, though we could stretch a point to accept Dashiell Hammett as Sam Spade and Agatha Christie as Miss Marple, perhaps, and certainly Ian Fleming as Bond.

Probably more to the point, imagine the disappointment of seeing Raymond Chandler as Phillip Marlowe or the cringe-worthy spectacle of Robert B. Parker as Spenser. Spillane was the rare author of popular fiction who physically resembled the type of superhero he writes about—broad-shouldered, steely-eyed, with a Dick Tracy hawkish noise and a commanding physical presence, Mickey Spillane IS Mike Hammer ... which is exactly the way he's billed in "The Girl Hunters."

If the film version of "The Girl Hunters" was, then, something of a stunt—part of canny Spillane's attempt to make up for lost time after a self-imposed hiatus of a decade, meaning to reinstate himself as *the* writer of suspense fiction—he was not entirely successful.

Though his books in the 1960s and '70s were invariably bestsellers, the pop culture landscape was changing beneath him. A writer who Signet Books, Spillane's reprint publisher, had promoted as "the British Mickey Spillane"—Ian Fleming—was destined to bump Hammer's creator out of the top spot. Spillane would even create his own secret agent, Tiger Mann, to compete with James Bond.

Tiger Mann, however, has as of this writing found his way to neither the large nor small screen. In the pages ahead, we will take a look at the Spillane adaptations that have.

But first we will take a brief look at the remarkable life and career of the creator of Mike Hammer.

Prologue: I, the Writer

Spillane, early 1950s, wooing his "mistress—Miss Smith Corona."

"I like people to enjoy what I've done," Mickey Spillane told *Memories Magazine* in 1990, "but you don't have to go crazy over it. If you just enjoy what you read, you'll buy the next one. I have an axiom: The first page will sell this book, the last page will sell your next one. Because people don't read a book to get to the middle, they read a book to get to the end. And they hope the end justifies the time they spent."

In an undated handwritten addition, Spillane continued: "Writing should be fun—then, so should any job."

In interviews, Spillane often came across as a gregarious blue-collar guy, an unpretentious guy you could enjoy a beer with (presumably Miller Lite, though Spillane himself drank straight Miller). But some readers and many critics overlook or ignore Mickey Spillane's humanity, overwhelmed by his larger-than-life antiheroes and their world of violence and sex. That blind spot limits the appreciation for the magnitude of his work, which includes novels, short stories, film scripts, comic book writing, non-fiction, children's books and acting.

The facts about Spillane's life are available, but they are mixed up with so many more fictions—some extrapolated by a public eager to know more about the man behind two-fisted, promiscuous Mike Hammer, but most created by the writer himself in an elaborate backstory for the media. Spillane was his own press agent, considering himself a marketer and merchandiser as much as a writer. Howard Stern once proclaimed himself the master of all media, but Mickey Spillane beat him to the punch by decades.

First the facts. Frank Morrison Spillane was born in Brooklyn, New York, on March 9, 1918, the son of Anne and John Spillane. He was baptized with the middle name "Michael" in the Catholic church of his father; in the Protestant church of his mother he was christened with the middle name "Morrison," which was the name teachers used at school. His mother nicknamed him "Babe," his father called him "Mickey." The affectionate motherly gesture of "Babe" proved the less lasting of the two pet names, and surely would have been a much less appropriate one to appear on the covers of the best-selling, controversial mystery novels that would make the name Mickey Spillane synonymous with "sex and sadism."

Mickey grew up in a rough Elizabeth, New Jersey, neighborhood where his father was a bartender. Young "Mick" was an affable youth, with a flair for football and swimming, the latter leading to jobs as captain of the lifeguards at Point Breeze, Long Island, for summers as late as 1940. He had a knack for spinning ghost stories that would "scare the hell out of the kids" who were bigger and tougher than he was.

His writing career began after his 1935 graduation from St. Erasmus High School in Brooklyn, New York. Spillane provided the original details for the short glimpse into his life on the back of his early paperbacks, which picture a handsome and impossibly young Spillane: "In the winter he wrote for nearly all the pulp and slick magazines (an avocation he had begun at college). His success decided him against becoming a lawyer and to concentrate on his writing."

According to Spillane, he worked under house names and pseudonyms (Frank Morrison, among others), contributing short fiction to various slicks and pulps, including *Collier's* and *Hollywood Detective*, continuing to sell short stories during his brief college stint. This began in 1939 at Kansas State Teachers College in Manhattan, Kansas, where his campus passions were football and the intramural swimming team, not his pre-law studies. He soon found himself back in New York.

Ruth Boyer, one of his Kansas State classmates, reveals that Spillane was always talking about receiving checks for the stories he wrote, but her friend never actually told her the name of the magazines. Tracking down Spillane's late '30s and early '40s fiction in both the pulps and slicks has been a frustrating task for researchers.

By the fall of 1940 Spillane was in New York for a brief stint in Gimbel's basement. There he met fellow comic-book writer, Joe Gill, who introduced him to his brother Ray who worked for Funnies, Inc., a comic shop that produced stories for various titles, among them *Bull's-Eye Bill, Human Torch, Sub-Mariner* and *Blue Bolt.* A post office requirement meant that each comic book needed at least one page of text; among the many one-page prose pieces Spillane produced was a lifeguard story featuring Captain Mickey Spillane.

A pioneer in the world of comic books, Spillane matched the output of any other three writers in his average single day, inventing a new style of comics writing that consisted of outlining the books so that each sentence stood for a picture and each paragraph for a full page. The earliest of these stories dates to February 1942, and the last December 1942.

"They were the happiest days of my life," Spillane said many years later. "I could walk anywhere and nobody knew who I was."

The young comic-book writer enlisted the day after Pearl Harbor, attacking the Army Air Corps (precursor of the Air Force) with the same zeal he had brought to the comic book industry. Although Spillane was among the first young Americans to enlist, he was not assigned for training until early 1942. The Army had so many volunteers, it did not have space to train them all immediately.

Spillane was originally assigned for training in Florida, while his buddy Joe Gill joined the Coast Guard and served in Saipan and in the Philippines. The writer-turned-pilot would forge many lifetime friendships in the Army. Witness this memorable dedication to his 1965 novel *Bloody Sunrise*: "To Nat Drutman and the days of the Kaydets and the AAF when the blue yonder was really wild and even wilder when you got shot out of it." While stationed in Mississippi, he met future fellow mystery writers Charlie Wells and Earle Basinsky. Both were helped by their friend Mickey to achieve publication, their books elaborately endorsed by their famous friend.

Unfortunately, the patriotic young pilot proved to be *too* good—his ease of communication led his superiors to believe he was best-suited for the position of fighter pilot instructor at the base in Greenwood, Mississippi (with his usual enthusiasm, he had learned to fly as a teenager).

Spillane served most of the war in Greenwood. He did land a fighter assignment toward the war's end, though apparently too late in the conflict to see action. That he never saw action was a sore point with Spillane, and friends knew not to bring it up. In Mississippi, he met and married Mary Ann Pearce; they would have four children, Kathy, Ward, Michael and Caroline.

Returning with his young wife to the New York area in 1945, the couple and the country were facing an immediate housing shortage. Spillane bought a patch of land in Newburgh, New York, announcing to one and all—despite having zero experience in construction—that he planned to build himself and his family a house. The property was eight miles out of that city on the Hudson River, near an Army base and West Point, and sixty miles from New York City.

To build his house, the veteran needed one thousand dollars for materials. His close friend Ray Gill once said that Spillane would "tell you what seems like the most outrageous lie, and then, after you've laughed at him, he hits you over the head by making it come true." His method of obtaining the money for this ambitious project was to start another ambitious project. He would write a book—a mystery novel.

Spillane, center, with producer Victor Saville, left, and director/screenwriter Harry Essex, on the set of "I, the Jury" (1953).

The comic book industry he had tried to return to was in a slump, and a stalled independent comics project of his—a private eye character called "Mike Danger"—would provide the basis for his book, he told his friends. They laughed. He turned the comic story into a mystery novel in less than three weeks (possibly in as few as nine days). The book was *I, the Jury*.

How Mike Danger became Mike Hammer remained an unanswered question until artist (and longtime crony) George Wilson revealed some backstory that was not merely Spillane self-press agentry. Seems a joint on Great Lake Street in Newburgh called Hammer's Bar became a hang-out for Spillane, Wilson and other buddies, including fellow writer and World War II vet Dave Gerrity. Over the course of that summer Spillane adopted the Hammer name for his new character.

Written in 1945, published in hardcover by E. P. Dutton in 1947, *I, the Jury* not only provided the money to build Spillane's house, but laid the foundation for the literary phenomenon of his private eye hero. A paperback blurb calls the book "one of the toughest (private eye novels) yet written" and another, from *The Oakland Post Enquirer*, insists that "this isn't good fare for the squeamish, but the writer has certainly produced a dramatic climax ... guaranteed to chill your blood."

Spillane then submitted his second novel, originally titled *Whom the Gods Would Destroy*, which Dutton rejected in part because of disappointing hardcover sales for *I, the Jury*, and also because the central idea—a father using experimental scientific means to create a genius in his young son—seemed too fantastic.

The paperback reprint of *I, the Jury* that would change everything was almost two years away, and the rejection left Spillane struggling financially. He returned to comic book writing while seeking employment unsuccessfully in the Newburgh area.

It appears he also returned to writing for the pulps under the name Frank Morris (a reduction of Mickey's first and middle names) in various pulps, including *Hollywood Detective* and *Thrilling Detective*. Stylistically, the hard-hitting Morris stories read like early Mickey Spillane, and have the sort of comic book feel favored by the pulp's publisher, Trojan Publications.

Then came the softcover edition of *I, the Jury*, which sold more than eight million copies, a figure that does not include the many translations and hardbound editions. This slender novel—along with the six more that followed it in Spillane's first great creative period—assured Mike Hammer's creator of a position among the best-selling authors of all time (the latest sales figures exceed 200 million books).

Mickey and his wife lived in a tent for four months while he and some friends built his house. The tent was a World War I Army surplus number that friend George Wilson's father helped them obtain. Mickey called the building site "Little Bohemia."

"There was no running water," Wilson remembered. "Everything had to be carried in. And the bathroom facilities were primitive." They even took baths in wash tubs. Eventually three buildings stood on the property: the main house, the artist's shop (George Wilson worked there) and the writer's building (where Mickey worked).

In typical Spillane fashion, the writer boasted that his friends were jealous of his new home and wanted him to build one for them. That's at least partially Spillane self-press agentry. But in 1946 it may have been serious—building his friends' houses was work he could use, because the Mike Hammer/Mickey Spillane tsunami would not hit until 1948, when that paperback edition of *I, the Jury* changed Spillane's life and American popular fiction forever.

Most of what the reading public of the fifties knew about Spillane derived from a *Life* magazine article of June 23, 1952, entitled "Death's Fair-Haired Boy" by Richard W. Johnston. It had many pictures of Mickey and his friends, but scant praise. At the time of the article, only five Mike Hammer novels had been published. The sales for these five Hammer in their paperback editions exceeded eleven million copies. At one cent per copy that's $110,000—huge money in 1952. And the royalty was probably more like a nickel. At those rates Spillane didn't have to build his next house himself ... not with the E. P. Dutton hardbacks averaging 15,000 copies per title, an enormous figure for a hardcover mystery novel of the day (and not bad now).

The unflattering *Life* article described Spillane "as a bantam-sized, slightly educated, self-professed roughneck who now lives in Newburgh, N.Y., but who grew up in Brooklyn and still talks like it." Continuing on in this patronizing fashion, the writer describes 26-year-old Mary Ann Spillane as "a subdued little bespectacled brunette." Photos of Mary Ann without her glasses reveal a prototype of Velda, dark haired and very pretty.

The photo of the exterior of the Spillane-built house reveals a rustic cinder block place with a chimney, and a scrubby yard where Spillane rides on a small wagon with his son Ward while Mary Ann holds baby Kathy, two dogs roam, and writer pals Joe Gill and Charlie Wells lean against a bug-eyed truck. The lifestyle of America's bestselling novelist displayed not the slightest resemblance to opulence.

But Spillane had grown up during the Depression and being careful with money was ingrained. Over the many decades of his career, Spillane remained particularly consistent on one key subject: he only wrote when he needed the money. The stop-and-start fashion of his writing career backs this statement up.

The *Life* article also displays a picture of Spillane typing on a manual typewriter. For many years the writer kept several such machines on hand (he had a mistress, he would tell reporters—"Miss Smith Corona"), sometimes working on different projects simultaneously. The look of the work area is spartan. The most prominent feature is a bulletin board on which Spillane has tacked unfavorable book reviews.

Looking for the real Mickey Spillane in the *Life* article is a mystery even Mike Hammer couldn't crack; but one revealing quote is attributed only to "a friend": "[Joe] Gill is not Mike Hammer, except maybe in his physical appearance. Mickey is Mike Hammer. He'd like to be big like Mike Hammer, which he never can be, and he'd like to be really tough, like Mike Hammer, which he never can be either."

Who *was* the real Mickey Spillane? Anyone who ever talked with the writer when he wasn't doing self-promotion, sensed his passion, his emotion and his dedication to himself, his family and his art (though he would never himself characterize his writing as such ... craft, maybe). Some critics have stated flatly that Mickey was not an artist and had no real creative vision, just a blue-collar hack serving up sex and bullets. Open up a copy of his second published novel, *My Gun Is Quick*, read the first paragraph and be the jury:

Spillane directs (from his own script) the test film for Jack Stang as Hammer (1953).

> When you sit at home comfortably folded up in a chair beside a fire, have you ever thought what goes on outside there? Probably not. You pick up a book and read about things and stuff, getting a vicarious kick from people and events that never happened.... But remember this: there are things happening out there ... Oh, yes, you can find them all right. All you have to do is look for them. But I wouldn't if I were you because you won't like what you'll find....You have to be quick, and you have to be able, or you become one of the devoured, and if you can kill first, no matter how and no matter

> who, you can live and return to the comfortable chair and the comfortable fire. But you have to be quick. And able. Or you'll be dead.

In this preamble to a novel—more an essay than a page of fiction—Spillane craftily justifies the melodramatic, even surrealistic world his readers are about to enter. It's a technique used, at times, by Alexander Dumas and Sir Arthur Conan Doyle, two authors Spillane admired. The speaker welcomes the reader to the state of mind that is Mike Hammer, and the New York City that is his version of Tarzan's jungle.

Many readers and critics alike have expressed wonder about the volcanic rage expressed in the first seven novels. But in his storytelling, Spillane was describing exactly the mind set of the returning and struggling World War II veteran. The boiling frustrations the writer expressed in his wildly successful fiction were eventually channeled into another, surprising passion.

During the winter of 1951, Spillane—raised in the Catholic church—converted to the Jehovah's Witnesses, possibly influenced by wife Mary Ann. This time his self- press agentry took on a different tone: "I've changed my work and course of action to be in harmony with Jehovah's Kingdom." By this time every early Spillane novel had been completed but *Kiss Me, Deadly*.

In more traditional self–PR moments, Spillane notes that the sex in the memorably titled *Kiss Me, Deadly* had been altered to "something even more exciting." This appears to mean Hammer does not sleep with any of the typically beautiful, sensuous damsels he encounters. The violence, Spillane indicated, had also been transformed. Perhaps he was referring to the Biblical Battle of Armageddon, a theme Robert Aldrich mined in the film version. Even Aldrich's comma-free alteration of the title fits into Spillane's new vision: Mike Hammer is not the only deadly one anymore; all the universe has now become toxic.

In the wake of the sex-and-sadism master's highly publicized religious conversion, readers worldwide wondered if the shocking conclusion of *Kiss Me, Deadly* spelled the end of Mike Hammer. Other than the first-person narration implying survival, the novel itself holds no clue:

> The flames were teeth that ate, ripping and tearing, into scars of other flames and her voice the shrill sound of death on the loose. I looked, looked away. The door was closed and maybe I had enough left to make it.

That ending is worlds away from the bloodied, battered yet wholly triumphant Mike Hammer at the end of *My Gun Is Quick*: "[The villain] had his mouth open, screaming with all the furies of the gods dethroned, but my laugh was even louder. He was still screaming when I pulled the trigger." The key words for Spillane are gods, death and the end of time. Those are key Spillane themes—not the sometimes senseless violence they engender.

But while Spillane the man struggled with his own personal issues, all the worldly success his pre–Witness writings had generated meant thirty-three-year-old Mickey Spillane was a very rich man ... if a still very much controversial one.

Spillane always had a love-hate affair with being a celebrity: appearing on TV and in the movies, self-promoting on the radio and in newspaper interviews, hobnobbing with the likes of Marlene Dietrich and Rocky Marciano in the early '50s, all seem to be something he got a kick out of. But being the target of the smug likes of Dr. Fredrick Wertham and Malcolm Cowley was nothing he relished, and at one point he said in quiet but seething frustration, "I just wish people would get off my neck."

For all his bluster about ignoring the critics and their opinions, Spillane—a simple soul and a complex man, and in his own way moral and even spiritual—was nonetheless stung by the attacks upon him and his work. He retreated to his image as the beer-drinking, blue-collar mystery writer that nobody but the public likes, "the chewing gum of American literature," a persona he crafted with even more care than he had brought to Mike Hammer.

A professional wordsmith with few literary pretensions—but with the love for language of a pure storyteller—he had simply tried to bring two elements to the mystery novel: the excitement and action of the comic books, where he'd learned his craft; and a level of realism, where sex and particularly violence were concerned, that had not yet been seen in American popular fiction.

The latter was Spillane's instinctive response to a reading public that consisted largely of ex-servicemen, who had fought a tough, brutal war; who were primed to have even their entertainment reflect the loss of innocence of that war ... and in the case of an action yarn, this meant sex and violence. These male readers were (to put it succinctly) a bunch of horny ex–GIs looking for a hot read. The seven novels Spillane produced between 1947 and 1952 have a level of sex and particularly violence that seems to come out of nowhere; but where it comes from is World War II.

The last of the seven novels—*Kiss Me, Deadly*—rapidly became one of Spillane's most popular, appearing on "the nation's most significant" bestseller lists (as the blurbs on the back of the paperback reprints put it): the *New York Times* and the *New York Herald Tribune*, the first mystery to achieve that distinction. Yet with this novel, which left its hero apparently dying in a burning building, the flow of books ceased. Mickey Spillane, at the peak of his popular success, had apparently stopped writing.

The take in the media was that Spillane had become a religious fanatic and that he was repenting for his "sins" by refusing to write any more fiction tainted by "sex-and-sadism." But despite the nine-year gap between novels, Spillane did not stop writing, nor did he change his subject matter. Though Mike Hammer remained on the shelf, a succession of similar, Spillane-crafted tough guys stepped up to fill his shoes, if temporarily.

Spillane's first appearance as Mike Hammer, recording the LP "Mickey Spillane's Mike Hammer Story" (1954).

Spillane wrote more than a dozen short works about such heroes during his so-called "drought," most of which are full-length novelettes, published in men's magazines and many reprinted two or three to a paperback. In addition, he wrote a number of non-fiction pieces, scripted and released the radio-drama-style record album *Mickey Spillane's Mike Hammer Story* (appearing as Hammer himself for the first time), and wrote nearly a year's worth of the Sunday-page scripts for a "Mike Hammer" comic strip. He was also involved, at least peripherally, with the Saville films and the Darren McGavin television series.

All of the magazine stories reveal effort by Spillane to modulate his style without abandoning his trademark elements and themes, including of course sex and violence. The 20,000-world novelette length was one Spillane preferred above all others, where he displays some of his best-crafted work.

In an article for *TV Guide* in 1961—responding in part to critics who blamed fiction writers for society's ills—Spillane himself criticized books, movies and TV shows that overused violence, calling for a more measured, effective and realistic use of violence in fiction. This declaration clearly reflects how he felt about his own work at the time: "There was a time when wild, gory scenes of violence were stock items in a story or script. I certainly went all out myself when that was the trend. Now times have changed." What Spillane doesn't mention is that he started that trend.

Nor does he mention that the work he was doing now—he had begun writing novels again—continued to include those "wild, gory scenes of violence." What had changed was Spillane's attitude about using violence (and sex): "Sex and violence are exclamation points in a story ... and you don't over-use exclamation points."

During the near decade away from novels, the writer traveled with Clyde Beatty's circus (as a trampoline artist and a human cannonball); appeared in the motion picture "Ring of Fear" (which he co-scripted for no screen credit); and indulged in such macho pursuits as stockcar-racing, fencing, flying, and diving for sunken treasure. If money means freedom, Spillane exercised his freedom by fulfilling all his childhood fantasies.

Spillane's return to novel-writing in the early '60s coincided roughly with his divorce in 1962 from wife Mary Ann and a separation from the Jehovah's Witnesses (he was apparently disenfranchised at least once, presumably for his provocative fiction-writing). Influenced by the novelettes, his crime novel *The Deep* (1961) was followed by a new Mike Hammer, *The Girl Hunters* (1962), the detective surviving the fiery finish of *Kiss Me, Deadly*. The film version of the new Hammer was co-scripted by co-producer Spillane himself, who of course starred in the film, his credit reading: "MICKEY SPILLANE IS MIKE HAMMER." His acting in "The Girl Hunters" was widely praised, including both *Time* and *Newsweek's* critics, his notices as an actor better than most reviews he'd received as a writer.

Mike Hammer's loyal secretary Velda—the love of his life, and virtual second lead of the series—had been entirely off stage in *The Girl Hunters* ... she is, in fact, the girl being hunted. But in Spillane's follow-up novel, *The Snake* (1964), she is at the center of the action, and the apparent consummation of their long smouldering love provides an atypically tender conclusion for a Hammer yarn.

By the time of his return to publishing in 1961, Spillane was quite savvy about contracts. According to the writer himself, the long wait between Mike Hammer novels had more to do with his displeasure with New American Library's money offers than with pleasing his Jehovah's Witness brethren. Among the novels Spillane delivered under his new, highly remunerative contract was the rejected 1948 novel, now retitled *The Twisted Thing*.

Spillane's editor Victor Weybright had tried as early as 1953 to get the shelved novel—now a highly valuable property—as a follow-up to *Kiss Me, Deadly*. Spillane had ignored these overtures. How frustrating it must to have been to Weybright that cash cow Spillane was no longer writing and refused to simply pluck an existing Mike Hammer down from that shelf. Now, a decade later, Spillane was ready to deliver the old manuscript as his new Hammer, for a hefty paycheck.

There was only one problem. Spillane now lived in South Carolina. He didn't have the manuscript, but believed a copy remained in his old house in Newburgh, New York. A fire in the writer's building, however, had seen some things destroyed. Dave Gerrity's son Devin found the manuscript; some of the pages, particularly the ones on top, were scorched ... and the final page was black. Spillane wrote a new final page, and when the scorched page was finally restored to readability, only a few words were variant. Spillane was obsessive about crafting "socko" endings to his tales, so perhaps it's not so surprising that he was able to summon the memory of the missing page eighteen years later. The novel's dedication affirms the story: "To Sid Graedon who saw the charred edges."

Spillane continued acting occasionally, appearing in 1973 as a best-selling author on the *Columbo* TV series, and began in the early 1970s appearing as himself in the phenomenally popular series of Miller Lite Beer commercials. For eighteen years, often appearing with actress Lee Meredith as "the Doll," Spillane spoofed himself in Hammer-like trenchcoat and porkpie hat.

In 1994 and 1996, Spillane appeared as criminal lawyer Wayne Ekhardt in the Iowa-produced indie films directed by co-author Collins, "Mommy" (a Lifetime movie of the week) and "Mommy 2: Mommy's Day." By that time Spillane the actor had became as well known as Spillane the writer.

After appearing as Hammer in "The Girl Hunters," Spillane on occasion played his famous detective in photo shoots for the covers of paperback editions of the books. Actress/model Sherri (Selma) Malinou posed with him for several, along the way becoming the second Mrs. Spillane in November 1965. Over the years the new couple were frequently in the media; they both would claim to having nothing in common, spending much of their time in separate cities, she in New York City and Hollywood, pursuing her singing and acting career, he in small-town Murrells Inlet, South Carolina, pursuing fish from the deck of a 22-foot boat.

Sherri appeared in a supporting role in Spillane's own film production of "The Delta Factor" (1970) and posed in the nude for the dustjackets of *The Erection Set* (1972) and *The Last Cop Out* (1973), a typical Spillane publicity gimmick, and an indication he was likely on the outs with the Jehovah's Witnesses at the time. Despite one legal separation, husband and wife were quoted describing the marriage in highly positive terms until their divorce in April 1983, which typically attracted tabloid attention.

In October 1983, Spillane married Jane Rogers Johnson, fitness teacher, former beauty queen (Miss South Carolina runner-up) and a "local girl" of 37 who lived "just down the lane" from Spillane in Murrells Inlet. The vivacious, energetic Jane kept her husband entertained and on his toes in a happy union that lasted some twenty-three years (until the writer's death).

Spillane published a young adult novel, *The Day the Sea Rolled Back*, in 1979; the book won a Junior Literary Guild award and its 1981 paperback edition by Bantam brought a renewed round of media interest in the toughest of the tough guy writers having written "a kid's book." The novel is the lyrical tale about two boys, Josh and Larry, who have numerous adventures when the tide goes out—way out—leaving the bottom of the ocean, and its many secrets and treasures, exposed.

The book reflected Spillane's interest in and love for the ocean, in a manner not unlike that of Peter Benchley, who ironically "borrowed" the title of Spillane's 1961 bestseller *The Deep* for one of his novels. Spillane, who admired Benchley's *Jaws*, sent the author a telegram wishing him luck, saying specifically, "Hope yours sells as many as mine!"

Spillane as Mike Hammer in "The Girl Hunters" (1963).

Spillane wrote two more young adult novels, *The Ship That Never Was* (Bantam, 1982) and *The Shrinking Island*, announced for 1984 but as yet unpublished. In addition, Spillane may have done the book for the unproduced Mike Hammer Broadway musical, *Oh, Mike!* (with a Johnny Mercer score), though the play has not yet turned up in his papers.

By the 1990s Spillane had become "the grand old man" of the tough mystery. In 1983 he received the Eye, the lifetime achievement award of the Private Eye Writers of America, as well as an award from that group for best short story of 1990 for "The Killing Man," an abridgement of his novel appearing in *Playboy*, December 1989. In 1995 he received a much-overdue Grand Master "Edgar" Award from the Mystery Writers of America. Recognition from his peers came some forty years after Spillane had been carelessly denigrated as a pariah by the critics and commentators who had blamed him for everything from ruining the mystery genre to fomenting juvenile delinquency.

Mike Hammer returned in two additional books before Spillane's 2006 death: *The Killing Man* (1989) and *Black Alley* (1996). These novels received a warm critical reception and allowed older readers to meet up with an old friend even as a new, younger audience got a taste of an authentic *noir* master.

Spillane designated the co-author of this volume, fellow mystery writer/filmmaker Max Allan Collins, to complete a number of unfinished manuscripts, including no less than six Mike Hammer novels. At this writing four have appeared—*The Goliath Bone* (2008), *The Big Bang* (2010), *Kiss Her Goodbye* (2011) and *Lady, Go Die!* (2012). The critical response has been overwhelmingly positive, further indicating the changing attitudes toward one of the most innovative and popular mystery writers of the 20th century.

The addition of six new Mike Hammer novels, developed from substantial Spillane manuscripts, is in part significant because Mike Hammer appeared in only thirteen novels between 1947 and 1996. Other fictional sleuths of similar fame—Hercule Poirot, Nero Wolfe, Spenser, for example—appeared in literally dozens of novels. The power and popularity of Spillane's relative handful of Hammer novels has a lot to do with the enduring legacy of the writer and his character.

But the films and TV series adapted from Mickey Spillane have also played a significant role.

Spillane at the Movies

1. "I, the Jury" (1953)

Biff Elliot, the screen's first Mike Hammer, in "I, the Jury" (1953). Much maligned, Elliot created a tough, impulsive, passionate Hammer consistent with the novels.

Six years after the initial hardcover publication of *I, the Jury*, British producer/director Victor Saville brought Mickey Spillane's first Mike Hammer thriller to the screen. Spillane himself described the film—and virtually all subsequent big-screen Mike Hammer films—as "lousy" (with the notable and understandable exception of "The Girl Hunters").

Spillane often told interviewers—including Johnny Carson on the "Tonight Show"—of attending a neighborhood theater showing of the movie "introducing" Biff Elliot as Hammer. When Elliot/Hammer rushes up the stairs of an apartment house, where the body of his dead friend Jack Williams has been found by the police, he grabs the nearest bystander roughly and says, "I'm Mike Hammer."

Then, according to Spillane, a patron stood up and pointed at the screen and said, incredulously, "*Dat's Mike* Ham-*muh?*" Upon this reaction, Spillane said he got up, walked out, and never saw the film in its entirety until a TV late, late show, many years later.

This proved to be typical Spillane self–PR when, in an unguarded moment some years later, he admitted to the authors that he had sat through a premiere showing of the "I, the Jury" film, 3-D glasses and all. In fact, he went on the road presenting and hyping the film at theaters, doing appearances with Biff Elliot, who at that time was expected to portray Hammer in all of the upcoming films (Saville had signed the Boston actor to a multiple-picture deal).

Spillane and Elliot remained lifetime friends, and while the writer remained critical of Elliot having been cast as Hammer, he made sure to underscore this opinion with another—"Biff is a damn good actor"—and on several occasions intended to use Elliot in film and TV projects himself.

Considered "a founding father of British filmmaking," producer/director Victor Saville was an unlikely impresario for the large-screen presentation of Mike Hammer to an eager public. Saville considered the books "raw sex and violence," but saw the potential Spillane's bestsellers had to be money-makers. He hoped to bring to the screen Thomas Costain's Biblical epic, *The Silver Chalice*, and wanted to "warm up" on the Hammer pictures, even as he filled his coffers.

"I arranged a meeting with Spillane," Saville told his biographer, Roy Moseley. "But not in an office, that was not the Spillane way. He insisted we meet under the clock at the Pennsylvania Railway Station."

From there Spillane and Saville "repaired to a dark bar on Third Avenue to make a deal." Their initial agreement—a fifty/fifty split of the profits, a partnership between the two men—was scuttled when Columbia pictures made a cash offer of $140,000 for four novels—*I, the Jury*, *My Gun Is Quick*, *The Long Wait*, and *Kiss Me, Deadly*. Saville set aside his previous offer and matched Columbia's.

"If Spillane had stuck to my original proposal," Saville claimed, "he would have made half a million dollars as his share of the first two pictures. He never really forgave me."

When the first Saville film was released, a movie tie-in edition of *I, the Jury* included backcover photos from the film version, labeled "MICKEY SPILLANE IN HOLLYWOOD."

"Mickey Spillane's bestselling mysteries," cover copy proclaimed, "can now be seen in exciting 3-D motion pictures produced by Victor Saville and released by United Artists."

This indicates Saville's intention of using the then popular 3-D process for all four Spillane novels whose screen rights he had acquired. But the 3-D fad fizzled before any subsequent Spillane films could be shot in that manner, and "I, the Jury" itself was screened in many theaters by way of standard "flat" two-dimensional prints.

The 3-D gimmick seemed a perfect way to exploit the curvy dames and fist-in-your face violence that were assumed to be the secret of Mike Hammer's—and Mickey Spillane's—success. But no gimmick could convey the special relationship that existed between readers and the unconventional, even psychotic hero who was Mike Hammer.

Seldom has a narrator been more effectively used by an author as a point of identification for readers; as previously noted, this personal connection was an elusive element in screen adaptations. The state of mind that was first-person narrator Mike Hammer extended to a number of the book (and movie) titles, with their use of first-person pronouns.

Much as the original Hammer paperback book covers emphasized this reader identification by never showing the detective's face, several shots in the 1953 film echo those cover poses, as do staged production stills and movie posters (which show Peggie Castle about to unbutton her blouse, something she never got around to doing in the actual film).

Director/writer Harry Essex tackled this problem head on, and his "I, the Jury" transfers the first-person style of the novels to the film in the form of voiceover narration. Not an uncommon element in films *noir* of the forties—memorably utilized in "Murder, My Sweet" (1944), Edward Dmytryk's adaptation of Raymond Chandler's *Farewell, My Lovely*—voiceover has traditionally been a crutch in Hollywood films, often a post-production attempt to clarify a muddy narrative.

"I, the Jury" might fairly be considered a muddy narrative, but the use of voiceover is one of its strengths, the language vivid, personal and appropriately Spillane in tone: "Remember what I promised you? No matter who it turned out to be, Jack, I'd get the killer."

The initial scenes of the film show us Hammer's back, or otherwise obscure any view of his face. The evocative paintings on the paperback covers encouraged male readers to fill in Mike Hammer's face with their own; the initial scene in the first screen version goes for a similar effect. But short of the subjective camera of Robert Montgomery's Raymond Chandler adaptation "The Lady in the Lake" (1946), this effect could not be maintained—sooner or later, Mike Hammer had to turn around and be seen. *Dat's Mike* Ham-*muh?*

Not to Spillane, who thought Elliot was too small, though his chief complaints about "I, the Jury" were with the script and such details as Mike Hammer's trademark .45 automatic being traded in for a revolver. And he howled about Hammer recovering a perfectly formed spent slug from a brick wall, and moaned about his hero getting knocked out with a wooden coat hanger.

Further, he found director/screenwriter Harry Essex obnoxious and disrespectful, and was irritated that his handpicked Mike Hammer, ex-cop Jack Stang (who appears briefly in "I, the Jury" in a poolroom scene), was turned down for the part. Spillane also griped that his pal Biff was "left-handed and had a Boston accent."

While it's true that Hammer appears to be a big man in the novels, whether he's right-handed or not wouldn't seem to be much of an issue, and Elliot's "Boston accent" isn't readily apparent. But even Mickey Spillane seems to have had his own ideas about what Hammer looked like, despite never sharing them with readers.

"I was hired as an actor to play Mike Hammer," an 86-year-old Elliot told the authors in 2010. "I was not Mike Hammer. Mike Hammer is a cartoon character like Superman. I am not Superman. I'm an actor.... I took a cartoon character and turned him into a flesh-and-blood human being similar to what Mickey Spillane was. It's impossible to please a writer who's writing, without knowing it, his own autobiography."

With all due respect to Mike Hammer's creator, Elliot was indeed a terrific Mike Hammer—an emotional hothead who could be as tough as he was tender. He fights hard and loves hard, and may not be as smart as most movie private eyes, which gives him a nice everyman quality. It's a shame Elliot, with a screen presence similar to James Caan's, was not better launched by the film.

While Elliot is hardly small, producer Saville and director Essex required him to wear padded shoulders, particularly in his camel-hair trenchcoat, which with the flat porkpie hat lends him an expressionistic, almost comics hero appearance that is wholly appropriate. For Mike Hammer to lumber down dark, wet streets like a good-guy Frankenstein monster is not all bad.

Of all the Saville films, the 1953 version of "I, the Jury" best captures the sleazy-side-of-Manhattan look and the bittersweet flavor of the novels; it is fun and tough and sexy, drenched in film *noir* shadows, with an atmospheric Franz Waxman score, and director Essex's dialogue has crackle.

Still, what disappointed moviegoers at the time remains disappointing: the most overtly sexual aspects of the plot (a dance studio may or may not be a brothel, several characters may or may not be homosexual) are incoherent due to censorship issues, and the famous striptease finale reduces lovely Peggie Castle's disrobing to ... taking off her shoes!

Nonetheless, the screenplay is remarkably faithful to the novel's plot, even if it does on occasion turn that plot into incoherent nonsense, due to the early 1950s necessity of censoring out drug and prostitution references. This moody, energetic film remains in some ways the best of the Hammer adaptations, with director Essex building an appropriate sense of tension and paranoia—Hammer peeks around corners, looks over his shoulder, when walking down shadowy city streets—while Elliot brings a crude enthusiasm to the role, his effectiveness bolstered by his being an unknown, and his bullying tactics offset by his partial lack of size. A six-foot-three Hammer (like Jack Stang) might have made Spillane's hero come across as a thug; Elliot's light-heavyweight look overcame that problem.

The film is further aided by that Franz Waxman score, a masterpiece of melancholy, discordant, off-kilter jazz themes, instruments wailing and prowling and mocking. The jazzy, jarring score of "Kiss Me Deadly" by Frank Devol, with its memorable Nat King Cole rendition of "Rather Have the Blues," is an outstanding contribution, and the television music of Dave Kahn and Melvyn Lenard provides a perfect musical landscape for Darren McGavin's 1958 Mike Hammer. But Waxman's little-discussed, barely-remembered music for "I, the Jury" is not just the finest Spillane score, but among the finest of any private eye *noir*. (While no soundtrack has been issued, Waxman's mini-suite of "I, the Jury" themes—"Three Sketches: Nostalgia, Song, Blues"—is featured on the "Crime in the Streets" LP and CD.)

The look of the film is of course due to that legendary "painter with light," John Alton, perhaps the most famous film *noir* cinematographer. He had already won an Academy Award for "An American in Paris" (1951) and his next picture was the justly famous "The Big Combo" (1955). The difficulty of seeing "I, the Jury" in its intended 3-D format stands in the way of this underrated crime-film gem receiving a proper reconsideration.

Seen "flat" on TV, the film doesn't seem to be much of a 3-D movie, with only a few instances of objects and people coming out of the screen, including the notorious "back scratcher" moment when one of the sexy Seitz twins extends that implement toward the viewer. "House of Wax" paddleball, anyone? But a 3-D theatrical screening reveals the brilliant Alton's mastery at creating depth, bringing the viewer inside the images.

A common misnomer about Spillane and his characters is that the Hammer novels are misogynist—the ending of "I, the Jury" has a lot to do with that misconception. While there is no shortage of beautiful women in the Essex film, the two central women are portrayed clearly as Hammer's equals, Peggie Castle as femme fatale Charlotte and Margaret Sheridan as Velda anything but weak, kitten-ish sex dolls.

Charlotte is educated, an author, a psychiatrist, and is treated with deference and then adoration by Hammer. Velda is Hammer's partner and friend, and possibly lover, and when she is invaded by thugs, holds her own—she witnesses Hammer's brutal dealings with these goons and in a singularly effective moment, actress Sheridan reacts to her partner's sadism by tossing her hair back in cool contempt of Hammer's victim.

The only problem with Peggie Castle's smouldering performance is the limitations of her final striptease. It's the most famous scene in the book, the one readers were anxious to see how Hollywood would manage, only to be faced with the disappointment of the scene essentially being skipped. While the famous violent punchline is retained, the sexy build-up is not. No wonder audiences were disappointed—you don't go to "Gone with the Wind" to hear Rhett Butler say he doesn't give a darn.

The film opens with a dramatic display of the villain's sadism. One-armed Jack Williams—his prosthetic arm draped over a chair—is shot, only to crawl toward the camera, extending his remaining arm toward the viewer (one of the few overt 3-D effects in the film) as he attempts to reach the chair on which his police revolver is slung. The mostly off-screen murderer draws back the chair, in cruel cat-versus-mouse manner, while the Franz Waxman score punctuates the tragedy with hammer-like brass.

No time is wasted establishing facts about Mike Hammer that the reading audience already knows. He's tough and acts impetuously. He's loyal to his friends, in this case Jack Williams, who lost his right arm protecting Mike from a Japanese bayonet. Learning that his friend Jack has been murdered, Mike rushes up the stairs and declares, "I'm Mike Hammer."

His friend Captain Pat Chambers quickly reminds him, "You're not the law, Mike." Hammer quickly tells Pat that the killer will get what he deserves, "a .45 right in the gut, just like he gave it to Jack." Elliot sounds as if he's out of breath, but it could be just the beginning of the notorious Hammer rage.

Within the first five minutes, another major Spillane character appears—the rain. In voiceover Mike tells us, "The weather was just about as happy as I was." The private eye is on his way to visit Jack's girlfriend, Myrna, a torch singer at a Greenwich Village club. Jack has saved her from drug addiction. Hammer says, "It'll be good to cry." He hears her scream as he leaves, Waxman's score echoing it with a tenor sax.

At Hammer's office the next day, Velda displays the front page newspaper story: "I, THE JURY, Says Mike Hammer/Adds Mystery Angle to Jack Williams Murder." In the first paragraph Mike is quoted: "I am the jury." Mike knows that Pat is using him as bait, because the cop really doesn't know who the killer is yet. But the private eye doesn't mind. He's game.

Pat has even sent over a list of the people at Jack's recent party: George Kalecki, the Bellamy twins, Hal Kines, and Charlotte Manning. Mike and Velda leave the office and head for the elevator. Pete, the operator (portrayed by bouncy Joe Besser of Three Stooges fame), tells Mike he should go up and out the adjoining building. Mike uses Velda as bait to go out the front way. She considers this and gives him a kiss under the mistletoe.

That mistletoe cues the time of year, as does Joe Besser singing "Jingle Bells." A key ironic touch provided by writer/director Essex is a succession of sentimental Christmas cards (with carol-like scoring beneath) to make his scene transitions.

Elliot's Hammer confers moodily with the screen's first Velda, Margaret Sheridan, among the best portrayals of the detective's secretary/partner. The Christmas tree in the background is evidence of the film's ironic holiday motif.

At George Kalecki's Westchester house, Mike lands a few blows on Hal Kines, a student that George is helping through college. As he leaves, Mike sees Kalecki and Kines having a fight. A homosexual relationship is implied, at least as much as a 1950s mystery film can manage.

Hammer's next stop is Charlotte Manning, psychoanalyst, whose maid Kathy tries to stop Mike from going in at such a late hour. Charlotte says, "What is it, a patient?" The maid replies, "Well, if he ain't, he ought to be." While Mike waits for her to come out of her inner office, he spots a book: *Analyze Yourself* by Charlotte Manning.

Charlotte comes out in a long-flowing dress, the lovely blonde a fluid vision of feminine sexuality. She has been expecting the detective. Mike shows her the shoulder rig under his right arm (Spillane is right—Elliot's Hammer is indeed left-handed). Charlotte had treated Myrna for her addiction.

As Mike leaves he spots Pat sitting outside. Pat purposely lets it slip that Hal Kines and the Bellamy twins kept apartments at the Midworth Arms. He bribes his way into Kines' digs. There he sees some old photographs from the 1930s indicating Kines is much older than he's pretending to be. Kines surprises him with a gun, but Mike takes it away and roughs him up.

On his way out, Hammer spots the fashion model-ish Bellamy twins, who are pretty in an offbeat, angular manner. One goes into Kines' place, the other into her apartment on the next floor up. In perhaps the first line of sexual innuendo, one twin, Mary, says to Mike as he enters her apartment: "How did you know what I wanted for Christmas?" She's a tall blonde with a long braided ponytail. She tells Hammer that she's the twin with an identifying strawberry birthmark. The other sister is Esther. Mary kisses him and locks the door. He unlocks it and leaves, handing to her the backscratcher she's been playing with: "Here. Scratch." She's smiling to herself as he leaves.

At Manuel's Spanish-American bar it looks as if Mike is finally getting a break. In all of the Saville films (in keeping with the novels), Hammer hangs out with underdogs, working class and ethnic types. Manuel is getting ready to tell him about how Kalecki controls the numbers racket when three thugs enter and attack Mike. In a scene Spillane justly criticized, the well-dressed top hoodlum takes a wooden suit coat hanger and knocks Mike down and out. "Enough," he says. Not really.

At Charlotte's apartment Mike is getting the royal treatment while he licks his wounds. The psychoanalyst tells her guest that he might end up being a chapter in one of her books. Inevitably, he leans in and kisses her. Interrupting what promises to develop into a tryst, Charlotte asks if Jack had left him a message. Soon Mike is sneaking into Jack's apartment through a window. Inside he finds a note: "Expected you here before this, Mike. If you find anything let us know. Pat."

Mike does find something: Jack's old diary. He returns to his office after a paranoid walk down the mean, dark streets. Velda says, "Where have you been?" He replies, "Looking for a needle in a haystack." Velda parries with "In whose haystack?" She, like the readers in the 1953 audience, knows Mike very well. She refers to Charlotte as "Miss Haystack."

In the diary, Mike has seen the name Eileen Vickers, the daughter of a vet in upstate New York. Eileen met a fellow at school—John Hanson—and ran away with him. But he was a rotter and the girl was in bad shape. John Hanson was a picture in the yearbook shown at the beginning of the movie right before Jack was killed.

Dr. Vickers, portrayed by venerable Hollywood character actor John Qualen, tells Hammer about Carlos and Bonita's studio, where Eileen works as a dance instructor. Mike goes there; she's now using the name Mary Wright. She doesn't know that Jack's been murdered. Jack had wanted her to get help from Charlotte Manning. She seems to be a prostitute, but the movie isn't quite telling.

Pat and Mike head to the public library to look at the college yearbooks that were missing from Jack's apartment. They discover a picture of John Hanson alias Hal Kines. Mike says, "He's been going to college for the past twenty years. What's his racket?"

Pat tells Mike that Hanson is supposed to be with Eileen Vickers that very night. That's why Jack, in his role as an insurance investigator, wanted the dance studio raided. When they arrive both Hal Kines and Eileen Vickers have been shot. Kalecki is broken up about Kines' death. That's as close to the truth as the movie can hint, where either prostitution or homosexuality are concerned.

Charlotte is at Mike's office. She wants to know if he's spotted the pattern: only the people who attended Jack's party are being targeted. Velda walks in on them as Charlotte and Mike are about to kiss. As they leave, someone shoots at them from a passing car. Pat promises to give them more protection. Charlotte and Mike finally get their kiss after Pat leaves.

At Mike's place Bobo Harper—one of the many little people that Mike knows (portrayed by eternal screen nebbish Elisha Cook, Jr.)—comes by to warn the detective that the "Mr. Big" has given the word to get Mike, a mysterious kingpin of rackets the movie can only hint at. Bobo is learning about bee keeping and has just bought himself a queen bee. Bobo tells Mike that, according to books he's read, "queens don't need no kings."

Mike thinks the chief suspect for shooting at him is Esther Bellamy, because she's an award-winning skeet shooter. Mary pretends to be Esther, but Mike spots the back scratcher, though she finally does get her kiss. She advises him enigmatically, "Mary's not the killing kind. She's not like me."

Charlotte is all lovey-dovey at her place. She kisses Mike and tells him to get a haircut and get pretty for her. She says a long "Goodbye, darling." This is the first instance of director/writer Essex not caring that he is tipping Charlotte as the "bad guy"—aware that the ending of the novel is ridiculously well-known. While Mike gets his haircut, he hears an ambulance and soon discovers that Bobo has been shot ... and the queen bee got away.

At Parkdale College, Mike finds Kalecki going through John Hanson's room. Mike throws open the door, but steps aside as the hood blasts away. Mike shoots him, then tries to hide the gun, but winds up in jail anyway. Pat comes to bail him out. Kalecki was looking for some notes that Kines had made about their illegal activities.

Back in the city, Pat and Mike open Kalecki's safe deposit box and find a wealth of diamonds. Jack must have found out who the real "Mr. Big" was. By now, the audience is dizzy trying to figure out what crimes are going on—prostitution? Numbers? Drugs? Now it's diamond theft and smuggling. Pat thinks that Myrna must have had something to do with it because of her addiction. (Drugs!) But Mike thinks Charlotte can explain it all.

Myrna is at Manuel's talking to two hoods. She says, "Look who's here—Sir Lancelot." She's drunk and Mike and Charlotte haul her back to the psychoanalyst's place to sober up. Myrna keeps calling out for Jack. Charlotte gives her an injection. She wants to know if Jack said anything about her. "What was it Jack said?" All pretense has flown: Charlotte is the murderer.

Mobsters are in Mike's office holding Velda, but subvert her attempt to warn Mike. They tie Mike to a chair and beat him up and say he's going to have an accident. A big, well-staged fight breaks out on the ornate open staircase in Mike's building. The boss hood had been holding Velda while he watched the fight. But Mike breaks away from the hoods and gets him. He grabs the man's hand and breaks it, which Velda seems to dig. But the guy does not know anything.

Myrna Devlin has left Charlotte's apartment. The police find her body shortly thereafter, victim of a hit and run. A disgusted Pat tells Mike, "No, Myrna couldn't lie. Take a look at her arm. Merry Christmas."

Mike goes into a smoky daze until he figures it all out, a light literally going on over his head (an obvious yet somehow effective touch). Charlotte had hypnotized Kines and found out about the jewelry smuggling racket.

"No," says Mike. "It wasn't Mr. Big. It was Miss Big. Beautiful Miss Big."

Mike is walking toward Charlotte's place, in full Frankenstein monster mode, going in and out of darkness. An icon of the private eye genre, he is wearing the hat and has the trench coat on, fully buttoned for the first time. It exaggerates his (padded) shoulders, giving him an almost ape-like gait. He has become the embodiment of revenge.

Mike goes in through Charlotte's darkroom, sits on her couch with his gun out waiting for her return. The scene is framed exactly like the original 1948 paperback book cover: Mike sitting on the left side of the screen with his gun pointed toward Charlotte at the far right. But as has been pointed out many times, the gun is a .38 revolver, not Hammer's trademark automatic. She, too, wears a trench coat.

The famous striptease finale of "I, the Jury" with Elliot's Hammer facing down Peggie Castle's sultry Charlotte Manning. The striptease would be truncated but the violent finish would be uncensored.

She removes her scarf. "Listen to me Mike. You're not making sense." She steps slowly toward him, taking off her coat. "My coat, Mike, don't you trust me to take off my coat?" She takes one more step, takes off her glove and removes her hair band. She takes off her high heels and kicks them away. That's all she wrote for the famous striptease.

Charlotte says, "My mistake was falling in love with you. That's why I couldn't pull the trigger from across the street at the barber shop." One more step. "And that's why you couldn't pull that trigger any more than I could."

In time-honored femme fatale fashion, she tells Hammer that the world could be theirs and comes into his arms. As they embrace—as every Spillane reader knows—she reaches around him for a gun she's placed in a planter. She points it at him from behind but he shoots her twice.

"Goodbye, baby," Mike says.

Charlotte says, "How could you?"

And in his famous reply, a line tossed off perfectly by Elliot, Mike says, "It was easy."

She slumps to the floor dead.

The book ended there, but on screen Mike must continue: "There was only one more thing to do—order a basket, a real pretty one. And wait for Pat. He had his killer and I had my memories."

One of the nicest things about director/writer Harry Essex's mildly sexy, violent little film is that it was made at the peak of Spillane's popularity and consequently reflects the early fifties of which the books were so much a part, in a manner that none of the later films (even "Kiss Me Deadly") really approach.

Of the Saville-produced films, "I, the Jury" is the most faithful adaptation of the source material and the only one set in Mike Hammer's signature New York. Though filmed in California, "I, the Jury" does a commendable job of transferring the surrealistic, even nightmarish urban landscape that Mike Hammer moves through in the novels. The use of the baroque Bradbury Building for Hammer's home base may employ a famous L.A. landmark, but the shadows and gothic feel of the place are perfect for Mickey Spillane's fever-dream New York.

"I, the Jury" (1953)

Parklane Pictures, Inc. • Running time: 87 minutes • Release date: August 14, 1953

WRITER: Harry Essex; DIRECTOR: Harry Essex; PRODUCER: Victor Saville; CINEMATOGRAPHER: John Alton; MUSIC: Franz Waxman;CAST: Biff Elliott (Mike Hammer); Preston Foster (Capt. Pat Chambers); Peggie Castle (Charlotte Manning); Margaret Sheridan (Velda); Alan Reed (George Kalecki); Mary Anderson (Eileen Vickers); Tom Powers (Milt Miller); Frances Osborne (Myrna Devlin); Bob Cunningham as Robert Cunningham (Hal Kines); Tani Guthrie as Tani Seitz (Esther Bellamy); Dran Hamilton as Dran Seitz (Mary Bellamy); Joe Besser (Pete, Elevator Operator); Paul Dubov (Marty); John Qualen (Dr. R.H. Vickers); Nestor Paiva (Manuel); Robert Swanger (Jack Williams)

2. "The Long Wait" (1954)

Anthony Quinn as Johnny McBride with returning Spillane "doll" Peggie Castle in "The Long Wait." This posed publicity shot invokes the moody, expressionistic sequence that elevates this non-Hammer adaptation to the upper reaches of Spillane on screen.

"The Long Wait" (1954) is the only one of the Victor Saville-produced quartet of Spillane movies to have been signed by Saville as director (he co-directed "My Gun Is Quick" under the non-de-plume "Phil Victor"). As the only non–Hammer novel of Spillane's early period, *The Long Wait* may have been chosen as *I, the Jury's* follow-up adaptation partially because it forestalled the problem of finding a satisfactory screen Mike Hammer. Despite the relative box office success of "I, the Jury," Biff Elliot had not scored a strong enough impression as the private eye to earn a second go-round.

As of this writing, there has never been an official home video release of "The Long Wait," which (like 1953's "I, the Jury") seldom if ever appears on television. Oddly, the other two Saville/Spillane films, "Kiss Me Deadly" and "My Gun Is Quick," are regularly shown on Turner Classic Movies.

Like "I, the Jury," this second Spillane adaptation is long overdue for a critical re-evaluation. Under-estimated by many critics (including the authors), "The Long Wait" is a fine film *noir* with outstanding cinematography by Franz Planer, a strong central performance by Anthony Quinn, a serviceable screenplay by Alan Green and Lesser Samuels that hews closely to the source novel (despite Spillane's own opinion to the contrary), with assured direction by Saville himself that lags only occasionally. The major weakness is a so-so score by Mario Castelnuovo-Tedesco that features a rather syrupy title-credits ballad, "Once," written by Harold Spina and Bob Russell.

Music aside, "The Long Wait" surprises as a strong *noir* that combines two sub-genres: the amnesiac thriller and the small-town corruption tale. Quinn as amnesiac Johnny McBride has retained a startling toughness, much as the violence of Spillane's early novel has lost none of its impact. Further, the hot-headedness of McBride serves two functions well: establishing the brutality of a typical Spillane hero while indicating the capacity of the amnesiac McBride to potentially be guilty of the murder he is accused of having committed, prior to his amnesia.

The central gimmick of Spillane's novel—that one of four women is McBride's former girlfriend, her appearance changed by plastic surgery, make-up and hair dye—gives Saville an excuse to trot out an array of "Spillane Dames" (as PR spreads publicizing the film put it). They are all beauties, if occasionally attired in ridiculous outfits that strain too hard to be sexy. Back again is "I, the Jury" femme fatale Peggie Castle, this time in a positive role as the mysterious "Venus" who may or may not be the missing Vera West.

A solid cast features Charles Coburn as the banker who befriends his former, disgraced clerk, and Gene Evans (on apparent loan-out from Sam Fuller's stock company) plays Servo, a gleefully malevolent casino boss. He and heavy-set Bruno Ve Sota make a memorable pair of over-the-top hoodlums who seem to have walked right out of a Spillane novel. The supporting players consist of mostly familiar faces, including an uncredited Lawrence Dobkins (soon to direct "Mike Hammer" TV episodes) as the doctor who provides amnesia exposition; and Jay Adler is on hand as a comically somber but greedy overage bellboy. In addition to Castle, the Spillane dolls include petite Mary Ellen Kay as Wendy, pin-up model/Marilyn lookalike Dolores Donlon as Troy, and Shawn Smith somewhat overplaying smiling seductress Carol. McBride appears to bed all four "suspects," or so Saville's sly dissolves imply.

Almost all of the major action in the film occurs at night—light and shadow, black and white, good and evil, all appear in stark contrast. The script is good but the photography is better, establishing an ominous tone in the nighttime sequences.

Two scenes of action in particular bring out the best in cinematographer Planer, starting with a tense confrontation in a quarry at night between a bound-and-gagged McBride and

Bruno VeSota as Eddie Packman, left, joins his boss Gene Evans as Servo, right, in contemplating which of Johnny McBride's four "Long Wait" love interests (Peggie Castle, Mary Ellen Kay, Shawn Smith, Dolores Donlon) might be the missing Vera.

three of Servo's thugs. Confusion and gunfire in the darkness of the quarry, where feet shuffle dangerously near the edge of a two-hundred-foot drop-off, create a nightmarish mood and considerable suspense.

But it is the violent finale in an expressionistically lit "abandoned power station" that raises this strong *noir* to a high position among Spillane adaptations. Director Saville credits Russian-born art director Boris Leven for designing this "escapologist scene," including extensive storyboarding.

"I directed the scene matching the camera to the drawings, shot for shot," Saville said, "eighty-seven (set-ups) in one day."

In this striking sequence, Peggie Castle's Venus is a lovely pile of femininity on the floor of a vast space whose shadows are broken by a spotlight making the tortured, bound woman the center of attention. When McBride fails to rescue her, getting sapped by thug De Sota, he is tied into a chair. With Gene Evans' Servo sarcastically, sadistically encouraging Venus to crawl across the vastness of the cement floor to take one last kiss from McBride, the actress strikes seductively victimized poses, crawling like a serpent as Evans hurls a table at her, just another sharp, abstract shape in a room of shadows and shafts and pools of light, revealed in off-kilter camera angles. This is Spillane's nightmare world made real and unreal at once, perhaps the single strongest sequence in any of the films, with the possible exception of the restored fiery ending of "Kiss Me Deadly."

The film opens with jagged credits appearing over an extremely wide shot of a stark landscape with a copse of trees in the center of the screen. Anthony Quinn's character enters screen right and slowly walks past the trees and exits screen left.

The walker is revealed to be Anthony Quinn, humming the theme song and hitchhiking along a lonely highway. It's night and his character has on a white shirt and tie, suit coat slung over his shoulder. A road sign shows US 66. Images are exaggerated, chiacachuro visuals predominating, conveying a dream-like quality.

A farmer wearing a fedora stops his truck and picks him up. Quinn wears a morose expression. Neither he nor the driver speak a word, adding to the dream-like mood. The audience sees the old truck veer to the right off the paved road, then sees the right front tire blow out. This causes the truck to go off the road, down an embankment and burst into flames.

Quinn is thrown from the truck and appears at first unconscious. He picks himself up and runs to help the driver. He tries to open the truck door but only succeeds in burning both his hands (which will provide an important plot point).

In an unnamed county hospital, Quinn is in the Chief Medical Resident's office, in a wheelchair, hands heavily bandaged. He clumsily tries to look up something in a phonebook on the doctor's desk. The doctor appears like Bugs Bunny behind Elmer Fudd and asks him: "Any luck? Maybe we can find a name that'll ring a bell." Apparently that's not the case because Quinn angrily throws the phonebook to the floor. This is the first of many outbursts of rage.

As he cuts off the bandages, the doctor explains that Quinn's lack of memory is "general amnesia." Memory will probably return but that could be a matter of days, weeks or even years. The scene ends with a closeup of Quinn's healing hands, just as the ensuing scene shows him using these hands on a oil pipeline.

Two coworkers are (rather improbably) making fun of his amnesia. An enraged Quinn beats up one of the guys. Over this fight, the brooding worker is fired and paid off: $739.50. His boss asks: "Ain't you got no feelings? You just nearly killed a man. I've had a bellyful of you for two years."

Quinn goes to Tom's Place, a little bar with a Pabst Blue Ribbon sign in the window. He spots his blonde girl friend talking with a guy in a dark hat. Quinn has on a work hat that resembles a western hat. She calls him Allen.

The guy is the girl's old boyfriend. He's just back into town, after visiting Lyncastle, Quinn's old stamping grounds. The fired oil worker immediately gets rough with the boy friend because no one knows where Quinn came from, even himself. The guy then proceeds to say he saw Quinn's picture in the window of a photographer's shop in Lyncastle ("across the state line").

After Quinn dumps his girl into the hands of her former beau and heads out to find himself, the boyfriend gloatingly informs the blonde that he indeed did see the photo, but it was on a poster: "WANTED FOR MURDER, Johnny McBride, Description—Height 6 ft., 2 in., weight 195 lbs, dark brown eyes, black hair. Wanted for the Murder of District Attorney Robert Minnow of Lyncastle."

Quinn arrives via bus in Lyncastle unaware that he's a wanted man. He even asks a motorcycle cop for directions to a good hotel when he arrives. As he steps into the lobby of the Lyncastle Hotel, three attractive women give him the eye (one wears a ridiculous Scottish Highlands outfit). The desk clerk turns out to be an old friend, Pop Henderson (played by veteran character actor Frank Marlowe), who immediately calls Quinn "Johnny" and tells the bellman to take Mr. McBride up to Room 408. Hearing the name, our impulsive hero changes his registration card from William Smith to Johnny McBride. Pop tells him he'll come up to his room to talk when he's off duty. As McBride leaves the lobby, one of the mysterious dames is making a call from the phone booth.

After McBride gives the ancient bellboy $10 to answer any questions he might have, two policemen enter his room. A plainclothes cop named Tucker (Barry Kelley) tries unsuccessfully to get rough with McBride. They want him to go downtown to the station since he had been recognized immediately at the bus station. They tell McBride he's wanted for murder. "We have a piece of evidence that doesn't lie. That says for sure that you're the killer."

At the station, Captain Lindsey (James Millican) does not buy McBride's amnesia. Supposedly McBride was a bank teller who stole $250,000 from the Lyncastle Bank and subsequently killed District Attorney Robert Minnow for having the goods on him. They have his fingerprints on the .38 used to kill Minnow, but are frustrated to find they cannot match them to McBride because his hands had been burned in the truck accident.

McBride goes to the public library to read about the murder. Logan (John Damler), the reporter who wrote the original article about the crime, approaches McBride and asks to see his fingers. He'd heard about McBride not having fingerprints and wanted to check for himself. Seems McBride and bank secretary Vera West had been an item, and she skipped town only two weeks after McBride left.

The reporter's needling manner makes McBride boil over and the hotheaded hero starts to rough Logan up right there in the library. "I'd say you were guilty, McBride," Logan says. "You've got it in you to kill a man." McBride tears out the newspaper article with Vera's picture, shooshes the guy who sees him do it and leaves.

As he exits the library, McBride is almost hit by a bullet from a silenced weapon. Pop Henderson walks up at the same time and is hit by a second silent bullet. Before Pop dies, he tells McBride that Vera has been back for over a year, but that she's changed her appearance and McBride won't recognize her. Pop's final words are: "You'll find her at Servo..."

At Servo Enterprises, McBride discovers secretary Carol Shay (Shawn Smith) crying. Pop Henderson was a friend of hers, took care of her when she first "hit town." McBride goes into see Servo (Gene Evans), who is trying to trick his visitor by having one of his boys, Packman (Bruno Ve Sota), sit behind his desk and play boss. McBride doesn't fall for it. Almost immediately Packman gets mad and tries to jump McBride. Servo steps in to break up the fight. Servo gives McBride three hours to get out of town.

As McBride leaves, Carol asks him to join her for a drink at a "cozy little place." McBride notes that there's one thing that Servo's afraid of: "Me getting my memory back." The cozy little place turns out to be Carol's apartment. She has a false bookcase in the wall that revolves to reveal a bar. She turns on some Latin dance music and tells him to make himself at home. They dance, sharing long lingering looks and eventually kiss. "Man," she tells him, "you're smooth. Like we've been stepping together for years." Carol asks him to wait while she washes her hair. She wants to prove to him that she's not really a blonde and at the same time show a little leg. They are dancing when the director dissolves away from the sexual encounter he can't show.

As McBride walks away from Carol's place, two hoods in hats pick him up, dump him into the trunk of a Ford and take him to the local quarry, hauling him to the edge of the cliff overlooking the quarry lake. The hood in charge decides to untie their victim, to make it look like an accident. Bad mistake. McBride asks for a final cigarette, then lights a match close to the eyes of the hoods, temporarily blinding them; he rolls away and mayhem ensues. The first two hoods accidentally shoot their leader, Harry; McBride tricks them and gets Harry's gun, then shoots them both, with one of them falling two hundred feet into the water.

McBride's next stop is Servo's (as a neon sign announces) CAN CAN CASINO. Packman and Servo spot McBride from a window overlooking the parking lot. They wonder how he got away from the hoods and decide he needs special treatment. Inside, McBride trolls for blondes. He asks a female dealer if Vera is working tonight.

"I don't know any Vera," she says. "But we have a Mollie."

"Who's she?" wonders McBride.

"Me."

This kind of repartee appears in all the Spillane movies, then in the 1950s TV series and the 1980s/1990s Stacy Keach TV series, as Mike Hammer and his clones are found to be immediately irresistible to good-looking women. Of all the tropes in the films, this one has worn the least well.

Blonde floor manager Wendy Miller comes over and encourages McBride to gamble a little. He wins big at the craps table, then tries to get Wendy to talk about Vera. He checks out her dark roots. She tells him Vera might not want to be found. He gives her the hood's gun and tells her to tell Servo that he'll find three bodies at the quarry: "If he waits till daylight he'll be able to see through one of them."

McBride goes to the bank to try to figure out how his fingerprints got on the murder weapon. McBride looks out through his teller window, invoking prison bars. He meets bank president Havis Gardiner (Charles Coburn). He notes that the teller drawers have a slot for a gun next to the money.

After depositing his casino winnings, McBride gets the ancient bellboy to provide info about Servo's latest moll, Troy Avalon (Dolores Donlon). As McBride knocks on her apartment door, the film's theme song "Once and Only Once" can be heard. Inside Troy is singing along. She's a leggy blonde in tight pants wearing a low-cut halter, with a collar and bare back. Her hair is short and has wavy curls. At the door she says, "I bet your name is Johnny McBride." He says, "You win." She replies, "So do you."

McBride wants to know how she knew who he was. Her reply pays homage to the first Spillane movie: "It was easy," she says.

McBride checks the roots of her hair and then kisses her. "Oh, mister, I haven't been kissed like that in a long, long time." He asks to go out, but she says she has nothing to wear. When he doesn't believe her, he checks out her three closets—all empty. Her clothes are locked up by Servo in a fourth closet. She shows him a long box containing many nylons. The name on the box—Venus of Lyncastle—leads McBride to yet another blonde, a modern day Venus (Peggie Castle).

McBride asks Venus many questions regarding a woman's ability to change her appearance, including plastic surgery. He asks her what her real name is, but she says, "Knowing that wouldn't help." He buys some perfume for Carol Shay—Venus will know where to send it, because she and Carol have the same boss.

As McBride and Carol arrive at the Can Can Casino, McBride is welcomed by another silenced shot. He cautions Carol, then runs upstairs trying to find the shooter. A rough-and-tumble fight breaks out between Servo, Eddie and McBride on the stairs. Wendy joins McBride to run upstairs to the room the shot came from. Both Carol and Venus watch McBride (and the rival blonde) from the bottom of the stairs. After McBride turns over some furniture in typically frustrated rage, Wendy claims not to know who shot at him. McBride says the gun used will have a mark on it from the kickback of shooting from the window ledge.

McBride goes into the next room to continue his search, and Wendy bends over to get a safe deposit box key that has been exposed while McBride was tossing furniture around. McBride knocks over a lamp, leaving the room in darkness. He continues to pressure Wendy and then kisses her in semi-darkness.

"Hold me, Johnny," she says. "I'm scared. Hold me tight. Love me."

He complies.

In a rare scene with McBride off-screen, Tucker the cop is seen to also work for Servo. He's been following McBride and reports to Servo, sharing the fact that McBride has been with Servo's girl Troy. Carol comes into Servo's office and sees the pictures of Vera West on the table. Servo sarcastically tells Tucker that they need to call a meeting of the Ladies Aid.

Meanwhile, McBride goes to see the Gardiner the banker, who offers McBride money to leave town, not because he doesn't sympathize with him, but to quell the accelerating violence. The banker wants McBride to stay away until a new DA is in place, but the amnesiac refuses. Gardiner is repairing a toy for his grandson while they have this conversation.

In a somewhat absurd and not entirely effective scene, McBride re-enters his hotel room, carrying a huge blowup of Vera's newspaper picture, which he places on his desk, and tries to reason his way to who she is. He keeps writing her name until it morphs into Venus: Vera, Vera, Venu, Venu, Venus.

This apparently leads him to call on Venus, who also favors tight pants and halter

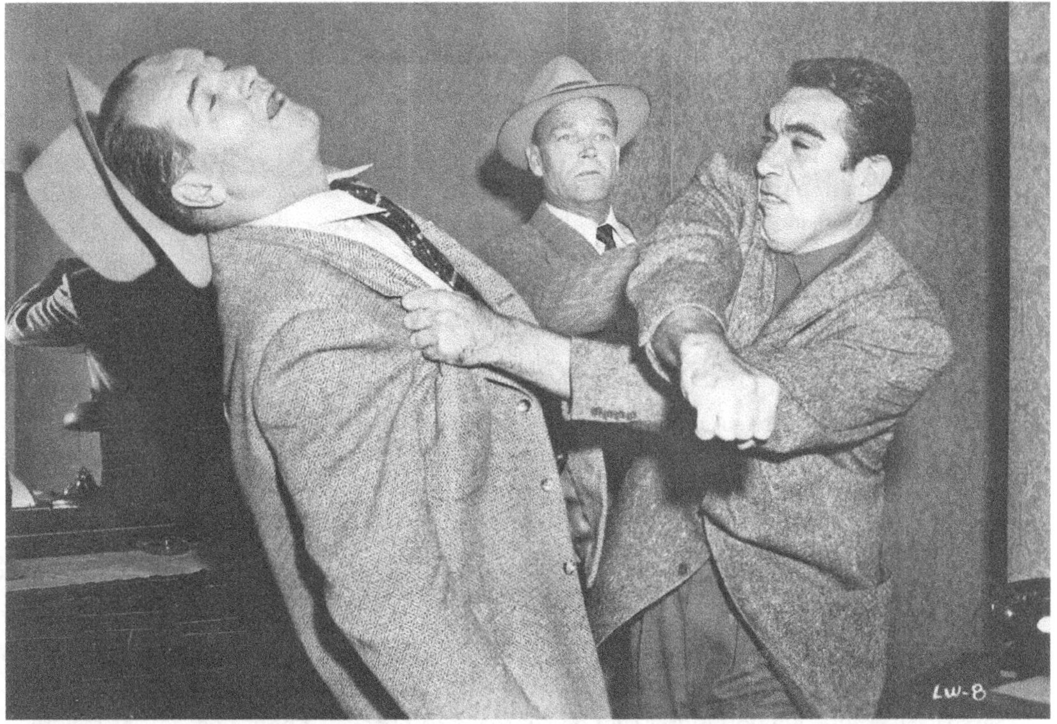

A hotheaded Quinn as McBride punches his way through "The Long Wait." Here he slugs corrupt cop Tucker, portrayed by perennial heavy Barry Tucker.

outfits, this one with a long flowing wraparound scarf all in white, one of the few sexy outfits in the film that isn't risible. She says, "How about a drink? You drink bourbon." McBride wants to know how she knows this. Venus makes a point of getting some special bourbon glasses from the top shelf, for McBride and the camera to admire her assets.

Venus tells him she would not like to be treated the way he treated Carol, leaving her at the casino in lieu of Wendy, who she notes is very pretty. She seems smitten with McBride, vulnerable and jealous over Wendy and especially Vera. Or are they the same person? Soon she receives a phone call summoning her to the casino, where Servo assembles the four girls McBride has questioned—Venus, Wendy, Carol and Troy—for roughing up, to find out if they know anything.

Wendy claims to be Vera, apparently to get Servo to lay off McBride, while Venus says she is not Vera. But Servo doesn't believe her and she tries to escape. He and Packman drive off with Venus. A call tips McBride that Servo and his minion have taken Venus to the power station.

Wendy is in McBride's hotel room. She came to keep him from going to the power station. Corrupt cops have given Servo twenty-four hours to find Vera.

"Johnny, don't go," Wendy says, "I love you."

He takes Wendy's garter (with a French quotation: *Evil to him who evil thinks*, introduced in Venus's first scene at the lingerie shop) to use to hide and secure a little revolver around his ankle.

The power station appears as an overpowering black image under a shimmering moon. The interior of the station is a sado-masochistic showroom, with Venus lying tied up on the floor in a white circle of light. Then the two hoods walk into a closer shot of Venus still in a half-circle of light. These so-far faceless antagonists produce long shadows.

McBride comes in to see Venus all alone on the floor in her white semi-circle in utter darkness. Servo has gone to fetch a gun. McBride comes down a spiral staircase. Packman creeps up on him and slugs him from behind and ties him in a chair facing Venus. In a starkly expressionistic set-up, Servo opens the door screen right and all that is visible is the normal-size man and a huge elongated robotic-appearing shadow that extends past the middle of the screen. All else is totally black—an image of pure evil.

Servo walks in with Venus still on the floor in an oval of light and McBride tied to a chair in the parallel light from the open door. Servo's shadow is elongated and menacing. McBride tells the story about the King and Queen and evil to them who evil think. Venus understands he's signaling her, and her eyes show that knowledge. Venus says wants to kiss her guy once more and Servo strangely allows this. She crawls across the floor trying to get to the gun. Servo pushes a table in her way, which she has to crawl around. The moving table perfectly frames her. She reaches McBride, kisses him, gets the gun from the garter, turns and shoots Servo. But Servo shoots Venus and she is forced to crawl around to shoot the ropes from McBride's hands. Packman comes back in, fires at McBride, who returns fire and kills him. His body falls over the railing.

McBride goes to the workshop where reporter Logan has just finished fabricating a box that holds a gun similar to the one that incriminated McBride in the DA Minnow's murder. The device would leave fingerprints on the gun and the trigger, fired by use of a wire.

Meanwhile, Wendy has returned to the Can Can to get the safe deposit key (417) from Servo's. She calls Captain Lindsey (not one of the corrupt cops) at police headquarters with important information in the McBride case. She then adds, "My name is Vera West."

McBride is breaking into Gardiner's house. The banker hears him and calls Tucker.

Once inside McBride finds the gun with the scratches and the silencer. Gardiner was the one who had been doing all the shooting at McBride. In a confrontation between the two men, Gardiner is revealed as Servo's silent partner, having lent Servo the $250,000 for 51% of casino racket. McBride had figured out Gardiner was the one when he saw how handy he was with making toys for his grandson. Tucker comes in and tries to shoot McBride, who bests him in the ensuing fight. McBride calls Logan to give him the exclusive.

McBride goes to Wendy/Vera. He tells her that Venus is okay in the hospital. She tells McBride that she should have realized immediately that the key was to Gardiner's safe deposit box—after all, she had been his secretary. She tells McBride that she knew he was innocent, but to prove that had to get in with Servo. McBride tells her he loved her face before and now he'll love learning her new one, "remembering everything, forgetting nothing."

While "The Long Wait" is worthy of both rediscovery and reconsideration, it does suffer from a somewhat disjointed narrative whose (blonde) roots can be found in Spillane's own novel. The gimmick of McBride needing to search out his true love—the woman who may help clear his name—from a bevy of beauties by kissing and presumably sleeping with them is fun and entertaining, but also a little silly.

Seldom has a film's appeal been so tied to its chief weakness, which is that amateur detective McBride's idea of sleuthing is to kiss dames and check for dark roots. The harsh critical response that has relegated the film to a lesser status than it deserves probably stems from its violent action scenes alternating with sexually charged ones. Saville may have considered this an ideal way to serve up Spillane's two tasty dishes—violence and sex—but the result remains at least somewhat jarring.

Nonetheless, Quinn is so strong a Spillane hero that it's tempting to call him the Mike Hammer who got away.

Only in recent years has film *noir* been taken seriously enough for a set piece like the mini-melodrama in the abandoned power station to be justly admired. Now the work of cinematographer Planer and art director Leven can be lauded for expressionistic flare and not dismissed as misogynist pandering.

A closer look at "The Long Wait" reveals that of the four Saville-produced adaptations, only the final one ("My Gun Is Quick") was worthy of Spillane's scorn.

"The Long Wait" (1954)

Parklane Pictures, Inc. • Running time: 94 minutes • Release date: May 26, 1954

WRITERS: Alan Green and Lesser Samuels; DIRECTOR: Victor Saville; PRODUCER: Lesser Samuels; CINEMATOGRAPHER: Franz Planer; MUSIC: Mario Castelnuovo-Tedesco; CAST: Anthony Quinn (Johnny McBride); Charles Coburn (Gardiner); Gene Evans (Servo); Peggie Castle (Venus); Mary Ellen Kay (Wendy Miller); Shirley Patterson as Shawn Smith (Carol Shay); Dolores Donlon (Troy Avalon); Barry Kelley (Tucker); James Millican (Police Capt. Lindsey); Bruno Ve Sota (Eddie Packman); Jay Adler (Joe the Bellhop); John Damler (Alan Logan); Frank Marlowe (Pop Henderson)

3. "Ring of Fear" (1954)

Spillane gets third billing in "Ring of Fear" (1954), but the poster art puts him front-and-center, and swinging.

In 1954, John Wayne hired Spillane to star with Pat O'Brien and lion-tamer Clyde Beatty in the decidedly odd "Ring of Fear." For Spillane enthusiasts, "Ring of Fear" has been both Holy Grail and Guilty Pleasure. It is considered here because the film represents Mickey Spillane's screen debut, referencing and frankly exploiting the Mike Hammer franchise that Victor Saville was pursuing at United Artists, with Spillane in a major way contributing (though un-credited) to the screenplay. Further, the confrontation between the villain and Spillane as pseudo–Hammer qualifies "Ring of Fear" as a legitimate, if odd and extreme, example of Spillane on screen.

Long accessible only in a pan-and-scan black and white TV version, the film has never seemed very good. Now a beautiful transfer of the CinemaScope film has finally appeared on DVD and in occasional Turner Classic Movies presentations.

Even with dynamic sound and flawless picture, "Ring of Fear" is still problematic, if great fun and historically fascinating. Troubled during production, the film was rescued to a degree when Wayne approached Spillane well into filming to do a rewrite. Spillane did, reviewing existing footage and fashioning a number of new scenes. His work uncredited (the official screenwriters are Wayne cronies Paul Fix, James Edward Grant—who also directed—and mystery writer Philip MacDonald), Spillane received a white Jaguar as payment from Wayne himself.

Spillane's rewrite made the film worthy of release, creating a compelling little 45-minute crime drama—unfortunately the film is 93 minutes long. Spillane-written scenes—particularly prominent in the film's last half hour—are easy to spot, crisp little crackers of pulp in a soggy sawdust soup.

From the opening credits, the good and the bad of the movie come jarringly to the fore—the film often uses two themes by Stan Purdy written for Spillane's rare, interesting 1954 LP, "Mickey Spillane's Mike Hammer Story"; these dramatic, punchy pieces are well-used in an otherwise routine score. As the credits begin, a blast of the Purdy "Mike Hammer" theme is unfortunately followed by a childish song, "Here Comes the Circus," played over one of the film's three (count 'em, folks, three) circus parades.

And this, in microcosm, represents the frustration of watching "Ring of Fear"—an interesting suspense yarn about an escaped psycho (Sean McClory) who infiltrates Clyde Beatty's circus to take revenge on Beatty and to pursue a now-married former lover/trapeze artist, alternates with endless, often mind-numbing circus footage.

Grant's direction is almost non-existent. This is an early Cinemascope feature, and the director mostly plants his camera and presents many of the scenes in single-take master shots. Some of the circus footage works—Beatty in a cage handling eight lions at a time still astounds, and the trapeze act excites (though we see the latter in full *twice*). Unfortunately most of the rest is of unfunny clowns and nothing-special acrobats, intercut with dull shots of crowds (if you delight at watching eight year-olds eat junk food, this is your movie). The humor is painful in that special 1950s way—a kid who has to go to the bathroom having to wait till a line of elephants passes by; Gonzales Gonzales doing his Mexican version of Willie Best, a performance as squirm-inducing as it is unfunny.

Spillane doesn't enter until twenty-five minutes into the picture, but thanks to him, "Ring of Fear" finally comes alive. He is a natural actor, delivering his self-written lines with his distinctive East Coast cadence. Obviously working with scant direction, he finds pieces of business in each scene, straw to chew, ice cream cone to nibble, fedora to tilt, perhaps overdoing it; but his final showdown with McClory in a claustrophobic trailer is pure Mike Hammer. Suddenly a glorified short subject about the Beatty circus has become a full-fledged, full-color *noir*.

Spillane's sidekick in the film is Jack Stang, that real-life upstate New York cop who was the writer's personal choice to play Mike Hammer. "Ring of Fear" hints that Stang is actually Hammer, and Stang certainly had the hulking build and forbidding face for the role, but he is blown off the screen by Spillane himself. This, of course, sets the stage for Spillane playing Hammer in "The Girl Hunters" (the writer had already portrayed Hammer on the aforementioned "Mike Hammer Story" LP, though Stang's picture was on the jacket).

"Ring of Fear" remains a quirky, frustrating, fun, unique film of its period, and evidence of the enormous celebrity Spillane enjoyed in the 1950s. Marion Carr, the female lead in "Ring of Fear," would have a key role in the following year's "Kiss Me Deadly," making her the only actress to appear opposite characters called "Mickey Spillane" and "Mike Hammer," in two movies likely shot back-to-back.

"Ring of Fear" opens and closes with voiceover narration appropriate to a documentary about the Clyde Beatty circus, in the manner of a short subject of the 1940s or '50s. But the documentary, inside-circus aspect of the film soon makes way for a subplot involving Dublin O'Malley, a mental patient who haunts the circus, obsessed with a young woman who married another man.

Dublin had been wounded in Iwo Jima and never recovered ("no man can ever recapture a dream"). His review board calls him homicidal and that is soon established as he overcomes

Looking very much like Darren McGavin in the later "Mike Hammer" TV series, Spillane has a word with future "Kiss Me Deadly" starlet Marion Carr.

his jailers and escapes in a truck and hops a train. He subsequently jumps to another train to avoid capture, overcomes a train guard and pushes him under the oncoming transcontinental. He has disguised the body in his own prison clothes in hopes the police will call off the search for him.

O'Malley returns to Clyde Beatty circus intent on killing Clyde, who once laughed at him when Dublin attempted lion taming. He wants to persecute the show for those who made fun of him. He blackmails Twitchy, an old circus worker, into pouring acid on the rope that Clyde uses to restrain his new lion.

A series of "accidents" begins to hit the show and the performers begin talking about a jinx. After three of these incidents, Beatty calls in famous mystery writer Mickey Spillane, to investigate.

When star-billed Spillane first appears, the tempo of the movie is immediately energized. He asks a vendor how to find Clyde Beatty. The vendor is reading a Signet edition of *My Gun Is Quick*. Spillane, wearing a suit with an untied tie and his characteristic porkpie hat, asks: "How do you like that book?" The vendor likes it fine, but tells Mickey that this guy Spillane has ruined his life. All he ever does now is read Spillane. He has all the Spillane paperbacks on his counter.

Mickey is amused and says, "Let's get you started on the new one." He pulls a paperback from his inside suit pocket and gives it to the vendor. The title reads: *Tonight I Die*, a nonexistent Signet paperback.

Mickey next appears with Pat O'Brien, who plays the manager of the circus. He tells Mickey about all the accidents and how much money the circus has been cost. In his third scene, Mickey, Clyde and Pat O'Brien are watching a woman balancing herself headfirst on a swing. Chewing on straw, Mickey says, "You'd think all the blood would rush to her head and get her dizzy." Dublin O'Malley joins them. He was Clyde's ring director six years before and Beatty hires him on to take the place of the recently "accidentally" injured ringmaster.

As O'Brien and Spillane walk around the circus tent, they encounter a beautiful blonde sword swallower who wants peppermint flavor on her sword. After being introduced to Mickey, she asks, "Hello, Mr. Spillane, are you married?" His reply is interesting: "Slips my mind at the moment." After Pat and Mickey leave, the girl says, "Slips his mind. Well, that's a new answer."

New ringmaster O'Malley soon encounters his old love, Valerie St. Dennis, now part of the Flying St. Dennis aerialist troupe. She has a young daughter born on June 6, and a very jealous husband Armand. Valerie is played by the lovely Marian Carr, who would later play Friday in *Kiss Me Deadly*.

Mickey's fourth scene is with O'Brien, Beatty and Jack Stang playing Paul Martin, a writer from Signet books who wants to do a series of articles on the circus. He asks, "Are you *the* Mickey Spillane?" Mickey replies, "Yeah." Stang says, "Quite a character you got there." Mickey says, "He sure is."

Of course Martin is a cover story. Martin is really one of Spillane's policeman buddies he's called in to help out. Signet has given Martin some credentials to help with the story. Mickey says he has three-hundred suspects, the number of people who travel with the circus. But he can eliminate the new ring master O'Malley, because he joined after the trouble had taken place. "That's just great," Stang replies. "One out of three hundred eliminated."

In his fifth scene, Mickey tells Beatty that Paul Martin is "really Jack Stang, a hot-shot copper out of New York." They go to check lockers for the compound that decayed the rope.

Dublin tells St. Dennis that his daughter's nose doesn't look like her parents, implying that it looks more like his. Valerie says, "If you made that plain to my husband, he might kill you."

In Mickey's sixth scene, he's lounging on a bale of hay, closing observing a young lovely blonde filling a water bucket. Mickey says to Stang, "I've been looking all over for you." Jack replies, "Yeah, in funny places." They decide that O'Malley might be a suspect after all. Mickey says, "Come on. Let's go see Little Boy Blue."

Next Mickey is lounging in a folding chair with his hat down over his eyes. He and Jack are talking with O'Malley about Beatty. They suspect someone tampered with Clyde's rope. Jack says, "It was one of the ideas my friend Mr. Spillane cooked up." O'Malley tells Mickey he thought he was gathering material for his new book. Mickey replies, "It's no secret." As O'Malley leaves he says, "We should get together, Michael." As O'Malley leaves the scene, Spillane winks at Stang under his hat.

{Spillane's name is, of course, not "Michael." It's Frank and the nickname Mickey is not derived from Michael. But the use of the name further associates Spillane with his famous Mike Hammer character.}

Stang and Spillane observe O'Malley giving a doll as a birthday present to Valerie's daughter, who he has chosen to call Angel. Spillane is wearing a mostly blue Hawaiian print shirt instead of a suit. They soon see O'Malley punched by Armand St. Dennis, who has noticed that Dublin's presence always brings tears to his wife Valerie's eyes. O'Malley picks up a tent stake to go after St. Dennis, but doesn't use it. Jack wonders what caused the attack. Mickey responds that it was the girl, Beatty having told him they were, "Old pals ... or something."

Dublin goes to pressure Twitchy to mess up the rigging for St. Dennis so he will fall. Seems Twitchy is wanted for murder in California. He was an aerialist but is now a drunken clown. During the performance, Mickey and Stang appear. Spillane's now wearing a yellow v-necked polo shirt; Stang has on a light grey suit with a light grey hat. There are two other quick cuts to them. St. Dennis falls but catches himself on a rope, landing hard. Jack says, "That wasn't part of the act. He could have been killed." Mickey replies, "Who do think that would make happy?"

O'Brien soon realizes it had to be Twitchy, because the clown always checked the rigging, and begins a search for him. Twitchy tells O'Malley he's going to tell Clyde. Dublin gives Twitchy a really strong drink and offers him a chaser of water in the tiger trough. When Twitchy leans over, O'Malley drowns him.

Dublin's fingerprints are on the bottle of rum. So he tells Mickey that Twitchy stole the bottle from his trailer. That forces him to race to his trailer and break his own lock.

Mickey is very suspicious, even asking Dublin if he's ever killed a man. Dublin walks in on Mickey searching his trailer. He continues to call him Michael and wonders if he's found his killer. Mickey tells him that he suspects Dublin. In lines that are clearly Spillane-crafted, he tells him that his eyes are those of a "homicidal maniac." All the while Dublin has been fooling with his flash camera. He suddenly shoots it, temporarily blinding Mickey. Dublin slugs the writer and ties him up with the string from his Venetian blinds.

Dublin is going to blind Mickey with acid, but Jack comes to his rescue. O'Brien tells Valerie that Dublin is insane. She races to her trailer to be safe, but when she opens her curtain, there stands O'Malley. Armand comes into the trailer and Dublin runs out.

O'Malley races to the cat tent and lets one of the tigers loose. They all rush to the tent, and Beatty goes in to get the cat back into the cage. There's a short scene with Mickey: "If that cat gets into town..." Dublin races to a nearby train car. The tiger decides to enter the

Movie-star Mickey mixes it up in "Ring of Fear."

same car. Beatty closes the door. It's the car that Dublin is in. He screams out as the cat attacks: "*Mike!*"

Jack says: "Couldn't happen to a nicer guy."

The movie concludes with the documentary narrator bookending the movie with a circus song.

Spillane-the-famous-mystery-writer character is clearly patterned upon Mike Hammer, as "Ring of Fear's" showdown scene between Spillane and psychopath-on-the-loose Dublin O'Malley reveals. O'Malley calling Spillane "Michael" and "Mike" further cements the Spillane/Hammer confusion/association.

Surrounded by professionals like Pat O'Brien and Sean McClory, Spillane appears in twenty five scenes with over twenty minutes of screen time. He exhibits good presence and appears comfortable.

The co-producer was Robert M. Fellows, a man who would work with Spillane several times thereafter. But as a second, bigger-time screen test for Jack Stang as Mike Hammer, "Ring of Fear" was a failure ... whereas in terms of presenting Mickey Spillane himself in the detective's role, it was a success.

"Ring of Fear" (1954)

Wayne-Fellows Productions • Running time: 93 minutes • Release date: July 24, 1954

WRITERS: Paul Fix, Philip MacDonald and James Edward Grant; DIRECTOR: James Edward Grant; PRODUCER: Robert Fellows; CINEMATOGRAPHER: Edwin B. DuPar; MUSIC: Arthur Lange and Emil Newman; CAST: Clyde Beatty (himself); Mickey Spillane (himself); Pat O'Brien (Frank Wallace); Sean McClory (Dublin O'Malley); Marian Carr (Valerie St. Dennis); John Bromfield (Armand St. Dennis); Pedro Gonzalez as Pedro Gonzalez-Gonzalez (himself); Emmett Lynn (Twitchy); Jack Stang (himself); Kenneth Tobey (Shreveport); Kathy Cline (Suzette St. Denis)

4. "Kiss Me Deadly" (1955)

Mike Hammer (Ralph Meeker) is surrounded by the "dolls" of "Kiss Me Deadly" (1955): (clockwise) Marion Carr, Cloris Leachman, Maxine Cooper, and Gaby Rodgers. This light-hearted, sexy publicity still is part of a bait-and-switch publicity campaign designed to attract Spillane's vast readership.

In addition to being the best Spillane film, the next Mike Hammer adaptation, "Kiss Me Deadly," is among the finest of all private eye films, on a very short list including "The Maltese Falcon" (1941), "Murder My, Sweet," (1944), "The Big Sleep" (1946) and "Chinatown" (1974). "Kiss Me Deadly" (minus Spillane's characteristic punctuation: *Kiss Me, Deadly*) is a remarkable and frightening vision of mid–'50s America, a quirky, cryptic examination of an era dominated by McCarthyism and the atom bomb.

At the same time, the film is a commentary and criticism of the Mike Hammer phenomenon itself, a somewhat hypocritical, left-leaning attack on the character and author by director Robert Aldrich and screenwriter A.I. Bezzerides, who were after all exploiting that phenomenon. In an outcome as surprising as the ending of a Mike Hammer novel, the filmmakers wound up inadvertently capturing the magic of Spillane's fever-dream storytelling at the moment of its popular peak.

Critics Elliot Lavine and Bob Stephens state that "'Kiss Me Deadly' is unquestionably the great *noir* film of the Fifties.... Robert Aldrich's film relentlessly focuses on a world at the brink of madness." They point out that by the 1960s, Jean-Luc Godard and Francois Truffaut "were citing 'Kiss Me Deadly' as the one American film most responsible for influencing the French New Wave."

Spillane himself, for years dismissive and even scornful of the film, came to appreciate it late in life, citing Ralph Meeker as his favorite screen Hammer (next to himself). The film's influence on Spillane's work is evident in his 1970 Hammer novel, *Survival ... Zero*, which returns to the same ideological, apocalyptic territory; and again in the posthumously published *Dead Street* (2007), in which stolen radioactive material again serves as the "The Great What's-It" (as Velda describes the McGuffin of "Kiss Me Deadly").

The Hammer portrayed by Ralph Meeker is a self-proclaimed "stinker," whose L.A. firm is kept nicely afloat by divorce cases. Spillane's Hammer, of course, works in New York and spurns divorce work. But these and other changes are not sloppy screenwriting: they demonstrate that much of the film is purposely backward, beginning with opening credits that roll down but read up:

SAVILLE
VICTOR
Presents
SPILLANE'S
MICKEY
DEADLY
KISS ME

Riding in the backseat puts the viewer behind Hammer, re-creating the faceless hero of the paperback covers. As those upside-down credits roll, composer Frank De Vol accompanies Nat King Cole on a haunting ballad on the radio ("I'd Rather Have the Blues"), overshadowed by hitchhiker Christina's heavy, even orgasmic breathing. The nighttime, delirious-dream world of Mike Hammer is already enveloping us.

Frequent Aldrich collaborator De Vol is an overlooked hero in the creative team behind "Kiss Me Deadly." His score is first-rate, brassy, percussive, but also dreamy and discordant, with jazzy, disturbing piano figures often adding tension and anxiety, atonal passages suggesting a science-fiction film. A rather atypical work for De Vol ("Pillow Talk" and "Cat Ballou"), "Kiss Me Deadly" rivals Franz Waxman's "I, the Jury" score and is long overdue for soundtrack release.

Bezzerides, who was as much of an eccentric character as Spillane himself, loved to brag that he threw out the "lousy" book and started over. Exaggeration or outright lie? Either way, it's typical Hollywood bluster. The basic plot and most of the characters originate in Spillane's novel. Everything from the startling girl-in-the headlights opening to the bomb in Hammer's gift car, from the key in Christina's stomach to the killing of Carl Evello at the beach cottage, you will find in the original text. Aldrich and Bezzerides do jettison the first-person, strong identification of the novels—no Chandler-esque voiceover here—and depict Hammer from the outside. From their perspective, the view is a troubling one.

Not that there aren't major changes. The shift of the location from moody, gritty Manhattan to modern, soulless Los Angeles removes a key ingredient from the Spillane recipe. But Aldrich offsets the problem by shooting much of the film in the baroque Bunker Hill area (largely gone now), which only emphasizes the *noir* feel. Still, this seems a modern lifetime away from Essex's post-war "I, the Jury," not a mere two years.

The major change, of course, is the contents of the box, that Great What's-It everyone is pursuing—narcotics in the novel and some nameless radioactive substance (or device) in the film. The film's reputation is so caught up with this atomic McGuffin that Bezzerides claiming to have ignored Spillane's novel has gained a certain credibility. The fiery climax of the film, however, remains a reworking of the fiery climax of the novel, right down to a gut-shot Hammer crawling out of a burning building.

Whereas even minor characters, in most cases, retain the names given them in the novel, Hammer's good friend, Captain Pat Chambers of Homicide, becomes the increasingly patronizing Pat Murphy of the film. Murphy, as portrayed by Wesley Addy, is a smug, possibly alcoholic upper-echelon copper who nonetheless begins the film as Hammer's friend. It's clear they have a close relationship—Hammer continually "borrows" Pat's cigarettes (setting up the moment where Murphy will spot the atomic burn on Hammer's wrist), Pat has a key to Hammer's apartment, and the cop helps himself to the contents of Hammer's liquor cart.

Despite the attempt to play up Hammer's divorce work, the film makes clear—through Pat and Velda—that Hammer has gone off on vendetta-tinged murder investigations before.

"You want to get even for what happened to Christina, don't you?" Hammer says to Lily Carver. "See what I can do."

This comes well after Pat says, "You'd like to take (the law) into your own hands. But when you do that, you might as well be living in a jungle."

This is commentary courtesy of Bezzerides and Aldrich, yet Pat Chambers has said much the same thing to Hammer in many a Spillane yarn.

Later Pat says with grudging admiration, "I've gotta say it—he's got a nose. He can sniff out information like nobody I ever saw."

But ultimately Pat is disgusted with his friend, saying he can "go to hell." There is a sense that this is (as was the case of the novel, at the time) the final Hammer story. That both Pat and Velda are finally fed up with Hammer's impulsive, self-centered, extra-legal ways. Pat's last scene implies he and Mike are through.

Velda, however, remains loyal to Hammer even in this variant version of the loyal secretary/partner. Spillane had not yet revealed the character's last name (Sterling) and Bezzerides provides one (Wickman). Her personality shifts from the gun-toting dame of the novels who has her own "P.I. ticket" to a sensitive, caring young woman whose hobby is ballet ... and who gradually becomes Hammer's conscience. She sarcastically speaks of the faceless bad guys he pursues: "They ... a wonderful word. And who are they?"

Still, she won't abandon him like Pat. She still loves the big lug.

Traveling through Bezzerides' typewriter, the detective himself has gone from idealist to opportunist, as seen early on, when Hammer/Meeker asks, "What's in it for me?" Significantly, when Hammer poses this question to Pat Murphy, off-screen elevator doors open to flood Hammer in light, prefiguring the opening of the deadly box.

Ralph Meeker is an excellent choice to play Hammer, rugged-looking with the consid-

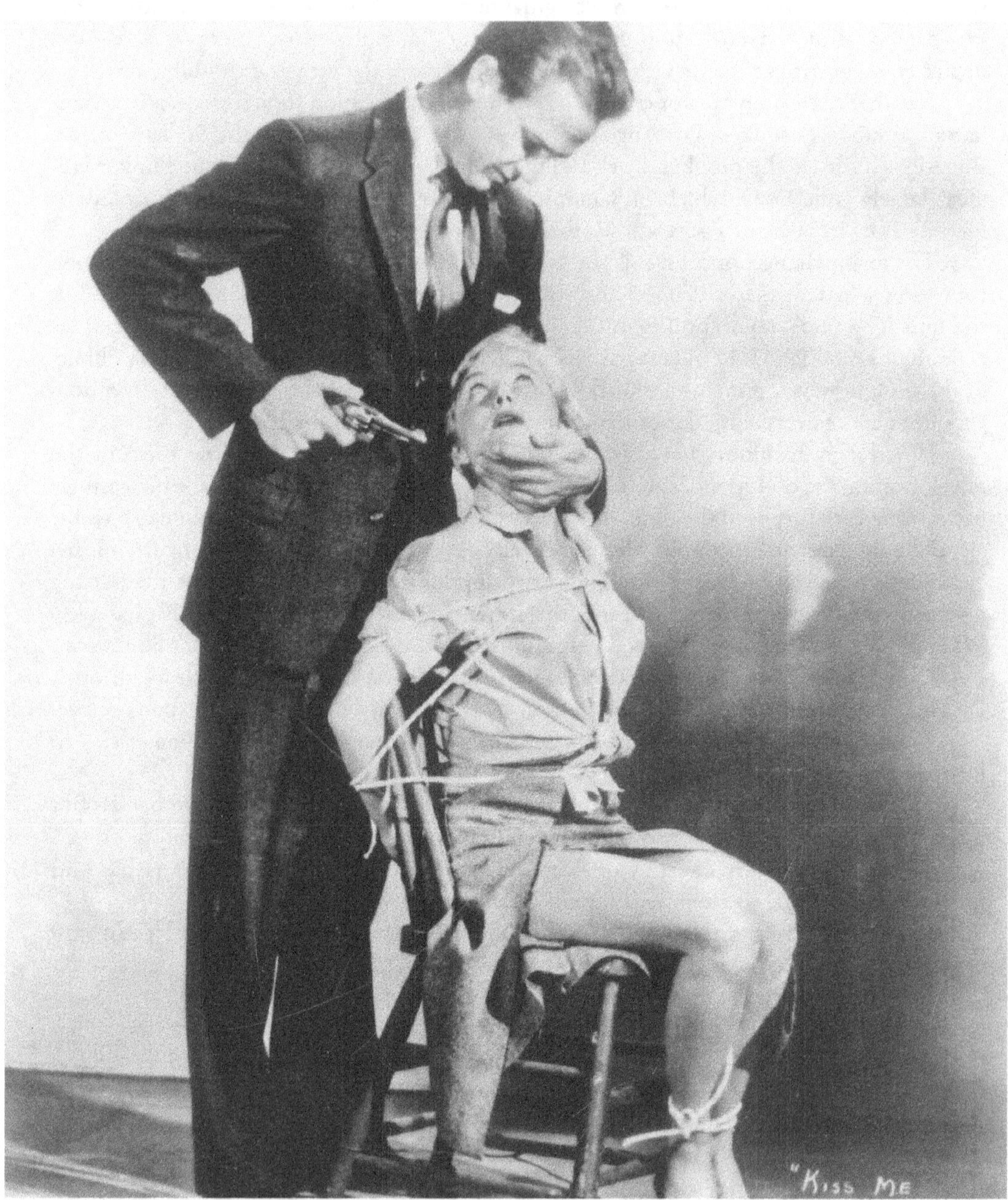

Ralph Meeker, considered by many the greatest screen Hammer, wields a gun in this publicity still that represents no scene in the film. Hammer never uses or even displays a gun in the Robert Aldrich film, and the woman tortured therein is Cloris Leachman, not the pictured Gaby Rodgers.

erable skills of an Actors Studio-bred Broadway actor, coming across smooth and self-contained. He had just won the Critics' Circle Award for his performance in "Picnic" and followed Marlon Brando in the role of Stanley Kowalski in "A Streetcar Named Desire."

Meeker displays enough brawn to fit the basic Hammer type, but the array of "Spillane Dolls" that Aldrich casts are not standard issue sex kittens. With the exception of Marion Carr, the three actresses are attractive but unusual in their looks, carriage and personality.

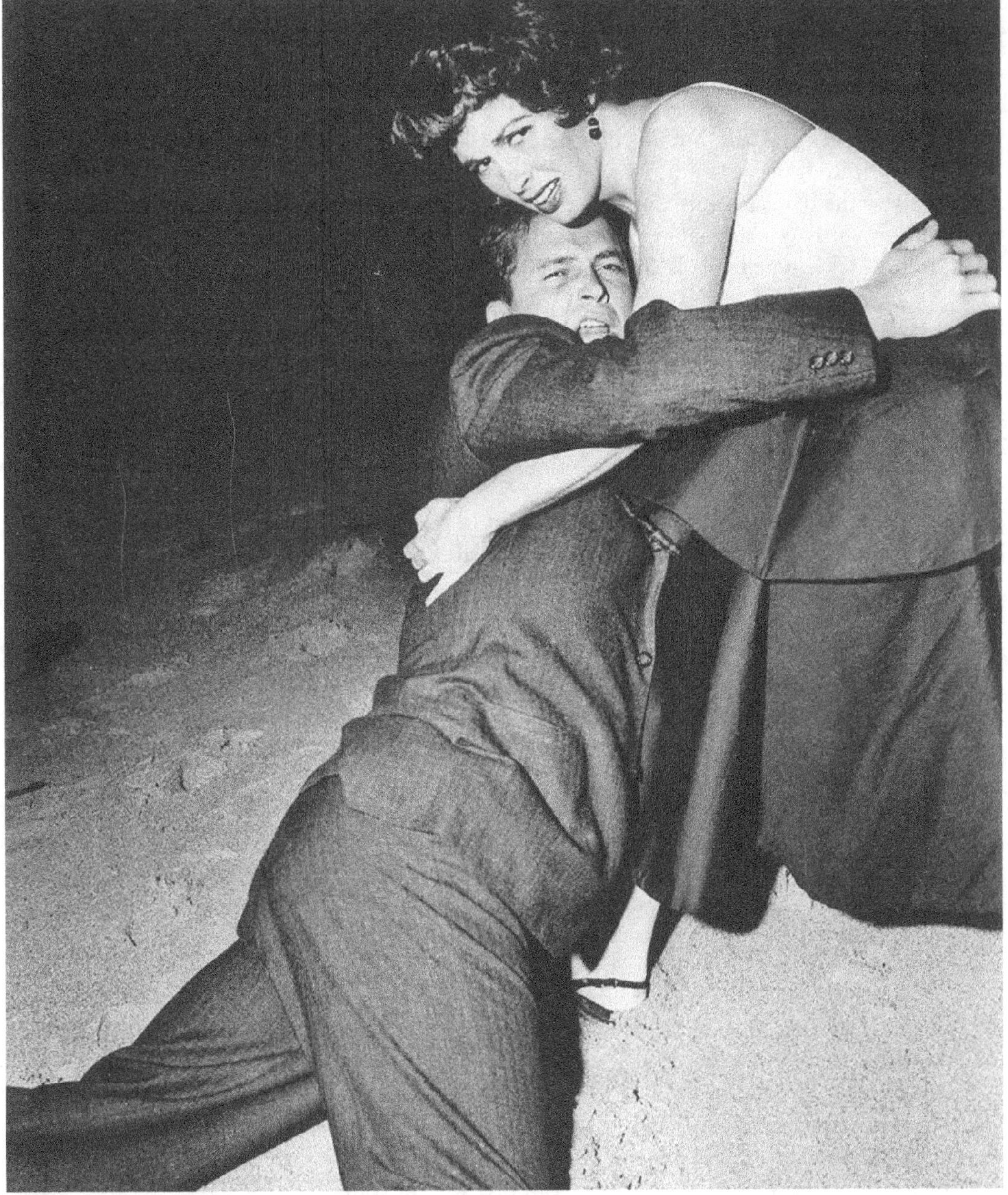

Meeker as Hammer and Maxine Cooper as Velda flee the apocalyptic climax of Aldrich's "atomic" reworking of Spillane's fiery ending to "Kiss Me Deadly."

Though on screen for less than ten minutes, Cloris Leachman—in her film debut—makes a strong impression as doomed Christina Bailey, her intelligent, even wise persona, tinged with fear and sadness, hanging over the movie like a blonde shroud. When late in the film she turns up on a morgue slab, it's an oddly shocking, touching moment.

In their brief time together, Christina needles Hammer (later he says he liked it): "You have only one, real, lasting love ... you."

He tells her to knock it off, not very threateningly, but she goes mockingly on: "Woman ... the incomplete sex, and what does she need to complete her? Why man, of course, wonderful man."

Not a conventional beauty, Maxine Cooper as Velda displays a sinuous quality, her lips plump with promise but her eyes lidded with regret. Like Leachman, she is not an unapproachable sex goddess, but a real woman, the kind you might meet at work, or after.

Gaby Rodgers, a stage actress with only a handful of screen credits, displays an off-beat beauty as the damaged Lily Carver, her manner alternately bird-like and childish, her eyes bedroom sultry one moment and as dazed as a drug addict's the next. Her last-act transition into suicidal femme fatale is chillingly believable.

The only "doll" who is at all typical is Carr (who after all is a veteran of "Ring of Fear"), playing Friday, the half-sister of mob boss Carl Evello. She comes on to Hammer all sexy-baby, cooing and doing a sort of third-rate Marilyn Monroe impression. Hammer goes along with it, kisses her a couple of times at her request—performances, not attraction, much less passion—and when Hammer has gone off to snoop in Evello's poolhouse, she drops her act, speaking to her brother, who asks, "Are you kidding?" Without a hint of Monroe, she says, "Why not?"

Hammer shows surprisingly little interest in these attractive women, although there is some awkward chemistry between him and Christina. Even so, he asks Christina sarcastically, "You always go around with no clothes on?" Later, when Lily kisses him, he seems unmoved, saying, "Okay. You made your point."

Despite his using Velda as "woo bait" who sidles up to men to gain information—a distortion of her role in the novels—Hammer clearly loves her. When he wakes in the hospital and sees her, his smile is genuine, as is their kiss.

"You're never around when I need ya," he tells her.

"You never need me when I'm around," she replies.

Later, in his apartment, he holds her in his arms and there is both passion and tenderness in it. Does he take her for granted, and even mis-use her? Yes. But he does love her, and her him. That much is pure Spillane.

So much for sex—what about violence? Early in the film, Captain Pat Murphy revokes Hammer's P.I. license and takes away his gun permit. Publicity stills aside, Mike Hammer never touches a gun in the entire movie. In the first two Saville/Spillane adaptations, Mike Hammer and Johnny McBride are shown hurling bad guys (and sometimes witnesses) around with a casual if rage-fueled brutality. But Aldrich rarely shows Hammer's act of physical violence—he implies that Hammer has martial arts skills that disable and even kill his opponents. Keeping off-screen all but a punch or two, and various slaps, makes an almost mystical force out of Hammer.

As the detective tells gangster Carl Evello, "I figure it's a good thing to speak a lot of languages—any country you go to, you can take care of yourself."

In the most violent on-screen confrontation, Hammer calmly walks along, unimpressed, between attacks by a knife-wielding thug, as if this kind of thing is commonplace, just something he takes in stride. Finally he punches the thug, sending the man careening down several endless flights of cement stairs, very likely killing him. Hammer's glance at his victim registers only the slightest, smirkiest smile.

So is the Aldrich/Bezzerides Hammer a sadist? The director in the above-mentioned scene, and in the notorious sequence in which Hammer slams Doc Kennedy's hand in a drawer, repeats the action to emphasize it, elongate it, and make Hammer look worse. Yet closer examination of the film suggests Hammer is not so much a sadist as single-minded.

The two old men he slaps—Doc Kennedy at the morgue and the older gent at the health club—he first offers money. Kennedy takes several helpings of green, then greedily demands more, and in Hammer's view deserves being spanked. The health club gent turns down the bribe and regards Hammer with snobbish disdain. This gets him slapped. Hammer needs the information; he's not sadistic—he's just not kidding around. Later he shows concern to the old boy, after the dangerous atomic box is found in a locker.

Earlier in the film, when he visits Christina's apartment, Hammer helps a nice elderly fellow—an Italian, like the opera singer Trivago—with a heavy trunk. Several exchanges between Hammer and the old man show the detective respectful and even warm to him. Significantly, this Italian is helping Hammer. Even when Hammer smilingly snaps a Caruso record in two, in order to get cooperation out of failed opera singer Trivago, he seems to be doing so out of the single-mindedness of his mission, not meanness. When he leaves, he compliments the old opera singer on what he's listening to, with no wise-guy sarcasm at all: "It's a lovely record." The only irony is Aldrich's (the line is not in the Bezzerides screenplay).

For a movie shot in under three weeks, the mastery of the camera-work and art direction is dazzling. The three- minute take at the boxing gym—one continuous shot that starts on a punching bag, follows a fighter to the stairs to pick up an ascending Hammer, follows Hammer for his conversation with Eddie Yeager (Juano Hernandez), then over to the phone for a call to Pat Murphy—is a stunning piece of sustained narrative filmmaking.

Similarly striking is the camera set-up that shows Velda in her ballet/exercise room only to reveal the first image was a reflection in a wall of mirrors, as Hammer enters. Don't accept anything in this film at face value, Aldrich warns us.

Simpler but also effective is the uninterrupted master shot of Hammer questioning truck driver Harvey Wallace, who accidentally ran down a potential witness. In the midst of conversation, we pick up Wallace (Strother Martin, unbilled in this early screen role) at his kitchen table with his family around him. The camera pushes barely perceptibly in as the fine character actor in the briefest of scenes conveys distress over having accidentally killed a man.

Credit the great cinematographer Ernest Laszlo as well as Aldrich himself for these and other striking images. The film shows an interesting preoccupation with introducing characters by way of their walking or running feet (starting with Christina on the pavement). Shots prefigure, as when the gas station attendant serving Hammer and Christina uses a jack like the one that will lead to Nick's death. Others recall previous images, as when the obnoxious landlady at Christina's waits at the bottom of the stairs as Hammer and her husband go up—the director positions her at the top of frame, cutting her off in imitation of Christina's dangling legs during the torture sequence. Velda waking up in bed with Mike hovering ("Hello, Mike") recalls Mike waking up in the hospital with Velda hovering ("Hi, Velda").

Constantly Hammer goes up baroque staircases, climbing, climbing, answers always out of reach. He cheerfully complains that a guy could get a heart attack coming up the stairs to an apartment house, where the crone clerk says, "Who invited you?" Needing nothing from her, Hammer thanks her instead of slapping her.

Whether the distinctive, persistent uses of "X's" through the film is Aldrich's work or art director William Glasgow's is unknown. Howard Hawks had used "X's" to represent death in *Scarface* (1932). Here Aldrich and Glasgow pepper frames with X's as an ironic combination of X as death but also kisses, as in the XXXXX's at the bottom of a naive love letter.

Here is a partial list of the X motif found in "Kiss Me Deadly":

X shadows on the floor made by the brass bed Hammer has been flung on while Christina screams as she's tortured.
X legs of the table Christina is tortured upon.
Row of gingerbread X's under the billboard at Nick's garage.
X-shapes on front of Hammer's building where thugs (or feds) are parked out front.
X-shapes of camera bags hanging on Hammer's apartment wall inside the door.
Windows cast X shadows in Hammer's apartment.
X-shape in white dominates abstract painting in Christina's apartment (also recalls Christina's outstretched hands as she stands in highway, flagging down Hammer's car).
Lily Carver's room, semi-sheer drapes have X and O pattern.
Overhead view of intersection forms an X.
Low angle at Nick's reveals ceiling's wooden beams forming X's above Hammer's head as Nick looks for the bomb in the gift car.
Chairs in Velda's reception area are metal with X-pattern.
X's on windows of Evello's poolhouse.
X shadow on hallway wall outside Trivago's apartment.
Hanging laundry in Trivago's apartment form X's and recall Christina's outstretched arms as she stood in the highway.
X in canopy draping over Velda's bed.
Undercarriage of beach cottage is X-shaped.
Hammer tied face down to bed forms X (recalls Christina's outstretched arms in highway).
X shadow on wall at coroner's office.
X-legged liquor cart in beach house.

There are surely others, just as some viewers will think this recurrence of X's is accidental. Those viewers are wrong.

Aldrich and Bezzerides may not have cared for Spillane's novels, but they knew their audience would be heavily populated by Mike Hammer fans. They were not stupid men. Despite what the latterday critics may think, the Mike Hammer of *Kiss Me Deadly* is primarily a positive character. From the very start, irritated or not, he gives Christina a ride. He helps her make it through a roadblock, putting himself at risk with the law. When the Interstate Crime Commission interrogates him (he barely acknowledges them with a word or a glance), they come off unctuous and smug, as does Pat Murphy, who finally doesn't seem to care about Velda's fate. Hammer hangs out with the underdogs of society, Greeks like Nick, person-of-color Eddie Yeagher at the gym, blacks like his friends at the Pigalle. Pat and Velda may be frustrated with Hammer, but they are in his shadow and his sway—they live in his world.

Further, the common critical notion that Hammer in "Kiss Me Deadly" is surrounded by art he doesn't understand—and it *is* fun that tough guy Mike must solve the mystery by interpreting a poem (which he does!)—Hammer's own apartment is filled with the same kind of modern art seen at Velda's, Christina's and even William Mist's art gallery. Much has been made of Hammer turning on Christina's radio and having classical music play, as if this brute is being confronted by something he doesn't understand ... *but when Hammer turns his radio on at home, it's tuned to the same classical station.*

When Hammer meets Christina, he's cool, cocky, self-assured. These qualities emerge from time to time later in the film, but there's also a sense that Hammer has been shaken by nearly getting killed. He moves through much of the first act like a distracted zombie, edging down his own hallway in abject paranoia. His mechanic pal Nick asks him, "Are you all right, Mike?" Hammer, with a contradictory smile, says, "I don't know. Maybe not."

Just prior to this conversation, Nick has risen from his grease pit as if from the grave (he'll soon inhabit one) to greet Hammer oddly: "Hey, look, Sammy, my friend just return from the grave!" In case we missed it, Nick adds, "Like Lazarus."

Hammer "dies" twice in the film (and possibly a third time, by radiation poisoning, after its conclusion). Christ figure Christina dies for real, but it's Hammer who's resurrected after the "accident." Throughout the investigation, he returns gradually to a more vital life until he's as cocky as at the start.

But after discovering the atomic box, getting himself burned and then beaten by Evello's "cannons," with Velda kidnapped because of him, Hammer is beaten down. He looks a mess, and for the first time, a character other than Hammer is given the dominant, higher angle in over-the-shoulder two-shots. Hammer looks small, defeated, as Pat gives his great speech:

"Now listen, Mike. Listen carefully. They're harmless words, just a bunch of letters scrambled together. But their meaning is very important. Try to understand what they mean. Manhattan Project. Los Alamos. Trinity."

Defeated, alarmed, Hammer turns over the locker key to his now contemptuous friend.

But once again, like Lazarus, he rises, and soon Hammer appears in a beautiful suit, his hair perfectly slicked back, his confidence high, a force of nature. The hell with the atomic box. He's going to find Velda. He's Mike Hammer again. Both Mickey Spillane's *and* Aldrich/Bezzerides'.

Ironically, Hammer shares only one short scene with Dr. Soberin, the villain of the piece, earlier, when Hammer is briefly captured. Soberin speaks in poetry, too: "As the world becomes more primitive, its treasures become more fabulous." Actor Albert Dekker gets his face on screen in just one sequence, at the beach house, where his mistress Lily Carver barely seems to hear his high-flown dismissal of her and certainly ignores his final, gut-shot warning: "As if I were Cerberus, barking with all his heads, at the gate of hell ... don't ... open ... the box."

Of all the Spillane films, "Kiss Me Deadly" has the strongest finish—a real Spillane ending, if considerably reworked. When Lily Carver opens that hissing box with its valuable but, of course, deadly radioactive substance, she is consumed by fire, and so is the beach house. In the original, now restored ending, the wounded Hammer manages to rescue Velda, who then rescues him, helping him down the steps of the beach house to stand in the lapping waves of the ocean to witness in Lot's Wife horror as an explosion whose end-of-the-world implication is emphasized by suggestions of a mushroom cloud.

For years, the TV print had concluded with an alternate ending—unknown to director Aldrich, who rode to the rescue with his own vault print for a DVD release in 1997—that implied Hammer and Velda died in the explosion. Some argued that this ending was accidental, due to missing footage that had been damaged. But the alternate ending has "The End" superimposed over the exploding house, while Aldrich's original, restored conclusion plays "The End" over Hammer and Velda standing in the water. Somebody changed it. Who? Why? It's a mystery even Mike Hammer can't solve.

"Kiss Me Deadly" opens with Christina Bailey (Cloris Leachman) running down a deserted California highway clad only in a trenchcoat. She flags down Mike Hammer's Jaguar convertible by holding her spread hands high in the air and standing in the middle of the road. The quite sane Christina has escaped from a mental hospital where she is being held against her will by as yet defined forces.

Mike swerves at the last second to avoid hitting her. As he restarts his stalled car, Mike says with open hostility: "You almost wrecked my car. Well?" When all Mike gets in reply is Christina's labored breathing, he says, "Get in." As Nat King Cole sings "I'd Rather Have the Blues (Than What I've Got"), the iconic backward credits begin to roll. The audience hears only the blues lyrics and Christina's combination of panting and stifled sobbing. The credits lack the usual author acknowledgment: no "From the Novel by Mickey Spillane"; only "Screenplay by A. I. Bezzerides."

Mike wants to know, "What's this all about?" Just before his car is stopped in line at a police roadblock, Christina—clad only in a raincoat—takes his hand and places it on her leg. Mike lies to the police about his "wife." As he drives off, Mike asks, "Can I have my hand back now?"

Mike wants to know who forced the hitchhiker to go to the "laughing house."

"I wish I could tell you that," she says, then adds, "But you know the old saying."

Mike finishes her thought: "What you don't know can't hurt you?"

Shortly Mike notices his steering is off and pulls in at a Chevron gas station. Mike asks the attendant to check his right front wheel. Christina jumps out to go the rest room and Mike waits for the young man to check the car. The attendant jacks up the front end and soon pulls a small branch stuck under the car. Subsequently when Christina asks the attendant to put a stamp on a letter, and mail it for her, he leeringly tells her the car picked up a branch when they took that "little trip off the side of the road."

Christina's expression registers disappointment but not surprise at this sexist remark.

Soon Mike is back on the highway. Christina tells Mike that a person can tell a lot about a person by the kind of car he drives. "You're one of those self-indulgent males," she says. "You're the kind of person who never gives in a relationship. You only take."

Christina continues to give Mike a hard time and finally he says, "All right. Let it go."

Mike asks his passenger's name. She responds by asking him if he ever reads poetry, gets a sideways smirk, then answers her own question: "Of course not." She was named after Christina Rossetti, who wrote love poetry. She knows Mike's name because she read it on the steering-column-mounted registration certificate. This also hints who the letter was sent to.

Her last words to Mike make him take his eyes from the road for the first time to look at her: "If we don't make that bus stop, remember me."

Mike is typically confident that he'll get her to the bus stop. For all her needling, he likes her. Then a car screeches into view, running them off the road.

After that, all we hear from Christina are her screams, as she is being tortured. Her raincoat is shown on the floor and all the viewer can see are her dangling legs and feet.

Heads cut off in the frame, the bad guys are differentiated by their shoes. Mike is passed out on a iron frame bed with exposed springs, lighting emphasizing the shadows from the austere metal headboard. The viewer can see the snazzy shoes with highlighted white stitching around the soles of the wing-tipped shoes, which crisscross the parallel shadows of the bed. (Christina continues to scream in this scene, but soon her legs are not moving at all. These screams seem intended to milk the scene, since she is clearly dead at this point.)

When the screaming stops, one hood tells the leader he can revive her. The leader responds that such an act would be resurrection, the first of many biblical and mythological allusions wasted on all his underlings. Who does the hood think he is that he can raise the dead? The headless hood is holding a large pair of pliers used to torture Christina.

The hoods load Mike and Christina back in his Jag and push them over the side of a cliff. The small fire that erupts prefigures the last scene at the beach.

So far the audience has seen a nude woman (at least under the trenchcoat) flagging down a car, a suggested sexual favor for Mike helping her, both a literary and biblical reference, a torture scene and an "accidental murder." Not bad, for the first ten minutes of a movie in 1955.

But Mike is not dead. He awakens in a hospital bed to angelic faces—one a pretty nurse, the other the iconic Velda. Mike's world is framed by women. All the action of Mike's apocalyptic journey will be controlled by his response to their love or animosity. This dichotomy is the first of several instances in the film that show Aldrich and Bezzerides could not control the emotional connection of Spillane's ethos with their own propagandistic reworking.

There is a kiss of greeting between Mike and his partner (she is clearly more than a secretary—also true in the novel). The scene is shot off-kilter, often suggesting Mike's point of view, harkening briefly to Spillane's first-person approach (no voiceover here, remember).

Police captain Pat Murphy comes into the hospital room, tells Hammer he's been out for three days and that he thought he'd have to buy a new tux for Mike's funeral. He wants to know if Mike remembers what happened, but the screen goes out of focus as Mike slips back into unconsciousness. We have now met the two most important people in Hammer's world—best girl Velda and best friend Pat.

As Mike and Velda walk down the steps from the hospital, Mike admires passing females (really the sole indication in the film of such an interest in him) only to be interrupted by the police and driven to the office of the Interstate Crime Commission (read: FBI). Pat waits patiently and laconically outside Room 724—he knows appealing to Hammer's better instincts will do no good, though he'll make that mistake repeatedly himself throughout the film.

Five men are interrogating Hammer, though only three speak. They know the "facts" but they want a "little more fill in." Mike quips, "I almost get myself killed and you want a little more fill in."

One of the interrogators reads from Mike's file: "Michael Hammer. 1401 Wilshire Boulevard, Los Angeles, California. He calls himself a private investigator. He specializes in divorce work. He's a bedroom dick." The feds continue to pound him with what they consider salacious details. "He has a secretary—at least that's what he calls her—named Velda Wickman." The cop says Mike sends Velda to attach to the husbands while he goes for the wives, thus playing both ends against the middle. Mike interrupts them: "OK, you've got me convinced. I'm a real stinker." After one penultimate snide comment about Mike's being anxious to get back to his life's work, the lead interrogator intones as Mike walks out of the room: "Open a window."

Pat wants to know the story as well. As usual Mike wants to go it alone and tells Pat very little. Pat asks him to step aside so that law enforcement can do their job. Mike's response: "What's in it for me?"

Mike goes to Nick's garage via Yellow Cab to find out about his car. Left in frame is an MG logo and on right is a JAGUAR oval. The oval covers part of a billboard which reads: "Season's Greetings" (Christmas again, but minus its ironic/thematic use in Essex's "I, the Jury"). Nick is in the grease pit working.

Ecstatic to see his friend, Nick tells Mike the Jag is totaled ("No more va va voom") and that "some very tough guys" have been looking for Hammer.

The cab drops Mike off at his apartment. Two beefy hoods (or maybe feds) are sitting in a big Cadillac waiting for his return. Mike looks back over his shoulder before he gets into the elevator to go up to his apartment. He stands in the shadows close to his door, assessing the situation. His apartment number is 904. He pushes the door all the way back before he enters.

Mike looks around the room as if entering a strange space, not his apartment. There are three camera bags hanging on the wall. One corner shows a large console TV; a complete drink cart stands in front of him; phonographs are visible on a side table close to the TV; a modernistic nude statue is on the wall near the fireplace. Mike continues through to his bedroom. Two pieces of abstract art hang above his bed.

His phone rings and a reel-to-reel tape answering machine (a very exotic, pre–James Bondian device for the era) switches on, a female voiced intoning: "This is Crestview 5-4124. Mister Hammer, whom you are calling, is not available. Please leave a message at the sound of the tone." The caller is Velda. She tells him she'll be right over.

Mike's picture window overlooks a six-lane tree-lined highway. The frame soon dissolves from Mike's pensive look to a loving kiss with Velda. She tells him that a man named Ray Diker has been trying to get in touch with him. Their kissing is interrupted by a knock on the door. Velda says, "Don't answer it." It's Pat on "official business." Velda says "Maybe he'll go away" and continues kissing Mike.

Pat lets himself in, sees them kissing, and says, "Go ahead. Don't mind me."

Then Pat shows Mike an official letter revoking Hammer's P.I. license and gun permit. "If I catch you snooping around with a gun in your hand, I'll throw you in jail." He says all this in a sing-songy way that is at once scolding and chummy. Mike asks Pat about Ray Diker, but then answers his own question. Diker was a science reporter for the news. Mike wants to know why he dropped out of sight.

Helping himself to his friend's booze, Pat continues to press Mike about the death. Showing Pat abruptly out, Mike says if he knew anything he'd tell the cop. Pat responds, "Suuuuure you would."

Velda does not want Mike to see Ray Diker. She sits down in a leather arm chair and picks up a magazine—*Physical Culture* with a leggy blonde on the cover. Mike wants Velda to call "Mr. Friendly," a guy she had on the hook for another job to get some information. He tells her, "Call him up. Tell him you're sorry. Give him some of that sincerity." Velda looks at him askance.

Velda tells Mike about Christina Georgina Rossetti (1830–1864) and wants to know why he's interested in the dead girl. Mike responds telling her that his Christina told him he could forget about her if they got to the bus stop. But if they didn't make it: "Remember me."

Velda comes over to Mike: "She's dead. But I'm not." She leans over to kiss him: "Hey.

Remember me?" When she starts to kiss him, he reminds her that she should be working on Mr. Friendly. Mike tells her to give him some of that "honey stuff" and says the tape recording she made of them "sure was nice." All of this is spoken with heavy but sarcastic innuendo. Velda leaves, telling him to do her a favor and "keep away from the window. Someone might blow you a kiss."

When Mike wakes from a nap, the room is dark. He looks at his note pad: "Ray Diker. 121 Flower St. Los Angeles, Calif." He drives there in another convertible, an MG with bug-eye headlights. The accompanying music conveys a strong sense of foreboding. As he parks, a hood in a doorway observes him, tails him down the street. Mike knows the hood is there, stops to get directions from an all-night newsstand, then pauses to a buy a bag of ten-cent popcorn from a vendor who seems to know him.

A large illuminated neon clock shows the time as 2:16 A.M., an oddly surreal deco touch. Mike stops at a cigarette machine and smirkingly observes the hood in the mirror on the machine. As Mike walks away, the hood pulls a switchblade. As soon as Mike hears the "click," he turns throws the bag of popcorn into the hood's face, and pulls the guy's arm behind his back. Mike forces him to drop the knife, hits him a few times, then slams his head against a brick wall more times than necessary, until the guy slides senseless down to the pavement.

Casually, Mike picks up the knife and walks away. The hood recovers and tries to get Mike from behind, but Mike throws him down a long flight of outdoor stairs to a street far below.

On Flower Street, a bruised-and-beaten Ray Diker will only tell Mike two things: Christina's last name, Bailey; and her address, 325 Bunker Hill. The only other thing he says: "If you knew you'd be afraid, like I am." Whether Diker's scars indicate he's been beaten for information already, or are burns courtesy of (the as yet unmentioned) atomic box, remains ambiguous. But Aldrich stages Diker's response at the door in an oddly surreal fashion, giving only a slice of his roughed-up face.

At Christina's place, Mike befriends an old man moving furniture utilizing a back-and-head-brace gadget to balance a trunk. A mildly comic episode follows, involving the super and his obnoxious wife, who Hammer regards with bored disgust. In Christina's apartment hundreds of books ride a wall of shelves; on her night stand is *Sonnets of Christina Georgina Rossetti*, which Mike takes with him. When Mike notes an empty birdcage, the apartment super tells him Christina's roommate, Lily Carver, had let the bird die. He doesn't know where Carver is. Outside, however, the old man who earlier Mike had helped gives the detective Lily Carver's new address.

Mike parks his convertible in front of a walk-up rooming house. This is the third set of stairs utilized by the director. Just as Christina's death had been framed by the slates in the steel bed, the viewer's introduction to Lily Carver is shown from behind vertical slats in her bed, echoing cell bars. She's showing off a shapely leg as she reads a magazine. As Mike enters, she points a .38 at him in a tableau that echoes various Spillane paperback covers, including *Kiss Me, Deadly*.

The quirky woman's very name conveys death and destruction: "lily" as the flower of death and "carver" with all its slashing resonance. This, of course, is a name from Spillane's book—no wonder Bezzerides kept most of the names from the "lousy" book he "threw away."

Mike questions her but doesn't find out anything except that Christina was "scared, more and more scared," and after a few visits by mysterious strangers, "they" took her away. Why did she let that bird die? She tells Mike she liked the bird, that it reminded her of

Christina. The scene closes with Carver once again on the bed, her face obscured by two suitcases. Only her legs and hips are visible. So often in this film the director reduces characters to limbs.

Mike returns to his apartment and receives a message from an unknown man who tells him that his (Hammer's) world has been interrupted, but if Mike will just forget about Christina, everything will be fine. The detective should check the street in front of his apartment house the next morning.

The next morning, Nick drives up, spots a brand-new Corvette convertible with the keys in it. Mike stops him from cranking it; they check and find a "torpedo" (in this case a few sticks of dynamite) wired to the starter. They start up the car and head to Nick's garage. When Nick encourages Hammer to open up the new vehicle, Mike says no—there is a second bomb. They find it wired to the speedometer. Nick agrees to find out who had the ability to wire a car like that. He says he knows someone in Culver City with connections. Mike tells Nick he can have a car just like the Corvette, if he finds out.

Mike opens the door to Velda's apartment—obviously he has a key. In addition, his own office seems to be attached. Velda is doing ballet moves while listening to classical music on a phonograph. Her outfit is tight black ballet pants and a bare midriff exercise top with a plunging neckline accented by parallel black-and-white stripes. The flooring in her apartment is large black-and-white tiles. Mike lights a cigarette with a lighter and lifts the tone arm from the record. The music stops but Velda keeps doing her ballet moves as if the music were still playing. Mike replaces the tone arm, the music begins again and he tells her to forget the divorce job with Mr. Friendly, he's on to something big.

Mike wants her to find out more about Christina. She tells him that Ray Diker called and left some names for Mike to check:

LEOPOLD KAWOLSKY
HARVEY WALLACE
    OVER BOMBA CAFÉ, CAHUENGA STREET
NICOLAS RAYMONDO
CARMEN TRIVAGO
    HILLCREST HOTEL, TEMPLE STREET.

Velda says, "Nick tells me your name in Greek would be Mikhail Spherios. But under any name would it be as sweet?" Oblivious, Hammer muses, "Kawolsky," a comic moment that may in part be a riff on Meeker's Broadway role in "A Streetcar Named Desire." On Velda's desk, next to her manual Royal typewriter, a small black poodle is sleeping on a white cushion. She tries to kiss Mike but he's only interested in finding out about the case and the names on the list. Nicholas and Lee are both dead: one fell out of cab, the other run over by a truck. Automobile "accidents" like Mike and Christina's. Carmen is an unemployed opera singer; Harvey Wallace drove the truck that killed Kawolsky.

Mike asks Wallace if Kowalsky stepped out in front of his truck or he was pushed in front of his truck. Wallace tells him it was more like he was pushed.

At a boxing gym, Mike's buddy Eddie is a smalltime fight manager known for selling out his boxers. Mike asks about Kowalsky. Eddie's mood drops as fast as the big cigar in his mouth and he tells Mike about a visit from two hoods, Charlie Max and Sugar Smallhouse. Mike offers to top their offer for silence. Eddie says Hammer can't top their offer: "They said they'd let me breathe."

Pat tips Mike off that the two hoods work for crime boss Carl Evello, a name Hammer clearly recognizes as big-time. Mike drives into the drive at Evello's palatial digs in his new Corvette. He's followed into the driveway by a busty blonde named Friday ("I'd have been named Tuesday if I had been born on Tuesday"), who turns out to be Carl's half-sister, "same mother, different father." She says, "Crazy," leans into him, giving him a full body kiss. She says, "You don't taste like anybody I know."

Friday takes Mike into Carl's house for a drink. She wants to be his "close friend." He says he wants to go for a dip in Evello's pool. Friday walks him out to the pool house. Once Evello sees Mike, he orders Charlie and Shug to take care of Mike. But Mike's real goal is to see the shoes in the pool house to identify their owners as participants in Christina's torture—like us, Hammer's view of the bad guys was headless. Mike sees a pair with white stitching but it's not an exact match. The two hoods enter; in mostly off-camera action, Mike quickly floors Sugar and a confused, terrified Charlie retreats.

A disgusted but amused Evello tells Friday to send Mike into the house. Evello immediately makes a phone call to his superior (as yet unnamed), telling the big boss that he doesn't know what Mike knows, just that he's there.

Greeting Mike with smiling contempt, Evello admits that they keep "underestimating" the detective, but notes that Mike doesn't know what he's looking for except "trouble." Evello seems to want to make nice with Hammer but never can bring himself to do so, his remarks always starting out complimentary but winding up insults. Evello wants to know what Hammer's price would be "to turn your considerable talents back to the gutter you crawled out of." But Mike's attitude turns Evello off, and no bargain can be struck: "It's too late," he tells Hammer, walking out on him (in his own house!). "Suddenly it's too late."

Mike heads for the former opera singer's place at the Hillcrest Hotel in the Bunker Hill area. It is reached by yet another high set of stairs. The leitmotif of Hammer's inability to climb to the heights necessary has by this time become apparent. Aldrich and Bezzerides cannot quite find a way to make Mike the villain. He's still on the quest, one which he will not relinquish even though he doesn't know what he's doing or how he will get there.

The sound of operatic singing is evident and the dumpy female hotel manager tells Hammer to "follow his ear" to the singer's apartment, number 2. There Mike commits the act that most surely conveys the Aldrich/Bezzerides contempt for their own hero—before he questions Trivago, he breaks a collectible Caruso, part of a 78 album, to make him cooperate.

Trivago has hundreds of albums, just as Christina had hundreds of books. The portrayal of Mike is meant to convey his insensitivity to culture and the arts (the Hammer of the novels is quite well read and enjoys classical music}, but this is contradicted by the film Hammer's artwork-filled apartment and the radio there tuned to a classical station. Trivago tells the detective that Raymondo had something small enough to hide that some very bad people wanted. Their question was: "Where is it?" But he doesn't know.

Mike returns to Lily's hotel, once more showing the stairway and the parallel patterns. The flooring of the hotel resembles that of Velda's apartment, black-and-white tiles, though smaller than those at Velda's. The cinematography emphasizes black over white, the camera shooting through the landing bars of the stairway, with more than half the screen in darkness.

"They came last night," Lily says. "I hid in the basement."

Mike tells Carver he's going for his Corvette: "When you hear the car, come running." Lily runs down the stairs, the camera showing her both from the top and the bottom. The overhead shot looks like a descent into madness or perhaps hell. She jumps into his car, he hides her beneath the convertible's pull-out canopy, and roars off.

Mike drops by Nick's—the mechanic has a lead about the car bomb, but Hammer wants to go with him to Culver City to follow it up. Carver, out of sight, listens. After Hammer departs, the cheerful Nick (a sure sign of tragedy) hops back to work under a car. The man with the pin-striped suit and white-stitched wing tips arrives at Nick's place and kills him by releasing the jack of the car.

Mike takes Carver to his place; she still has on the terrycloth robe. She thanks him with a kiss. As Mike leaves he tells her not to answer the phone and keep the door chained and she'll be safe. She replies, "But if they pay you off, where will I be?" He doesn't bother answering.

Mike returns to Nick's place only to find him dead. "They kill Nick, Mike," says Sammy, the mechanic's assistant. A morose, guilt-racked Hammer leaves and goes to Velda's place. She's in bed asleep. She kisses him as soon as she wakes up. "What kind of trouble are you in this time? ... I'm always glad when you're in trouble because then you always come to me." He tells her Nick is dead. Velda knows all too well that Mike's friends lead dangerous lives. Mike tells her "they" are after the girl because of something Raymondo had.

Velda analyzes all this quickly in perhaps the most famous, memorable speech of the film: "They. And who are they? The nameless one who kill people for the Great What's-It. And does it exist?" This would appear to be Bezzerides commenting not just on Spillane, but on all tough detective stories.

Velda is quietly seething, but goes on discussing the case with Mike. She met Ray Diker for a drink; he has pointed out an abstract art dealer who eventually, after a few drinks, drops the name of a Dr. Soberin. Velda says she's sure she could get more information if she "dated" the guy again.

"Well, do you want me to date him?" Mike replies: "I want to get my hands on the guy who killed Nick."

This comment sets her off on Mike's propensity for revenge. Here Bezzerides (and presumably Aldrich) finally hone in on the vengeance aspect of Mickey Spillane's Mike Hammer that so outraged liberal reviewers of the day.

"You want to avenge the death of your dear friend. How touching. How sweet. How nicely it justifies your quest for the Great What's-It." After a long pause, she says, "Why don't you leave, Mike?" She goes into her bedroom but comes back, her disgust and anger trumped by her love for the lug, saying, "Meet me at the Pigalle. Two o'clock."

At the Pigalle, a young black woman is singing "I'd Rather Have the Blues." She caresses the phallic microphone in an openly erotic manner that somehow made it past the censors. Everyone in the club is black except Mike, who tells the bartender to bring him a double bourbon and leave the bottle. They drink to Nick. "Va-va voom," the bartender says, unaware of their mutual friend's demise. "3-D Pow!"

Mike passes out at the bar. A hood comes in with a message that the bartender urgently relates: "They've got your girl. They've got Velda."

Hammer leaves and heads back to the gas station on the highway where he stopped when he first picked up Christina. He wants to know to whom the letter was addressed that she gave him: "It was some guy named Mike."

Mike roars off to his office in search of the letter. Charlie Max and Sugar Smallhouse are there in the dark, waiting for him to return. They found the letter, but can't figure out what it means. All it says: "Remember Me!"

Sugar slugs the detective and the two "polite cannons" drive him to a beach house in the car they gave him. There is of course another set of stairs. Mike tries to escape but they chase him down the beach. They slug him a few times, he escapes again, and they corner him in the ocean, a direct foreshadowing of film's finale.

Mike awakens from the beating tied face-down on a bed. He's questioned by the mystery man in the white-stitched shoes. "You will die, Mr. Hammer, but you can save your friend." He injects Mike with sodium Pentothal. The big boss wants to know what "remember me" means.

"Pleasant dreams, Mr. Hammer," he says.

A crime boss reduced to lackey, Evello comes in to listen to Hammer's mumblings. All that can be made out is a slurred, "Velda." Evello exits.

Mike works his right hand out of the knots of the rope binding him and, when Evello comes back into the room, the detective tells the gangster that he's ready to talk—but wants to whisper. When Evello leans over, Mike grins—he has him.

Mike calls out in Evello's voice: "Sugar, he's yours." Sugar opens his switchblade and slides it into what he thinks is Hammer's side—but he's actually just murdered his boss, Evello.

Hammer then jumps him and—in mysterious, off-camera martial arts action—kills Sugar, likely snapping his neck. As a radio announcer does ironic play-by-play on a prizefight in the background, Charlie hears his scream, comes in, finds both men dead and hears Mike's car speed off. Again, Hammer is almost a supernatural force. A terrified Charlie retreats to nowhere ("his eyes are glazed") and never has actor Jack Elam's odd visage been put to better use.

Mike returns to his apartment to check on Carver. She has on a black-and-white outfit brought by Velda. Carver reads part of a Rossetti poem for Mike to interpret, which sends Mike (with Lily) to the morgue. He figures out that Christina swallowed something. It turns out to be a key. Mike tries to pay the greedy weasel of an autopsy surgeon for it, but when the doc wants too much, Mike slams his hand in a drawer.

The key reads H.A.C. He and Lily drive to the Hollywood Athletic Club. When the old man at the desk won't cooperate for money, Hammer slaps him. (In his script, Bezzerides plays this scene for comic effect, with the clerk stereotypically British—"By jove!"—but Aldrich wisely drained all the humor out.)

The key belongs to Nicholas Raymondo. Inside is an oblong leather case. Mike lifts the leather top and, when he notices that the metal box inside is hot, he does not open it at first. He then lifts the lid slightly and a hissing, inferno-like noise leaps out and bright light blazes; he quickly shuts it, having received a burn on his right wrist for his trouble. He leaves the box behind, telling the clerk not to let anybody near it and to call the police. When Mike leaves the club, Carver is gone.

Pat is waiting for Mike at his apartment. He wants the key that Hammer got from Doc Kennedy at the morgue. Mike resists and rattles off a list of people that are dead. He wants Pat to help him rescue Velda. Then he mentions Lily Carver and Pat solemnly tells him that the real Carver's corpse was found over a week before. Pat sees Mike's wrist and gravely intones the famous "Manhattan project" speech that finally convinces Hammer just how over his head he's gotten himself. And Velda.

Quietly Mike gives Pat the key.

The other policemen want to know what to do with Mike. Pat says, "Let him go to hell. Let the big slob sit there and think about his girl, what's likely to happen to her." Mike says, "I didn't know." Pat retorts, "You didn't know. You think you'd have done any different if you had known?"

Perhaps Pat is right, because a renewed Hammer, his mission now to save Velda, goes into full throttle mode, his first stop: Ray Diker's place. Diker tries to hide from Hammer, who enters and notes a cigarette going in the ash tray. Hammer pretends to leave and then Diker finds himself confronted by a sneering, almost monster-like version of our hero. Mike slaps the smaller man around until Diker gives Mike the name of the art collector Velda told him about: William Mist of Mist's Gallery of Modern Art.

An unstoppable Mike breaks into the gallery. Mist hears the noise and reaches for the sleeping pills that Dr. G. E. Soberin has prescribed. Mist tries to take the whole bottle. Mike has been slowly climbing up another set of stairs, moving past modern art images. He tries to beat the info out of Mist, who has fallen quickly to sleep—there's black comedy in Hammer's inability to beat the truth out of a sleeping, snoring man. Then Mike notices the bottle with Dr. Soberin's name, calls his answering service, and learns about the doctor's beach cottage.

The next scene begins on the shoes with the white stitching, except this time the camera pans up to finally reveal the face of the mystery big boss ... and, as the big boss had earlier warned Hammer, seeing his face tells us nothing and solves no mystery.

The false Lily Carver is by his side. She had called him and they recovered the box from the Hollywood Athletic Club, killing the old clerk. She keeps repeating: "What's in the box?" Her real name is Gabrielle. Dr. Soberin says her real name should have been Pandora, who also had curiosity about a famous box, opening it and letting loose all the evil in the world.

Gabrielle's unimpressed response is worthy of Hammer: "Never mind about the evil, what's in it?" *What's in it for her?*

Soberin answers her mentioning Lot's wife, who was turned in a pillar of salt, and refers cryptically to the head of the Medusa and that whoever looks upon it will be turned into brimstone and ashes.

She wants half.

Soberin says he agrees that she deserves *at least* half, but that the box's contents can't be divided. She pulls a revolver on him and replies, "Then I'll take it all." And shoots him.

As he sways in pain, he warns her: "I'll tell you where to take it. Just don't ... open ... the box."

But he falls dead before he can tell her anything more.

Unarmed, Mike bursts in on her. As he walks toward her, she says, "Kiss me, Mike. I want you to kiss me. The liar's kiss that says I love you, but means something else. You're good at giving such kisses." She says one last "kiss me," then shoots him.

Gabrielle's curiosity gets the best of her. She notices that the box is hot. Still, she opens the box, lifting the lid to expose its contents, which seems to hypnotize her as she stares into it, screaming, as the nuclear contents set her aflame.

Mike recovers enough from his wound to crawl from the flames in search of Velda. He starts down the stairs but hears Velda calling to him in a locked room. Velda assists the wounded Mike down the stairs of the burning cottage and they stagger toward the water. They fall once on the beach, but arise and make it to the lapping waves before the house explodes in flames. The film ends with a shell-shocked Mike and Velda embracing in shallow water as a wave breaks behind them.

Despite Aldrich and Bezzerides conceiving the film as a denunciation of Spillane, "Kiss Me Deadly" evokes Spillane's (if not Mike Hammer's) bizarre vision of the universe as none of the other films do. The occasional but rapid and brutal scenes of violence, the constantly sexually available beautiful women and the uneasy, vaguely psychotic atmosphere are pure 1950s Spillane.

Ironically, producer Victor Saville didn't get it. He said, "This opus has become a cult film.... I cannot say why—I never completely understood our finished screenplay and my confusion was still there when we ran the completed film."

Plenty of others have understood the film. Aldrich and Bezzerides clearly intend Hammer to represent the baser aspects of man in general, and America in particular. Similarly, the villain Dr. Soberin (Albert Dekker) seems to represent the nobler aspects of the species turned decadent, his dialogue littered with literary and mythological references, his manner oozing culture and intellectualism. It is the efforts of these two opposite types—the crude Hammer/Meeker and the cultured Dekker—to find out "What's in it for me?" that brings global destruction, figuratively and perhaps literally, in "Kiss Me Deadly."

Only Christina—the female Christ-figure "crucified" at the film's opening, the only "dame" Hammer doesn't bestow a deadly kiss—suggests an alternative for apocalypse. She and Velda are the only small hopes for mankind that Aldrich and Bezzerides hold out.

Spillane, of course, offers a hero. And despite the filmmakers' best efforts, so do they—it's a shabby world Aldrich and Bezzerides present, but Mike Hammer is the best man in it.

"Kiss Me Deadly" (1955)

Parklane Pictures, Inc. • Running time: 106 minutes • Release date: May 18, 1955

WRITER: A.I. Bezzerides; DIRECTOR: Robert Aldrich; PRODUCERS: Robert Aldrich and Victor Saville; CINEMATOGRAPHER: Ernest Laszlo; Music: Frank De Vol as Frank Devol; CAST: Ralph Meeker (Mike Hammer); Albert Dekker (Dr. G.E. Soberin); Paul Stewart (Carl Evello); Juano Hernandez (Eddie Yeager); Wesley Addy (Lt. Pat Murphy); Marian Carr as Marion Carr (Friday); Marjorie Bennett (Manager); Mort Marshall (Ray Diker); Fortunio Bonanova (Carmen Trivago); Strother Martin (Harvey Wallace); Mady Comfort and Madi Comfort (Nightclub Singer); James McCallion (Horace); Robert Cornthwaite (FBI Agent); Silvio Minciotti (Mover); Nick Dennis (Nick); Ben Morris (Radio Announcer); Jack Elam (Charlie Max); Paul Richards (Attacker); Jesslyn Fax (Horace's Wife); James Seay (FBI Agent); Percy Helton (Doc Kennedy); Leigh Snowden (Cheesecake); Jack Lambert (Sugar Smallhouse); Jerry Zinneman (Sammy); Maxine Cooper (Velda); Cloris Leachman (Christina Bailey); Gaby Rodgers (Carver); Sam Balter (Radio Announcer, voice); Joe Hernandez (Radio Announcer, voice)

5. "My Gun Is Quick" (1957)

Mike Hammer (Robert Bray) and Velda (Pamela Duncan) convey the romantic attraction between boss and secretary in one of the most faithful aspects of "My Gun Is Quick" (1957).

Is it overstating the case to say moving from "Kiss Me Deadly" to "My Gun Is Quick" takes us from the sublime to the ridiculous? Probably not, although the final of the three Mike Hammer films produced by Victor Saville has its guilty pleasures.

Robert Bray, an actor who a decade before had been touted by RKO as the next Gary Cooper, was awfully seasoned to wear an "introducing" designation as a big, tough Mike Hammer who more nearly fit Mickey Spillane's visual notion of the character than either Elliot or Meeker. Location shooting returns us to the Bunker Hill area of "Kiss Me Deadly," if briefly, and the film depicts the seedy side of Hammer's world perhaps better than any other. Spillane "dolls" are on hand, too, and Mike is out to avenge the death of one of them. What's not to like?

Almost everything. While "My Gun Is Quick" (1957) is occasionally entertaining in its vapid, trashy way, Robert Bray delivers probably the most ordinary portrayal that this unique private eye has ever been subjected to; the most distinctive aspect of Bray's performance is that he shouts most of his lines.

The suspicion lingers that with better direction, Bray might have been up to the job. Just a year away from Darren McGavin's charismatic star turn as an affable yet still incredibly brutal, vengeance-leaning Hammer, Bray's Mike is humorless, hotheaded and just not very smart. Bray himself seems to have to work hard to do the shouting, and in quieter moments acquits himself well. The director must take the blame, because the other actors—even pros like Donald Randolph and Whitney Blake—often deliver their lines in an over-the-top manner seemingly designed to wake up the crew.

The "director" is two men—George White, a well-known film editor earning his only director's credit (and a half a one at that) and "Phil Victor," a pseudonym for producer Victor Saville. Saville thought so little of this film, his autobiography makes no mention of "My Gun Is Quick," which is even left off his filmography. This was the final novel on the Spillane contract, and Saville appears to just be playing it out.

In addition to four Spillane film adaptations, Saville produced at least one Hammer TV project, the 1954 Brian Keith "busted pilot" written and directed by Blake Edwards. In an interview, actor McGavin indicated there were at least two pilots made before his version of Hammer finally made the grade, one of them the Keith/Edwards effort. Looking at the two listed directors, and a cast and creative team mostly drawn from television—the two writers, Richard Powell and Richard Collins, were veterans of sitcoms, westerns and crime dramas—the notion that "My Gun Is Quick" began as a TV pilot film makes a certain sense.

It would explain the two directors—White directing a one-hour pilot and Saville stepping in to film additional scenes—and would justify the inclusion of some obvious padding. But this remains just a theory. Equally credible is the notion of White getting fired on the basis of lousy dailies and producer Saville, a seasoned director, stepping in to save the project. At least one sequence might show the assured hand of the man who directed "The Long Wait."

After director Aldrich abandoned Manhattan to create a modern, even science-fiction setting for Mike Hammer in the Los Angeles of "Kiss Me Deadly," producer Aldrich uses the seamier side of L.A. in "My Gun Is Quick" to represent the kind of ravaged urban landscape implied by the original novel. We meet Hammer under effective opening credits as, on location, the camera follows the brutish detective moving inexorably through an area rife with low-end movie theaters and burlesque houses. Dramatic music accompanies him, jungle drums that recall Pat Murphy warning Meeker's Hammer of the jungle-like result of vengeance, with occasional slashing brass to hammer at us—not melodic, but promising danger and even violence.

Unfortunately, composer Marlin Skilles—a Hollywood journeyman whose scores of scores included entries in such B movie series as Blondie and the Bowery Boys—seldom returns to this jazzy approach. Much of the music here is of the "Mickey Mouse" variety, spelling action out in an embarrassingly obvious, cliched manner. Franz Waxman and Frank De Vol have nothing to worry about.

The basic Hammer of Spillane is here, as are Velda and Pat (now "Chambers" again), but Mike's two closest associates are presented in a simplistic manner. The numerous Mike and Pat scenes (some may be padding, if this is indeed an expanded TV pilot film) are repetitious nonsense, with Hammer yelling at Chambers, who often yells back. Their dialogue is risible, as when Pat says to the detective, "You've got thoughts in that scrambled brain of yours that could make the track nice and muddy."

In a phone conversation with Pat, Mike—taking a break from yelling at his friend—suggests, "You might want to pick up a butler type ... called Lou or Louie if you prefer." Bray delivers this stilted line with a stilted reading—perhaps the actor was distracted, wondering what a "butler type" was.

A letter in Spillane's files from Saville has the producer promising the writer that more of his dialogue will turn up in this picture than previous ones. Now and then a good line pops up, but seeming strangely out of context, and the Spillane afficionado recognizes it as an actual line from the novel, shoe-horned into a script that has otherwise abandoned its source. Bezzerides claimed to have thrown out the novel of *Kiss Me, Deadly*, but producer Saville really *has* thrown out *My Gun Is Quick*.

Oh, the first ten minutes are very close to the novel, including dialogue, though awkwardly staged and acted. After this, Spillane's plot—which had to do with prostitution (Saville told Spillane this was the reason for the censor-sensitive departure from the original)—devolves into a very tired re-hash of *The Maltese Falcon*. We will meet a Brigid O'Shaugnnessy clone and a skinny Kasper Gutman, as well. The falcon has become "the Venacci jewels," one ring of which had been in the possession of the dead hooker Hammer is avenging.

Hammer, by the way, constantly wears a battered fedora. This is apparently somebody's idea of characterization, but the result is unintentionally comic. Otherwise attired in a decent suit, Hammer apparently jumps up and down on the hat before he applies it to his thick skull in just the right haphazard way. Like previous screen Hammers, he carries a revolver, probably a .38, not the detective's trademark .45 Colt automatic of the novels. At first, he needs a shave, but in an early instance of product placement, he uses a Norelco electric shaver in his office with a prominently positioned bottle of Mennen Skin Bracer in frame.

As for the Spillane dolls, dark-haired Pamela Duncan—something of a minor league B-movie scream queen—certainly looks the part of Velda, so much so that when she scolds Mike about those "bosomy types" he goes for, she rates a full-bodied unintentional laugh. Not a bad actress, she is given impossible lines and made to spend most of her screen time striking unlikely pin-up poses in doorways and on desks and couches.

Two of the "dames"—Pat Donahue as Dione and Gina Core as Maria—are attractive if not quite beautiful, and fit in well with the sleazy side of Hammer's world, the low-end strip club and grimy hotels where his investigation first takes him. Red, the victim prostitute, is pretty and actress Jan Chaney is competent in her single scene, more waif than broad. Dione is a good-looking blonde who makes a credible B-girl pick-up for Hammer, and stripper Maria has pretty features that seem ravaged and hard in the unflattering (if appropriate) lighting.

Robert Bray's Hammer smacks around an over-eager john (Richard Garland), coming to the rescue of prostitute "Red" (Jan Chaney) in the only scene in "My Gun Is Quick" that derives directly from the source novel.

Despite the burden of impossible, wretchedly written expository speeches, the lovely blonde Whitney Blake makes a fine Charlotte-like femme fatale. Recalling Kim Novak, she struts confidently around in eye-popping white short shorts, a skin-tight swim suit, a teddy-style nightie, and other provocative attire. Like Peggie Castle, she conveys cool intelligence with a promise of hot sex.

Unfortunately, her sections of the film are set chiefly in a bland, unimpressive, even middle-class-looking bungalow whose primary appeal is its location on the water. A big open living room is the only room of the apparently small house that we are ever in.

The bungalow's dockside location leads to many inherently ridiculous scenes in which Mike Hammer is turned instantly into the assured captain of her motor cruiser. After several reels of crawling through a nighttime world of tenements, greasy spoons and strip joints, Hammer is suddenly a seasoned sailor, using nautical terms and adept at motor-boat engine repair.

Though he shows up at Nancy's house by following a potential murderer there, Hammer is soon kissing her and piloting her boat, the P.I. decked out in a pull-over sport shirt that he apparently produced out of thin air, like Bugs Bunny materializing a carrot. One such sequence is accompanied by jaunty travelogue music as the little cruiser skims along the water in a sequence about as *noir* as a postcard from your Uncle Carl and Aunt Edna.

That potential murderer, by the way, is supposedly Nancy's butler (or is that "butler type"?), in this house of maybe six rooms. Perhaps he sleeps at the foot of her bed. When she fires this slick hoodlum (actually putting on a show for Hammer, but no one in the audience is fooled), she replaces Louie (or Lou if you prefer) with a British butler who Hammer even calls "Jeeves."

The film's worst offense—and the clearest indication that this may be a shorter film, again possibly a TV pilot, fleshed out by producer Saville—is what is almost certainly the worst, most boring chase scene in film history.

After a Bunker Hill sequence that recalls "Kiss Me Deadly," right down to an endless cement staircase, Hammer spots the probable murderer of a snitch and follows him by car to Nancy's dockside bungalow. The film and Hammer abandon the gritty Manhattan-esque side of Los Angeles to head out to the freeway, where Hammer at a snail's pace follows the suspect. Jaunty, dumb music accompanies this tedious exercise in abysmal filmmaking. This most tedious of "chases" lasts an astonishing five minutes, an eternity of screen time.

This is followed by the improbable scene in which the skimpily bathing-suit-clad Nancy greets the total stranger who has turned up in her backyard as warmly as if he were her latest boy friend, which Hammer soon will be. She almost immediately invites Mike inside for a drink. (A similar scene in "The Girl Hunters" reveals Spillane's ability to make this kind of inherently unlikely "tough guy meets cute with doll" situation play effectively.)

Absurdities abound. A secondary group of villains, French sailors, wear striped shirts and stocking caps or berets and lack everything but baguettes under their arms. Gutman clone Colonel Holloway introduces himself to Hammer at the strip club, with a brunette on one arm and a blonde on the other, and then spends his first several lines telling Hammer that the strip club's bar is the perfect place to be "gay"—coming from an effete actor who is wildly over-the-top from here till his *the-diamonds-are-finally-mine* death scene, that's a little much.

One of the two really effective scenes—Hammer follows a diamond cutter, recently arrived on the docks, through a menacing junk yard, only to have a load of scrap iron narrowly miss falling on him—is flawed by the absurdity of the writing. Why would the diamond cutter exit customs and walk through a junkyard? How did one of the striped-shirt French guys get access to a crane to drop junk on Hammer?

The strongest indication that Saville directed part of the film comes late in the proceedings, by way of the other really strong sequence. Hammer, suddenly wanted for questioning, goes to Nancy's dockside bungalow, which at night finally gains some *noir* mood. He sneaks past cops, vaults up onto the roof, climbs onto a balcony and through a window looks down on a tableau that shows Pat and the cops on the scene. Via purely visual storytelling, much is explicated: crime scene procedure in full sway (with flashbulbs flashing), Lou the former butler dead on the floor, the diamond cutter having a sudden heart attack, Nancy going into histrionics for the cops, and finally Pat coming upstairs to the hole in the brick wall from which the missing jewels were obviously recovered. Hammer is on one side of the frame, outside on the balcony, and his friend Pat is inside, looking out, unaware of Mike's side-by-side presence. It's an effective, wordless sequence topped with a final memorable moment.

The climactic shoot-out with the French sailors on the pier is decently staged, though minus any music until toward the very end, when Mike finally clashes with the hook-handed baddie, who—like the probable murderer/butler—has a key role but few lines. Earlier fights are similarly well, if not spectacularly, handled.

The final confrontation between Hammer and femme fatale Nancy—on the little yacht, of course—is a tired reworking of the endings of *The Maltese Falcon* and *I, the Jury*. This time, however, Hammer does not execute the bad girl—he simply heads to shore to turn her in. No Spillane film—probably no Hammer TV episode, either—had so limp and disappointing a denouement.

As "My Gun Is Quick" begins, Mike is walking down a crowded street in Los Angeles when he turns into a greasy spoon, the Star Café, and calls Velda. He's beat, he's been up fifty two hours straight. "I feel like I just crawled out of a sewer," he says, providing no specifics. "There's not a decent person left in the world."

Velda replies, "I'm here Mike," but that doesn't seem to matter to Hammer.

There's a pretty young woman sitting at the counter. Shorty the ex-con counter man merely calls her Red, and wants her to quit using his joint as her "office." She tells Hammer she's from Nebraska and wishes she could go back. Mike buys her a bowl of soup because she's out of money.

A slick ascot-sporting hood comes into the café and accosts Red. Mike, feeling sorry for her, protects Red from this "greaseball" (a description from the novel that no longer applies) and roughly runs him off.

She says, "Now I feel like I've got a friend." Mike gives her money to buy new shoes, a dress and a bus ticket back home. He tells her to call to say she's safe and gives her a piece of paper with his contact info. Mike leaves the café with the chopped egg sandwich he promised to take to Velda.

When he arrives at his office, Velda has put a hand-written sign on his door so that, under

MIKE HAMMER
PRIVATE INVESTIGATOR

have been added the words:

OUT TO LUNCH
WON'T BE BACK

Mike stops her as she's leaving, gives her the fat wad of cash he's made over the last few days to bank. Velda is attractive and voluptuous with short black hair and form-fitting attire. She has attitude and is basically the Velda of the novels, if more subservient. We'll see no example of her packing a gun or doing anything but minding the office.

Mike keeps his hat on while he shaves with an electric razor. Velda stands in the doorway eating her sandwich, then sits on his desk. She tells Mike she turned down a divorce job and a bodyguard assignment, and Hammer complains that she should stop making decisions for him.

A uniformed cop comes into his office with a message from Captain Pat Chambers. (Apparently the phones do not work in Los Angeles.) Mike goes to see Pat (Booth Coleman), portrayed as a fairly mousy bureaucrat. Red is dead, her neck broken in a hit-and-run accident—Pat had found the note with Mike's address on the girl's body. But the elaborate ring that Mike noticed on her hand in the café is missing. She had new clothes but the flesh on her ring finger is badly bruised as if someone had ripped it off. Mike describes the ring as having a black stone with an antique setting: a large V with many small stones set on the outside edge in concentric circles.

Pat goes to his files and brings back a picture that Mike identifies. The ring is part of the Venacci jewels that disappeared during World War II. Mike doesn't know this because he was in the South Pacific fighting (so was actor Bray). It seems a Colonel Holloway confiscated the jewels back in 1945 and was given prison time for his trouble—why, exactly, is typically vague. The jewels, however, were never recovered. Of the late Red, Mike tells Pat, "She was a nice kid who was murdered. I don't like it."

In an uncomfortable scene that makes a bully out of him, Mike returns to the Star Café and intimidates Shorty into telling him that Red worked at the Bluebell, a strip club. When Mike arrives at the club, he writes a large note on the menu that the stripper can read as she comes by his table: IT WAS NO ACCIDENT—RED WAS MURDERED.

The stripper, Maria, continues her act to "Why Don't You Do Right." Dressed all in black, Maria is trimly curvy. The camera lingers on the club's unlikely crowd of middle-aged, middle-class couples as Maria completes her strip off camera (yes, there's nothing that June Cleaver likes better than having Ward take her to a strip joint). Maria returns to take a bow as she extends a long slender leg around the curtain and bends to pick up her discarded outfit.

Mike and Maria soon leave to go to her place. She and Red lived at the same hotel. He's driving a Ford convertible. Red's crummy room has been torn apart, even her Teddy Bear cut open.

Maria tells Mike, "I don't like men like you. I have no luck with men." Red got the ring from a Frenchman who works at the club, but he will not be back until later. An openly seductive Maria wonders what they can do for the next several hours and Mike suggests gin rummy—is this a joke, or just a stupid line?

"Three hours is a long time to wait for such a violent man," she says nonsensically. "I don't play cards. I kiss."

But Hammer, improbably, leaves after that kiss, promising to return to take Maria along on his interrogation. The dissolves of "The Long Wait," indicating a randy Spillane hero making it off-camera with a doll, are not part of Saville's approach here.

Mike and Maria question the Frenchman at the club—this apparent janitor cannot speak, because the Nazis tortured him in some manner. Hammer bullies him and the actor playing the Frenchman hams it up weirdly. Getting a few shreds of information, Mike leaves, sending Maria off on her own. He has barely left when he sees numerous cops and at the bottom of a long outdoor stairway where someone lies dead—Hammer goes down there and it's the dead Frenchman. The timing is strange here, the body barely shown, and viewers are likely to be confused—just a few moments ago, Hammer was talking to this guy.

Mike spots and follows the probable killer (the guy who accosted Red at the café) to a house at the beach. There he finds Nancy Williams, a leggy blonde in a one-piece black bathing suit, who (improbably) invites him in for a drink. The driver of the car turns out to be her butler, Louie. When Mike catches Louie eavesdropping on his conversation with Nancy, she fires him on the spot. While Mike makes her a drink, Nancy tells Mike of dating a married man whose wife committed suicide when she discovered her husband was unfaithful. Nancy's so afraid of Louie now that she hires Mike for a few days as a bodyguard/companion. This entire sequence—from the prolonged car chase through the scenes at Nancy's—makes very little sense, either logically or narratively.

On a ride in her speedboat cruiser, Nancy tells "Captain" Mike Hammer (who is at the wheel) the whole convoluted story about marrying young, her husband's subsequent death and then being involved with the married man. Actress Blake does the best she can.

Mike tells her, "My whole life is mixed up with up people who make mistakes" and

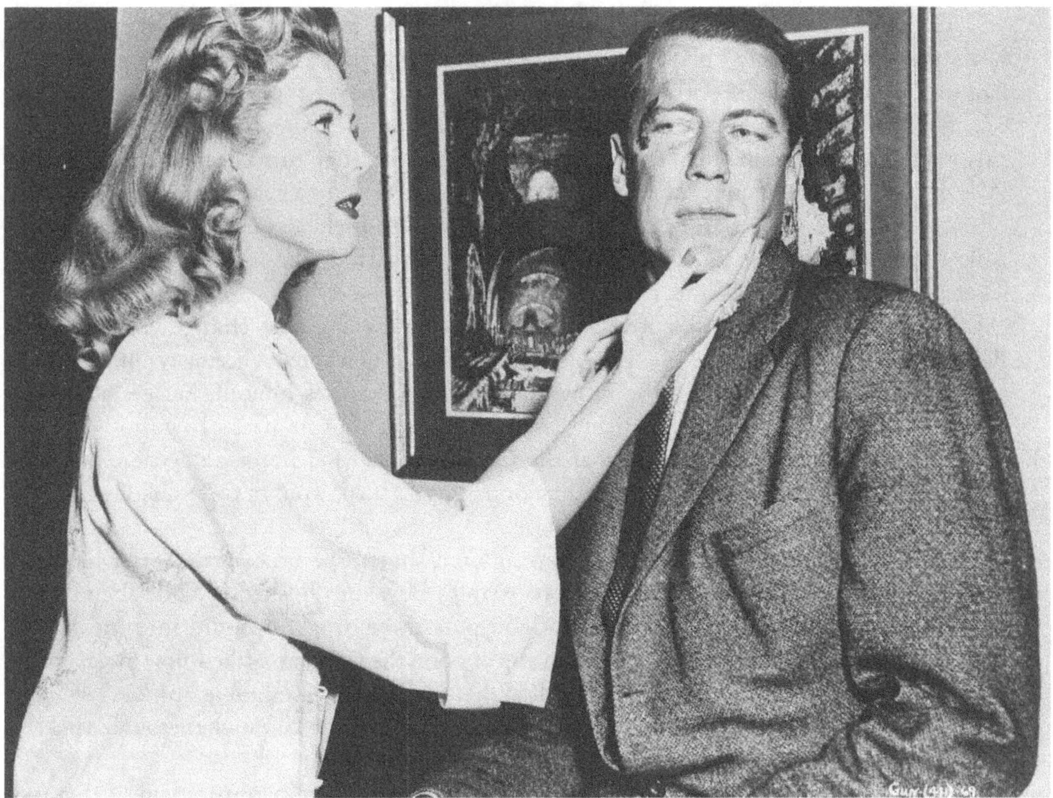

Nancy Williams (Whitney Blake) administers first-aid to Bray's battered Hammer in "My Gun Is Quick," the final and much the weakest Spillane adaptation from producer Victor Saville.

that sometimes he feels "cold bitter rage." She tells him it's been two years since she's been with a man and kisses him as lush, romantic, cliched music plays.

Returning to the beach house, they find Red's "V" ring. Mike spots an intruder, a fight ensues and Mike is subdued at the boat dock by a guy in a striped shirt and beret who has a hook instead of a left hand.

Nancy comes running down to the dock wearing tight white shorts and a tight top. After Nancy and Mike give fruitless chase, he calls Velda on the ship-to-shore phone and ends the conversation with, "love you." This piques Nancy's interest. Mike tells her that Velda has been with him for five years, and offers up a rare Spillane-derived line: "She's got a brain that figures all the angles. Mine only figures the curves."

Back at the office, Velda has the data on Colonel Holloway and the missing jewels. She shows Mike a *Life Magazine* dated July 19, 1946 with a cover story on the "Venacci Jewels." Inside are many pictures of the jewels, including the one Red had, as well as a picture of the Colonel surrounded by many lovely women. But Mike leaves to see what new information Pat has. There is nothing new, in this latest pointless Mike/Pat shouting match, the cop saying, "The only thing that will satisfy you is an eye for an eye."

At the strip club, Mike can't find Maria but is sought out by Colonel Holloway, in the presence of two beauties, and behaving in a somewhat drunkenly jaunty manner, making several odd "gay" references to Mike (yes, it's 1957, but the gay term was known in hipper circles).

Holloway's curvy blonde gal pal at the bar gives Mike her room key. At her door, he hears the song "Bluebells" playing, changes his mind and goes around the back entrance. Colonel Holloway is there with her. Mike knew all along that she was too good to be true.

Colonel Holloway tells Mike he did not kill Red, but he's spent the last ten years in prison and feels like he deserves the jewels. Mike plays along, then turns dark on the colonel: "Oh, you've got a bad temper, Mr. Hammer. I'm not so sure that's a good sign." The Colonel offers him 25% of the take ($250,000), which Mike seemingly accepts. The colonel tells Mike that he believes the Frenchman, LaRoche (the guy with the hook), has the diamonds. There's a little gun brandishing by the fey colonel.

In a decent attempt at conveying atmosphere, the lighting changes light/dark, light/dark, light/dark while Mike is looking for Maria at her hotel. Three guys jump him, beat him up and leave him on the filthy floor. When he rouses himself, he sees another copy of the old *Life* with jewels on the cover. He reasons that he needs to go to Nancy's place because Velda has discovered that the Colonel rented her house some time before, and that the Colonel probably hid the diamonds there. (If so, wouldn't the Colonel know where the jewels are? Why hire Mike?)

Nancy comes down her stairway throwing on a short robe on over a shorter teddie, and offers Mike a drink. Mike looks a mess, saying, "Boy, am I bushed." While she makes Mike's drink, Nancy takes out a little vial and puts three drops of liquid into his glass. Shades of Charlotte drugging Myrna. Waking up at noon the next day, Mike—now in pajamas (where did Nancy get those?)—is mildly miffed that his hostess gave him a "mickey," which she freely admits, saying he needed the rest. Pat calls (how does he know where to call Mike?) to tell Hammer that Maria has been found dead in her bathtub.

The Colonel has learned that a Mr. Teller, a jewel cutter from Amsterdam, is due to arrive in Los Angeles by ship. Mike goes to the port and trails him through a junkyard. One of the French gang is suddenly a crane operator who tries to kill Mike by dropping scrap metal on him from a giant magnet. Mike escapes, but so does Mr. Teller, picked up by Louie.

As Mike is driving, trying to locate Teller, he hears on the police band that he's wanted—this plays twice, in a another obvious instance of padding—and that there's been a disturbance at Nancy's house, 34 Harbor Drive. The police description of Hammer: "Thirty-five. Six feet two and a half inches. One-hundred-and-ninety pounds. Brown hair. Blue eyes. Gray sports coat and slacks."

At Nancy's, Mike ducks cops and goes in the back way and climbs on the roof to her balcony. From there he can see the open living room of her bungalow. Louie is dead on the floor and Teller promptly has a heart attack, while Nancy is in hysterics. When Mike gets in his car, the Colonel pops up in the back seat. He tells Mike that the Frenchman has the jewels at the pier.

"I must have them," the road-company Gutman says. "Faster. Faster. Faster!"

At the pier, the Frenchman and his crew are busily loading up their boat, the Rough & Ready. A gun fight starts up, with Mike and Colonel jumping from small boat to small boat, trying to get on board the bigger vessel. The Colonel shoots one of the bad guys but is eventually hit himself. Mike shoots the other thug. That only leaves La Roche, the man with the hook. He and Mike fight from one side of the boat to the other, and it looks like La Roche will spear Mike with his hook when Mike maneuvers La Roche into falling, fatally, onto his hook. Mike recovers the jewels from La Roche's body and gives them to the Colonel. All he can say is, "Beautiful. Mine." And then falls dead.

Nancy pulls up in her speedboat. Mike jumps in and gives the diamonds to her. He says, "Beautiful collection. Are they all there?" When she replies, "Yes, all but the ring," Mike knows she's the killer. She tells him she was desperate for money and simply had to kill. Mike says, "I told you I had moral objections to murder." Told her when?

Nancy replies, "I thought I could count on you ... that you saw things as I did." When she pulls a gun on him, Mike revs the boat, throwing her backward. As they wait for the harbor police, she says, "You're the biggest fool of all." Mike replies solemnly, "Look me up in about thirty years and we'll talk."

The movie ends with the screen all in darkness except for Nancy's boat on the far right side of the screen and a streaming spotlight from the police boat coming in from the left. It's an attempt for a stylish *noir* finish with little or no impact.

The years have been surprisingly kind to "My Gun Is Quick," though its proximity to "Kiss Me Deadly" does it no favors. Despite its considerable faults, "My Gun Is Quick" has the benefit of being produced in the 1950s, Spillane's big decade, a factor that elevates the McGavin TV series over the later, more lavishly produced Keach version. The *noir* aspects of "My Gun Is Quick"—Maria's dressing room and hotel room are evocative hovels of misery and poverty, the latter subject to a constant neon pulse out her window—make the film the equivalent of a cheap but entertaining paperback of the era. Not Spillane level, but in that vein.

A DVD release by MGM presents this most minor of Hammer adaptations in the best possible light, a crisp, wide-screen transfer. The Spillane fan who survives one viewing may find that subsequent visits—after the shock of the script's incompetence and the disappointment of Bray's braying, humorless Hammer have worn off—will bring modest rewards.

"My Gun Is Quick" concludes the run of Victor Saville-produced Spillane films.

"My Gun Is Quick" (1957)

Parklane Pictures, Inc. • Running time: 90 minutes • Release date: August 1957

WRITERS: Richard Collins and Richard Powell; DIRECTORS: George A. White and Phil Victor (Victor Saville); CINEMATOGRAPHER: Harry Neumann; MUSIC: Marlin Skiles; CAST: Robert Bray (Mike Hammer); Whitney Blake (Nancy Williams); Patricia Donahue as Pat Donague (Dione, Blonde Bar Girl); Donald Randolph (Colonel Holloway); Pamela Duncan (Velda); Booth Colman as Booth Coleman (Det. Pat Chambers); Jan Chaney ("Red," Café Girl); Genie Coree as Gina Core (Maria Teresa Garcia); Richard Garland (Louis, Henchman); Charles Boaz (Gangster); Peter Mamakos (LaRoche, Smuggler Chief); Claire Carleton (Proprietress); Phil Arnold ("Shorty," Café Proprietor); John Dennis (Al); Terence de Marney as Terrence De Marney (Jean the French Janitor); Jackie Paul (Stripper); Fred Essler (Ludwig Teller)

6. "The Girl Hunters" (1963)

Mickey Spillane as Mike Hammer in full Colt .45, trenchcoat and porkpie-hat regalia, in the UK-lensed "The Girl Hunters" (1963). James Dyranforth played old-time reporter Bayliss Henry.

As previously noted, Mickey Spillane had—for various reasons, including the critical pummeling he'd received and his well-publicized religious conversion to the Jehovah's Witnesses—stopped writing Hammer novels at the peak of his early '50s popular success. Driven by "the urgent need for money" (Spillane's definition of inspiration), the writer returned in 1960 with a non–Hammer novel, *The Deep*, following up quickly with Mike Hammer in *The Girl Hunters*, which explained the private eye's absence in terms of a seven-year drunk due to blaming himself for his beloved secretary Velda's (apparent) death.

To further emphasize the return of Mike Hammer and Mickey Spillane, a film version was planned, with the stunt casting of the writer himself as his famous creation designed to attract attention, which it certainly did. With his co-starring role in "Ring of Fear," his guest shots on television, and occasional commercials he'd appeared in, Spillane felt confident he was up to the challenge. And this increased participation—including co-writing the script—was an opportunity to show Hollywood how Mike Hammer should really be handled on screen.

It would be nice to be able to say that "The Girl Hunters" (1963, directed by Roy Rowland) is the best of the Spillane films, but in a list that includes "Kiss Me Deadly" that would be difficult for any film. But it rivals Essex's "I, the Jury," and ranks first in terms of putting the Hammer of the books literally on screen.

The plot is hardly Spillane's strongest—"derivative drivel," a *Newsweek* film review said, going on to advise that "if one checks his brains at the popcorn counter, 'The Girl Hunters' is outrageous good fun." The film's modest budget slightly undercuts the proceedings, as does the nagging feeling that Hammer just doesn't work as effectively in James Bondian 1963 as he did back in the vintage years 1947–1959 (i.e., from the publication of *I, the Jury* through the Darren McGavin TV series).

Ironically, "The Girl Hunters" gained its widest release in America in re-release a year or so later, after Spillane's co-star Shirley Eaton had become the "golden girl" of "Goldfinger" (1964). Eaton's presence in "The Girl Hunters" is only one of several ironies that signify the passing of the popular-culture torch from Hammer to Bond, starting with the film itself being a British production, and an often crafty slice of cinematic slight-of-hand.

Prior to director Rowland shooting the main, studio-bound footage in England, an American second unit had shot Spillane as Hammer walking familiar Manhattan streets, showing the detective entering the Blue Ribbon Restaurant (a haunt of Hammer's in the novels and Spillane in life) and in a context of other immediately identifiable NYC landmarks. A sprinkling of American actors—Spillane's friend Scott Peters and venerable Lloyd Nolan, former screen Mike Shayne—added to the illusion of an American-made film. A number of English accents—including Eaton's—do intrude; but—as Spillane's Manhattan is a dream landscape anyway—it's only occasionally distracting.

Unfortunately, "The Girl Hunters" over-uses the second-unit material, as scenes of Spillane as Hammer walking New York streets, going in and out of buildings, getting in and out of cabs (not to mention his trenchcoat) eventually become unnecessary and pace-dulling.

The story of "The Girl Hunters" is at once simple and convoluted, not a rarity in a Spillane (or any hardboiled detective) tale. Mike Hammer is retrieved from the gutter—where he's spent the past seven years in guilt over his secretary/lover's death—by his old friend Captain Pat Chambers of Homicide. But Chambers is no longer friendly to Hammer, sharing the private eye's belief that Hammer is responsible for Velda's death—turns out Chambers loved her, too. Hammer is hauled to the bedside of a dying FBI informant, who informs the P.I. that Velda is still alive but in hiding, and sought by an assassin called the Dragon. Promptly, the informant dies, and just as promptly, Hammer sobers up.

Watching the unshaven, bum-like Spillane transform into crisply trench-coated, porkpie-hat-sporting Mike Hammer is a genuine treat, even a thrill—like seeing Clark Kent enter the phone booth only to emerge as, well, you get the picture. Hammer chases leads, instructs a voluptuous nurse to "lick her lips," discovers numerous corpses, ducks a bullet or two, gets in an occasional scuffle, and—despite pining for the missing Velda—begins a romance with Laura Knapp (Eaton), the widow of a senator whose murder is linked to Velda's disappearance.

Laura—whose favorite attire is the flimsiest of bikinis—is rather transparently a black widow, and Hammer's investigating consists primarily of one scene after another in which the detective chats with various middle-aged men, getting one scrap of info after another (real-life NYC newspaper columnist and Spillane crony, Hy Gardner, is terrible as himself, looking at the camera, stumbling over his lines).

The final confrontations, however—two of them, as the Commie assassin the Dragon is a team, "tooth and nail"—are memorable, to say the least. Hammer's major fight scene—in which Spillane seems to be doubled only in a few instances—is as brutal as anything in the writer's novels, which is plenty brutal. And his showdown with the showering Laura remains the only finale in a Spillane-derived film to capture the shocking, hypnotic, sexy, violent, abrupt endings that so characterize the books.

Perhaps the boldest storytelling trick of the movie—which, of course, is in the novel as well—is the absence from the screen of Velda herself. The search for Velda is resolved by Hammer going to retrieve her—off-screen—after the film's conclusion. The only image of Velda in "The Girl Hunters" is a photo—with the head torn off, leaving just a shapely body and lovely legs for us to contemplate just how beautiful the object of Hammer's search must be.

Interestingly, the violent Hammer kills nary a soul in "The Girl Hunters"—though he does, in the movie's most indelible moment, literally hammer a bad guy's hand to the floor, as well as trick the beautiful bad girl into blowing off her own head. Another famous sequence (absent from the novel) has Hammer using merely his eyes, a sneer and a reach-inside-his-jacket-hand to force a saloon tough guy to eat a .45 slug. The narrative strategy of having Hammer stumble onto grisly corpses, even as everybody else reminds us how deadly Hammer himself is, works well—although "The Girl Hunters" falls short of being as classic a pro–Spillane film as "Kiss Me Deadly" is an anti–Spillane one, due to a handful of flaws.

The first flaw comes from Spillane's own screenplay—Rowland and co-producer Bob Fellow share credit, but Spillane clearly did the heavy lifting. For the most part, it's a first-rate if over-literal translation of the novel, including many mind-numbing expository scenes. In later years, Spillane himself said he wished the film had been trimmed by ten or fifteen minutes. If veteran director Rowland was going to take a co-scripting credit, the least he could have done is some trimming either at the script stage or in the editing suite.

Spillane the screenwriter, however, deftly handles a typical problem of transposing the first-person private eye to the screen (avoiding the overdone voiceover of the fun, flawed 1975 version of "Farewell, My Lovely") by using narration only in moments when Hammer is lost in alternately romantic and violent reverie over the missing Velda.

The second flaw is the somewhat flat-footed direction by aging Hollywood veteran Rowland. The *noir*-ish trappings—pulsing neons through Hammer's office window, gritty saloons, grimy alleys—are all present, but minus the visual flair of many films *noir*—including Saville's "I, the Jury," "The Long Wait" and "Kiss Me Deadly." On the other hand, the Cinemascope images are well-composed, even striking.

While "The Girl Hunters" falls short of "Kiss Me Deadly—and most films do, after all—it succeeds in bringing to the screen a true rarity: the author of the source novel's vision. The rough-tough violence of the final fight scene, the enticing presence of Shirley Eaton in one bikini after another, the snappy dialogue right out of the novel, all join with Spillane's remarkable central performance to create a time-capsule Hammer novel-on-film, a pulpy paperback come to life.

And Spillane's performance is remarkable indeed. Never mind that writers usually make lousy actors (Stephen King and Norman Mailer, anyone?). Never mind that the production was falling down around him (Spillane had to sell four collections of his work to a British publisher to raise money to complete the film, which was supposed to have been shot in color, not black and white). Self-proclaimed "amateur actor" Spillane dominates every scene with a hard-eyed ease worthy of Robert Mitchum. He is in virtually every scene, almost every frame—controlling the screen even when paired with the seasoned likes of Lloyd Nolan and Shirley Eaton.

Spillane even plays some of the trumpet solos in the nice if repetitious Philip Green score—the writer had insisted on a trumpet theme for Hammer, considering it more heroic than the usual *noir*-ish sax, as in Franz Waxman's "I, the Jury" score. (The Dave Kahn/Melvyn Lenard "Riff Blues, theme of the McGavin series, also employs trumpet to good effect.)

The movie's November 19, 1963 release was nothing if not the epitome of bad timing—there is no one of a certain age who does not know that President John Kennedy was assassinated on November 22, 1963. Even with the generally good reviews the movie received, the public predictably was not poised to accept a rough-and-tumble Mike Hammer at that moment. A general release six months before might have made a huge difference

The series of Spillane-as-Hammer films that "The Girl Hunters" was to have initiated never came to pass: the black-and-white movie—way past the *noir* curve—wasn't seen much in the United States till its "Goldfinger"-inspired re-release. The private eye heroics of Hammer seemed quaint and, not surprisingly, tied to the 1950s, compared to the garish color and suave antiheroics of the early Bonds. Though released only a year after "Dr. No," the world of Mike Hammer was already looking dated.

The novel begins: "They found me in the gutter." After bold credits establish the iconic New York City skyline, the film starts exactly the same way with two cops in a patrol car stopping to pick up a drunk and finding Mike Hammer instead ("a private jingle who gets around"). Captain Pat Chambers (Scott Peters) had put the word out he wants Hammer. When they call the captain on the phone ("We don't want this on the air"), Chambers tells them to bring Hammer to his home.

Pat has a doctor there to bring Mike around. Obvious animosity exists between the two former friends. Pat blows smoke in Mike's face, tells him his clothes are in the garbage. When Mike calls him "a lousy slob" for a second time, Pat slugs Mike so hard, the drunken detective flips over in his chair into the wall.

Pat needs Hammer only because a dying man has some information valuable to the police but insists on speaking just to Hammer. Another man has been killed with the same gun that killed Senator Knapp. When the dying man doubts Mike is the man he's been looking for, Mike tells him: "I haven't been feeling well."

Hard-bitten Mike asks the dying man his name and who shot him. He's Richie Cole and he relates the story about a team called the Dragon, making up "Tooth and Nail."

"But you'll never get her," Richie says.

"Who?" asks Mike.

"The woman ... Velda."

"You *knew* her?"

"I know her."

The words jolt Hammer. Richie says she's alive and the Dragon is after her. Cole has left some information with a newsstand proprietor who Mike knows, but expires before he can share Velda's location.

Pat wants to know what Cole said. Mike just wants to know who the guy was and, as usual, doesn't answer questions. Pat wants to beat it out of his "old buddy" and hits him again. Unimpressed, Mike says, "You're right, doc—he's really sick."

When Mike awakens the next morning, Hammer's in a hospital bed. The doctor admits he's worried about Pat, who has changed since Velda disappeared and Mike became a drunk. The doctor believes that Pat was in love with Velda. Mike only says, "She was in love with me, doc."

Mike relates the story of Velda's disappearance to the doctor. "It was supposed to be a routine job," a jewel protection gig arranged by Rudolph Civic. Mrs. Civic's jewels were stolen that night and Civic and Velda were never seen again. Typically, Mike just says, "Kismet, buddy."

The doctor figures Cole told Mike who the killer was, and that Hammer wants to go out on his own, just like the old days. He leaves and a cute brunette nurse comes to check on Mike. He flirts with her and tells her to get his clothes.

As she leaves, federal agent Arthur Rickerby (Lloyd Nolan) comes in. He wants to know about Cole as well. Rickerby offers "a certain amount of immunity." Seems Cole was like a son to Rickerby, who will arrange for Hammer's release from the hospital. Rickerby says, "You come and see me so I don't have to go looking for you."

The cute little nurse brings Hammer's clothes. When he kisses her, she says, "You're crazy," and backs out of the room. Her patient replies, "Mad, kitten. Out of my mind." Inside the drunk, Mike Hammer is stirring.

We next see Mike in his traditional trench coat and hat on the streets of New York City. He gets out of cab and goes through the back entrance of an office building only to emerge at Dewey's newsstand. Dewey's not there, just a kid who tells Hammer that his buddy has not been at his stand for "two days running." Behind the kid, men's magazines Spillane wrote for in '50s and '60s can be seen: *Stag, Male*. As Mike walks away from the stand, you can read more titles: *Man's World, Whisper, Confidential, Bachelor* and *Playboy*.

The Hammer theme trumpet solo first heard during the opening credits plays in the background as Mike walks toward Dewey's place, in the basement of a brownstone. Sensing danger, he takes a rolling leap into Dewey's apartment. There he finds his friend's dead body.

Over the corpse, he says somberly, "I'll find him, Dewey."

Mike returns to his old office in the Hackard Building. His office is still listed: "HAMMER MIKE—808." Nat Drutman, the building manager (named for Spillane's wartime friend) has kept the office intact, using money from an old case that Mike never collected.

Drutman tells Mike, "You know, you don't look the same except for the eyes. That's the worst part. That'll be bad for somebody." As Mike leaves the office, he takes a plant that belonged to Velda.

Mike puts Velda's plant on the windowsill and looks around his office. He calls Rickerby. "Bring a sandwich and a couple of beers." He checks under his desk drawer and finds an old friend. In reverie voiceover, he muses, "Colt automatic. Caliber .45. The day of the guns back again. Could I make it? But I had no choice. One mistake and Pat has me. And if he misses me the Dragon has me." (Spillane would use *Day of the Guns* as the title of his first Tiger Mann novel.)

Mike continues his thoughts: "Old Pat. Could he have loved her too? Something sure loused him up." Mike finds one more thing in the drawer—a necklace with "V. S." engraved on a medallion. V. S. stands for Velda Sterling, a last name Spillane would not reveal until the posthumous *The Goliath Bone* (2008).

Rickerby comes in with sandwiches and two cans of Pabst Blue Ribbon beer, and some information: Richie Cole was working as a seaman with a full card. As soon as Rickerby leaves, Mike bolts to the *Herald Tribune* office to see Hy Gardner, who briefs him on the Knapp murder and his "stacked" wife Laura.

Mike takes the Knapp clipping file and drives to Laura Knapp's upstate New York home. He leaves New York City driving a Ford Galaxie 500 convertible, but he arrives at Laura Knapp's place driving a Ford Thunderbird convertible—reflecting the difficulties of maintaining continuity when B unit footage is shot in the USA and principal photography takes place across the pond. After ringing the doorbell to no effect, Mike walks around to the back and finds Laura Knapp lying prone in a bikini on a pool float. He retrieves her from the middle of the pool with a gentle pull from a convenient rake.

Mike Hammer (Spillane) gets the attention of bikini beauty Laura Knapp (Shirley Eaton). Eaton would soon meet James Bond in "Goldfinger" (1964).

Spillane and Shirley Eaton (as Laura) have immediate on-screen chemistry. He tells Laura that another man has been killed with the gun that killed her husband, and he's trying to make a connection. Laura, aware of Hammer's reputation, wants to know what happens if she doesn't cooperate: "If I don't talk, will you belt me one?"

Mike replies with a grin: "Hell. I never hit dames. I always kick 'em." (This is a line first used by Spillane in his 1950s "From the Files of Mike Hammer" comic strip.) She replies, "I'll talk. Do I get a reward if I do?" Mike laughs, "Sure, I won't kick you."

While he's there, Mike checks out the Senator's safe including the alarm function that brings the county cops in quickly. He learns from an officer that the alarm was not engaged on the night of the robbery and murder.

Mike returns to the city to again meet with Rickerby, who knows all the details about the break-in and acts as if Mike is only wasting his time. (The audience's time is being wasted, too, by these frequent dull expository conversations.) Mike asks for an additional week to work on the case and gets the agent's agreement.

Mike returns to his office building, greets the old man security guard, signs the after-hours log book, and is promptly slugged when going into his office. The hood who slugged him runs out when Mike's phone begins to ring. Mike struggles to his feet, sees that his office has been searched and wrecked, and in a fit of rage lashes out at the clutter, sending it smashing to the floor. He calls Nat Drutman to get someone to clean up his office.

As he leaves the building, he discovers the night watchman's dead body. He tears the sign-in sheet out of the watchman's book and hails a cab. He goes to Joe Grissi's bar near the waterfront. A hood tells him to stay out, private party, but he goes in anyway.

A sleazy type in a wide pin-striped suit, tries to act tough and intimidate Mike with an ice pick. He sticks it into the bar, pulls it out and says, "Now you blow, eh?" Mike doesn't answer, but takes out a .45 clip and ejects one of the shells onto the bar. It rolls toward the hood. Mike sticks his right hand into his jacket like he's reaching for a gun, looks down at the bullet on the bar and says, "Eat it." The hoods does and walks out in shame.

Grissi, the bar owner, comes over and tells Mike he's ruined the guy and he doesn't need any more tough guys in his bar, especially old tough guys. Mike takes Grissi's revolver, empties the shells onto the bar, sticks the gun in Grissi's pocket and encourages him to beat it. Bayliss Henry, the old reporter Hammer is there to see, approaches Mike at the bar.

Bayliss knows Richie Cole and is not surprised to learn he's dead. He figured Cole for a smuggler until Mike marks him as a federal agent. Bayliss tries to warn Mike away from following up on the case. Mike says, "I've been shot before." To which Bayliss replies, "Yes, but you've never been dead before."

They leave the bar and go to Cole's place. There, Mike finds a photo book: ALBUM 1941–1945. It contains a photo of a woman that shows only gorgeous legs and is signed, "With affection, Velda." The album shows pilots in a briefing room and two pilots looking at an engine.

Mike and Bayliss leave by the back way. As they climb over a fence into an alley, shots ring out in their direction. Mike draws his .45 and returns fire, to no avail. Old Bayliss, terrified, says, "I'll never learn to keep my mouth shut."

Mike heads for the Blue Ribbon restaurant, where he's meeting Rickerby yet again. Mike wants to know if Cole had any friends. Rickerby says there was a stewardess named Greta King, a sister of someone he served with in the Army. And there was another guy he served with, Alex Bird, who retired upstate to a chicken farm. Also a woman, an old friend, but Rickerby did not know her name.

After Rickerby leaves the restaurant, Mike wraps up his .45 in a newspaper and gets bartender George to mail it to his office. He then returns to the alley where the hoods fired on him and Bayliss, and digs the slug out of the fence.

In his office, he finds Pat and Laura Knapp. Pat has heard about the killing in his building. Mike wants to know how Velda become a PI. Hammer knows that a person needs three years of experience in a qualifying agency, but he never bothered asking her where she got that experience. As a trade, Mike hands Pat the slug from the fence and says he'll tell the cop where the slug came from ... *if* he gets the straight dope on Velda's background.

As Chambers leaves, Mike asks, "Pat, did you love Velda too?" Pat doesn't answer, just abruptly turns away. Laura Knapp has heard the question about Velda.

Laura asks if Velda is alive. Mike replies with quiet conviction, "If she's alive, I'll find her. If she's dead, I'll find the one who killed her." Laura offers him money to continue his investigation, but she calmly stops him from kissing her.

Pat swaps Hammer the info on Velda for Mike's on the bullet. Mike figures the slug came from the same gun that killed Senator Knapp. But Pat also knows there was a .45 fired at the same location: 1800 J Street. And he suspects that Mike is "playing guns again."

The report on Velda reveals that she was an active member of OSI during World War II. Mike tells the doctor, who is also in Pat's office, that Pat is a sick man who won't admit he loved Velda. As Mike leaves, he says, "Go ahead. Admit it. You were in love with Velda, too. Weren't you, Pat?" Pat slowly says "Yes," and then as Mike is walking out the door adds, "Damn you."

Back at the Blue Ribbon, Rickerby has new information about Richie Cole. (Good as Lloyd Nolan is, these scenes are becoming endless and hamper the film's flow.) Seems Cole was big in the war, especially working against Butterfly Two, a spy ring that supported the Nazis before the war. Cole and Velda met during the war, trying to get info on Butterfly Two. Their chief adversary was a guy named Gerald Ehrlich, who headed the spy ring.

Mike springs the name "the Dragon" on Rickerby, who he identifies as Richie's killer. Rickerby knows that the Dragon is a Communist hit man. He tells Mike that he knows too much and he might become a target himself. But Mike knows more, and he wants Rickerby to get him into an official capacity in some agency, so he can carry a gun like in the old days.

Mike visits Hy Gardner to see if the newspaper man can get a coded message about the Dragon to his contacts in Europe. Hy also takes a picture of Gerald Ehrlich from Hy.

At Laura's place, Mike once again finds her at the pool, this time in a black bikini. He shows Laura the picture of Gerald Ehrlich and asks if she has ever seen the picture in her husband's files. She tells him she doesn't think so. Ehrlich has slick-backed hair and a very mean stare. A shot rings out and hits the portable radio between Mike and Laura. Mike races to the gate leading to the pool, but he hears a car pulling away. Hammer tells her the shot was from an assassin called the Dragon.

Laura takes Mike inside to show him Leo's effects. At the pool, she mentioned having a gun for protection. While he's looking through the material, it begins to rain and Mike once again goes into voiceover reverie: "A summer rainstorm. How many times have Velda and I walked in it, our shoulders and legs touching? Okay, kid, the odds are lousy but I'll find you."

Laura comes in to find him staring out the window. She leans in for a kiss but Mike steps past her. "I'll be back."

Rickerby is sitting in Mike's office chair when he returns. He gives Mike his ticket to carry a gun ("in any state") and wants to know about finding Richie's killer. The fed passes on the information that Ehrlich has been dead for five years and that the "Commies" have taken over Butterfly Two. Because of that takeover, anyone who knew the Russians were now in control had to be killed. This meant Cole and Velda.

Hy calls and tells Mike to come quickly, he has some new data. Then Laura calls to tell him she's coming into town to meet with Pat and wants to see him. He suggests Morarity's, 50 East 54th Street. Hy's info relates that the Dragon has the assignment to kill a dark-haired beauty who knows enough to blow the Butterfly Two network. Mike tells Hy that the girl is Velda. Gardner's delivery is abysmal and the expository lines he's handed are no help.

Pat is also at Morarity's. Pat suggests that somehow Mike was in a shady deal with all the gems, and involved in Senator Knapp's robbery. He then shows him a photograph of Civic. It's a match for Ehrlich, but Hammer keeps that to himself. Pat leaves and takes the photo with him.

Mike and Laura return to her place. Mike crashes on her couch. He looks up to see her coming down the wide staircase in a dressing gown, radiantly lovely. She joins him on the couch and kisses him. (This is the famous scene in which the actors ignored the director's order to "cut.")

The next morning, sitting around the pool, Laura asks if Mike loves her. He tells Laura he's not sure and then briefs her on what he knows about the case. Laura suggests a swim.

Hammer and Laura make love on the couch in the infamous "Girl Hunters" scene that found Spillane and Eaton going on enthusiastically after the director yelled cut. (See Chapter #27.)

In the pool house Mike finds a shotgun stuck in a planter, barrel down. He goes ballistic that the gun is plugged and tells her in excruciating, gory detail the way a backblast would kill her. This is also Laura's third bikini, a light print number.

Mike cleans the clay out of the shotgun barrel. When she comes out of the pool, Laura says, "You're going to leave me now, aren't you? It's between your Velda and me." Before he goes, they share another passionate kiss.

Back in the city. Mike stops by the newsstand to see if Dewey had left him a message. The boy says no and asks him about his magazines. Mike tells him to hold them for him. Mike walks away and the boy notices a letter with Mike's name on it falling out of a copy of *Cavalier*. The boy can't get Mike's attention.

Mike goes back to see Bayliss at Joe Grissi's bar. He wants to know what ship Cole sailed on—it's the Vanessa. Cole had a buddy named Red, the one he played chess with. Red knew the girl hidden on the ship—Velda! Dennis Wallace, a buddy of theirs, got her off the ship in a crate. Then Red tells Mike and Bayliss about the big guy who also wanted to know about Dennis and the girl. He was "bigger than you," and looked like an Indian—the Dragon. Bayliss and Mike then go to Dennis' place. They find him strung up, dead, on his Murphy bed.

Mike's third voiceover comes to grips with situation: "The night of the girl hunters had finally come. The truck that delivered Velda had been labeled Alex Bird. And I could have known it if I had read the note old Dewey had left for me."

He drives the Corvette to Bird's farm. He sneaks into Bird's house only to find him dead with a belt around his neck. The Dragon is standing in the dark on the stairs overlooking Bird's den. Mike flips on the light, the Dragon flips his derby at Hammer a la Bond secondary bad guy Odd Job (this, a year before *Goldfinger* was filmed), and shots are exchanged. The Dragon runs for his car but Mike shoots at it and the Dragon ducks into the barn. Mike's .45 has jammed and he enters the barn unarmed.

A long and grueling fight ensues. The Dragon tries to cut off Mike's head with a saw, but the private eye escapes. Both fighters are physically winded and the fight returns close to the turning saw. Finally Mike clubs the brute with both fists, until he falls on the floor. Mike turns off the saw and goes over to pick up an axe, which he drags over, clearly ready to kill his opponent in a gruesome, brutal manner. Then he remembers his promise to Rickerby to leave the Dragon to him, and instead of splitting the spy open with an axe, nails a large spike through the man's right hand, pinning him to the floor. Tooth had been hammered. (British prints substitute an alternate shot that shows a wrist clamp being hammered into place, negating the scene's effectiveness.)

Mike walks away exhausted, sits down at the phone in the garage and calls Rickerby. "He's on the floor of Alex Bird's barn. They just don't make dragons like they used to." Next to the phone is an issue of *Cavalier*. Hammer realizes that he could have known where Velda was days before—Dewey often slipped messages in the *Cavalier* that Mike picked up from his newsstand. Mike just had not checked.

He returns to Laura's place. This time she's back in the black bikini. They chat walking into the pool house. As she steps into the shower, Mike says, "It'll be over today." Laura asks, "Today? Are you sure?"

As Mike explains to Laura what he has learned, he slowly checks the shotgun to see if it's loaded, then methodically replugs both barrels. He explains that Senator Knapp had set a trap for his wife by hinting that his safe held some important military papers. When he discovered what she was doing, he was killed. Mike tells her he knows where to find Velda, the address is in a copy of a magazine. Velda holds the secrets to a nasty spy ring. He tells her as he walks out of the pool house, "I may be wrong but now there's only one way to find out."

He walks away from the pool house. Laura calls to him, "Mike... Mike!" She points the shotgun at him. The camera rack-focuses to bring the clogged barrels into sharp view.

Mike says, "So long, baby."

She pulls the trigger and the audience hears the blast. Mike winces at the nasty off-camera sight, then walks quickly away toward the gate. The camera pans upward and never shows Laura's body. The scene fades into the credits rolling over an aerial shot of New York City as the theme music starts. The end credits read

MIKE HAMMER
is
MICKEY SPILLANE

And was there ever any doubt?

Despite the film's sometimes sluggish pace, Spillane himself as Hammer is letter-perfect ("I knew the lines," he would say, "because I wrote the script"). The transformation of Hammer from gutter-bum to trench-coated classic private eye is handled with humor and style (and in an echo of that Brooklyn patron's doubt about Biff Elliot, several characters profess surprise that this is Mike Hammer).

While Ralph Meeker remains the most memorable big-screen Hammer, and Darren McGavin and Stacy Keach each made the character work within the confines of television, Spillane's is the definitive portrayal of the Mike Hammer of the books. That an actor of as little experience as Spillane could carry an entire motion picture is a tribute to the writer's natural charisma and imperturbability. Some authors have appeared in films, but Spillane alone seems to have had the makings of a movie star (as his Miller Lite Beer commercials indicated).

His position in the pantheon of mystery writers is unique, but—if there were such a thing—it would be made "more" unique by Spillane having portrayed his famous creation on screen. The novelty, even the historical importance of that, however, is surpassed by his having done it well.

"The Girl Hunters" (1963)

Fellane • Running time: 98 minutes • Release date: June 1963

WRITERS: Mickey Spillane, Roy Rowland and Robert Fellows; DIRECTOR: Roy Rowland; PRODUCERS: Robert Fellows and Charles Reynolds; MUSIC: Philip Green; CAST: Mickey Spillane (Mike Hammer); Shirley Eaton (Laura Knapp); Scott Peters (Police Captain Pat Chambers); Guy Kingsley Poynter (Dr. Larry Snyder); James Dyrenforth (Bayliss Henry); Charles Farrell (Joe Grissi); Kim Tracy (Nurse); Hy Gardner (himself); Lloyd Nolan (Federal Agent Arthur Rickerby); Benny Lee (Nat Drutman); Murray Kash (Richie Cole); Bill Nagy (Georgie); Clive Endersby (Duck-Duck); Ricardo Montez as Richard Montez (Skinny Guy); Larry Cross (Red Markham); Tony Arpino (Cab Driver); Nelly Hanham (Landlady); Robert Gallico as Bob Gallico (Dr. Leo Daniels); Michael Brennan (Policeman); Howard Greene (Policeman); Grand Holden (Policeman); Francis Napier (Detective); Larry Taylor (The Dragon)

7. "The Delta Factor" (1970)

Christopher George as Morgan the Raider in "The Delta Factor" (1970) with Yvette Mimieux as CIA agent Kim Stacy, as Morgan admires the black-leather wardrobe of his "wife."

In 1967, with some fanfare, a new Spillane hero was introduced in the novel, *The Delta Factor*. As the writer's "answer" to James Bond, Tiger Mann (1964's *Day of the Guns* and three sequels) had been somewhat disappointing, particularly in the area of motion pictures. In an arena rife with spy films, Spillane's new spy series remained untapped by Hollywood. Modern-day pirate Morgan was a second attempt by Spillane to work in the espionage/thriller genre, and the book was extremely well-received. Much was expected of Spillane's new series character. And then a movie was announced.

"The Delta Factor" (1970) did not, however, give the James Bond films a run for their money—a low-budget affair, indifferently directed by seasoned pro Tay Garnett ("The Postman Always Rings Twice"), and co-produced by Spillane himself, the failure of the film on both artistic and commercial levels soured the writer on the much-lauded character. The second Morgan the Raider novel, *The Consummata*, would not see publication (and completion, by co-author Collins), until 2011.

Christopher George (from TV's "Rat Patrol") portrays Morgan and eternal starlet Yvette Mimieux ("The Time Machine") is CIA agent Kim Stacy, posing as Morgan's wife. The charismatic George makes a fine Spillane hero, and plays his role with enthusiasm, humor and energy. Mimieux is able to convey kitten-ish sexuality and intelligence, though (as in the book) she is not centerstage often. Mostly she makes attractive window dressing, lovingly arrayed in various bikinis and lingerie.

The film has its moments—particularly Morgan's rescue of a political prisoner from an "impregnable" castle/prison, bringing to life a strong sequence from the novel—but remains an undistinguished effort, clearly beset by budgetary and other production problems. The filming technique, alternately under- and over-lit, makes for gaudy visuals, the result strictly that of a sub-par TV movie.

Chief among the production problems was the death of Spillane co-producer and friend Bob Fellows, who had also produced "Ring of Fear" and "The Girl Hunters."

"'The Delta Factor' should have been buried with Bob," director Garnett says in his autobiography. "As a kindness to many people, including Mickey Spillane, I shall forego a recital of most of the tragedies of that misbegotten film."

Garnett then goes on to describe an accident during the shooting of the climactic chase scene that put him in a wheelchair for the duration of "Factor's" shooting. In an interview with the authors, Spillane recalled having to re-cut the film himself, to salvage it as best he could; and it is perhaps the memory of this troubled film that put the writer's film production company on the inactive list.

Again, screenwriter Spillane (he is uncredited but his fingerprints are all over the Garnett's screenplay) does himself no favors by trying to film the entire novel. This time it's not slow pacing and exposition that harms the picture (per "The Girl Hunters"), but a stubborn insistence on remaining true to the novel's text when the budget won't allow. A hurricane that threatens the island remains largely off-screen, for example, and would have been better written out of the scenario.

The plot centers around some of Spillane's personal interests: the sea, modern-day pirates, the CIA and other various "alphabet" agencies, rescues from fortresses, and numerous damsels in distress. This allowed the writer to use the tough-guy approach of his private eye novels in a yarn reflecting not just his nautical interests but his love for the work of such swashbuckling authors as Alexandre Dumas and Anthony Hope. Further, it provided a different, non-urban kind of cinematic backdrop for this non–Hammer James Bond-era thriller. But the film's budget scuttled any possibility for a change-of-pace, big-landscape, exotic-locale Spillane film.

Instead, "The Delta Factor," despite its old pro director, has a home-made quality to it. Sherri Spillane, the writer's wife at the time, is given a major supporting role and a nightclub scene meant to showcase her singing ability. This sequence is so poorly shot, costumed, and choreographed that the former Sherri (Selma) Malinou—who had starred on Broadway—is presented in an unintentionally unflattering manner. Her singing comes off shrill, her acting uneven. A talented performer, Sherri Spillane is done no favors at all by director Garnett.

An embarrassing cameo by a long-in-the-tooth Yvonne De Carlo, a bit from TV veteran Ralph Taeger, and an uncomfortable, past-stardom turn by Diane McBain (subjected to an awkward topless insert by a body double) represent a ragtag team of has-been's likely rounded up by producer Fellows. An interesting presence, in one astoundingly poorly lighted scene, is perennial second-string screen tough guy Ted De Corsia, an actor who portrayed both Mike Hammer (on the radio) and Pat Chambers (in a single episode of the McGavin TV series).

The film opens with a '70s TV-style police chase, right down to the brassy, bouncy, unmemorable musical cues. One nice Spillane touch, at least, is that the scene takes place at night in the rain. Morgan the Raider, having just escaped from prison, is in a phone booth, a spectator to a high-speed chase that concludes with the booth getting rammed.

After credits emphasizing the word "Delta," Morgan is seen next in a hospital bed being coerced by CIA agent Ames (De Corsia) into performing a service for his country in Nuevo Cadiz. Morgan has been convicted of stealing $40 million in currency, but has recently escaped. Thanks to the "kismet" of that phone booth getting rammed, the CIA has captured him, only this time they want him to break into a prison instead of out of one. Ames promises to reduce his prison sentence of thirty years by twenty, which still leaves Morgan with twelve years to go. Despite such strange logic, Morgan decides to cooperate. To keep tabs on him, the CIA assigns him a cover story that includes a "wife"—Kim Stacy (Mimieux).

After a quick escape from custody, Morgan checks in with his lady friend (and apparent madam) Valerie (De Carlo) at a party. Several young ladies {billed as The Party Girls) are thrilled to be seen with notorious Morgan the Raider. (Several are seen topless in a European print).

In Nuevo Cadiz, Morgan (despite escaping, he still goes through with his bargain with De Corsia, who has already disappeared from the film) prepares for the rescue operation of scientist Victor Sable, who now resides in the local impenetrable prison. He and his "wife" Kim Stacy go to a local nightclub to meet his contact, the girl singer Rosa (Sherri Spillane), who performs a sultry number, "Playing It Cool." Rosa's wardrobe is strictly '70s kitsch, tight-fitting with a large circle cut in front revealing her flat stomach.

Morgan tells Rosa that he needs some heroin to bribe the prison guards and asks her to obtain it. Later, Rosa is strangled while broadcasting on a clandestine radio arranging for the drugs.

A secondary plot has Morgan helping attractive blonde Lisa Gordot (McBain), trapped in Neuvo Cadiz because a corrupt local cop has made her his mistress, forbidding her to leave. Morgan has a lucky streak at the craps table and gives her some money to get away.

Morgan has been trying his best to get to "know" his "wife." Kim has staved off his advances, but eventually they kiss. Soon Kim is getting increasingly jealous of Morgan's way with women ("You and your damn broads"). She even explains the concept of the delta factor to him: "The Greek letter D. The phallic symbol for women." In other words, the female pubic triangle.

Morgan the Raider (George) rescues scientist Victor Sable (actor unidentified in credits) from a castle-turned-prison.

Morgan returns to his hotel room after being questioned by the police. As he turns on the TV, he hears a clicking sound. He quickly grabs his wife and they dive behind a free-standing bar as the TV explodes. Angelo, Morgan's contact in the hotel, brings in a portable radio and they contact the operatives who are going to help them with the boat escape after the prison raid.

In typical Spillane "big ending" fashion, "The Delta Factor" builds to the prison raid, this time with the added complication of a potential hurricane. The castle prison sits right on the sea. The prison captain he's bribing gives Morgan a tour of his unescapable castle, complete with prisoners, including the most famous guest, Victor Sable, the man Morgan must spring.

Morgan returns to the prison with his "drugs," really baking soda wrapped in a nice package. The corrupt guards give Morgan $20,000 for the fake drugs, but he shoots them as they try to betray him. He says, "Why did you give me the money? Do you enjoy taking money off a dead man's body?"

On his way to Sable's cell, Morgan releases all the prisoners and begins to shoot his way out. The action moves fast and furious, in true grindhouse feature form. Morgan and Sable climb down the prison wall toward the VW that Kim has left for their escape, as the prisoners push their jailers over the edge of the cliff.

Their red VW is chased by a yellow Mustang until the VW pulls down a side road to the rescue boat that awaits them. For onto five minutes, not a single word of dialogue is exchanged in what is a fairly exciting chase sequence, made amusing by the hero's car being a VW. After the Mustang crashes into a river, Morgan and Sable are chased by the island commander and his soldiers, who blow up the VW.

But Morgan escapes to the awaiting plane. Unfortunately, Sal Decker—the man who framed Morgan for the big heist, posing as a tourist, hiding behind plastic surgery—holds Kim hostage there. He had been driving the Mustang. Morgan kills him in the ensuing shoot-out and Morgan and Kim depart in the plane.

Kim tells Morgan she loves him and will wait for him. He overpowers the CIA agent on the plane and jumps out to an awaiting ship, very much like the ending of a James Bond movie. As she looks out, Kim draws a red delta in lipstick on the plane window. The name of the boat which picks up Morgan is the "Sea-U-Later."

In its own low-end, pulpy way, "The Delta Factor" is a passable time-waster, particularly for the Spillane fan. Morgan's creator called himself an entertainer, writing material that his "customers" could enjoy in the moment and then move on. This film qualifies by that standard, if barely.

Never again would Spillane participate on the production end of a film.

"The Delta Factor" (1970)

Medallion Television and Spillane-Fellows Productions, Inc. •
Running time: 91 minutes • Release date: May 15, 1970

WRITER: Tay Garnett; DIRECTOR: Tay Garnett; PRODUCERS: Tay Garnett and John Monks, Jr.; CINEMATOGRAPHER: Ted Saizis and Vincent Saizis; MUSIC: Howard Danzinger and Raoul Kraushaar; CAST: Yvette Mimieux (Kim Stacy); Christopher George (Morgan); Diane McBain (Lisa Gordot); Ralph Teager (Art Keefer); Yvonne De Carlo (Valerie); Ted de Corsia as Ted De Corsia (Ames); Rhodes Reason (Dr. Fredericks); Joseph Sirola (Sal Dekker); Sherri Spillane (Rosa); Caren Chatham (Party Girl); Georgine Darcy (Party Girl); Francine Farrar (Party Girl); Valerie Hawkins (Party Girl); Leslie McRay (Party Girl); Elizabeth Thompson (Party Girl)

8. "I, the Jury" (1982)

Armand Assante as Mike Hammer in "I, the Jury" (1982)—a hardhitting, raunchy PI in a hardhitting, raunchy film that finally delivers on the sex and violence promise of the source novel.

In 1981, Mickey Spillane began his long association with TV producer Jay Bernstein. Their first Mike Hammer made-for-TV movie for CBS, "Mickey Spillane's Margin for Murder," is loosely based on *I, the Jury*. Of course, it couldn't be directly based on that novel, because Spillane had sold those rights in perpetuity to producer Victor Saville. And much to Spillane's displeasure, a rival, theatrical version of "I, the Jury" was shooting simultaneously with the Bernstein TV version.

Without either Spillane's blessing or even knowledge, the Victor Saville estate had sold the remake rights to "I, the Jury" (and the other three Spillane properties) to controversial writer/director Larry Cohen, perhaps best known for his three "It's Alive" films. Spillane received no direct financial reward from the Cohen deal, and was understandably irritated by the prospect of a production that he saw as a rival to a TV film that he had profitably sanctioned.

On the other hand, a new "I, the Jury" film seems a natural outgrowth of the Spillane revival of the early '80s spearheaded by the writer himself by way of his popular Miller Lite Beer commercials. A new theatrical Mike Hammer film could only serve to bolster Spillane's reputation, and keep the money coffers filling up, as reprints of his books—including a new movie tie-in edition of *I, the Jury*, and paperbacks adorned with his Miller Lite image—continued to appear in a period when Spillane's only literary output was a couple of kids' books.

But Spillane saw "I, the Jury" as a renegade production, and rejected Cohen's advances when the director attempted to solicit the writer's promotional participation. Further, Mike Hammer's daddy had read the screenplay and considered it trash.

After reading Cohen's screenplay, understanding Spillane's reaction is easy. Cohen has a solid understanding of the Hammer character, updating him to the '80s—he is a Vietnam vet, for example—and retaining memorable bits from the novel—Hammer and Velda trap a guy shadowing them in a revolving door. But much of Spillane's famous plot is abandoned to a degree that rivals "My Gun Is Quick."

Keeping in mind how conservative Spillane had become by the 1980s, the womanizing Hammer of the screenplay might well offend him—it opens with Hammer bedding the wife of a client in a divorce case. Even factoring in changing times and mores, this casual immorality lends a hypocritical edge to the moral outrage Hammer expresses when his buddy Jack Williams is killed.

To Spillane's delight, Larry Cohen was fired from his own production—by the "money men"—after less than two weeks of shooting (for going over budget). But Cohen's screenplay remains the engine of "I, the Jury" (1982); and does, finally, bring the famous "It was easy" confrontation scene to the screen.

Replacement director Richard Heffron's "I, the Jury" is a gritty, witty, crisply-edited action flick. Blessed with extensive location shooting in Manhattan, and a dynamic, jazzy score by Bill Conti of "Rocky" fame, the second "I, the Jury" is among the stronger action films of the period. With better distribution, the film might have made of Armand Assante an action star of the magnitude of Charles Bronson or Sylvester Stallone.

When it was announced he would portray Mike Hammer, Assante—previously best-known as Goldie Hawn's French boy friend in "Private Benjamin"—seemed bizarrely miscast. But with his brooding good looks, he makes a rough-and-mumble Hammer, muttering to himself like Brando playing Popeye, reflecting a wryly existential outlook on life that is quintessential Mike Hammer.

Assante is on the short list of great movie Mike Hammer's. He is as true a Hammer as Spillane in "The Girl Hunters"; but where Spillane's Hammer is the older, post-gutter one, the Assante version is the younger, more psychotic P.I. of Elliot in "I, the Jury," only with the screen presence and dangerous charisma of Meeker in "Kiss Me Deadly." And because this is the '80s, not the restrictive '50s that burdened Elliot and even Meeker, Assante is able to blossom in all of Mike Hammer's berserk glory.

If the womanizing aspect of the character seems more extreme than in the novels, remember that this is not the Mike Hammer of 1947; this is an updated Hammer, his mores shaped by a different era, his war not the Holy One against Adolf Hitler but that Godforsaken fiasco in Vietnam. This Hammer still smokes Luckies, but he also subscribes to *Soldier of Fortune*.

And no screen Hammer is tougher, more reckless than Assante's. When he finally gets within reach of the homicidal killer he's been tracking, he is in the awkward position of being in the back of a truck driven by the killer at 60 mph; still, Hammer does not hesitate to shoot the son of a bitch, consequences be damned—Hammer will take his chances.

When a Japanese fry cook turns out to be an assassin who slashes a woman in a restaurant, Hammer slams the cook's face into the hot grill, and steam rises.

When a mob chief's underling gives him too thorough a frisk, Hammer casually closes the door of a cab on the hood's coat, insulting the cabbie, prompting the latter to pull quickly away without realizing he's dragging the helpless, hapless hood behind him.

When Hammer comes calling on Charlotte at film's end, he greets her with a long narrow box of flowers—that turns out to contain not roses, but his dead friend's artificial arm.

Assante carries all of this off with a macho charm and a nice sense of the black humor that pervades the script. The fish tank in Hammer's office reflects the dark nature of the detective's world: Hammer cannot keep the fish alive, and whenever someone in the film

In the "I, the Jury" remake, Assante's Hammer can't keep his pet fish alive, but he has the support and love of Laurene Landon's Velda, one of the truest portrayals of the detective's secretary, partner and chief love interest.

dies, a scene shortly follows showing Hammer discovering another dead fish (or two) in his tank. His secretary Velda (Laurene Landon) suggests he try another type of pet: a coyote, perhaps.

And it is with the treatment of Velda that "I, the Jury" outshines all the other films. (In "The Girl Hunters," of course, Velda is off-stage.) Though a blonde—presumably so-cast because Charlotte is portrayed by brunette Barbara Carrera—Laurene Landon's Velda is the Velda of the books: a big, beautiful broad who packs a revolver in her lacy drawers, who stands side by side with Hammer and trades slugs with the bad guys, who wants to marry Hammer but stoically wipes the lipstick off his face for him while informing him that once they're married, her "Sicilian grandmother" will strangle him if ever he cheats.

When Velda is kidnapped late in the film by a homicidal slasher programmed to kill by the CIA, she is no passive female victim; she is nearly free of her own accord when Hammer finally crashes in to rescue her. In perhaps the nicest bit in the film, Hammer—about to pursue the killer, who has just leapt from the several-story window to the street below—hesitates to see if Velda is all right, not bothering to untie her, just ascertaining she's okay. Mike says to her, "You exhaust me," and resumes pursuit.

The shot lingers on the still-tied up Velda whose little girl grin is full of the love that readers of Spillane's books know Velda has for the tough/tender Hammer.

This "I, the Jury" begins after the pre-credits bedding sequence with the murder of Jack Williams and ends with the death at Hammer's hands of the murderess Charlotte.

These scenes are remarkably faithful to the book—though Charlotte does not do a striptease, exactly, having already been to bed with Hammer, although she is mostly naked when he shoots her—but what happens in between those scenes bears only occasional resemblance to Spillane's story.

Assante as a Hammer who dishes it out and takes it, on the trail of a CIA-mind-controlled serial killer in "I, the Jury" (1982).

Charlotte Bennett (not Manning) runs a sex clinic where Jack Williams, there for treatment of sexual dysfunction—vaguely suggested to be a homosexual yearning for his friend Hammer—stumbled onto a CIA brainwashing scheme. The twins, one of whom has the novel's famous strawberry birthmark, are sex surrogates at the clinic ("hookers" in Hammer's view). This CIA aspect is trendy but somehow acceptable, as are the occasional scenes that are not from Hammer's point-of-view, which reveal early on that Charlotte is a bad "guy"—no attempt to surprise here.

But the spirit of the story is

intact, and Cohen and Heffron clearly know their Spillane: elements of *The Girl Hunters*, *Kiss Me, Deadly*, and *One Lonely Night* are utilized, to fine effect.

From *The Girl Hunters* comes a suggestion that Pat Chambers (Paul Sorvino) loves Velda; a one-on-one fight reminiscent of Hammer slugging it out with the Dragon; and the gimmick of plugging the barrel of the villain's gun, so that it explodes on said villain.

From *Kiss Me, Deadly* comes the kidnapping of Velda, and from *One Lonely Night* comes Hammer's one-man assault on an enemy fortress. In *One Lonely Night*, more than any of the other books, Hammer seems an ex-soldier, using combat-style, commando-like tactics, when he attacks the nest of Commies holding Velda captive, and machine-guns 'em down.

In the 1982 "I, the Jury," in a manner none of the other films approaches, Hammer is an ex-soldier; his attack on the stronghold of CIA-agent Romero (a reference to "Dawn of the Dead" director George Romero, no doubt) portrays him specifically as a Vietnam vet—a sequence, incidentally, absent from Cohen's original screenplay. After he has killed any number of CIA agents, Hammer stands in a swamp-like area over a body that lies dead in the water (like another fish in his tank). When the walkie-talkie he's taken from the dead CIA agent's body calls out "Romero One to Romero Three," Assante replies in his best Brooklynese, "Romero One, this Hammer One—you wanna rock 'n' roll wid me?"

When Romero is dead, it is time to take "flowers" to Charlotte.

Assante's performance has a psychotic edge that makes his Hammer, updated or not, the definitive screen portrayal to date of the young Mike Hammer. Somewhere in there with the Brando and Stallone bits is a sense of the Mick himself: Assante has watched Spillane, obviously, and has the bantam walk down pat—as with Biff Elliot and Spillane, Assante confirms that a small, broad-chested Hammer has a bulldog rather than bully quality needed for character empathy in the page-to-screen transfer of the brawling hero.

The Assante Hammer is outraged; he's prepared to risk anything for his goal, because his Hammer simply does not give a damn; if he dies in the course of his quest, so be it—"You take life too serious," he advises several terrified unwilling participants in his various war games. Another time he tells Charlotte that he "may take a few suspects out along the way—I'm not perfect." Dat's Mike Hammer, '80s style.

Predictably, Spillane despised the film; most of his objections stemmed from Cohen's script, understandably displeased that his straightforward detective plot had been abandoned. He reserved his most dismissive comment for Assante: "He wore Italian heels," as if this were enough to invalidate the film.

Even the update's most obviously strong point did not impress Spillane—he dismissed the portrayal of Velda as "a preppie." If so, this is a pistol-packing preppie, who likely shot the alligator on her shirt.

And what became of this hard-hitting, sexually explosive action movie? 20th Century-Fox—who had inherited the movie from bankrupt American Cinema—shelved the film for over a year, despite the fact that a *Playboy* March, 1982, cover story provided the sort of publicity that could have turned "I, the Jury" into the "10" of private eye movies. Not until October of that year was the picture even given test runs. The studio put the film out with an uninspired ad campaign (referring to the hero not as Mike Hammer but "The Hammer"—shades of Fred Williamson) and withheld it from broad, national release. (The film has since been seen on cable television, and on VHS, but to date not on DVD or Blu-ray in the USA.)

In the midst of the film's initial release, fired director/screenwriter Larry Cohen got on the national wire services by claiming that Heffron had put "obscene" scenes into "I, the Jury" that he hadn't written; and that his intention had been to make a "lighter, James Bond" sort of film. The added material Cohen wanted excised included an orgy scene intercut with the death of the twins, and the Japanese cook sequence. Despite Cohen's claim, these scenes are in his original screenplay.

Still, the scenes Cohen wanted cut even today seem shocking, disturbing; but so was the ending of the original novel when it first appeared in 1947.

"I, the Jury" (1982)

American Cinema Productions, Larco Productions, Pellepont, Solofilm • Running time: 111 minutes • Release date: October 9, 1982

WRITER: Larry Cohen; DIRECTOR: Richard T. Heffron; PRODUCERS: Michael Leone, Andrew Pfeffer as Andrew D.T. Pfeffer and Robert H. Solo as Robert Solo; CINEMATOGRAPHER: Andrew Laszlo; MUSIC: Bill Conti; CAST: Armand Assante (Mike Hammer); Barbara Carrera (Dr. Charlotte Bennett); Laurene Landon (Velda); Alan King (Charles Kalecki); Geoffrey Lewis (Joe Butler); Paul Sorvino (Detective Pat Chambers); Judson Earney Scott as Judson Scott (Charles Kendricks); Barry Snider (Romero); Julia Barr (Norma Childs); Jessica James (Hilda Kendricks); Frederic Downs (Jack Williams); Mary Margaret Amato (Myrna Williams); F.J. O'Neil (Goodwin); William G. Schilling as William Schilling (Lundee); Robert Serva (Breslin); Don Pike (Evans); Timothy Meyers as Timothy Myers (Blake); Leigh Harris as Lee Anne Harris (First Twin); Lynette Harris (Second Twin); Gwyn Gilliss as Gwynn Gillis (Receptionist); Mike Miller (Victor Kyle); Alex Stevens (First Cab Driver); Bobbi Burns (Sheila Kyle); M. Sharon Madigan (Bonnie); Richard Russell Ramos (Second Cab Driver); Norman Blankenship as Norm Blankenship (Kelsey); Daniel Faraldo (Danny); H. Richard Greene (Gentleman at Bar); Felicity Adler (Jogger); Jodi Douglas (Party Girl); Lee H. Doyle (Maitre D'); Cheryl Henry (Brunette); Michael Fiorello (Man in Revolving Door); Herb Peterson (Policeman); Richard Dahlia (Doctor at Clinic); Aaron Barsky (Guard at Gate); Ernest Harada (Chef); Larry Pine (Movie Director); Joe Farago (Assistant Director); Alan Dellay (Cameraman); Jack Davidson (Eric Clavel); Loring Pickering (Soap Opera Actor); Corinne Bohrer as Corrinne Bohrer (Soap Opera Actress)

Spillane on TV

9. Mike Hammer TV Pilot (1954)

Though neither porkpie hat nor trenchcoat is in sight, Brian Keith plays an authentically tough Hammer in Blake Edwards' "busted" TV pilot of 1954.

Prior to the filming of "Kiss Me Deadly," Victor Saville produced a "Mike Hammer" TV pilot, which is somewhat surprising since he and Spillane were then at odds. Yet the existence of this production shows the two men doing business beyond the confines of their four-novel/four-picture deal. The pilot was rejected by the networks as too violent, and there appears to have been a subsequent pilot, also deemed too violent, similarly rejected by network television. (See the "My Gun Is Quick" chapter for speculation that a second pilot was the basis of that film.)

Chosen to helm the pilot was talented young writer/director Blake Edwards, creator of radio's popular "Richard Diamond, Private Detective" with film star Dick Powell. (The radio show was later adapted to television for David Janssen, in a series whose first two seasons were scored by "Kiss Me Deadly" composer Frank De Vol).

On the cusp of a major film directing career, Edwards would also create TV's very successful "Peter Gunn," a beat generation spin on Mike Hammer that sparked a wave of private eye television series. The Hammer influence on Edwards would continue on in the unsuccessful 1967 big-screen remake "Gunn," which "borrowed" the famous transvestite ending of Spillane's *Vengeance Is Mine!* Mike Hammer's creator felt the famous music by Henry Mancini for "Peter Gunn" was heavily influenced by the Stan Purdy themes used in "Ring of Fear" and on the "Mickey Spillane's Mike Hammer Story" album.

That the pilot is an effective if unimaginative rendition of Spillane's famous detective is no surprise—in addition to various versions of Peter Gunn, Edwards wrote and directed such big-screen thrillers as "Experiment in Terror" (1962), "The Carey Treatment" (1972), and "Sunset" (1988). What perhaps is both surprising and disappointing is the humorlessness of his approach to Hammer by way of a dour, sleepy Brian Keith. It would take Darren McGavin's affable tough guy to make Hammer palatable to TV audiences in the late 1950s.

This is not to say Keith makes an uninteresting Hammer, and the broad-shouldered actor would become a major TV star in years to come (Sam Peckinpah's "The Westerner," the long-running sitcom "Family Affair," and the Stephen Cannell hit "Hardcastle and McCormick"). Keith even played another famous literary private eye in the short-lived Ross MacDonald-based "Archer" (1975).

But Keith's Hammer is alternately shouting and mumbling, and his size makes a bully of him, even to roughing up a gangster's moll, who predictably falls for him (quickly—it's a half-hour pilot). His relationship with Pat Chambers (Robert Bice) is strictly adversarial, prefiguring Meeker and Addy in "Kiss Me Deadly," but reduced to a shouting match. This Hammer wears neither hat nor trenchcoat, carries a revolver (even though Chambers revokes his gun and PI license), and is never seen at his office. As with the McGavin series, the half hour makes no room for Velda.

Otherwise, Edwards—in rather perfunctory style—touches all the Spillane bases in that very short running time: a newsboy pal of Hammer's is accidentally killed and Hammer swears vengeance; Chambers dresses Hammer down for his vigilante ways; Hammer dishes it out and takes it; a damsel falls for him in a big way; said damsel gets herself killed; and Hammer shoots bad guys down with nary a twitch of remorse. The music accompanying all this is strictly overly familiar "library" cues, hardly the Mancini musical masterpiece that Edwards would have for "Peter Gunn" in just four short years.

Like the McGavin series, the Edwards/Keith pilot utilizes voiceover, sometimes quite evocative of Spillane: "The city was quiet and the sharp wind blowing off the river smelled like rain." Other narration seems like leftover "Richard Diamond," as when Hammer says that waking up after a beating is "like wading through an acre of glue."

Still, it's a fast, hard-hitting half hour and the violence is dished up unstintingly, with a particularly well-staged brawl between Hammer and two hoods waiting for him at his apartment. Guns are soon blazing and Hammer cleverly sets a trap for them with a spray of hot shower in the bathroom they break in to. A brief but moody waterfront sequence gives the little pilot some *noir* credibility, and as a smooth mob boss, Donald Randolph—so over the top and fey in Saville's "My Gun Is Quick"—oozes understated menace.

Had this pilot led to a series, it might have been a winner, particularly if Brian Keith had been allowed to warm up, perhaps with a more friendly Chambers relationship and maybe with a humanizing Velda at the office.

Certainly Blake Edwards learned that lesson, as his "Peter Gunn" was noted for its cool humor and clever back-and-forth dialogue (quite unlike his "Hammer" pilot). Gunn (Craig Stevens) and his Pat Chambers—Lt. Jacoby (Hershel Bernardi)—and his Velda, Edie Hart (Lola Albright)—made a warm if hip and very human family.

The opening titles, over stock footage of a car moving fast through the city, follow the familiar pattern of Spillane getting billing over Hammer:

Mickey Spillane's
"Mike Hammer!"

This time, however, the writer's name—in a font similar to that used on the covers of the Signet reprints of Spillane novels of the era—is larger than that of his creation. And Brian Keith gets no billing at all, nor does Blake Edwards.

Mike is walking down Beacon Street between 54th and Jefferson heading to his favorite restaurant, The Purple Peacock. Outside Mike talks with newsboy Roger Poe, who jokes he's saving his money for a yacht. The restaurant is run by Jimmy, a product of Prohibition: it caters to everybody from politicians to hoods.

Jimmy and Mike talk about gangster Harry Lund, who's going to testify against his former boss, Carl Muuse, on the next day. Both are aware that it's not good for the gangster and his party to be at the restaurant. Suddenly, after Lund has just left, shots ring out. Everyone ducks inside, but outside, Harry and a newsboy named Roger Poe lay dead and one of two federal agents protecting Lund has a stomach wound. Lund's girlfriend showing off lots of cleavage is screaming about "a new dimple in her knee." In a nice moment, Hammer snatches the screaming moll's fur to provide the wounded fed with a pillow.

This sequence appears inspired by the famous shooting of Mickey Cohen, while in protective federal custody, outside Sherry's restaurant on the Sunset Strip in Los Angeles in 1949.

At Captain Pat Chambers's office, Mike complains about Pat (Bice) not arresting Muuse for murder. But Muuse has an alibi: he was with his girlfriend, Janice Graham (Virginia Lee). Two hoods were with them as well. Pat has combed-back salt-and-pepper hair and wears dark-rimmed glasses, looking more like a lawyer than a police captain. Mike wants to know what Pat is going to tell Father Crump about Roger.

Pat says, "What gives you the right to make this a personal vendetta?" Pat says Roger's death might just be the last step to getting Muuse. Before Mike leaves Pat demands his gun. Mike gives it to him. It's a .38.

Janice Graham is an ex-showgirl and currently Muuse's personal property, living at the fancy Regency House. Mike busts in by pushing Ray Kittle, one of Muuse's goons, back into the apartment. Janice, Muuse and another hood are there. Muuse says he'll send the priest a donation for the orphanage. Mike says the gangster will get it back in his teeth. Muuse tells him his has ten seconds to leave. Janice says to Hammer, "Please." Kittle is eager take Hammer on. Mike tells Janice, "Better get him to lie down. He's dead and don't know it." After Mike leaves, Muuse tells Kittle if Hammer starts anything to bury him.

Mike walks the streets until nearly one in the morning. He stops for a smoke in front of a movie poster: "The Battle Cry of China." Mike knows that "he's on a tight, simple schedule. Get Carl Muuse before he gets me."

Mike sneaks back into Janice's apartment, where she's in bed, and puts his hand over her mouth. He asks her where Carl and his boys were at 10:30 and pulls her by the hair on her neck. She says, "What are trying to do, strangle me or scalp me?"

Mike asks, "What kind of a dame are you? Don't you care about a poor little kid?" She says she's just "a dame that got tired of being pushed around. And then she met a man named Muuse who didn't push her around anymore." Mike responds, "Well, whaddya you got now?" He leaves.

Mike goes to Ray Kittle's place, catching him after a night of celebratory, post-hit drinking. Hammer roughs him up some and tells him he's going to get his boss. The private eye shoves the hood against a wall, hard, and the hood slides down, in a very direct prefiguring of a similar scene in "Kiss Me Deadly."

Next morning, Mike goes to Father Crump's orphanage where Roger lived. The father tells him, "Roger liked you. He thought you were quite a guy." The father gives Hammer Roger's pen to remember him by. "It's rather old, but it writes." Captain Chambers has already been to see the Father. Angry Mike refers to Pat as an "Irish wetback."

Mike stops by the Purple Peacock and makes an anonymous call to Muuse's place. With a small, rare smile, Hammer plants the story that Kittle is getting ready to rat on his boss. Back at his apartment, Mike laments that after a day of interviews, he can't get anybody to talk about Muuse. The mob boss has been controlling things for over three years and people are scared. On his dresser there is a picture of a blonde woman (Charlotte?). On his bookcase are several hardbacks. Janice Graham calls asking to meet Hammer "someplace out of the way. Around eight. Someplace safe." He tells her to meet him at warehouse number three down at the end of 108th street.

She drives there in a Ford convertible. Mike makes her wait until 8:15 before he steps out of the shadows, wanting to make sure this wasn't a trap. She says he scared her to death, making her wait. They drive away and park at a safe and secluded place. She tells him he made her think about her life with his questions the night before. She admits Lincoln and Kittle were not in her apartment the night of the shooting. Mike is still worried that this may be a trap. "It's not," she says, and he leans over and they kiss.

When Mike returns to his apartment, the two hoods are waiting. A fire fight breaks out. He runs to his bathroom, locks the door, turns on the hot water and aims it at the door. Then he jumps out the window to the fire escape. The hoods come in and get doused/scalded. Mike drops to the ground and hides in the trash as the hoods look for him.

"It's easy to sleep after a beating like that," Hammer's voiceover tells us. "You just close your eyes and bleed a little."

Upon awaking, Mike rushes to Janice's apartment. Even if she didn't set him up, he figures, she's in trouble. He finds her on the floor, apparently shot. He tells her he's sorry. She says, "I never was much good to anybody anyway" before dying. He calls Pat to let him know about Janice's death.

Hammer then takes the dead woman's convertible, puts the top up, and goes out to Muuse's place. He hopes that the guard will recognize the car and let him in. Mike knocks the guard out and goes in to get Muuse to write a confession before his two hoods come back in. "I, Carl Muuse, ordered Ray Kittle to kill Janice Graham and Harry Lund." At gunpoint, Hammer forces him to sign, making the gangster use Roger Poe's pen.

The two hoods come in. They draw on Hammer. He shoots Lincoln, then tells Kittle that Muuse ratted him out in the confession. Kittle turns and shoots Muuse. Then Hammer cold-bloodedly shoots Kittle, three times.

When Pat arrives Mike tells him to try to prove it wasn't self-defense and then walks down the driveway.

Mickey Spillane's "Mike Hammer" (1954)

A Charles B. Moss and Richard Lewis Production

WRITER: Blake Edwards; DIRECTOR: Blake Edwards; PRODUCERS: Richard Lewis and Victor Saville; CAST: Brian Keith (Mike Hammer); Robert Bice (Pat Chambers); Virginia Lee (Janice Graham) Donald Randolph (Carl Muuse); Donald Harvey (Ray Kittle); Dale Van Sickle (Charlie Lincoln); Robert Foulk (Jimmy Shipp); William Woodson (Father Crump); Leon Burbank (Rodger Poe); Carol Brewster (Barbara).

10. "Mickey Spillane's Mike Hammer" (1958–59)

Darren McGavin brought humor to Mike Hammer in the 1958–1959 MCA-TV series without compromising either the brutality or the vengeance-seeking ways of Spillane's famous private eye.

After at least two rejected pilots, Mike Hammer finally appeared on the home screen in the Revue syndicated series, "Mickey Spillane's Mike Hammer" (1958–59). Hammer's debut was greeted with the same critical enthusiasm as his large screen ones: a critical hammering. But revisiting these black-and-white adventures—or seeing them for the first time—reveals a high degree of pulp artistry and a particularly memorable star turn from Darren McGavin as one of the best screen Hammers.

McGavin had several things going for him—he was a rising stage and screen star, he was masculine but not a bruiser, he bore a resemblance to Mickey Spillane himself, and had the charisma and wry humor required of a leading man for the intimate medium of television. Though he carried a .38 not a .45 (much to Spillane's displeasure), McGavin "knew how to wear the hat" (much to Spillane's approval) and he tempered his roughhouse ways with an affability previously unseen in a screen Hammer.

Many episodes are right out of the Spillane playbook: vengeance-driven stories that put Hammer at odds with his friend Captain Pat Chambers. Gunfire is rampant in a Spillane landscape that makes the Wild West out of Manhattan, willing "chickies" abound by way of some of Hollywood's most fetching starlets, and the fights are brutal, with Hammer smashing, kicking, slapping, and throttling bad guys, frequently tossing them headlong into the furniture. Sometimes dismissed as too good-natured, the McGavin Hammer is easily as brutal as Spillane's.

In "Kiss Me Deadly," Ralph Meeker breaks one collectible opera record to make a potential witness talk, and comes across as a brutal heel; in the TV episode "To Bury a Friend," McGavin similarly destroys one collectible clock after another to force a supposedly crippled collector out of a wheelchair, potentially a far more extreme scene that McGavin performs without losing the viewer's sympathy and support.

Captain Pat Chambers is only occasionally featured, and less so in the second season. As a cost-saving measure, Hammer frequently talks with Pat on the phone, with Pat's side of the conversation unseen and unheard. Still, his relationship with Chambers as played by Bart Burns is among the better screen depictions of the pairing. Burns, a fine, natural character actor (he was one of the jurors in the original "Studio One" version of "Twelve Angry Men"), maintains a nice rapport with McGavin.

Velda does not appear—she is mentioned in the pilot, but in the series that followed, Hammer is shown alone in an office with no reception area. Perhaps these stories took place between Velda's disappearance and "The Girl Hunters." The reality is, a half-hour rendition of Hammer makes it very difficult to find the time or place for Velda.

All seventy-eight episodes bear titles revealing their pulp roots, starting with episode one—"The High Cost of Dying," which could have been the title of a *Dime Detective* story. One memorable episode, "Crepe for Suzette," was the title of a story in the September, 1948 issue of *Thrilling Detective* (one of *Dime Detective*'s competitors). Writers of scripts and source stories on "Mike Hammer" make a Who's Who of pulp fiction: Robert Turner, Stephen Marlowe, Richard Deming, James Gunn and especially Frank Kane. Three episodes were based on stories by Curt Cannon, an Evan Hunter pseudonym (ironically, Hunter had published an acid Spillane parody, "Kiss Me, Dudley," in *Manhunt* in 1955).

In all, the series had nineteen writers, five contributing only the source story. Kane—whose own private eye Johnny Liddell was strictly second-string—wrote twenty-four episodes, many adapted from Liddell short stories. Kane had the habit of calling the women in his teleplays "chickie." Spillane used "kitten" and "doll."

Some of the best scripts come from B.X. Sanborn, a pseudonym for crime writer Bill S.

Ballinger, whose celebrated novel *Portrait in Smoke* (1950) was filmed as "Wicked as They Come" (1956). Other gems were courtesy of "Steven Thornley," identified by TV scholar Stephen Bowie as a young Ken Pettus, who under his real name would go on to an impressive small-screen career, writing the likes of "The Big Valley," "Mission: Impossible" and "Hawaii Five-O."

Thornley contributed teleplays for twenty-one episodes, Ballinger twelve. Lawrence Kimble wrote seven; Fenton Earnshaw five; Robert Turner four; and Barry Shipman three. Eight other writers contributed one episode each.

The music alternates between generic dramatic "library" music and original material written by Dave Kahn. The second season, influenced by the success of Henry Mancini's "Peter Gunn" music, has considerably more of Kahn's original scoring, much of it written specifically for the RCA Hammer "soundtrack," capitalizing on the success of Henry Mancini's "Gunn" albums.

The haunting, melancholy theme ("Riff Blues") by Kahn plays over the NYC location-shot opening and close of each episode. While the Keach era "Harlem Nocturne" is now the most famous Hammer theme, the Kahn original is at least as memorable. Kahn shares credit with Melvyn Leonard, but (in an interview with Hollywood music expert Jon Burlingame) the composer dismissed Leonard's credit as "designed to capture composer royalties for the publisher."

In a stable of pros, future top TV (and occasional big-screen) director Boris Sagal is dominant, particularly in the first season. Seasoned serial director William Witney contributes nine episodes to the second, his work perhaps the most cinematic and stylish of the series ("Dixie Is Dead," "Curtains for an Angel"). Some sources credit Richard Irving (director of eleven episodes) as the producer, but there is no on-screen producing credit.

The premiere episode was first broadcast on January 7, 1958, toward the beginning of the private eye "fad" on American television. "Perry Mason" was first seen on CBS-TV on September 12, 1957, "Peter Gunn" on September 22, 1958, and "77 Sunset Strip" began October 10, 1958. Though "Peter Gunn" and "77 Sunset Strip" ignited the popularity of the genre on TV, "Perry Mason" and "Mike Hammer" lit the fuse—"Mason" matter of fact and procedural in nature, "Hammer" edgier, more realistic in its melodramatic way, certainly more violent, overtly sexual, and yet more amusing.

Characteristically, the first episode begins in voiceover: "'Maybe, as the saying goes, iron bars do not a prison make, but they help.'" For the remainder of the series, Hammer's cynical sense of humor gives context to the rough-stuff action, and McGavin's throwaway narration provides character and a distinctly New York flavor.

Episodes operate as miniature examples of film *noir*, displaying fluid photography—frequent long takes, master shots worthy of Joseph H. Lewis ("Gun Crazy"), with effective integration of excellent New York "B" unit work seamlessly woven into Hollywood-produced studio principal photography. The series works effectively within its limited budget (under $50,000 an episode), practically making the limitations a plus via the gritty look of low-end apartments, seedy burlesque house dressing rooms, and shoddy offices.

The series was shot on the ancient Republic Studios back lot in the San Fernando Valley. So, apparently, was "My Gun Is Quick," made just a year before the "Hammer" series began, as artwork seen on the walls of the flophouse apartment in "Quick" turns up in several episodes of "Hammer."

In the first-aired episode, Mike is called to Sing Sing prison by Floyd Ingalls, a dying inmate whose wife Evie has been kidnapped to force Ingalls to reveal the location of missing loot from a robbery. Mike doesn't like criminals, but he also hates mistreatment of the innocent. When Floyd reveals the loot's location, Mike withholds it from the police and goes his own way.

Mike's office is PI basic: wooden client chair, a wooden desk out of Army surplus, and a wooden roller chair, all well-used. The entire office is only nine steps deep. The desk holds a black rotary phone, a banker's light, an ash tray, a wooden in-box, and an office supply store desk calendar/writing surface combo. Behind the desk is a small side table with half a dozen reference books. On the walls are a United States map and several nondescript picture prints, mostly of horses. A well-worn sofa sits under one of the pictures; a steam radiator is next to the entrance. A small room on the left has a lavatory and a hot plate for making coffee. The office door reads

"812
MIKE HAMMER
PRIVATE INVESTIGATOR."

Nothing about the office gives the appearance of prosperity.

Mike's first visitor is Captain Chambers, an old friend and Hammer's co-worker from his previous stint with the New York police force. In the first of many verbal (and some physical) sparring matches, Mike tells Pat he's wasting his time trying to find out anything about what Sing Sing inmate Ingalls wanted. Pat demands to know if Mike wants "to do it the hard way" by hauling him "downtown for questioning." Mike says they are "both too old to play trick or treat."

Meg Hollister, Ingalls' sister-in-law, calls Mike asking for his help. As Mike rushes from his office, the viewer sees a mysterious man in the hallway waiting to follow Mike. This ploy will be repeated many times in the series. Meg seems too eager to get Mike to turn over the money to ransom her sister, so Mike baits her by saying, "Are you afraid someone might mistake you for a woman?" He then kisses her and she responds by slapping him.

Mike takes that as proof she is not part of the kidnapping plot. As he leaves, Meg thanks him for offering her encouragement, but she avoids his attempted kiss. She is not a raving beauty and the casting of this moderately attractive non-starlet gives the proceedings genuine poignance.

In the hallway, the man who followed Mike is overcome by a judo move. But the guy draws a gun and tells Mike he needs to go downtown to see Captain Chambers. Mike tries to rebuff that request, but the much taller man forces him to leave by waving the gun around.

As it turns out, the guy really is taking Hammer to police headquarters. Pat's office door reads: "PATRICK CHAMBERS." A picture of J. Edgar Hoover is prominently displayed. Mike talks Pat into a plan to use the holdup money to rescue Evie, recover the $60,000 robbery loot, and arrest the kidnappers. Reluctantly Pat okays Mike's scheme.

The loot is buried near an old farmhouse between Tarrytown and Dobbs Ferry New York. Mike digs it up in the light of an old-style lantern; he then returns to the sister's apartment. The kidnappers instruct Mike to carry the money to Long Lake, not far from Martin's Landing in upstate New York.

Meg accompanies Mike on the three-hour trip in his '57 Ford Fairlane convertible. At the lake, Mike rents a small boat for one dollar. The quoted price is $2 per hour but Mike tells the guy if he's not back by the price of the buck, then he probably won't be back at all. As Mike crosses the lake, a man with a rifle follows his progress with binoculars.

Once Mike steps from the boat to the ramp, he's stopped by the man with the rifle, who tells him to drop the briefcase with the money in it, take off his coat, and drop his gun. (Mike has the gun in a shoulder rig under his left arm.) The guy makes Mike sit on his hands while he looks into the briefcase. But Mike tricks him out of his rifle, knocks him unconscious, and goes to rescue Evie. She tells him the kidnapper is Herb Garth (her "erstwhile boyfriend" from the restaurant where she worked). But Mike gets a queasy feeling when the phone in the cabin has no dial tone. The viewer can see Mike thinking: How could she have called? A typically well-acted moment from McGavin.

Mike confronts her with his suspicions, telling her she needs to do one decent thing in her life by being nice to her dying husband. Mike then hauls the kidnapper off the dock as the music comes up for the end of the episode.

Let's review the violence quotient of the first aired episode: one prison stabbing leading (eventually) to the inmate's death; one instance of police intimidation (toward Mike); two fights (Mike loses to the policeman but knocks out the bad guy); two weapons are brandished but no shots are fired. Such restraint is not in evidence for most of the remaining episodes, in which violent fights, brutal beatings and sudden death by gunfire are the norm. This episode was likely chosen for the opening show to toss a softball to critics ... for all the good it did.

The sexual quotient is mild by modern standards but considerably above the norm for 1958 TV—one unrequested kiss, a slap, and the later promise of a date ("Just one?" asks Meg). So, all in all, for a 25-minute episode, plenty of action, a little violence and the hint of sex. Much more of those elements awaited viewers in subsequent episodes.

Still, this first episode has all the ingredients of a fast-moving *noir* B picture, and also serves as a precursor of the Stacy Keach "Mike Hammer" of the '80s/'90s with its voiceovers, sexual innuendo and random violence.

Like Keach's version, McGavin's Hammer had a way with the ladies, but could be counted on dropping them by the next episode. The only variation to the love-'em-and-leave-'em motif was provided by a Barry Shipman-scripted episode, "Wedding Mourning," in which Mike meets and proposes to a beautiful brunette named Kathy Dean.

Mike sees Kathy in a little restaurant while he is on a date with another woman, but they cannot keep their eyes off each another. Before the second act, Mike has proposed, set the date and asked Pat Chambers to be his best man. Tragedy strikes when Kathy is murdered on their wedding day by someone from Mike's past with a overwhelming desire for revenge. He even leaves a note on Kathy's dead body next to the flowers: "Till Death Do Us Part."

What follows is a prime example of the series hewing close to Spillane: Mike becomes enraged with finding her killer, telling Pat, "I killed Kathy as sure as I'd pulled the trigger myself." The only variation to the Spillane theme occurs when Mike is overcome by her killer, leaving Pat to ride to the rescue.

The only other recurring character pops up in this episode. Hammer occasionally uses as a snitch a shady, creepy character named Geta (Vito Scotti), who runs a candy store/soda shop as a front for selling contraband items, including guns. Geta has extremely thick glasses and loves to read to better himself. In this episode he's studying up on yoga. Mike always roughs up Geta—no exceptions. This time he sticks Geta's head through the back of a chair, pulls his tie, and squirts soda on him, and in general treats him like dirt. Yet Geta calls Mike his "friend." In this episode Geta sold the gun that killed Kathy to a hood but gets remorseful and calls Mike.

This character may have morphed into Ozzie the Answer in the Keach series, mellowed in tone. Keach's Hammer sees Ozzie the Answer in the Lite 'n' Easy Bar, but the 1950s series does not include recurring bar scenes. The McGavin Hammer appears not to have many friends except Pat, the people from his old neighborhood (who only call when they need help), and the showgirls he always dates.

More than a dozen episodes involve showgirls—chorus girls, singers in oddly named low-end bars, out-of-town cuties trying to make it in the modeling business. On one occasion Mike follows a showgirl girlfriend to the 1958 Brussels Worlds Fair, where she is performing. Not to miss a chance to re-use a set, two entirely unrelated shows are set at the fair.

Half a dozen episodes utilize a carny show or some variation of the Coney Island Arcade. Mike himself becomes a pitchman for a girlie show in one episode. No opportunity to depict girls in skimpy costumes is overlooked. Most are full-bodied and buxom. Mike's perfect beauty has a classic hour-glass figure, with the exception of lanky Lauren Bacall-lookalike Nita Talbot, who appears in two episodes. Mike is always backstage in the girls' dressing rooms. He never watches a show from the from the audience—he's always catching it from the wings.

Other than Pat, who does not appear in every episode, Mike has no "family" on the show, which makes the series a showcase for McGavin. The entire production seems to be on the actor's shoulders, but he carries it with ease and aplomb. He plays it big and at times puts the "ham" in Hammer, but without his swaggering, self-confident, self-amused performance, the show would not work.

Mike's relationship with Pat rings true to the novels. They have a mutual respect as former partners on the police force. Pat knows that Mike cannot conform to the rules of society. In one compelling episode, Pat loses his cool, detached demeanor and tells Mike that he wishes he could act as Hammer does and dispense rough justice. In another, Mike tricks Pat and ends up slugging him to get away; Pat repays him at episode's end by returning the blow and pushing him against a wall. Mike goes down hard but realizes that he deserves it and starts laughing. This relationship is depicted similarly in the Keach 1980s version.

In the novels, Spillane makes reference to some unrecorded bread-and-butter cases that pay his bills. The McGavin series illustrates many such cases. These involve badger games in Central Park with visiting small-town businessmen; fake relative scams; phony modeling schools; ex-cons pressured to help in new robberies; blackmail for revenge; blackmail over marital indiscretions; blackmail for keeping the knowledge of past larceny from the new rich family's knowledge; scamming old guys with the "love" of a pretty young thing; murder witnesses refusing to talk because they are too close to the killer; hoods being overly possessive of showgirls, particularly when the girls have found rich potential husbands; clients framed in small towns for various "crimes"; even murder at a fraternity hazing at a rich graduate brother's lake house.

The cases have a common denominator: money. And the amounts inspiring the bad guys seem incredibly small by twenty-first century standards: scamming the public with a phony investment company run by a man named Lonzi (as in Ponzi); conning a beauty contest winner out of $50; overcharging a naive girl for a modeling fee; killing a drifter for less than $100; threatening to expose a businessman for a $500 gambling debt.

The houses and apartments Hammer visits swing between the lowest and highest levels of society. Occasionally Hammer works for the rich and visits their lavish mansions. More often he moves between small, poorly furnished apartments and shabby businesses. The characters seem hopeless, doomed to a mundane existence, and as often as not are caught up in loveless relationships. Still, money rarely provides the answer in this bleak, *noir* world, ironically made palatable by the affable presence of Mike Hammer. The rich in Hammer's world seem as unhappy as the poor, and steal and murder just as frequently.

As in the novels, a major character in that world is New York City itself, starting with the opening credits shot of Hammer staring out at the George Washington Bridge, then turning with a small smile and an air of contentment at being in this great town. Yet many episodes begin with city shots that dissolve into the streets below where the sun never seems to shine. And, as with the novels, when it rains, it's much worse. Rain doesn't cleanse this world, it complicates. It's always a jolt when there's an episode in which Mike is on a beach or even mentions the word vacation. The viewer just knows that the joy is strictly temporary.

A partial list of felonies and misdemeanors becomes almost overwhelming. Murder—or the very least accidental death—is the rule. In the seventy-eight episodes, at least fifty people are killed with fifty more struck by bullets. Countless bullet wounds, slappings, and scenes of intimidation take place (often by Mike), with at least one hundred fistfights (usually involving Mike) and the occasional scene of torture. Sympathetic characters die.

The TV Guide: Guide to TV (calling itself the "most definitive encyclopedia of television") quotes its own 1958 review, saying "['Mickey Spillane's Mike Hammer'] could easily be the worst show on TV." It continues by berating pulp-style episode titles such as "Dead Men Don't Dream" as the "stuff of parody." In less than one hundred words, it assigns the "violent tales of the hard-boiled hero of Mickey Spillane's popular private-eye novels" to the trash heap of early television drama. But the 30-minute episodes are listed as 60 minutes, indicating that yet again a reviewer has given an opinion on a Spillane project without having any real familiarity with it.

This same guide to TV calls "Peter Gunn" the "sleek and noirish Blake Edwards series about an ultra-cool, jazz-loving L.A. private eye." You'll recall that in 1954 Edwards had written and directed the "Mike Hammer" TV pilot with Brian Keith, and that "Peter Gunn" was a beatnik-era, Man-Who-Reads-*Playboy* updating of Spillane's concepts.

The Television Writer: Techniques and Practices utilizes part of a Frank Kane "Mike Hammer" script "Death Takes an Encore" (based on the Kane novelette "Return Engagement" from a 1955 issue of *Manhunt*) to inform prospective screenwriters of the "television obsession with 'strong action'.... We know little about the effects on violence in programming. All we know is that it wins audience response and that producers and sponsors have vied to satisfy it."

Darren McGavin went on to several successful series, including *Riverboat* (which for part of a season he filmed concurrently with "Mike Hammer"), *The Outsider* (a private eye show from *77 Sunset Strip* creator Roy Huggins), and the much-loved *Kolchak: the Night Stalker* (which grew out of a highly-rated TV movie co-starring fellow Mike Hammer, Ralph Meeker). Still, McGavin is perhaps best-known today for his role as the father in the holiday film favorite, "A Christmas Story" (1983).

One of the delights of revisiting "Mickey Spillane's Mike Hammer" is the array of famous faces, including such actors as Robert Vaughn, Lorne Greene and DeForest Kelley. In particular, the lovely actresses on the series represent a fascinating mix of starlets on the way up and B-movie queens on the way down.

Very much on the way up, Angie Dickinson appears in two episodes: "Letter Edged in Blackmail" and "Look at the Old Man Go." In the first, she is pushed down a flight of stairs; in the second, she is bilking an old and foolish man of his money.

On the way down was Charlotte from "I, the Jury": Peggie Castle again finds herself part of Mike Hammer's world in "The Big Drop," this time facing Darren McGavin, not

Biff Elliot. Another big-screen Spillane femme fatale, Whitney Blake, appears in the pilot, "Just Around the Coroner" (in which an off-camera Velda is prominently mentioned). In a remarkable change of persona, Blake went on to play Dorothy Baxter ("Mrs. B") on "Hazel" (1961–65). She was the mother of actress Meredith Baxter-Birney.

Among a dazzling array of lovely actresses featured on the series are Sue Ann Langdon, Nita Talbot, Lisa Gaye, Diane Brewster, Fay Spain, Marion Ross, Bethel Leslie, Ruta Lee, Abby Dalton, Allison Hayes and Yvette Vickers.

But for all of that pulchritude, the show hinges on the performance of McGavin, who managed to give Hammer a new affability, and to just slightly kid the material, without losing the character's tough, even brutal edge.

In a 1994 *Scarlet Street* interview with the late Richard Valley, McGavin said that the powers-that-be were unhappy with early episodes, because they felt the actor was making fun of the material.

"I'm not making fun of it," McGavin told them, aware that the grim Brian Keith pilot had been rejected by the networks. "I'm just treating it in a lighter manner."

Threatened with firing, McGavin said, "I got a farm in upstate New York, and I'm really very happy there. I don't wanna do this the way you wanna do it. Let's just call it quits today, and you can hire somebody else to do it."

Reminded he was under contract, McGavin said, "We have a contract for me to say the words that are put on the paper. I don't want anybody telling me how to do it."

McGavin said this directly to Universal's big boss, Lew Wasserman.

"After that," McGavin said, "they left us alone, and we went ahead and made them—and they were instantly successful."

Mickey Spillane's Mike Hammer (1958–59)

"Mickey Spillane's Mike Hammer" was a syndicated TV series airing 1958–1960, produced by Revue Productions in Hollywood, California. MCA-TV was the exclusive distributor. The series was in production for two complete seasons of thirty-nine episodes each, although whether all of the episodes aired during that initial period is in doubt. Although initial air dates are indicated below, as with any syndicated series, episodes were broadcast at various times and days by subscribing stations.

Series regulars are Darren McGavin as Mike Hammer and Bart Burns as Captain Pat Chambers, although Burns appears irregularly.

First Season (1958)

EPISODE #1 (JANUARY 7, 1958) "THE HIGH COST OF DYING"

DIRECTED BY: Lawrence Dobkin. WRITTEN BY: Steven Thornley.

Hammer promises a dying convict that he'll take care of the prisoner's wife.

CAST: Bart Burns, Lynn (Marilyn) Allen, William Allyn, Robert Patten, Eleanore E. Tanin, Don Kennedy.

EPISODE #2 (JANUARY 14, 1958) "JUST AROUND THE CORONER"

DIRECTED BY: Richard Irving. WRITTEN BY: Lawrence Kimble.

Private eye Mike Hammer tries to protect a mild-mannered old man from swindlers, but death results when some sleazy characters get in Hammer's way.

CAST: Whitney Blake, Raymond Greenleaf, Walter Reed, Charles Davis, Jonathan Hale, K.L. Smith, Stanley Farrar, Helen Spring.

EPISODE #3 (JANUARY 21, 1958) "HOT HANDS, COLD DICE"

DIRECTED BY: Boris Sagal. WRITTEN BY: Lawrence Kimble.

Hammer passes out in a young woman's apartment in New York and wakes up the next morning in Las Vegas.

CAST: Barbara Darrow, Paul Langton, Voorhies J. Ardoin.

EPISODE #4 (JANUARY 28, 1958) "DEATH GETS A DIPLOMA"

DIRECTED BY: Richard Irving. WRITTEN BY: Rik Volloerts and Frank Kane.

A gangland killing and a mysterious blonde plunge Hammer into a situation that almost destroys a young college student and Hammer himself.

CAST: Karen Sharpe, Bart Burns, William Swan, Ann Morrison, Richard Benedict, Steve Conte.

EPISODE #5 (FEBRUARY 11, 1958) "SO THAT'S WHO IT WAS"

DIRECTED BY: John English. WRITTEN BY: James Gunn and Fenton Earnshaw.

Hammer receives a phone call from a man who is later found dead in a Chinatown alley. While hunting the murderer he learns that the motive has to do with a previous killing. Based on Curt Cannon's (Evan Hunter's) short story "Good and Dead" (*Manhunt*, July 1953; collected in *I Like 'em Tough*, Gold Medal 1958).

CAST: Anna May Wong, Bart Burns, Barbara Luna, Robert Foulk, John Harmon, Keye Luke, Weaver Levy, William Yip, Charles Horvath.

EPISODE #6 (FEBRUARY 18, 1958) "DEAD MEN DON'T DREAM"

DIRECTED BY: Joe Parker. WRITTEN BY: Frank Kane.

Setting out to avenge the murder of his old friend Charley Dagerra, Hammer finds himself hunting the head of a protection racket. Based on Curt Cannon's (Evan Hunter's) short story "Dead Men Don't Dream" (*Manhunt*, March 1953; collected in *I Like 'em Tough*, Gold Medal 1958).

CAST: Bart Burns, Russell Collins, Lawrence Dobkin, Lisa Gaye, Kipp Hamilton, Richard Bakalyn, John Shaner.

EPISODE #7 (FEBRUARY 25, 1958) "LETTER EDGED IN BLACKMAIL"

DIRECTED BY: Boris Sagal. WRITTEN BY: Frank Kane.

Hammer gets into serious trouble for making a false accusation. Soon after he comes to suspect he's been framed, he encounters a beautiful young woman and starts to wonder whether she's behind his troubles. Based on Frank Kane's short story.

CAST: Angie Dickinson, Fay Baker, Herbert Rudley, Stacy Harris, John Gallaudet.

EPISODE #8 (MARCH 7, 1958) "DEATH TAKES AN ENCORE"

DIRECTED BY: Richard Irving. WRITTEN BY: Frank Kane.

Shortly after a man has been reported killed in an auto accident, a hoodlum confesses to Hammer that he murdered the same man six months before. Based on Frank Kane's short story "Return Engagement" (*Manhunt*, February 1955; collected in *Johnny Liddell's Morgue*, Dell 1956).

CAST: Diane Brewster, Ted de Corsia, John Dennis, Pete Coe, Lou Krugman, Ralph Gamble, Jan Arvan, Tim Graham. Ted de Corsia's only appearance as Pat Chambers.

EPISODE #9 (MARCH 14, 1958) "LEAD ACHE"

DIRECTED BY: Richard Irving. WRITTEN BY: Frank Kane.

Hired to find the murderer of a newspaper reporter, Hammer visits the dead man's apartment and is greeted by the killer. Based on Frank Kane's short story "Lead Ache" (*Manhunt*, May 1954; collected in *Johnny Liddell's Morgue*, Dell 1956).

CAST: Doris Dowling, Bart Burns, Doris Singleton, Richard Karlan, Raymond Bailey, Dan Seymour, Joi Lansing.

EPISODE #10 (MARCH 21, 1959) "OVERDOSE OF LEAD"

DIRECTED BY: Boris Sagal. WRITTEN BY: Fenton Earnshaw.

Hammer goes to the aid of a nightclub singer who's being blackmailed. Based on Curtis Cluff's short story "Overdose of Lead" (*Black Mask*, November 1948).

CAST: Constance Towers, Grant Richards, Eve McVeagh, Robert Quarry, Theodore Newton, Karl "Killer" Davis.

EPISODE #11 (MARCH 28, 1958) "A GRAVE UNDERTAKING"

DIRECTED BY: Boris Sagal. WRITTEN BY: Frank Kane and Fenton Earnshaw.

Hammer makes a late-night visit to a cemetery to exchange a bundle of cash for a bundle of letters. Based on Henry Kane's short story.

CAST: Peggy Converse, Fay Spain, Rebecca Welles, Frank Albertson, Tracey Roberts, Chester Stratton.

EPISODE #12 (APRIL 4, 1958) "A SHOT IN THE ARM"

DIRECTED BY: John English. WRITTEN BY: Richard Deming and Fenton Earnshaw.

Hammer tries to help a young debutante break the drug habit. Based on Richard Deming's short story.

CAST: Jacqueline Scott, Philip Ober, Katharine Warren, Sydney Smith, Robert Dix, Maudie Prickett, Herschel Bernardi.

EPISODE #13 (APRIL 11, 1958) "STAY OUT OF TOWN"

DIRECTED BY: Boris Sagal. WRITTEN BY: Frank Kane.

Hammer tries to find the killer of a gambler and his secretary who identified the gunman from a photograph just before dying. Based on Frank Kane's short story "With Frame to Match" which appeared in the 1965 paperback anthology *Come Seven, Come Death.*

CAST: Gloria Talbott, James Westerfield, H.M. Wynant, Jean Byron, Rusty Lane, Peter Miller.

EPISODE #14 (APRIL 18, 1958) "BEAUTIFUL, BLUE AND DEADLY"

DIRECTED BY: Boris Sagal. WRITTEN BY: Steven Thornley.

Hammer encounters a lovely female racketeer who attempts to use a foreign racing car for criminal purposes. Based on Burt Sims' short story "Swing Low, Sweet Mustang" (*Doc Savage*, October 1945).

CAST: Bart Burns, Nita Talbot, Robert Ellenstein, Tom Brown, Berry Kroeger.

EPISODE #15 (APRIL 25, 1958) "SKINNED DEEP"

DIRECTED BY: Richard Irving. WRITTEN BY: Frank Kane.

Hammer encounters a beautiful but unhappy young woman who has just lost a talent-search contest. Based on Frank Kane's short story.

CAST: Carole Mathews, Patricia Hardy, John Seven, Tom Palmer, Alan Paige.

EPISODE #16 (MAY 2, 1958) "PEACE BOND"

DIRECTED BY: John English. WRITTEN BY: Frank Kane.

Hammer's hopes for peace and quiet are shattered when a man is shot and killed in a woman's apartment with Hammer's gun. Based on Curtis Cluff's short story.

CAST: Bart Burns, Marion Ross, Edmon Ryan, Wesley Lau, George Eldredge, Frank Marlowe.

EPISODE #17 (MAY 9, 1958) "PLAY BELLES' TOLL"

DIRECTED BY: Boris Sagal. WRITTEN BY: Frank Kane.

Hammer hunts the murderer of an old girlfriend whose body was claimed from the morgue by a society woman. Based on Frank Kane's short story.

CAST: Bart Burns, Jean Willes, Joan Marshall, Douglas Dick, Dennis Patrick, Lillian Bronson, John Seven.

EPISODE #18 (MAY 16, 1958) "FOR SALE: DEATHBED—USED"

DIRECTED BY: Richard Irving. WRITTEN BY: Lawrence Kimble.

An enraged Hammer searches for a psychopathic knife killer.

CAST: Bart Burns, Sam Buffington, Judith Ames, Virginia Christine, Gail Kobe, Terry Becker, Joe di Reda, Lida Piazza, Dale Van Sickel.

EPISODE #19 (MAY 23, 1958) "MUSIC TO DIE BY"

DIRECTED BY: Boris Sagal. WRITTEN BY: Frank Kane.

Hammer tries to help a disc jockey who is forced to play only the recordings of syndicate-controlled singers. Based on Frank Kane's short story.

CAST: Joan Banks, Wally Vernon, Robert Nichols, George Keymas. Song by The Ames Brothers.

EPISODE #20 (MAY 30, 1958) "MY FAIR DEADLY"

DIRECTED BY: Richard Irving. WRITTEN BY: Barry Shipman.

Mike's girl friend Vergie has an dancing job at the World's Fair in Brussels. Her roommate is late for the plane. Mike discovers her missing roommate has been murdered and her expensive diamond necklace stolen. Mike flies to the Brussels to find the killer.

CAST: Jean Allison, Dan Barton, Betty Utey, Paul Lukather, Alan Dexter

EPISODE #21 (JUNE 7, 1958) "THE NEW LOOK"

DIRECTED BY: John English. WRITTEN BY: Lawrence Menkin.

Hammer is hired by a psychoanalyst who has learned that one of his patients is being blackmailed.

CAST: Doris Dowling, Mary Anderson, Walter Reed, Midge Ware, Steven Geray.

EPISODE #22 (JUNE 14, 1958) "THE BROKEN FRAME"

DIRECTED BY: John English. WRITTEN BY: Steven Thornley.

A convict condemned to death confesses to Hammer that he committed another murder for which an innocent man was executed.

CAST: Bart Burns, Dick Van Patten, Robert P. Lieb, Lisa Golm, Sara Anderson, Jack Weston, Charles Horvath.

EPISODE #23 (JUNE 21, 1958) "LOOK AT THE OLD MAN GO"

DIRECTED BY: Boris Sagal. WRITTEN BY: Lawrence Kimble.

Hammer takes a case that brings him as an uninvited guest to a penthouse party where he meets a lovely lady.

CAST: Bethel Leslie, Angie Dickinson, Peter Hanson, Steven Ritch, Howard Wendell.

EPISODE #24 (JUNE 28, 1958) "THE PAPER SHROUD"

DIRECTED BY: Boris Sagal. WRITTEN BY: Fenton Earnshaw.

While investigating a daring daylight holdup, Hammer discovers information that shatters and sickens him.

CAST: Bart Burns, Anthony Caruso, Lisa Montell, George Brenlin, Penny Santon, Jay Lawrence, Eddie Saenz, Jimmy Cassino.

EPISODE #25 (JULY 5, 1958) "MY SON AND HEIR"

DIRECTED BY: Sherman Marks. WRITTEN BY: Lawrence Kimble.

Hammer tries to help a rich man's son overcome his parent's opposition to his romance with a poor young woman. Based on Stephen Marlowe's short story "My Son and Heir" (*Manhunt*, December 1955).

CAST: Robert F. Simon, Douglas Dick, Barbara Turner, Virginia Gregg, Denver Pyle, Donald Foster.

EPISODE #26 (JULY 12, 1958) "FINAL CURTAIN"

DIRECTED BY: Richard Irving. WRITTEN BY: Frank Kane.

Attracted to a beautiful red-haired chorus girl, Hammer promises to protect her and find the killer when two other red-haired women are mysteriously murdered. Based on Richard Ellington's short story.

CAST: Bart Burns, Joan Taylor, Lawrence Dobkin, Herbert Rudley, Tudor Owen, Maurice Kelly, Barrie Chase.

EPISODE #27 (JULY 19, 1958) "A DETECTIVE TAIL"

DIRECTED BY: Boris Sagal. WRITTEN BY: Frank Kane.

After Jack Cordell has hired Hammer to find his missing girlfriend, Hammer learns that another detective is following Cordell. Based on Richard Ellington's short story; loose take-off on Chandler's *Farewell, My Lovely*.

CAST: Frances Helm, Ric Roman, Carl Betz, Grace Whitney, Joey Faye, Leonard Bell, Pat O'Malley.

EPISODE #28 (JULY 26, 1958) "IT'S AN ART"

DIRECTED BY: Boris Sagal. WRITTEN BY: Frank Kane.

Hammer combs Greenwich Village for a young art student who vanished from her home in Iowa. Based on Frank Kane's short story.

CAST: Helen Westcott, Ralph Clanton, Konstantin Shayne, Ellen Parker, Robin Hughes, Harry Landers, Richard Reeves, Franz Roehn, Barrie Chase.

EPISODE #29 (AUGUST 2, 1958) "FOUR BLIND MICE"

DIRECTED BY: Boris Sagal. WRITTEN BY: Steven Thornley.

Hammer becomes involved with a beautiful fashion model and her suspicious husband.

CAST: Bart Burns, Paul Langton, June Dayton, William Phipps, Patricia Blair, Vito Scotti.

EPISODE #30 (OCTOBER 12, 1958) "SCAR AND GARTER"

DIRECTED BY: Lawrence Dobkin. WRITTEN BY: Steven Thornley.

A young man who's been separated from his mother since childhood comes to Hammer for help after he encounters a veiled woman in a secluded house.

CAST: Margaret Lindsay, Yvette Vickers, Paula Hill, Barney Phillips.

EPISODE #31 (AUGUST 9, 1958) "NO POCKETS IN A SHROUD"

DIRECTED BY: Boris Sagal. WRITTEN BY: Frank Kane.

A beautiful nightclub photographer seeks Hammer's help when her shop is completely and inexplicably demolished. Based on Frank Kane's short story.

CAST: Bart Burns, Joan Taylor, King Calder, Clarke Gordon, James McCallion, Linda Leighton, Dick Crockett.

EPISODE #32 (AUGUST 16, 1958) "THE LIVING DEAD"

DIRECTED BY: Sherman Marks. WRITTEN BY: Steven Thornley.

Hammer gets mixed up in an intrigue involving a missing woman, a hermit who hasn't been seen in twenty-five years, and a man's love for a woman of questionable background.

CAST: Robert Vaughn, John Hoyt, Patricia Huston, Charles Davis.

EPISODE #33 (AUGUST 23, 1958) "OLD FOLKS AT HOME BLUES"

DIRECTED BY: Richard Irving. WRITTEN BY: Lawrence Kimble.

Hammer befriends a helpless young woman who's afraid her husband may be dead, and their search for the missing man takes them to New York's Bowery.

CAST: Ruta Lee, Arthur Batanides, Robert Clarke, Grace Raynor, John Day.

EPISODE #34 (AUGUST 30, 1958) "NO BUSINESS LIKE...."

DIRECTED BY: Boris Sagal. WRITTEN BY: Fenton Earnshaw.

Hammer becomes involved with a beautiful acrobat who performs on a high wire.

CAST: Anthony Caruso, Jeanne Cooper, Susan Morrow, Michael Miller, Theodore Newton, Addison Richards, Marya Stevens.

EPISODE #35 (SEPTEMBER 7, 1958) "CREPE FOR SUZETTE"

DIRECTED BY: Boris Sagal. WRITTEN BY: Frank Kane.

Hammer investigates the disappearance of a beautiful young drama student in New York. Based on Frank Kane's short story.

CAST: Alan Mowbray, Ruta Lee, Henry Hunter, Dick Crockett, Dale Van Sickel, Walter Maslow.

EPISODE #36 (SEPTEMBER 14, 1958) "LETTER OF THE WEAK"

DIRECTED BY: Boris Sagal. WRITTEN BY: Frank Kane and Lawrence Kimble.

Hammer receives a mysterious letter that leads him into a murder trap.

CAST: John Smith, Paula Raymond, John Hoyt, John Carlyle, Charles Watts, Evelyn Scott.

EPISODE #37 (SEPTEMBER 21, 1958) "THAT SCHOOL GIRL COMPLEX"

DIRECTED BY: Boris Sagal. WRITTEN BY: Steven Thornley.

Hired to investigate some strange events at an exclusive girls' school, Hammer encounters blackmail and attempted murder.

CAST: Andrea King, Katherine Squire, Maureen Cassidy, Francis McDonald, Carol Nugent, Susan Whitney.

EPISODE #38 (SEPTEMBER 28, 1958) "TO BURY A FRIEND"

DIRECTED BY: Boris Sagal. WRITTEN BY: Steven Thornley.

A friend's death takes Hammer to Chicago, where he becomes involved in an unusual con game.

Based on Stanley Anton's short story "To Bury a Friend" (*Ellery Queen's Mystery Magazine*, March 1956). CAST: James Westerfield, Jacqueline Mayo, Than Wyenn, Baynes Barron, Larry Blake, Jean Inness, Allen Pinson.

EPISODE #39 (OCTOBER 5, 1958) "MERE MAID"

DIRECTED BY: Boris Sagal. WRITTEN BY: Robert C. Dennis.

Hammer becomes involved in a murder at an exclusive resort. CAST: Allison Hayes, Neil Hamilton, Mary Webster, Peter Damon, Robert Riordan, Don Hix, Michael Hinn.

Second Season (1959)

EPISODE #40 (JANUARY 9, 1959) "ACCENTUATE THE NEGATIVE"

DIRECTED BY: Earl Bellamy. WRITTEN BY: Frank Kane.

Hammer's investigation of a charm school swindle becomes more complicated when a murder is committed at the school.

CAST: Ben Nelson, Barbara Bain, Jeff Daley, Patricia Huston, Ben Morris, Louise Lewis, Chuck Ross, Louise Truax.

EPISODE #41 (JANUARY 15, 1959) "REQUIEM FOR A SUCKER"

DIRECTED BY: Earl Bellamy. WRITTEN BY: B.X. Sanborn.

Hammer literally uses his nose as he attempts to solve a murder among the members of a small burlesque troupe.

CAST: Stewart Bradley, Joan Tabor, Evelyn Bunn, Len Lesser, Orville Sherman, Vito Scotti, Richard Benedict.

EPISODE #42 (FEBRUARY 7, 1959) "I AIN'T TALKIN'"

DIRECTED BY: Boris Sagal. WRITTEN BY: Frank Kane.

Hammer becomes involved in the case of a murder witness who refuses to speak even when he is himself accused of the crime. Based on Frank Kane's short story.

CAST: Marianne Stewart, Robert Fuller, DeForest Kelley, Frank DeKova, Bart Burns, Joan Tabor.

EPISODE #43 (FEBRUARY 14, 1959) "THE BIG DROP"

DIRECTED BY: Boris Sagal. WRITTEN BY: Carey Wilbers and B.X. Sanborn.

When an ex-steeplejack dies in a fall, Hammer investigates and learns that an unusual treasure hunt led to the man's death.

CAST: Peggie Castle, Berk Nelson, Jan Arvan, Karl Davis.

EPISODE #44 (FEBRUARY 21, 1959) "ACES AND EIGHTS"

DIRECTED BY: Boris Sagal. WRITTEN BY: Frank Kane.

A beautiful young woman who is also a bungling thief leads Hammer to a den of gamblers. Based on Frank Kane's short story.

CAST: June Dayton, Madlyn Rhue, Bern Hoffman, John Anderson, Frank Gerstle.

EPISODE #45 (JANUARY 2, 1959) "BAUBLES, BANGLES AND BLOOD"

DIRECTED BY: Richard Irving. WRITTEN BY: Frank Kane.

Hammer is greeted by violence and a blackmail threat when he investigates a crime at a carnival. Based on Frank Kane's short story.

CAST: James Bell, Suzanne Lloyd, John Goddard, Paul Lukather, Nancy Valentine, Lane Bradford, Paul Baxley.

EPISODE #46 (FEBRUARY 28, 1959) "HUSBANDS ARE BAD LUCK"

DIRECTED BY: Justus Addiss. WRITTEN BY: B.X. Sanborn.

Hammer becomes involved with a cowboy, his society girl-friend, and a pack of trouble.

CAST: Jean Willes, Allan Lane, Ann Robinson, Eric Sinclair, Owen Cunningham.

EPISODE #47 (JANUARY 30, 1959) "JURY OF ONE"

DIRECTED BY: Edward Ludlum. WRITTEN BY: Steven Thornley.

Hammer becomes involved in a judicial matter after a single juror blocks an otherwise unanimous verdict of guilty in the trial of a notorious mobster.

CAST: Robert H. Harris, Patricia Huston, Bill Mims, Priscilla Amidon, Steve Ihnat, Ted Knight.

EPISODE #48 (APRIL 2, 1959) "PARK THE BODY"

DIRECTED BY: Edward Ludlum. WRITTEN BY: Steven Thornley.

The murder of a parking lot attendant leads to Hammer's involvement with some ruthless garage operators.

CAST: Helena Nash, Johnny Seven, Frank Ferguson, Robert Fuller, James Chandler.

EPISODE #49 (APRIL 9, 1959) "TATTOO BRUTE?"

DIRECTED BY: Virgil W. Vogel. WRITTEN BY: B.X. Sanborn.

Investigating a theft from an apparently thief-proof room, Hammer encounters an ancient Chinese secret society.

CAST: Lisa Lu, Theodore Marcuse, Paul Dubov, Allen Jung, Anthony Jochim.

EPISODE #50 (MARCH 6, 1959) CONEY ISLAND BABY"

DIRECTED BY: Richard Irving. WRITTEN BY: B.X. Sanborn.

Hammer visits a waxworks museum in his search for a desperate killer.

CAST: Lloyd Corrigan, Dorothy Provine, Johnny Seven, Natalie Norwick, James Gavin.

EPISODE #51 (JANUARY 23, 1959) "ACCORDING TO LUKE"

DIRECTED BY: Earl Bellamy. WRITTEN BY: Steven Thornley.

Hammer has four homicides to solve when he tangles with a violent gang of hoodlums.

CAST: Tom Neal, Lewis Charles, Joseph Mell, Jan Harrison, Tom Gleason.

EPISODE #52 (MARCH 20, 1959) "SAVE ME IN SAN SALVADOR"

DIRECTED BY: Boris Sagal. WRITTEN BY: B.X. Sanborn.

A book of ancient languages embroils Hammer in a political intrigue involving a clever colonel and a pair of beautiful woman.

CAST: Nita Talbot, George Givot, Alberto Morin, Evelyn Ward, Jonathan Hole.

EPISODE #53 (APRIL 30, 1959) "THE LAST ALOHA"

DIRECTED BY: Sidney Salkow. WRITTEN BY: Steven Thornley.

Hammer goes to Honolulu in search of stolen gold. Based on Curtis Cluff's short story.

CAST: Mari Aldon, Don Kelly, Beverly Tyler, Victor Sen Yung, Kenneth Terrell, Eddie Saenz.

EPISODE #54 (APRIL 23, 1959) "SWING LOW, SWEET HARRIET"

DIRECTED BY: Edward Ludlum. WRITTEN BY: Steven Thornley.

Hammer becomes involved when a woman blackmailer receives as her payoff an iron ingot with a noose dangling from it. CAST: Lorne Greene, Andrea King, Merry Anders, Ross Elliott, Adrienne Marden.

EPISODE #55 (APRIL 23, 1959) "ANOTHER MAN'S POISSON"

DIRECTED BY: William Witney. WRITTEN BY: Steven Thornley.

A blind friend asks Hammer to find out whether the man claiming to be his long-lost brother is a phony.

CAST: Michael Connors, Tracey Roberts, Bern Hoffman, Jacqueline Holt, Wolfe Barzell.

EPISODE #56 (NO KNOWN DATE) "A HAZE ON THE LAKE"

DIRECTED BY: Sidney Salkow. WRITTEN BY: Kenneth Enochs.

Hammer tries to find the person who committed a crime during a fraternity hazing ritual on the college campus.

CAST: Lorne Greene, Elaine Edwards, John Carlyle, Richard Gerin, Ray Stricklyn, Bill Roerick.

EPISODE #57 (NO KNOWN DATE) "WHEN I AM DEAD, MY DARLING...."

DIRECTED BY: Boris Sagal. WRITTEN BY: B.X. Sanborn.

Aboard a French luxury liner, Hammer tries to help an attractive widow who insists that her late husband's ghost is haunting the ship. Like the film "Kiss Me Deadly," makes use of a Christina Rossetti poem.

CAST: Catherine McLeod, Paul Dubov, Jan Arvan, Carolyn Hughes, Eugene Borden, Rolfe Sedan.

EPISODE #58 (AUGUST 7, 1959) "STOCKS AND BLONDES"

DIRECTED BY: Ray Nazarro. WRITTEN BY: Robert Turner.

Hammer is hired by a former prizefighter who's been hospitalized after being beaten by two thugs.

CAST: Rita Lynn, Dennis Patrick, K.L. Smith, Roxanne Brooks.

EPISODE #59 (MAY 8, 1959) "EVIDENCE ON THE RECORD"

DIRECTED BY: William Witney. WRITTEN BY: B.X. Sanborn.

The murder of a helpless woman entangles Hammer with the owners of a crooked juke-box vending company.

CAST: Frank Maxwell, Gerald Milton, Helene Stanley, Vito Scotti.

EPISODE #60 (MAY 1, 1959) "SHOOT BEFORE YOU LOOK"

DIRECTED BY: Ray Nazarr. WRITTEN BY: Frank Kane.

Hammer becomes involved when a woman is murdered and the diamonds she's been carrying disappear. Based on Frank Kane's short story.

CAST: Charles Aidman, Georgine Darcy, John Milford, Gail Kobe, Bart Burns, Vito Scotti.

EPISODE #61 (MAY 28, 1959) "THE COMMODORE"

DIRECTED BY: Sidney Salkow. WRITTEN BY: B.X. Sanborn.

Hammer meets a vagrant who claims he's been the victim of a double-cross and also encounters a genial old man who admits he's a murderer.

CAST: Edgar Stehli, H.M. Wynant, Jean Allison, Ashley Cowan, Evelyn Scott, Michael Winkelman.

EPISODE #62 (JUNE 4, 1959) "SEE NO EVIL"

Directed by Ray Nazarro. Written by B.X. Sanborn.

When a bank guard accused of robbery refuses to defend himself, a gypsy fortuneteller brings Hammer into the case. CAST: Miriam Colon, Steve Peck, Walter Burke, Gene Saks, Ted Markland.

EPISODE #63 (NO DATE KNOWN) "CURTAINS FOR AN ANGEL"

DIRECTED BY: William Witney. WRITTEN BY: B.X. Sanborn.

While investigating a murder, Hammer is persuaded to act in an off–Broadway Shakespeare production.

CAST: Virginia Gregg, Abby Dalton, Robert Ellenstein, Richard Crane, Alexander Lockwood.

EPISODE #64 (NO DATE KNOWN) "DIXIE IS DEAD"

DIRECTED BY: William Witney. WRITTEN BY: B.X. Sanborn.

A feud between rival jazz café owners brings Hammer to Greenwich Village to investigate a club called The Velvet Cellar.

CAST: Sue Ane Langdon, Dick Wesson, Ray Daley, Walter Reed, Ken Lynch.

EPISODE #65 (NO DATE KNOWN) "M IS FOR MOTHER"

DIRECTED BY: William Witney. WRITTEN BY: Steven Thornley.

Hammer becomes involved in the violence that results when a mother and daughter discover that they're rivals for the same man's affections.

CAST: Coleen Gray, Bart Burns, Diana Barth, Harry Swoger, Vito Scotti.

EPISODE #66 (JULY 7, 1959) "PEN PALS"

DIRECTED BY: Ray Nazarro. WRITTEN BY: Frank Kane.

When a young man becomes terrified at the unexpected appearance of two strangers, his distraught wife goes to Hammer for help. Based on Frank Kane's short story.

CAST: Michael Connors, Betty Lynn, Edward Kemmer, Dort Clark, Angela Austin.

EPISODE #67 (NO DATE KNOWN) "NOW DIE IN IT"

DIRECTED BY: William Witney. WRITTEN BY: Steven Thornley.

Hammer becomes involved in the death of a beautiful young woman who harbored a secret love that affects two lives.

Based on Curt Cannon's (Evan Hunter's) short story "Now Die In it" (*Manhunt*, May 1953; collected in *I Like 'em Tough*, Gold Medal 1958).

CAST: Eddie Firestone, Barbara Turner, Richard Tyler, Tommy Ivo, Jo Kaiser, Howard Wright.

EPISODE #68 (NO DATE KNOWN) "SLAY UPON DELIVERY"

DIRECTED BY: Sam Strangis. WRITTEN BY: Frank Kane and Steve Thornley.

While out to break up a floating crap game, Hammer is nearly snagged in his own line by a ruthless operator. Based on Frank Kane's short story.

CAST: James Westerfield, Dorothy Green, Bart Burns, Stacy Harris, Alan Dexter, Cay Forester, Marianne Gaba.

EPISODE #69 (NO DATE KNOWN) "GROOMED TO KILL"

DIRECTED BY: Ray Nazarro. WRITTEN BY: Robert Turner.

Hammer is hired to investigate when a stag dinner for a prospective bridegroom is interrupted by blackmail and murder.

CAST: Bart Burns, Frank Albertson, K.T. Stevens, Joan Tabor, Ray Daley.

EPISODE #70 (NO DATE KNOWN) "DOLL TROUBLE"

DIRECTED BY: William Witney. WRITTEN BY: Barry Shipman.

Hammer is hired to investigate a young woman's claim to be the long-lost relative whom an older woman has been searching for.

CAST: Isobel Elsom, Dolores Vitina, John Archer, Carol Sydes, Marian Collier.

EPISODE #71 (NO DATE KNOWN) "I REMEMBER SALLY"

DIRECTED BY: William Witney. WRITTEN BY: Steven Thornley.

Carrying out a dying man's last wish, Hammer conducts a search for a beautiful woman.

CAST: Doris Dowling, Malcolm Atterbury, Steve Gravers, Fred Sherman, Asa Maynor.

EPISODE #72 (NO DATE KNOWN) "WEDDING MOURNING"

DIRECTED BY: William Witney. WRITTEN BY: Barry Shipman.

Hammer finally decides to get married, but his fiancée is murdered just before the wedding.

CAST: Linda Lawson, Bart Burns, Vito Scotti, Bernard Fein, David Fresco, Frank Yaconelli.

EPISODE #73 (NO DATE KNOWN) "MERCHANT OF MENACE"

DIRECTED BY: William Witney. WRITTEN BY: Robert Turner.

Through an unusual set of circumstances, Hammer is branded a coward and becomes a target for the underworld.

CAST: Barbara Stuart, Arthur Kendall, Vito Scotti, James Flavin, Eddie Marr, Larry Perron, Brad Trumbull.

EPISODE #74 (OCTOBER 3, 1959) "BRIDE AND DOOM"

DIRECTED BY: William Witney. WRITTEN BY: Robert Turner.

Hammer tries to solve the murder of a dancer he was hired to protect from her wealthy boyfriend's sister.

CAST: Frances Robinson, DeForest Kelley, Sue Ane Langdon, J. Pat O'Malley, Richard Angarola.

EPISODE #75 (NO DATE KNOWN) "SLAB-HAPPY"

DIRECTED BY: Frank Arrigo. WRITTEN BY: Steven Thornley.

Hammer tries to help an ex-prizefighter who has lost his athletic prowess to advancing age and his heart to a ruthless woman.

CAST: Jack Lambert, Mary LaRoche, Bart Burns, Ralf Harolde, Peter Adams, Joe Yrigoyen.

EPISODE #76 (NO DATE KNOWN) "A MUGGING EVENING"

DIRECTED BY: William Witney. WRITTEN BY: Frank Kane and Robert Turner.

Hammer is hired to clean up a hoodlum-infested park.

CAST: Yvette Vickers, Irene Vernon, Jack Hogan, Gene Collins, William Keene, J. Pat O'Malley.

EPISODE #77 (NO DATE KNOWN) "SIAMESE TWINGE"

DIRECTED BY: William Witney. WRITTEN BY: Steven Thornley.

Hammer investigates a case of blackmail with Asian overtones.

CAST: Sondi Sodsai, Bart Burns, Julie Scott, Arthur Batanides, Eric Sinclair, Eleanor Audley, John Duke, Richard Kiping.

EPISODE #78 (NO DATE KNOWN) "GOODBYE, AL"

DIRECTED BY: Frank Arrigo. WRITTEN BY: Steven Thornley.

Hammer tries to help a gambler running from a hoodlum who has threatened to kill him.

CAST: Ned Avery, Walter Coy, Melanie York, Ned Glass, Pete Kellett.

11. "Mickey Spillane's Mike Hammer In 'Margin for Murder'" (1981)

Dobson's Hammer with Cindy Pickett's Velda in "Margin for Murder." A talented actress, the light-haired, slender, almost boyish Pickett made an ineffective secretary/partner.

The first Mike Hammer made-for-TV movie, "Mickey Spillane's Mike Hammer in 'Margin for Murder,'" appears to be very loosely based on *I, the Jury*. Spillane had little directly to do with the production—the screenplay is credited to Calvin Clements Jr. and Alex Lucas—but he gave it his blessing, and his then-wife Sherri receives credit as "Technical Advisor." Most significantly, "Margin for Murder" marked the beginning of the writer's long-relationship with producer Jay Bernstein.

The telefilm's Hammer is Kevin Dobson—Crocker on the long-running CBS Telly Savalas cop show, "Kojak"—updated into a Vietnam-vet private seeking to avenge the death of a war buddy ... not one-armed investigator Jack Williams, but disco bouncer Joey DeFellita. The capable Dobson is handsome, brooding yet affable with the physicality needed to turn the corner into brutality when necessary. If he doesn't quite have the swaggering charisma of McGavin and Keach, Dobson nonetheless suggests he might have pulled off the task of playing Hammer in a weekly series.

This version of Hammer, however, is strictly a '70s/early '80s TV rendition, pushed through the network-television cookie cutter. It possesses little *noir* mood, despite some effective New York location shooting; hoodlums and mob bosses seem straight out of Central casting, and the viewer is subjected to corny mother-of-the-victim scenes, standard if well-staged action sequences, watered-down sex and violence, and sluggish pacing that builds to a soggy series of anti-climaxes in a film that simply refuses to end. At the point when the cops have hauled off the bad guys, an astonishing near six minutes remains of Hammer playing cute with Velda. The latter padding is perhaps the telefilm's greatest sin against Spillane, whose sudden "socko" endings remain a trademark of the Mike Hammer novels.

The original screenplay of "Margin for Murder" spent considerable time making the murdered Joey DeFellita seem real, a flawed friend Mike nonetheless seeks to avenge. It includes a violent, disturbing method of homicide—a small, steel fist used to beat DeFellita to death while leaving the false impression that his killer was female. So key was this point to the original screenplay that it was titled "Death by a Dainty Hand." A few sloppy references to the fist remain in the finished telefilm as loose ends.

Some care has been taken with the two key relationship's in Hammer's life, with the Hammer/Chambers friendship well-portrayed, thanks in part to the nice rapport between actors Dobson and Charles Hallahan ("The Paper Chase"). The screenwriters develop Velda well, making her affection for Mike evident and even allowing her to wave a little gun around, late in the proceedings. But Cindy Pickett is perhaps the screen's least sultry Velda—attractive, yes, but thin, wan, with short blonde hair, almost as if the casting director attempted to portray the exact opposite of Spillane's physical description of the raven-crowned, voluptuous Velda. A good actress miscast, Picket comes across as a nice, cute, an older sister (if with incestuous leanings), not the leggy amazon who can hold her own with the bad guys, and Mike Hammer.

The telefilm does not address Hammer's man-out-of-time, anachronistic nature, and—however one may wince at some of its campiness—the subsequent Keach series would effectively embrace Hammer's retro nature and luxuriate in his political incorrectness. Dobson does not, to put it in Spillane's terms, wear the hat well. The hat itself, a feathered sporty thing, is as miscast as Velda. At least he carries a .45 automatic.

Even the score by the usually first-rate Nelson Riddle ("The Untouchables") is an assembly of wah-wah guitar-driven cop show cliches, with the main brass line lifted the brass-driven rock song "Vehicle" by the Ides of March and the secondary theme a reworking of the theme of "City of Angels," a superior Riddle score for a superior private eye show.

Professional and watchable, "Margin for Murder" remains a disappointment. A decent understanding of the main character, well-portrayed by an actor with Dobson's experience, is not enough to make up for numerous shortcomings. Spillane's narratives confine themselves to Hammer and his point of view, but "Margin for Murder" includes scenes of the bad guys plotting in Hammer's absence—standard TV stuff of the era. The lack of any real mystery deprives a story that proudly wears the name "Mickey Spillane" of anything resembling a surprise ending, and the absence of a victim who deserves avenging—Jack Williams is a detective chasing down bad guys, but Joey DeFellita is a minor mob guy who probably got what he deserved.

After much ranting and raving ("They're gonna pay for it exactly the same way as Joey!"), the vengeance-driven Hammer decides he would rather see the bad guys die in prison than at his own hands ("Killing you would be too easy ... now you'll die little by little"). Hammer and Velda oooh and ahhh over puppies. Dat's not Mickey Spillane.

Mike Hammer's murdered friend Joey DeFellita had been working as a bouncer at a local dance club, the Planet. The club's silent partner is the mob and Joey falls out of favor when a illegal diamond delivery goes wrong. They turn on Joey, string him up by his hands in a warehouse, slowly beat him to death and then crash the car Mike had loaned to Joey. Just as in the uncredited novel, Mike tells Pat, "Somebody's going to pay for this." Pat (Hallahan) says, "Mike, you were a cop once. You know the rules." Mike replies, "Those rules don't apply anymore."

Mike entrusts three abandoned puppies into Velda's care. He doesn't want anything else to die on the day his friend did. The first several times we see Velda she's in her dressing gown in her apartment. Mike had been out of town and she's up waiting for him to drop by. Their friendship/sexual tension is apparent. Every time Mike spends time with an attractive woman, Velda wants the details.

At the Planet, several ladies make their availability known to Mike. He spurns them all except one, the lovely blonde B-girl Daisy (Donna Dixon). Mike forces his way past three goons to see Jerry Adams, the manager of the club. Adams tells him that Joey was just muscle and laughs when Mike relates that Joey had said he might be a night manager soon at the club.

But Joey's mother shows Mike a small package that Joey had left with her. She thinks it's drugs, but it turns out to be a handful of diamonds. Mike knows something's going on with this kind of stash and keeps pushing Adams.

Daisy overhears a conversation between Adams and a mob boss named Machetti. Unfortunately, Adams sees her calling Mike and she is quickly pushed out of a window at the club to her death.

Soon Mike is approached by a mob lawyer named Krone who offers up the killer if Mike will stay out of the limelight for a few days. Such an offer really intrigues Mike. He pretends to go along with the deal and a subsequent phone call leads him to an abandoned warehouse where Jerry Adams (supposedly Joey's killer) is hanging dead from the ceiling with a sign pinned to his suit: "Paid in Full." This makes Mike even madder. He wanted to have fun of punishing Joey's killer.

As in the novels, Velda goes with him. She carries her little .25 automatic, which Mike calls a "toy."

Mike links the need for him to be out of the limelight for a few days to an important local election. He breaks into a meeting between Machetti, Krone and crooked politician O'Hare. Even though Mike beats up two of Machetti's bodyguards, the level of violence in the entire show is restrained. Pat comes in with several policemen but no shots are fired.

The final scene is with Mike and Velda. Velda brings the last of the three puppies for Joey's mom. Mike has left the stolen diamonds with her. The diamonds are hers to keep because Joey paid for them with his life. Joey's mom offers Mike one diamond so he can give it to a special girl—obviously, Velda. When Velda and Mike are alone, Velda tells him, "I'm not that hard to take." Mike feels the pressure and says, "I'll think about it." This treatment is worlds apart from the Stacy Keach series Hammer, where women come and go with abandon, and Velda plays a sisterly role.

Despite its flaws, it's surprising "Margin for Murder" did not lead to a Dobson "Hammer" series. Noted film critic Judith Crist chose the telefilm as one of the best TV movies of 1981, the Mystery Writers of America nominated it for best TV movie as well, and the ratings were strong, with "Margin" beating out a World's Series play-off game that would seem to be a good bet for draining away Spillane's core audience.

The film did lead to a request for a second Hammer telefilm, but producer Jay Bernstein would not return Dobson to the role (and would abandon Picket and Hallahan as well). Instead, he chose a celebrated, versatile actor to play the private eye, and took an entirely different approach, bringing campy humor and a sense of retro fun to his next Spillane telefilm.

"Mickey Spillane's Mike Hammer in 'Margin for Murder'" (1981)

Hammer Productions • Running time: 98 minutes • Release date: October 15, 1981

WRITERS: Calvin Clements, Jr., and Alex Lucas; DIRECTOR: Daniel Haller; PRODUCERS: Jay Bernstein, Robert Hamner, Biff Johnson, Alex Lucas and Larry A. Thompson; CINEMATOGRAPHER: Michael D. Marguiles; Music: Nelson Riddle; CAST: Kevin Dobson (Mike Hammer); Charles Hallahan (Pat Chambers); Cindy Pickett (Velda); Donna Dixon (Daisy); Asher Brauner (Jerry Adams); Floyd Levine (Machetti); John Consindine (Krone); Renata Vanni (Mama De Fellita); Nicholas Hormann (Actor); Ivan Saric (Morgue Attendant)

12. "Mickey Spillane's Mike Hammer: 'Murder Me, Murder You'" (1983)

Stacy Keach dons the porkpie hat and trenchcoat of his signature role, accompanied by Tanya Roberts in her only appearance as Velda, in "Murder Me, Murder You" (1983).

Without question, Stacy Keach is the actor most strongly identified with Mike Hammer, a role many critics at the time (and even now) considered beneath him. But the actor's classical training and stage experience, as well as his years before the camera starring in major films, made him the perfect performer to bring a touch of class to this controversial character. That Keach was a broodingly handsome, wryly humorous performer with a physique suited to Hammer (without seeming a brute or a bully), added to what became, in the actor's own words, his signature role.

Keach has played Hammer in four telefilms and three television series, the latter accomplishment noted in *The Guinness Book of Records* (according to producer Bernstein). Since the 1980s, making good use of his mellifluous baritone, he has read ten Mike Hammer novels as audio books and starred in the three-volume full-cast radio-style series, "The New Adventures of Mike Hammer," the second volume of which ("The Little Death") won the Audie for Best Original Work in 2011. With his three-decade association with Mike Hammer, Keach rivals Spillane himself in identification with this iconic character.

While the telefilms range from excellent to good, the various series themselves have not always been up to Keach's high standard, who always displayed a remarkable ability to maintain Hammer's toughness and the integrity of the source material even when an episode was indifferently written or campier elements kicked in. The melancholy yet good-humored warmth of his voiceovers created *noir* poetry, even when the scripting didn't merit it.

Bernstein believed that the pure, unadulterated Hammer of the novels needed tempering for the times, that Spillane's private eye was at once anachronistic and politically incorrect. Though a Vietnam veteran, this Hammer's musical tastes run to 1940s big band, and he comes across more as a reminder of World War II than a survivor of the 1960s. Keach plays Hammer as a man out of time, a very hard-nosed conscience from the recent past turned loose on a debauched era. That this conscience is himself a womanizing tough guy who casually brutalizes and even kills his adversaries provides an ironic counterpoint.

Darren McGavin played Hammer affably, with his tongue slightly in cheek, in fairly grim little melodramas that depicted a seedy post-war world. While Keach's Hammer has humor, the formula here has been upended—Hammer is played straight while the world around him is consciously absurd, filled as it is with B-movie heavies too dumb to steer clear of the violent PI, and willing women in low-cut tops who find the fedora-sporting neanderthal instantly irresistible. This approach worked very well as an '80s TV series, but one could argue that Keach is the definitive small-screen Hammer in a far from definitive presentation.

The first and finest of the telefilms, "Murder Me, Murder You," premiered on CBS-TV on April 9, 1983. Where "Margin for Murder" is loosely based on *I, the Jury*, the follow-up film takes its lead from *Vengeance Is Mine! TV Guide* (in its May 28, 1983 edition) considered the Keach debut "the best TV version of a Spillane thriller yet." The interestingly plotted screenplay, hampered by some awkward dialogue, incorporates details from Mike's past—some from the novels, some via logical updating, in particular his Vietnam service—that underscore an underlying humanity in the hard-bitten character.

Tanya Roberts appears as Velda (she would be replaced by Lindsay Bloom in the series), perennial movie heavy Don Stroud is Pat Chambers, and Kent Williams as Deputy District Attorney Lawrence T. Barrington personifies the parade of weasel D.A.'s in the novels.

Embodying the Velda of the books, former "Charlie's Angel" star Tanya Roberts projects sex appeal, intelligence, and a lustful love for her boss, brandishing a gun and rescuing him at one point. It's fitting that she played Sheena in the movies, a comic book character

Spillane may well have scripted in his Funnies, Inc. days. While Lindsay Bloom did a fine job in the later series, the Bloom version of Velda is a sisterly, sometimes motherly one, whereas Roberts suggests an equal partnership and a sexual relationship. In this one telefilm, Tanya Roberts creates the most faithful, accurate screen depiction of Velda.

Rugged Don Stroud—surprisingly likable after a career of playing nasty heavies ("Coogan's Bluff")—convinces as both cop and friend, and is at least as good as McGavin's Chambers, Bart Burns. Kent Williams plays the slimy DA with aplomb, a little guy with a big opinion of himself.

The telefilm also introduces us to another important co-star: the big-band blues standard "Harlem Nocturne," which has become as associated with Hammer as Keach himself. This memorable, melancholy theme was written by Earle Hagen, who contributes music for not just "Murder Me, Murder You" but the first two Keach series. This signature music fits the Hammer world and sets the perfect atmosphere.

A typewritten (one-letter-at-a-time) title card again presents "Mickey Spillane's" in larger letters than "Mike Hammer," indicating that Spillane's Miller Beer ad fame had perhaps outstripped Hammer's in the early '80s.

The opening sequence of two attractive young women leaving an airport, only to be run off the road by bad guys, is damaged by laughable dialogue that has the blonde and brunette mingling casual conversation about a political assassination attempt with going skiing. The broad daylight attack on a freeway is similarly unbelievable. This odd, unconvincing opening is soon forgotten, however, as we move to Mike Hammer's Manhattan.

In a modest two-room office suite right out of 1947, Velda exudes smoldering sexuality, wearing a low-cut red blouse and a tight navy blue skirt. She brings Mike a single red rose, tells him she's made reservations at Antonio's. He takes the rose and gently rubs her cheek.

This tender scene is interrupted by obnoxious cops who tell the P.I. that the DA has subpoenaed him to appear before the grand jury. Once there, they take Hammer in to see one of witnesses, who has refused to testify until she speaks with Mike. The witness turns out to be Chris Jameson (Michelle Phillips of Mamas and Papas fame), a lovely woman Mike almost married twenty years before. She is to testify against helicopter manufacturing magnate Jack Vance, who allegedly is bribing government officials to boost sales. Chris's company makes confidential deliveries. One such delivery has been compromised and the two couriers are dead.

But Chris has another, bigger motive for seeing Mike. After all these years, she's finally decided to tell him that he's a father ... to a now nineteen-year old daughter, Michelle. He was on leave from the Vietnam War when the child was conceived, but Chris never told Hammer, after he decided to reup for another tour.

On the witness stand at the grand jury, Chris gets woozy and steps down. She plummets to the floor and is dead of an apparent heart attack within minutes. When Mike goes to her apartment later to get a recent picture of his daughter, he discovers all such photos have been removed from a scrapbook. He does find all the letters that he wrote to Chris from Vietnam as well as several she wrote to him but never mailed, with details of her pregnancy and the subsequent birth.

At Chris's courier company, Mike meets icily attractive co-owner Isadora Shepperton, who seems oddly unmoved by her trusted partner's death. Mike also meets and observes a moving tapestry of gorgeous women employed as couriers. Mike calls them "31 flavors." One such flavor is Paula Corey (Delta Burke, "Designing Women"), who gives him some information about his daughter. Michelle, it seems, was always mad at her father for not being there—her mother never told Michelle that Hammer was unaware of her existence—and took that aggression out by taking drugs and appearing in porno movies as the naughty, naked and hocky-masked Miss All Skate (who "makes the team"). Needless to say this depresses him.

But Mike still needs a picture to identify his missing daughter. He sneaks into the Graphics Industrial Films "studio," using Velda as bait (as in the novels). She poses at their surveillance camera as a potential actress, and Mike slips in when they hit the buzzer. Sleaze-movie mogul Saracen is eating his lunch while nearby his cameramen film two girls mud wrestling. Saracen, who has had a falling out with his former star, says all he knows is that Michelle had daddy issues, her abandonment sending her careening from college student into porno queen. Though Saracen doesn't know that father is Hammer, Mike flips out. When Saracen's men subdue him, Velda comes onto the balcony with her gun blazing. As Mike leaves, he pushes the pornographer into his own mud, right on top of the girls.

At the Lite N Easy Bar, "Moonlight Serenade" is playing on the retro jukebox. The drinks are being poured by Marty (Lee Meredith, Spillane's Miller Lite "Doll"). Mike tells Pat and Velda, "This is my most important case and I don't have a clue." Velda is mystified: "Important case?" And then he says, "I'm looking for my daughter." Pat and Velda exchange looks.

As they leave the bar, two attractive women see Mike. One hugs him and asks him why he hasn't called since Atlantic City. He beats a hasty retreat. Velda is irritated—again the signal here is that Mike and his secretary have a sexual relationship. When Roberts departs the role, so does this notion.

At his apartment, Mike finds Paula Corey waiting. She has brought Michelle's file. They end up in bed, of course, and later, as Paula is leaving, Mike hears her scream from the hallway. Shots ring out and goes to Paula, but she's dead. Her neck has been broken. One of the assailants is Cal Pope, a sleazy ex–PI who has been following Mike around, while the shadow of an as yet unseen second assailant appears mysteriously on the wall.

Vance, an ex–Marine who knows Mike was in the Air Cavalry in Vietnam, looks more guilty by the minute. Hammer seems to have contempt for Marines, which doesn't ring true. Vance, a stutterer whose statuesque secretary finishes his sentences, gets Mike to visit him on his boat "Lovely Lady" at the Yacht Basin. To prove how tough he is, Vance is taking a wintertime swim.

Mike goes back to see Isadora Shepperton. She appears cold to his questions at first but warms suddenly. Mike says, "After this is over you and I should have dinner together." She replies, "And breakfast." But Isadora has an unsettlingly well-sculpted, too-perfect beauty (not to mention a firm handshake!). Her curvy figure is shown off in a low-cut blouse with long sleeves. She wears collars that cover up her Adam's apple ... oh, wait, women don't have Adam's apples....

At the Lite N Easy, Marty tells Mike a new girl named Teresa has been coming in for several days. Some "punkers" (an embarrassing TV version of goth punks, who Pat earlier ran out of the bar averting a Hammer scene) hassle Teresa for a dance. Mike plays Glenn Miller's "In the Mood" on the jukebox and beats them up, running them out. Teresa says, "Now *you* I could dance with."

They leave the bar and go to Mike's place. After a while she says, "There's something you should know before you head to the bedroom."

Mike says, "You're a virgin?"

"No," she replies. "I'm your daughter."

"...I know."

Teresa, actually Michelle, had been the second girl in the car chased off the road at the start. Thrown from the wreck, she switched identities with the other courier, Mickey Pennoyer. Her mom switched the dental records so that even after the autopsy, the police would believe Michelle had perished. Her mother had taken the delivery briefcase of two million in cash, and hidden it. That's what everyone is *really* looking for.

But Michelle wants to know why Mike didn't marry her mother. The story is somewhat convoluted and involves the deaths of two more women that Hammer was close to—perhaps one is meant to represent Charlotte Manning. It's all about pain and guilt to him. She then goes into the bedroom.

Mike hears a noise at his door. He pulls his gun and Velda comes in. Velda notices Michelle's scarf and says, "Well, they don't call me Veldus Interruptus for nothing." But she's on a mission and holds up a handwritten card: "Office Broken Into! Look for Bug."

Mike calls Vance to set up a meet. The private eye pretends to have the briefcase of money and tells the industrialist to come to the Brooklyn Heights Cemetery. But the DA has used his bug to know about the meet, nab the money, and solidify his case against Vance and Mike. The police grab them and take them back to the station. Once there, the briefcase is opened to reveal nothing but a note from Mike, telling Vance he may be able to press a case of false arrest.

Pat says he knows a good place to hide Michelle out—his house. (Pat in the novels is a bachelor, carrying the torch for Velda. Here is married to "Linda," has some kids, but everybody's away right now.) Michelle tells her father she now knows why he didn't marry her mother: "You like your women." Mike's reply is poignant: "Michelle, I take women seriously and you know what it gets them? A body bag."

Mike leaves Pat and Michelle at the house while he goes to the McGrady Mortuary. He believes Chris hid the money in a body bag. While he's there, someone knocks him out. When he returns to Pat's, he learns that two guys pretending to be policemen have taken Chris hostage—a handsome young cop blind-sided Pat with a judo kick. With some deductive prodding from Pat, Mike suddenly thinks to look for a body bag at the mortuary labeled ... "Michael Hammer."

The pair who kidnapped Michelle want to swap her for the money. They tell Mike to come an old warehouse near 8th Avenue and West 27th Street. Once there, Cal Pope gets the drop on Hammer and they moving through a hanging sea of naked manikins, until they see Michelle tied in a chair.

This leads to a violent confrontation with a beautiful woman who turns out to be a transvestite—a confrontation that includes the death of Mike's daughter. In a fit of rage and violent abandon, Hammer returns to beat the transvestite senseless ... perhaps to death. "This is for Chris.... This is for Michelle.... And this is for me!"

Three days have passed, and Mike broods in his office, quietly drinking. Vance comes in to offer him a high-paying gig with his company. This is a frankly off-putting scene, because Vance morphs for no real reason from bad guy to good guy, and in a really dumb piece of throwaway TV-style humor, reveals that his stuttering is a put-on to keep his secretary busy (!).

After Vance leaves, Velda comes to Mike and says she's got those reservations at Antonio's: "If it's a family you want, I thought we'd have dinner first." Yes, a sexual relationship—Velda's rose is neatly pinned to the police dart target nearby. As the music swells,

Mike's voiceover comes in: "Two things you can't share. Pain and guilt. Anyway, thank God for Velda and the city."

"Murder Me, Murder You" is an outstanding start for the Stacy Keach version of Mike Hammer, setting in motion the style and format of the several series to come. With considerable location shooting in a snowy, sludgy Manhattan, the telefilm has a gritty quality later episodes would largely lack, and several scenes—notably one at a shadowy mortuary morgue room, and the eerie manikin warehouse showdown—help the film qualify as quality neo-*noir*.

The performances are solid all around, with bosomy Delta Burke giving a hint of comic potential to come by doing a gentle spoof of Marilyn Monroe, while Lisa Blount offers a very natural, understated performance as daughter Michelle. Blount and Keach together provide the film with a believable human center.

Keach is suitably tough, with a particularly nice moment coming when he steps on an elevator, baddie Cal Pope punches the button, the door opens on Keach, who then punches Pope on the button. At one point he salutes Darren McGavin by imitating the other Hammer's cocky gesture of pushing his hat forward.

Keach also makes some fairly deadly lines play well—"You got giant lizard breath" for example, and "I'm gonna dump these toads in their own burn bag." A tough guy saying, "You're gonna get maxed, Hammer," provides one of numerous head-scratcher lines from a screenwriter who appears to be inventing his own slang expressions.

Producer Bernstein said, "I knew when Ronald Reagan got in, Mike Hammer could get on." This catering to conservative sensibilities comes across unvarnished in a conversation between Mike and Pat at night on the stoop of a house, an exchange having nothing to do with the plot.

"It's about time we stopped bad-mouthing this country," Keach says, making that play as well. Pat's similarly regretful thoughts about where the nation has gone are well-delivered by Stroud.

Nonetheless, this appears to be Bernstein pandering to the Silent Majority. Hammer, after all, is a conservative's nightmare. "What happens to our values?" Hammer wonders, in between sleeping with every good-looking woman he meets, slugging law enforcement officials, and picking bar fights. Is it Keach's innate intelligence that makes us accept Hammer and his quaint double standard? This is, after all, a film that wants us to applaud Hammer terrorizing a pornographer while at the same time we're relishing buxom babes mud wrestling.

But "Murder Me, Murder You" has a different attitude toward women than the various Keach series that follow. Awkward dialogue aside, the screenplay explores the roles of women in an interesting fashion. Casual womanizer Hammer must deal with having driven his daughter into pornography. The "31 Flavors" of women include a beautiful transvestite, pointing out graphically the artificial means (make-up, hairdos, padding) used by women to attract men. Hammer himself admits to his daughter that he does not take women seriously—that he sleeps around in love 'em and leave 'em fashion—because, when he does get serious with a woman, the consequences are also serious. A woman you love dies, you are left with "pain and guilt" that can't be shared.

Unfortunately, Bernstein took the wrong message from the telefilm's success and went on to use the beautiful couriers as a springboard for filling episodes with a dazzling but silly array of what Keach has called "Hammerettes"—gorgeous women immediately attracted to Mike Hammer. From the serious theme of "Murder Me, Murder You," the series devolves into the campy approach that Spillane himself, privately, admitted to disfavor.

"Murder Me, Murder You" (1983)

Columbia Pictures Television and Jay Bernstein Productions • Running time: 100 minutes • Release date: April 9, 1983

WRITER: William Stratton; DIRECTOR: Gary Nelson; PRODUCERS: Jay Bernstein, Lew Gallo, Larry A. Thompson and Lana Wood; CINEMATOGRAPHER: Gayne Rescher; MUSIC: Earle Hagen and J.J. Johnson; CAST: Stacy Keach (Mike Hammer); Tanya Roberts (Velda); Don Stroud (Captain Pat Chambers); Delta Burke (Paula Corey); Tom Atkins (Jack Vance); Jonathan Banks (Janos Saracen); Kent Williams (Barrington); Lisa Blount (Michelle Jameson); Michelle Phillips (Chris Jameson); Bert Rosario (Duardo); Randi Brooks (Arla); Lee Meredith (Marty); Ric Manicini (Cal Pope); Eddie Egan (Hennessey); Madison Arnold (Conlin); Ava Lazar (Janice Wells); James Arone (Bumppo); Michelle Avonne (Betty Heraldo); Julie Hayek (Second French Courier); Quin Kessler (Karen Marshall); William Vincent Kulak (Paramedic); Carol Pritkin (Second Receptionist); Timothy Stack (Natty); Michael A. Andrews (Isadora Shepperton)

13. "Mickey Spillane's Mike Hammer: 'More Than Murder'" (1984)

Spillane specifically requested that Keach wear a porkpie hat, but the actor was displeased with the way it looked and felt in the first telefilm. For the second, "More Than Murder" (1984), he adopted a more traditional private-eye fedora.

The Stacy Keach Hammer series unofficially began with the telefilm "More Than Murder," airing in a two-hour time slot on January 26, 1984, two days before regular one-hour episodes began on Saturday 28, 1984.

All four Keach/Hammer TV movies have a bigger budget and better production values than a normal episode. But "More Than Murder" has an episodic TV approach that makes it a lesser film than its predecessor. Keach is comfortable and confident in the role, the Spillane-requested pork pie hat of "Murder Me, Murder You" replaced by a more standard Keach-dictated fedora.

Already, however, the parade of Hammerettes has begun, and a silliness undermines the proceedings. Keach, however, continues to maintain his (and Hammer's) dignity.

When a high stakes poker game ends in murder, Pat Chambers is arrested as an accessory. DA Barrington, whose opinion of Chambers is tainted by his dislike of Mike Hammer, believes that Pat had involvement with not only the murder but drug smuggling as well. Mike always sticks by his friends and Pat is his best friend.

In this episode Mike beds two lovely ladies and is well on the way to the third, Eve Warwick (played by the lovely Robyn Douglass), when she is killed helping him nab the bent DEA agent who is really behind the crimes. Along the way, Mike also finds time to romance wall-climber Sandy (Lynn-Holly Johnson, Olympic ice skater and Bond girl), who ends up strung up on her own equipment in Mike's bathtub.

After Eve dies in his arms, an enraged Mike chases the DEA man to the top of a ferry boat and shoots him. The bad guy doesn't die immediately but is hanging on the railing. He asks for Mike's help. Mike does nothing and watches him lose his grip and fall to his death. Whatever campiness has preceded, this moment is authentically Spillane. Variations on this ending appear in several episodes, most adding gallows humor.

Back in his office, Mike is drinking Jack Daniels and trying to sneak cigarettes. Velda is starting an anti-smoking campaign that is so long, it will last into the next actress.

Mike is looking forlorn in his office chair. Velda, knowing Mike is a womanizer, says to him, "You've always got me." That is the softer Lindsay Bloom version of Velda—the no-nonsense Tanya Roberts version would come sit in his lap. He ends the episode as usual in voiceover, this time slightly varying the line from "Murder Me, Murder You": "Thank God for Velda. Thank God for the city."

The viewer always sees producer Jay Bernstein at the end of the credits, picking up a cane and walking out of the scene with his back to the camera. This episode is also notable for Bernstein appearing as the mysterious poker player, Sprague.

"More Than Murder" (1984)

Columbia Pictures Television and Jay Bernstein Productions • Running time: 100 minutes • Release date: January 26, 1984

WRITERS: Stephen Dowling and Bill Stratton; DIRECTOR: Gary Nelson; PRODUCERS: Jon C. Andersen, Jay Bernstein, Daniel H. Blatt, Lew Gallo and Robert Singer; CINEMATOGRAPHER: James Crabe; MUSIC: Earle Hagen; CAST: Stacy Keach (Mike Hammer); Lindsay Bloom (Velda); Don Stroud (Captain Pat Chambers); Kent Williams (Lawrence T. Barrington); Tim McIntire (Malcolm Dobbs); Lynn-Holly Johnson (Sandy); Sam Groom (Phillips); Richard Romanus (Bordante); Denny Miller (Tallahassee); Robyn Douglass (Eve Warwick); Danny Goldman (Ozzie the Answer); Gail Ramsey as Gail Rae Carlson (Linda); Kevin King (Davey); Ingrid Anderson (Angela); John Hancock (Judge); Stephanie Blackmore

(Roz); David Haskell (Titus); Martin West (Ellison); Lee Meredith (Marty); Nora Grave (Nicky); Jineane Ford (Honey); Mindi Iden (Bonnie); Darcy Lee (Jolene); Michelle Michaels (Maisy); Jinaki (Millie); Carol Pritkin (Bidder); Celia Ward (The Face); Norman Matlock (LeRoy Applebaum III); Mike Glassman (Nitro); Bob Tzudiker (Doctor); Yung Sun (Gambler); Nick DeMauro (Moe); Brad Sanders (Dude); James Rosin (Bidder); Richard E. Butler (Garth); Jerry Taft (Auctioneer); Kirk Cameron (Bobby); Victor Magnotta (Patrolman); Deborah Jean Templin (Woman Passenger); John Coran (Male Passenger); Jena Greco (Child Passenger); Jay Bernstein (Sprague)

14. "Mickey Spillane's Mike Hammer" (1984–85) CBS-TV

Stacy Keach as Mike Hammer studies a glittering clue in "Hot Ice," the second episode of the CBS series "Mickey Spillane's Mike Hammer" (February 4, 1984).

The regular series began at ten o'clock Saturday night January 28, 1984 (nine central). If not a blockbuster hit, the series scored well enough in the ratings to justify its existence, and lasted for forty-six episodes, eventually leaving the CBS network in 1987. Its run might have been longer but for an unexpected nine-month break in production.

"24 Karat Dead," the first of forty-six regular episodes, continued the TV tradition of Hammer as a wise-cracking, hardboiled PI who punches and swaggers his way through a world over-populated by bosomy beauties finding him impossibly irresistible. The 1980s Hammer spent some time with rock and R & B groups, including Herbie Hancock and George Benson. The one-hour format—unlike the half-hour McGavin series—makes it possible for Velda to appear along with Pat Chambers. As in the novels, Velda does much of Mike's investigating, off-camera, and Pat is the PI's police contact who helps out with protected information.

The production values of this CBS series are first- rate. Producer Bernstein seems more concerned with guest stars and glitz than quality scripts, though a number of first-rate writers worked on the show, even if at times they were hampered by producer Bernstein's requirements for this take on the PI genre, a tricky mix of campy humor, leering sex, and hard-boiled action. What makes it all work is Keach's self-assured performance, genuinely tough, humorous without winking, an actor capable of conveying the tenderness and cruelty of Spillane's famous character.

The credits roll on a Venetian blind style opening focusing on the full-screen face of Stacy Keach as Mike Hammer. Lines move back and forth horizontally until Keach's face is revealed, all the cuts in the title sequence imitating the opening and closing of blinds. On a black screen comes bold lettering: MICKEY SPILLANE'S MIKE HAMMER. Earle Hagen's "Harlem Nocturne" plays under, heavy on the saxophone. Clips from scenes alternate between heavy action and serio-comic, and of course the ubiquitous sexy females. Mike is jostled by a biker, left hanging onto a slice of pizza with his teeth. (This somewhat out-of-character portrayal is mimicked in the opening of the later syndicated series, the pizza accident caused by a punching bag.)

The credits present the new Velda—Lindsay Bloom—a buxom brunette with big '80s hair and a winning smile. Then two shadow figures indicate Velda giving Mike a kiss. The credits close with the blinds criss-crossing horizontally on the shadow figures. This hint at character equality will not appear in the later "New Mike Hammer" credits.

In this first episode, the lovely and mysterious woman known only as "The Face" (Donna Denton) is introduced sitting in a limo next to the building. Hammer sees this gorgeous woman, they have a moment of connection, and poof ... she's gone. This is a Bernstein-created gimmick that becomes a running bit until she and Mike finally meet in the last episode of the CBS series. Actress Donna Denton is not identified in the credits until that final episode.

Considered by fans and critics an outstanding episode, "Seven Dead Eyes" was written by mystery writer Joe Gores, a former skip tracer and PI whose novels are noted for their attention to detail and realistic atmosphere. Gore also wrote memorable scripts for "Columbo" and "Remington Steele." He stated his goal writing for "Hammer" was to preserve Spillane's original vision as much as possible.

Mike meets PI Ridge Grundy at the Lite N Easy bar. Grundy wants Mike to watch his back at an upcoming private investigators' convention. Since Grundy had helped Mike get into the business after his return from Vietnam War, Mike agrees. But Grundy is blown up by a C4 bomb as he walks away from the bar. That's the first dead eye.

Mike goes to Grundy's office and finds a list with six names on it: Ridge's name is first, and now he's dead. Mike tracks down name number two, Ari Artel, at the convention. He makes his living doing society divorce work and using his attractive co-worker to entice rich guys into compromising positions. (This appears to be a sly reference to Meeker's Hammer in "Kiss Me Deadly.") Mike asks him a few questions, and, shortly after, Ari is strangled with some of the film he used against his clients. That's two dead eyes.

Mike next contacts Dan Forman, who not only does not cooperate with him but berates his former friend. Forman calls both of them "walking fossils" because the industry has passed them by. Still, Forman offers to throw some business his way; he needs help with an important client named Harry McBride. Shortly thereafter, as Forman goes into his office, a man dressed like a painter sprays him directly in the face and kills him. So far that makes three dead eyes.

Mike goes to Forman's office before the police can get there to look for clues. He's slugged and wakes up with the building on fire, saving himself by jumping. As he's recovering his breath on the street, wondering who is responsible, he muses, "Who is the snake?" This appears to be an homage to Spillane's Mike Hammer novel, *The Snake* (1964).

Subsequently, two more PIs whose names are on the list turn up dead in a car in the East River. Now it's five dead eyes. But Mike has some help on the case, in addition to Velda. Grundy had been mentoring young Artie Landon, much as he had Mike. Landon doesn't seem very effective and Mike mostly ignores him.

The sixth name on the list is Kim Warren, an attractive blonde PI. Mike helps her out on a case and ends up spending the evening with her. As they are walking out onto the street from her apartment, she is shot by a sniper. Mike returns to Kim's apartment, looking for details related to the list. Kim had revealed that the list is the secret committee that votes on the membership for the PI society. Once Mike sees the minutes for the society, he knows all he needs to: One of the names on the list had been turned down by the committee. Mike sets a trap for the killer in Kim's hospital room.

In a final confrontation with the bad guys, Mike gets help from Betsy. (It should be noted that Hammer only refers to his .45 as "Betsy" in the novels a handful of times.) Mike had been playing an old Glenn Miller song ("Pennsylvania 6-5000") during the confrontation, a fitting homage for his friend.

The story is quite layered for a TV episode, without a false note of dialogue, and a very subdued amount of sexual byplay. Gores even manages to work in a scene, after Artie tries to kill Velda, in which she spends the night at Mike's apartment. Nothing happens, of course, but the viewer—and Velda—could always hope.

Stacy Keach was in London to film part of a "Mike Hammer" episode and then planned to fly to France to shoot "Mistral's Daughter," a CBS-TV mini series. While in London on April 4, 1983, he was arrested for possession of 1.3 ounces of cocaine. Both Keach and his long-time secretary Deborah Steele were arrested. Keach posted $100,000 bail and moved on to France. It took Steele a few days to raise the $15,000 for her bail. Keach was convicted and began his sentence in December, 1984.

Keach had pleaded guilty on December 7, anticipating a light sentence. Instead he had received a nine-month term. The circumstances of Keach's arrest, conviction and prison term are themselves the stuff of mystery. Keach was never known to be a heavy recreational drug user. The very conservative Mickey Spillane stood behind his "Mike Hammer," and suggested enigmatically that Keach had not been guilty.

Several months before, a half-page *TV Guide* article about Stacy Keach revealed that he had to "strike a deal with ex-executive producer Jay Bernstein ... 'to avoid eating too much French food'" while he was in France filming "Mistral's Daughter."

Keach had been married five years to former model and actress Jill Donohue; his secretary had been with him for fourteen years. Donohue commented in the article that their Malibu house had a piano: "He plays ... beautifully." Many episodes of the Hammer series show Keach playing the piano (he scored and played the music for "The New Adventures of Mike Hammer" audio-book series).

In the same article, Jay Bernstein said he acquired the rights to Hammer in 1976, but had to wait until the 1980s, because TV then preferred what he called "soft detectives," like "Barnaby Jones" and "Cannon."

CBS issued a statement saying they stood by Keach and planned to carry "Mike Hammer" in the fall. Less than a month later, the show was on the fall schedule with an episode entitled "Torch Song," airing September 29, 1984.

Due to Keach's imprisonment, post-production issues plagued the final three episodes of season two: Mike's voiceover was ghosted (poorly) by comedian Rich Little. In addition, Pat and Velda both contribute narration. Producer Bernstein had offered the job to Keach's actor/director brother James, who was too distraught to complete the work.

Mickey Spillane's Mike Hammer (1984–1985) CBS-TV

"Mickey Spillane's Mike Hammer" was a CBS-TV series airing 1984–85. It was produced for by Jay Bernstein Productions and filmed at The Burbank Studios in Burbank, California, for Columbia Pictures Television (a Sony Pictures Entertainment Company).

Season 1 had 10 episodes; it was broadcast from January through April 1984. Season 2 had 14 episodes; it was broadcast from September 1984 through January 1985.

Series regulars were Stacy Keach as Mike Hammer; Lindsay Bloom as Velda; Don Stroud as Captain Pat Chambers; and Kent Williams as Assistant D. A. Lawrence Barrington. Other series regulars include: Danny Goldman as Ozzie the Answer; Eddie Egan as Hennessy; Eddie Barth as Richie; Lee Benton as Jenny; Ben Powers as Moochie.

Season 1 (January 1984–April 1984)

Episode #1 (January 28, 1984) "24 Karat Dead"

Directed by: Paul Krasny. Written by: Bill Froehlich and Mark Lisson.

Mike searches for the killer of Vincent and Lillian Becker, an elderly couple who asked Mike to help them recover their life savings from a bogus gold-investment firm.

Cast: Tracy Scoggins as Claire/Nicole; Barbara Stock as Lenore; Tom Hallick as Justin Herd; Larry Gelman as Kreiger; Hugh Gorrian as Slerick; Donna Denton as "The Face" (first appearance, uncredited).

Episode #2 (February 4, 1984) "Hot Ice"

Directed by: Bernard Kowalski. Written by: Frank Abatemarco.

A diamond heist goes wrong; one of the dealers is killed and Mei Ling, a friend of Mike's, is kidnapped. They want a diamond worth $1.3 million for her return.

Cast: Catherine Parks as Rachel; Michael Constantine as Mel Hurock; Dorlie Fong as Mei Ling; Christine Claridge as Rene Lovely; and featuring Key Luke.

EPISODE #3 (FEBRUARY 11, 1984) "SEVEN DEAD EYES"

DIRECTED BY: James Frawley. WRITTEN BY: Joe Gores.

Ridge Grundy (PI #1)—the man who taught Mike how to be a private cop—mysteriously asks for Mike's help. Before he can give details, Grundy is killed by a bomb. Mike discovers that his death is linked to a list of private eyes who are being threatened. Then someone starts killing them off one by one. There seems to be a connection to an upcoming election of new members to the PI Association.

CAST: Myron Healey as Ridge Grundy (PI #1); special appearance by Dr. Joyce Brothers.

EPISODE #4 (FEBRUARY 18, 1984) "VICKIE'S SONG"

DIRECTED BY: Michael Preece. WRITTEN BY: Joe Gunn.

Mike is in Greenwich Village at the Expectations Club for a set by Vickie Cornell, a girl Mike helped kick a drug habit. Soon Vickie is dead of what appears to be a drug overdose and Mike wants answers.

CAST: Linda Leilani Brown as Vickie; Steven Keats as Harry Welch; Lynn Herring as Georgette.

EPISODE #5 (MARCH 3, 1984) "SHOTS IN THE DARK"

DIRECTED BY: Michael Preece. WRITTEN BY: Larry Gross and Frank Abatemarco, and Bill Froehlich and Mark Lisson.

Mike rescues a young woman named Shelley from two hoods in Central Park. She's soon shot down and dies in Mike's arms. Her roommate Julie is then kidnapped.

CAST: Jenilee Harrison as Shelley Steele; Jeff Conaway as Owen Goddard; Sharon Stone as Julie Eland; Delta Burke as Linda Sloan; Burr De Benning as Cobb; Jacquelyn Ray Sellect as Dr. Marcia Forrest.

EPISODE #6 (MARCH 10, 1984) "DEAD ON A DIME"

DIRECTED BY: Arnold Laven. WRITTEN BY: B. W. Sandefur.

A mysterious blonde leaves a dime marked with a red x on the bar where she was having a drink with ex-cop Richard Austin. Austin subsequently pulls a gun, shoots a patron, and then turns the gun on Mike, who defends himself and kills Austin. Mike wants to know why.

CAST: Sam Chew, Jr. as Lacy; Barbra Horan as Dr. Jennifer Crane; Stephen Elliott as Kohlmyer; Greta Blackburn as Roberta.

EPISODE #7 (MARCH 24, 1984) "SEX TRAP"

DIRECTED BY: James Frawley. WRITTEN BY: B. W. Sandefur.

One of Mike's ex-girlfriends is blackmailing diplomats with sex tapes.

CAST: Brett Halsey as Tolnosk; Mike Preston as Griffin; Lee Benton as Jenny; Ben Powers as Moochie.

EPISODE #8 (MARCH 31, 1984) "NEGATIVE IMAGE"

DIRECTED BY: Leo Penn. WRITTEN BY: George Lee Marshall.

Photojournalist Bobby Indigo has been murdered in his darkroom and his friend Mike thinks a negative shows why. Soon some of his models also turn up missing or dead.

CAST: Steven D. Reisch as Bobby Indigo; Steven Keats as Harry Welch; Elyssa Davalos as Jackie Drake; Al Ruscio as Rosario; Paul Lambert as DeVita; Kitty Moffat as Joanna Wells; Lynn Herring as Kiki Small and "The Face" (uncredited).

EPISODE #9 (APRIL 7, 1984) "THE PERFECT TWENTY"

DIRECTED BY: John Patterson. WRITTEN BY: Joe Viola.

Mike investigates the fiery death of a beautiful model. He was led to the flames by Rocky her barking dog. Mike soon discovers it's all connected to some missing counterfeit plates.

CAST: Shannon Tweed as Karen Thorson; Dane Clark as Bremmer; Michael Currie as Gus Thorson; Ingrid Anderson as Monica; Asher Brauner as Tice; and "The Face."

EPISODE #10 (APRIL 14, 1984) "SATAN, CYANIDE AND MURDER"

DIRECTED BY: Michael Preece. WRITTEN BY: Stephen Downing.

Client Nancy Madden, owner of Ravel Fashions, is killed by a rifle shot in Mike's office. Hennessey thinks the bullet was meant for Hammer, but Mike's wants to learn more about Nancy: "She had her whole life to live and then she walked into my office." Final shoot out in a hall of mirrors.

CAST: Leigh Lombardi as Nancy Madden; Stepfanie Kramer as Lisa; Tracy Brooks Swope as Cynthia; Linden Chiles as Paul Madden; Leo Rossi as Tony Weston; Robert Miranda as Johnny Moretti; Eddie Barth as Ritchie; Danny Goldman as Ozzie; Timothy Carey as Kenny the Knife; and "The Face."

Season 2 (September 1984–January 1985)

EPISODE #11 (SEPTEMBER 29, 1984) "TORCH SONG"

DIRECTED BY: James Frawley. WRITTEN BY: Sy Salkowitz.

This season premiere was at a new time: Saturday, 9:00 P.M.

Joey Peel, a friend of Mike's who was convicted of arson as a teenager, dies in a fiery explosion his first day on the new job that Mike pulled strings to get him.

CAST: Maggie Cooper as Terry Bacon; Jim McMullan as Martin Stevens; Beau Starr as Al; Danny Goldman as Ozzie; Eddie Egan as Hennessey; Tegan West as Joey Peel; Christie Claridge as Maria; and "The Face."

EPISODE #12 (OCTOBER 6, 1984) "TOO YOUNG TO DIE"

DIRECTED BY: Russ Mayberry. WRITTEN BY: Ed Scharlach.

Mike protects a young girl (Sally Jordan) from her would-be pimps on her first day as a prostitute. He directs her to a real job, but a hood with a gun forces her into a big car. When Mike next sees her she's on a slab at the morgue.

CAST: Laurie Wilson as Sally Jordan; Ron Harper as Roger Payton; Wendie Malick as Louise; Neil Zevnik as Buck Derwin; Taro Meyer as Ellen Grant; Greta Blackburn as Jackie; Dr. Joyce Brothers as herself; and "The Face."

EPISODE #13 (OCTOBER 13, 1984) "KILL DEVIL"

DIRECTED BY: Russ Mayberry. WRITTEN BY: B. W. Sandefur.

Mike rescues Velda from a mugging. That's bad enough, but Betsy is stolen and used on a gang leader.

CAST: Faith Minton as Bertha; Ray Liotta as Tony Cable; Dan Lauria as Moses; Deborah Goodrich as Marilyn; David Labiosa as Sammy; Vincent Keith Ford as Krager; Debi Richter as Chi Chi; and "The Face."

EPISODE #14 (OCTOBER 20, 1984) "CATFIGHT"

DIRECTED BY: Christian I. Nyby, II. WRITTEN BY: Stephen Kandel.

A mobster's escape plans goes awry and he's killed in a car fire. But he leaves a strange puzzle to three women. Mike thinks the solution may lead to his friend Dave's killer. This might be the sexiest episode of the TV series.

CAST: Rebecca Holden ("Knight Rider") as Barbara; Barbi Benton as Susan; Ann Turkel as Gail; Lou Ferrigno ("The Incredible Hulk") as King Steele; David Prather as Dave Hunter; Joanna Johnson as Kerri; Allan Graf as Jack Rogan; and "The Face."

EPISODE #15 (OCTOBER 27, 1984) "WARPATH"

DIRECTED BY: James Frawley. WRITTEN BY: Sy Salkowitz.

Someone is threatening the Indian performers in Mike's ex-girlfriend Laura's wild west show. Mike winds up on a white horse chasing down the killer.

CAST: Shanna Reed as Anna Sanderson; Michael Ironside as Wade Bennett; Jaime Lyn Bauer as Laura Kimble; Richard McGonagle as Joseph Barry; and "The Face."

EPISODE #16 (NOVEMBER 3, 1984) "BONECRUNCH"

DIRECTED BY: Michael Preece. WRITTEN BY: Stephen Kandel.

The New York Marauders quarterback is shot right in front of a crowd of 60,000. Mike suspects a gambling connection.

CAST: Bubba Smith as Buddy Lofton; Hugh Gillin as Nick Stanton; Mary-Margaret Humes as Dana Lord; Janine Turner as Christie; Tim Rossovich as Tony Crier; Mindi Iden as May; the Los Angeles Raiderettes as the Cheerleaders; and "The Face."

EPISODE #17 (NOVEMBER 10, 1984) "THE DEADLY PREY"

DIRECTED BY: Paul Stanley. WRITTEN BY: B. W. Sandefur. STORY BY: Paul & Jean Blake.

An art collector is murdered with a ceremonial sword by an intruder wearing a cat mask. Velda's brother is murdered in a similar manner but not before he gives her a jade necklace on his return from a year long business trip.

CAST: Susan Anton as Noelle; Marcy Lafferty as Rhonda Rodale; Henry Gibson as Simon Rodale; David Winn as Gary (Velda's brother); Anthony De Longis as Caudell; and "The Face."

EPISODE #18 [18) (NOVEMBER 10, 1984) "DEAD CARD DOWN"

DIRECTED BY: Leo Penn. WRITTEN BY: B. W. Sandefur.

At the airport, Mike meets his friend Cozy Higgins, who tells him that a man tried to kill him in Paris. Cozy is gunned down in the airport walkway; he gives Mike half of a torn $10,000 bill before he dies.

CAST: Beah Richards as Mattie Higgins; Katherine Cannon as Linda; Aharon Ipale as Anthony Malan; Jeff Pomerantz as Peter Brett; Eli Cummins as Louis; and "The Face."

EPISODE #19 (NOVEMBER 24, 1984) "A DEATH IN THE FAMILY"

DIRECTED BY: Ray Danton. TELEPLAY BY: B. W. Sandefur. STORY BY: Marvin Paul Kupfer

Mike witnesses the killing of a mob leader Big Ed Huntley at Mama Zinetta's Restaurant. Mama Z is caught in the crossfire and Mike promises to find them. Mike suspects Big Ed's former partner Vince Randolph.

CAST: Barbara Bain ("Mission: Impossible") as Julia Huntley; John Ireland as Vincent Randolph; Dan Hamilton as Acker; Susan Walden as Carol; Twylva Littleton as Madeline; and "The Face." Dom DeLuise and Burt Reynolds: unbilled cameos.

EPISODE #20 (DECEMBER 1, 1984) "COLD TARGET"

DIRECTED BY: Jon Andersen. WRITTEN BY: Duke & Bill Sandefur.

Mike meets with Donnie Hendricks, an investigative reporter, but before he can talk with her, she is killed right before his eyes. In court, Mike gets enraged at the killer and jumps over the table trying to grab him.

CAST: Susan Strasberg as Judge Hullis; Dick Van Patten as Charles Behmer; Gail Rae Carlson as Linda Chambers; Ben Powers as Moochie; Timothy Carey as Kenny the Knife; Mindi Iden as Janet; and "The Face."

EPISODE #21 (DECEMBER 8, 1984) "A BULLET FOR BENNY"

DIRECTED BY: Ray Danton. TELEPLAY BY: Paul Bernbaum and Jack B. Sowards. STORY BY: Chester Krumholz.

Benny Winslow, who runs a local candy store, is killed by a lone gunman. His daughter Tina wants Mike to find her father's killer. But federal agents and racketeers may be involved. Nicely done twist ending.

CAST: Martin Rudy as Benny; Leslie Wing as Tina Winslow; Frank Schuller as Daniels; Danny Goldman as Ozzie; Michael DeLano as Leo Ratan; Abe Vigoda as Arthur; Brian Libby as Marlan.

EPISODE #22 (DECEMBER 29, 1984) "DEAD MAN'S RUN"

DIRECTED BY: Michael Preece. WRITTEN BY: B. W. Sandefur.

At a New Year's Eve party (December 31, 1984), Pat Chambers tells the story about their friend and former commanding officer, Colonel O'Hara, who hands Mike an envelope telling him who killed him. It involves Altos, a small country engulfed in a freedom movement, while Mike searches for the terrorist who killed O'Hara. The story is mostly told in flashbacks. The voice over at the end is by Rich Little.

CAST: Laurence Guittard as Stephan Konos; Barbra Horan as Lisa; Gerry Gibson as Colonel Tim O'Hara; Ingrid Boulting as Alina; Gene Dynarski as Zarubica; Reid Smith as Stan; and "The Face."

EPISODE #23 (JANUARY 5, 1985) "FIRESTORM"

DIRECTED BY: Cliff Bole. TELEPLAY BY: Stephen Kandel. STORY BY: Paul Ehrmann.

Lonnie Challenger, the lead singer of Firestorm, an all-girl rock group, and an old friend of Mike's, is electrocuted during rehearsal, but all the surviving band members care about is her missing demo tape. No closing voiceover.

CAST: Kim O'Brien as Lonnie Challenger; Dennis Cole as Dave Marquette; Anne Kerry as Shale; Jan Smithers ("WKRP") as Millicent; Lauren Tewes ("The Love Boat") as Chastity; John Calvin as Pete Kingman; Dallas Cole as Abigail; Casey Kasem as himself; Herbie Hancock as himself; and "The Face."

EPISODE #24 (JANUARY 12, 1985) "DEADLY REUNION"

DIRECTED BY: Sutton Roley. TELEPLAY BY: B. W. Sandefur. STORY BY: Jay Bernstein.

One of Mike's classmates is found dead at Mike's former teacher Viola Green's retirement party. An elite IQ club membership is Mike's only clue. No closing voiceover.

CAST: George Benson as George Langdon; Esther Rolle as Viola Green; Simone Griffeth as Sylvia; Chip Lucia as Dempsey; Steve Carlson as Lanzberg; Lana Wood as Virginia Warburton; Alex Henteloff as Errol Ford; Cynthia Cypert as Marilyn; Terrence McGovern as Taylor Wilson; Les Jankey as James Fuller; Michael Gregory as Rick Osgood. Rich Little did voiceover narration (uncredited); and "The Face."

15. "Return of Mickey Spillane's Mike Hammer" (1986)

Stacy Keach poses with other cast members of the "Return of Mickey Spillane's Mike Hammer" telefilm (1986): (left to right) Emily Chance, Keach, Lauren Hutton, Bruce Boxleitner.

Despite CBS' announced support of Stacy Keach, producer Jay Bernstein was asked to make what was essentially yet another pilot. This unusual procedure was not to try out an already known property, but to have a new Keach "Hammer" project to gauge audience response to the post-scandal Keach-as-Hammer. If the ratings were good enough, all would be forgiven, and "Mike Hammer" back on the air.

"The Return of Mickey Spillane's Mike Hammer" aired on April 18, 1986, five months before the start of the fall TV season. The telefilm is a child kidnapping caper that took Mike from New York to Los Angeles and back again. As usual with a Hammer TV movie, the production values were higher than a typical episode. The Hollywood setting also provided a context to present several cameo stars.

TV Guide critic Judith Crist hailed Keach's return in a TV movie deemed "stylish, sharp-tongued and sophisticated with a sensational helicopter sequence."

The action begins with a high angle shot of New York City finally zeroing in on a mime show near Central Park. A very sinister looking mime abducts Sasha Davidson, a six- year-old blonde girl, and we see an Ugly Man callously shoot the girl's father as he tries to stop the getaway van from leaving.

Mike is awakened at his apartment by a film crew. He goes down to the street, notices this same mime behaving oddly, and as the mime steals another little blonde girl, he gives chase. He shoots the mime in the leg, Ugly Man shoots several times at Mike, and the girl is protected. She turns out to be Megan (Emily Rose Chance), the daughter of film star Joanna Lake (Lauren Hutton).

DA Barrington arrives to harass Mike for actually stopping a crime. "Hammer, do you realize that every time there's a violent crime in the city, you're in the middle?" Mike replies, "I love my work." Mike gives Joanna a book of matches from the Lite N Easy bar, writes his office number in it and goes on his way. Joanna comes to the bar later to try to persuade Mike to return to Los Angeles with her to protect Megan. He turns her down, but as they leave the Ugly Man lets fly a hail of bullets.

A car is pulled out of the river the next morning. The mime is dead in the trunk. His back is covered with a distinctive dragon tattoo.

This attack convinces Mike to make the trip west and amusing moments follow as Velda prepares him an LA kit, including sun glasses and a loud Hawaiian shirt. Mike thinks that there's a pattern to these strange abductions and for input visits Simon Chapel, whose own daughter was abducted almost twenty years before.

In LA, Mike begins to complain about the peace and quiet until he takes Megan to her private school where she is abducted by the same group, this time disguised as nuns. One nun asks, "Where are you from Mr. Hammer?" "New York," he replies. The nun coyly replies, "I will pray for you." When a second nun says the same thing just moments later, he becomes suspicious. It's too late, however, because Ugly Man is trying to garrote him with a steel wire. Mike escapes but the kidnappers get Megan. As Mike fights with them, he notices another dragon tattoo, this one with a lily.

Soon a video tape arrives showing a frightened Megan. She holds up a little sign: "$500,000 used $100 Bills Get it Now." Joanna tells Hammer about Nick Anton (Stephen Macht), her former husband and Megan's father. He's a compulsive gambler who complicates her life.

FBI agent Frank Walker (TV icon Vince Edwards of "Ben Casey") notes that the tattoos have some connection with a special long-range patrol unit in Vietnam that went MIA. Pat Chambers is following up via telephone on this connection as well.

A package comes to Joanna's house with two New Orleans bus tickets for Mike and Nick. They are to take the money on this bus and wait for instructions. The bus driver has received instructions to drop them off in the desert at an intersection called East Lizard. A mailman in a Jeep stops and gives Mike a package with a compass and instructions to "Walk South."

Mike and Nick head in that direction until they reach the edge of high ledge. At that point, Ugly Man pops up in a helicopter; inside is Megan. The helicopter lands away from them and the girl gets out; it then comes over to Mike and he attaches the satchel of money. Nick goes over to check on his daughter and discovers that it's Sasha, not Megan. He starts running for the helicopter yelling, "You cheated me." The Ugly Man shoots Nick.

Mike tries to get the money but ends up in the air when the helicopter takes off. Ugly Man brings him back and drops him. Mike wonders why he didn't kill him. The FBI locates the helicopter. The now dead pilot was the nun in tennis shoes that Mike saw at Megan's school.

The FBI has located a member of the LRP unit and Mike visits him at the graves of some of his compatriots. The guy is extremely strung out, but shows him his tattoo of a dragon with a strawberry in his mouth. He also drops the nugget that the Ugly Man was DAK (sergeant in the unit, David Anson Kohler).

Before he died, Nick had told Mike that his bookie was a guy named Herschel Dean, who he owed over $100,000. Mike goes to Nick's little place overlooking a small backwater area. It's not very prosperous. He picks the lock and, as he is looking around, hears a key in the lock: it's Joanna. He thinks this is quite interesting and she declares she now wants him off the case. Joanna tells him that Nick was always coming around for money, and when she gave it to him, he would disappear until the next time he needed more.

Back in New York, Barrington—in a rare scene showing his human side—tells Pat and Mike that the tattoos all form one big scene, and that's the key to the kidnappings. Joanna has also returned to New York, to apologize to Mike for firing him. Mike never quits just because a client fires him, of course. They reconcile and share a brief kiss before Mike has to go to Sai Lahn's apartment. She was the wife of one of the LRPs. Mike finds Sai Lahn dead on the floor. Her body is also completely covered in tattoos. A lily and a temple or a church seems to control the imagery of the tattoos.

DAK has arranged another drop of the ransom money, but tricks them by placing a trash can over an open man hole. By now Mike has figured out that the real clue is not a temple or a church, but a man named Chapel. Mike learns from him that the unit had set up an orphanage to save the children of the war. Sai Lahn was Chapel's wife. Lily was the name of their dead daughter. In their confused logic, they believed that the baby broker business they were in helped the children.

Chapel was really the mysterious Captain Baker that the mellow guy at the gravesite had told him about. Mike and Chapel go to the house where all the abducted children are kept. DAK is hiding in the house with Megan as a shield. Chapel pretends he's still in control of the unit, and orders the sergeant to release the girl. He does, but he also shoots Chapel.

Mike chases DAK outside, into what resembles of a Vietnamese jungle. DAK has mined the entire area around the house and traps Mike. He takes a couple of steps backward, close to one of the trips for a mine. Mike shoots the trip and blows DAK up. All Mike finds are his dog tags. He picks them up and says, "David Anson Kohler. Sergeant. RA2931685. Dismissed." He then throws the dog tags into the hole created by the blast.

Megan is reunited with her mother and Mike muses that there never could be anything to the relationship ("too much space between them"). He contents himself with going to see the movie she was filming in front of his apartment: "Joanna Lake in 'Street Cop.'"

A solid, densely plotted thriller, "The Return of Mickey Spillane's Mike Hammer" is particularly satisfying in its depiction of Hammer in a relationship with a woman who is not a young bimbo. Lauren Hutton and Stacy Keach have a chemistry aided by neither being a kid.

If the film is in any way misjudged, it's in re-introducing Hammer in a largely non–Manhattan-based story. His TV family of Bloom and Stroud are largely absent—even Barrington is mostly sidelined.

Director Ray Danton, a former movie star himself ("The Rise and Fall of Legs Diamond"), was a mainstay of TV action shows of the era. In the early street scene next to Mike's apartment, his name can be read on the clapboard for the scene.

"Return of Mickey Spillane's Mike Hammer" (1986)

Columbia Pictures Television and Jay Bernstein Productions •
Running time: 94 minutes • Release date: April 18, 1986

WRITERS: Larry Brody, Janis Hendler and James M. Miller; DIRECTOR: Ray Danton; PRODUCERS: Gray Frederickson and Jeffrey Morton; CINEMATOGRAPHER: Héctor R. Figueroa; MUSIC: Earle Hagen. CAST: Stacy Keach (Mike Hammer); Emily Rose Chance (Megan); Don Stroud (Capt. Pat Chambers); Lindsay Bloom (Velda); Kent Williams (Barrington); Lauren Hutton (Joanna Lake); John Karlen (Chapel); Michael Preston (Dak); Leo Penn (Leo); Mickey Fooney (Jack Bergan); Stephen Macht (Nick Anton); Vince Edwards (FBI Agent Frank Walker); Bruce Boxleitner (himself); Dabney Coleman (himself); Dionne Warwick (herself); Tom Everett (Orville Tate); Lee Renton (Jenny); Kieu Chinh (Sai Luhn); David Chow (Prof. Lai); Peter Iacangelo (Norwood Fitz); Hunter von Leer (Sneakers Man); Dawn Mangrum (Dancer); Don Lewis (Mime); Andre Rosey Brown (Big Black Man); Frank Romano (Postman); Patrice Chanel (Nichols); Joseph DiSante (Lieutenant); Julie Hayek (Ticket Cashier); Malgosia Tomassi (Nun); Corinne Wahl (Sandra); Otto Felix (Agent Adler); Christina Jensen (Carla Arnell); Kathy Chaffin (Wanda); Tony Mann (Bus Drive #2); Laurie Cantwell (Sgt. Hooper); Laura Dankel (Sasha Davidson); Gregory Chase (George); Donna Snow (Paula); Ron Foster (Forensic Man); Bobby Babb (Bruiser); Gianni Russo (Card Player); Laurence Grant as Larry Grant; "The Face"

16. "The New Mike Hammer" (1986–87) CBS-TV

Stacy Keach as Mike Hammer and Lindsay Bloom as Velda. Bloom's Velda is voluptuous, desirable and yet somehow wholesome, providing the randy P.I. with a sisterly secretary/partner. If not as faithful to Spillane as the Roberts or Landon, Bloom is the most identifiable actress in this key role due to her long run on the series (and her natural charm).

Together, "Mike Hammer" and "The New Mike Hammer" comprise forty-six episodes, roughly divided into two partial and one complete season: "Mike Hammer" twenty-four, "The New Mike Hammer" twenty-two. Despite this relative paucity of episodes, and in part because of the four telefilms and the one-season late '90s syndicated series, Keach is one of the iconic television detectives of the '80s, and remains the actor most associated with Spillane's private eye.

Had the initial run of "Mike Hammer" gone uninterrupted, the series might well have enjoyed a lengthy run, like "Mannix" or "Cannon." That loss of momentum, and a poor time slot (up against Top 20 hit "The Golden Girls"), damaged Hammer irreparably.

As the Keach version continued, aspects of the character unrelated to the Spillane original emerged: Hammer a trout fisherman, can play the piano (courtesy of Keach), and his favorite song is "My Favorite Things" by John Coltrane. The combination to his office safe is 36-24-36, but he has to have Velda remind him. He has many friends and associates that he usually meets at the Lite N Easy Bar: comedy snitch Ozzie the Answer (Danny Goldman), Jenny the barmaid (Lee Benton—replacing Lee Meredith as Marty), Richie (Eddie Barth), Moochie (Ben Powers) and Vickie Chambers (Linda Leilani Brown), though earlier Pat's wife was "Linda." Secondary police contact Pat Hennessey is portrayed by Eddie Egan, the real-life cop who was the basis of the Hammer-like Eddie "Popeye" Doyle in the classic crime film, "The French Connection." Many guest stars are either former beauty queens or sports figures, including Simone Griffeth (Miss Virginia 1975), Mary-Marget Hawes (Miss Florida 1975), and Lynn Holly-Johnson (Olympic ice skater).

"The New Mike Hammer" has, appropriately, new opening credits that show Mike looking out through the blinds of his office window: "Mike Hammer Private Investigator." The shadow figures of the former opening do not appear and Velda does not receive a kiss, her role ever more sisterly now. The pizza-in-the-mouth clip remains, however, and "Harlem Nocturne" seems more mellow and melancholy. Mickey Spillane's name is displayed in huge block letters, more prominently, his Miller Lite fame ever-growing.

When "The New Mike Hammer" debuted in an 8:00 P.M. time slot—its earliest airing—violent deaths remain but the sexy edge dulled. According to a Bernstein press release, "There will be no more portrayals of women as bimbos." This promise is not really kept, but the producer hoped to "attract a larger feminine (sic) audience" and strove for "sexual equality." A *TV Guide* article reporting this shift offered an example: in a role written for John Huston, was Nina Foch, who noted: "They didn't change a thing in the script—except, of course, 'he' to 'she' and the name Mildred instead of Willis." The *TV Guide* writer concluded archly, "Man, oh man things really have changed on 'Hammer'!"

The first two seasons had customarily used three or more "Hammerettes," gorgeous young women who by their comments, actions or attire made it immediately known that the Hammer character was attractive to them and that they were available. Revealing outfits were worn and ample cleavage was shown. Season Three, while not entirely sexless, dropped for the most part such scenes. It's noticeable from the beginning of the credits: all the women shown have on more clothes, including Velda who previously was shown in lingerie, but in this version appears in a business suit with a high collar. Even the barmaids at the Lite N Easy don't show cleavage.

Ever the promoter, producer Bernstein started using credited and unbilled big-name guest stars. Most series of the era paid guest stars $2,500 an episode. "The New Mike Hammer" made news offering certain stars $35,000. This attracted such '80s TV royalty as Emma Samms ("The Colbys"), Heather Thomas ("Fall Guy"), and Mary Frann ("Newhart"). Frann did an effective comic turn as a female Crocodile Dundee PI, while Burt Reynolds and Dom De Luise showed up in an empty bus in the middle of a hot shootout that ended with Hammer ramming a bad guy between two giant rigs.

"Deirdre," the first new episode, was surprisingly subdued in tone. The music at the Lite N Easy Bar is more muted as Pat and Mike are talking quietly. Mike is not flirting with barmaid Jenny. He is searching for the missing Deirdre Corrigan, an investigation leading him to Reverend Blessing, the pastor of the Church of the Penitential Reward, a cult. The photography has a *noir* tinge, Velda does not appear, and the tone is strictly low-key with no sexual byplay and no humor. An odd choice for a return episode.

The second episode, "Dead Pigeon," is business as usual, with Mike accused of killing narcotics cop Eddie Forbes who lured away Mike's girlfriend Sheila. Mike has a fistfight with Forbes but doesn't kill him. After a hearing, Hammer is held over for trial. The ending is a lift of the famous "I, the Jury" denouement, with another lovely blonde standing in for Charlotte Manning.

In "Golden Lady" Mike is investigating the death of dockworker Sam Baylor for his grieving widow Ruth. The case involves the union management stealing money from their pension money. In "Mistress for the Prosecution," DA Barrington finally gets featured in an episode. The defendant in one of the cases sets Barrington up at a lawyer's party by taking pictures of him with a transvestite.

But some of the energy and creativity is on the wane in this new round of Hammer episodes. "Harlem Nocturne" is a shameless black-cast reworking of Raymond Chandler's "Farewell, My Lovely," which had relatively recently (1975) been a hit feature film with Robert Mitchum. Was Hollywood's penchant for theft ingrained enough to risk the ire of many PI genre buffs in the "Hammer" audience? Apparently so—the McGavin series had similarly plundered that famous novel in "A Detective Tail."

"Murder in the Cards" begins with an old adage: "A private detective who's dead tired better be careful. He could wind up just plain dead." Mike is telling the story of his recent adventures to current girlfriend Hilary (Penelope Jane Reed). The son of one of Mike's old friends has been framed for a robbery and Mike to helping him out.

"Requiem for Billy" is another friend-in-need episode. This time young Billy Wayne, who Mike helped out years ago, needs the detective's aid. "Little Miss Murder" is a missing daddy case. Sixteen-year-old Kim Farris comes to New York to get Mike to find her father Harry. "Kill John Doe" is a an espionage yarn. John Doe (Tony Dow, "Leave It to Beaver") wanders into Mike's office for help.

"Elegy for a Tramp" is the story of a fallen angel named Cassie Conroy (Claudia Christian), another Hammer ex-girlfriend whose Hollywood success wound up killing her. It's a stormy, rainy episode, during which Mike muses: "The storms make the city smell as good as it ever gets."

"Body Shot" begins with Mike saying "the city is only as warm as the friends you have." It's a boxing story about former champ Sonny Timmons. "Who Killed Sister Lorna" has Karen Valentine playing a spunky nun and Mike revealing that he spent the night with a woman who shall remain nameless ("only because I couldn't remember her name"). This sexist remark is courtesy of writer Judy Burns.

Another rare female-scripted episode (from Nancy Ann Miller), "Deadly Collection," explores the nefarious and backbiting fashion world. "Green Blizzard" is about a flood of counterfeit money—Mike hits a twelve horse $2 parlay bet and collects $610, but only the $10 bill is good.

Nancy Ann Miller is back as co-writer of "The Last Laugh," set in the world of comedy clubs, specifically The Comedy & Magician Club East. Comic Shelley Berman makes a special guest appearance. The episodes written by the female writers were among the raunchier ones this season.

In "Lady Killer," real-life shrink Dr. Joyce Brothers hosts a show called "Woman's World," on which Claire (Barbara Carrera), the editor of "Darling" magazine is a guest. The resonance here is that Carrera previously played a psychoanalyst herself as Charlotte in the "I, the Jury" remake. Both big-screen Charlottes—Carrera and Peggie Castle—made appearances on small-screen "Hammer" series.

Pauline's body is discovered the next morning. Mike then goes to see an expert—Dr. Joyce Brothers (her second "Hammer" appearance). What kind of man would do this, Mike asks? "A sociopath," she replies. This response also resonates, as a number of Spillane's early critics called Mike Hammer a sociopath.

In "Mike Gets Married," the detective gets a call from the INS (Immigration and Naturalization Service) saying they are holding a woman who claims to be Mrs. Mike Hammer (Barbara Stock). She's from French Polynesia—not Mike's wife, of course, but he goes through a sham marriage to keep her in the country until he figures out what's going on.

"A Blinding Fear" concerns a kidnapped dog named Max, and is the only Keach-directed episode. Hammer wants nothing to do with a kidnapped dog case until he meets Max's owner, Jennifer, the blind daughter of millionaire A. Walter Decker (Ken Kercheval). Seems Mike had a dog when he was a kid—"Ike." The inevitable "Ike and Mike" jokes roll out.

"Green Lipstick" might have been better titled "Mike's Other Daughter," concentrating on nefarious dealings in the music business, specifically stolen song rights and drug overdoses. But the real story is about another daughter Mike never knew of, this one named Jamie Jynx (Emma Samms). The recycling of the daughter idea, like the "Farewell, My Lovely" rip-off episode, reflects an incipient staleness.

The last CBS episode, "A Face in the Night," opens at midnight in Mike's office as he waits on a client. He's dozed off and is dreaming of the lovely Face. Australian PI Harriet "Harry" Quayle (Frann) comes around, trying to track down the elusive best-selling novelist, Frederick Flynn, author of popular thrillers about Nick Steele, a hard-boiled PI. She has a photo of "The Face" (Donna Denton, finally credited), who works for Flynn.

A message on Flynn's answering machine leads Mike to the Chinese Flower Mart. There he sees the Face pass an envelope to a man. He stops her. Mike says, "Hold it right there, sweetheart. You're not going to disappear on me this time." The Face replies, "I was wondering what you'd say if you had the chance." Her name is Laura.

A fire fight breaks out, and he and Laura flee to Frederick Flynn's place. Laura turns down a drink but kisses him instead. She works for Flynn and has been following Mike, doing research on the character Nick Steele, based on Hammer. That's why she's been turning up on the fringes of all his cases—"research." Hammer replies, "You mean like Jane Goodall and the chimpanzees?"

Mike is kidnapped and tortured by some seriously bad dudes, flashing back unpleasantly to Viet Nam. Mike has been grabbed to get info about Dick Bartlett, Flynn's editor and blackmailer. But Bartlett is shot in the back as Australian PI Harry/Harriet is talking to him.

Harry had been hired by the mysterious Mr. Milo, a man with a cane (producer Jay Bernstein). Laura is waiting at Mike's apartment when Harry goes there. Harry has the last Flynn manuscript, which contains a fictionalized version of a real murder that took place in Greece. Flynn knows a witness. Laura offers herself up in trade for Mike.

Harry and Pat suggest a sting, using Pat to play Flynn. This provides the show that supposedly abandoned T & A with an opportunity to show off the Face's figure as they put a wire on her.

Mike celebrates the successful conclusion of the case by spending the night with the Face. In the morning, she admits she's Frederick Flynn, but Mike already knew that. As he pours some champagne, Laura slips out into a waiting limo.

Mike muses, "I would remember the sweetness of this moment. And the pain." But Laura had said they'd meet again, and Mike believes her.

If the final season of "Hammer" on CBS did not live up to either its commercial or creative potential, Keach emerged unscathed. His ability to shift gears between affability and rage, his confidence and swagger and sheer macho charm, made him *the* Mike Hammer of several generations. The show Keach appeared in was good, solid entertainment, but the frustration for the Spillane fan is in knowing how better Keach was than his material.

Is it fair to ask which television version of Mike Hammer is better—the McGavin '50s one, or the Keach '80s take? It's a tough call. Both McGavin and Keach are fine Hammers. The Keach series has better production values, and the relationship with Pat is more deeply explored, and Velda—whether Roberts or Bloom—is a part of the mix, whereas she was MIA in McGavin's series.

Next to the Keach iteration, McGavin's looks shabby, even dingy, but that's part of why it may edge out the various Bernstein-produced series. Even a film as weak as "My Gun Is Quick" benefits from having been produced in Spillane's big era—the fifties. Darren McGavin is walking around in his porkpie hat, flinging spent cigarettes into Manhattan streets, chasing bad guys and willing babes with equal abandon, and all in black-and-white, with scripts based on real pulp stories going back as far as *Black Mask*. It all seems right somehow.

Stacy Keach must play a man out of time, a fifties PI who tumbled off a time machine into the '80s. This explains and justifies the campy side of the Bernstein-produced show. Keach seems to relish playing an anachronistic Hammer, alternately deft and bold in an approach that makes something positive out of political incorrectness, letting the show do the winking while he stays true to Spillane's character.

Call it a draw, or pick your own favorite. Either way, in the world of series television, Mike Hammer was a lucky guy to be represented by Darren McGavin and Stacy Keach.

"The New Mike Hammer" (1986–87) CBS-TV

"The New Mike Hammer" was a CBS-TV series airing 1986–87, produced by Jay Bernstein Productions in Los Angeles, California. Note: Mickey Spillane's name was not used in title for this iteration of the series. His credit appears just before the writers in each episode.

Unless noted the series regular appeared in each episode: Stacy Keach as Mike Hammer; Lindsay Bloom as Velda; Don Stroud as Captain Pat Chambers.

Season 1 (3) (September 1986–May 1987)

EPISODE #1 (25) (SEPTEMBER 27, 1986) "DEIRDRE"

DIRECTED BY: Ray Danton. WRITTEN BY: Herman Miller. (The show aired on CBS-TV Saturday at 9:00 P.M.)

At her sister Anne Marie's request, Mike is searching for the missing Deirdre Corrigan. His investigation leads him to Reverend Blessing, the pastor of the cult Church of the Penitential Reward.

CAST: Leslie Wing as Anne Marie Corrigan; John S. Ragin as Reverend Blessing; Peter Iacangelo as Howard Rosenwald; Michael DeLano as Augie; Lee Benton as Jenny; Steve "Stevo" Danton listed as a second assistant director. Neither Velda nor "The Face" make an appearance.

EPISODE #2 (26) (OCTOBER 4, 1986) "DEAD PIGEON"

DIRECTED BY: Bruce Kessler. WRITTEN BY: Fred Freiberger.

Mike is accused of killing narcotics cop Eddie Forbes, who lured away Mike's one-time girl friend Sheila.

CAST: Randi Brooks as Sheila; Robin Curtis as Officer Peggy Ryan; Elaine Wilkes as Nancy Holden; Christopher Stone as Lloyd Carmody; and "The Face." Velda is seen working out on an exercise bike because she has a new boyfriend.

EPISODE #3 (27) (OCTOBER 11, 1986) "GOLDEN LADY"

DIRECTED BY: Ray Danton. WRITTEN BY: Duke Sandefur.

Mike investigates the death of dockworker Sam Baylor for his grieving widow Ruth. It involves the theft of $2,200 from their pension fund. Hammer makes everything more than right; he returns the money at face value in rare coins.

CAST: Shelley Smith as Kate Wilkins; Nina Foch as Mildred Hofsteder; Paul Kent as Victor Panasetti; Gary Wood as Vernon.

EPISODE #4 (28) (OCTOBER 18, 1986) "MIKE'S BABY"

DIRECTED BY: Bruce Kessler. WRITTEN BY: B. W. Sandefur.

Mike finds a baby in a dumpster. He believes that the mother was murdered with poisoned drugs.

CAST: Robyn Douglass as Ellen Wasnaski; Cornel Wilde as George Burnett; Michael David Simms as Atamien; Kimberly Beck as Lisa Burnett; Anjanette Comer as Toni Caudell.

EPISODE #5 (29) (NOVEMBER 5, 1986) "TO KILL A FRIEND"

DIRECTED BY: Don Weis. WRITTEN BY: B. W. Sandefur. (The show moved to new day and time: Wednesday at 8:00 P.M.)

Hammer and one of his friends are wounded in a jewelry robbery.

CAST: Meg Wittner as Audrey Rothmore; Charles Bouvier as Merchason; Anna Nicholas as Lizetta; John Calkins as Conrad Baxter; Sydney Lassick as Philly; Gail Rae Carlson as Linda.

EPISODE #6 (30) (NOVEMBER 12, 1986) "MISTRESS FOR THE PROSECUTION"

DIRECTED BY: Bruce Kessler. WRITTEN BY: Arthur Ginsburg.

The defendant in one of Lawrence Barrington's case set him up at a lawyer's party by drugging him and taking pictures of him and a transvestite named Jerry Jayson. Barrington reluctantly hires Hammer to help him get the pictures back. Mike keeps calling this case "Larry Does Dallas."

CAST: Kent Williams as Barrington; Molly Fontaine as Jerry Jayson/Stephanie Stewart; Lisa Fuller as Ondine Walker (girl found dead in Barrington's bed); Lauren Koslow as Val Kearney; Radames Pera as Bernard Rocklin; Brett Hadley as Stanford Cole; Michael Ennis as Carey.

EPISODE #7 (31) (NOVEMBER 26, 1986) "HARLEM NOCTURNE"

DIRECTED BY: Ray Danton. TELEPLAY BY: Howard Berk. STORY BY: Ray Danton and Ed Scharlach

A huge black guy named Malachi Crown ("call me Bubba") walks into Mike's office and want him to find his girlfriend, Bess Irvine. She's been missing for eight years while he was in the federal pen in Atlanta.

CAST: Samm-Art Williams as Malachi Crown (cf. Moose Malloy in Raymond Chandler's *Farewell, My Lovely*); George Benson as Sweet Billy Marvel; Isabel Sanford as Hot Mama Vibes; Lynn Whitfield as Delia Marvel; Jeannie Marie Austin as the lady in red; Ernie Hudson as Digger Love (aka John Boy Pettijohn).

EPISODE #8 (32) (DECEMBER 3, 1986) "MURDER IN THE CARDS"

DIRECTED BY: Don Weis. WRITTEN BY: S. S. Schweitzer and Jay Bernstein

The son of one of Mike's old friends has been framed for a robbery. Mike's investigation leads him to a lake retreat where Mike and three armored car robbers are meeting. But none know each other because they always wore masks. They were to identify themselves by one half of a torn ace from a common deck of cards.

CAST: Jack Carter as Ruark; Tony Young as Gross; Gary Watkins as Norton; Kitty Holcomb as Donna; E. Danny Murphy as Mitchell; Brett Halsey as Forrest; Penelope Jane Reed as Hilary.

EPISODE #9 (33) (DECEMBER 10, 1986) "REQUIEM FOR BILLY"

DIRECTED BY: Sigmund Neufeld, Jr. WRITTEN BY: Herman Miller.

Billy Wayne, a kid that Hammer helped out in a police jam years ago becomes unknowingly involved in a mob money swap and is killed.

CAST: John C. Cooke as Billy Wayne; Lyle Waggoner as Leo Raffle; Martha Smith as Mindy; Byron Webster as Dutch Graber; Barbara Bosson as Emily.

EPISODE #10 (34) (JANUARY 7, 1987) "LITTLE MISS MURDER"

DIRECTED BY: John Herzfeld. WRITTEN BY: Ed Scharlach. STORY BY: Ed Scharlach and Jay Bernstein

This episode is a missing daddy case. Sixteen-year-old Kim Farris comes to New York to get Mike to find her father Harry. Mike shares some tender moments with Kim: "I never raised a daughter. But I did have one. I lost her."

CAST: Jeff Conaway as Harry Farris; Fran O'Neil as Fran Lasker; Danny Goldman as Ozzie; Madison Mason as Andrew Lasker; Edward Edwards as Stu Norris; Barney McFadden as Kruger.

EPISODE #11 (35) (JANUARY 21, 1987) "KILL JOHN DOE"

DIRECTED BY: Marc Daniels. WRITTEN BY: Howard Berk.

This episode is a spy adventure turning on the identity of Mr. X (John Doe) and the mysterious people who are following him.

CAST: Tony Dow as John Doe/Robert Miller; Bo Hopkins as Ted Sharpe of the Federal Security Agency; Malgosia Keach as Natasha; Jaclyn Zeman as Lisa Miller; Eddie Barth as Monroe.

EPISODE #12 (36) (JANUARY 28, 1987) "ELEGY FOR A TRAMP"

DIRECTED BY: John C. Andersen. WRITTEN BY: B. W. Sandefur.

A fallen angel named Cassie Conroy, another of Mike's ex-girlfriends, becomes disenchanted with stardom only to be thrown off the 24th floor of her apartment building. (This is the "Give me a hand" episode that seemed to enrage several critics. Mike applauds while the killer hangs onto a ledge, but eventually falls to his death because Mike won't help him.)

CAST: Robert Evan Collins as Nathan Bacchus; Bernie Kopell as Tony Beltzer; Theodore Bikel as Gerringer; Claudia Christian as Cassie Conroy; Foster Brooks as Manny.

EPISODE #13 (37) (FEBRUARY 4, 1987) "BODY SHOT"

DIRECTED BY: David Jackson. WRITTEN BY: Samm-Art Williams. STORY BY: Ray Danton & Samm-Art Williams.

Susan Timmons fears that her boxer brother Sonny is ill and that his next fight will kill him. She asks Mike for help. This episode reveals that Mike got his start in boxing with the Golden Gloves.

CAST: Louise Mandrell as Darlene Baxter; Larry Wilcox as Sonny Timmons; Genie Francis as Susan Timmons; Theodore Wilson as Booker; William Frankfather as Langston.

EPISODE #14 (38) (FEBRUARY 11, 1987) "WHO KILLED SISTER LORNA"

DIRECTED BY: Frank Beascoechea. WRITTEN BY: Judy Burns.

Sister Amelia comes to Mike's help in finding the missing Sister Lorna.

CAST: Karen Valentine as Sister Amelia; Alan Stock as Donnie Novak; Barbara Billingsly ("Leave It to Beaver") as Sister Superior Paula; Jared Martin as Ray Novak; Cathryn Damon as Aunt Dorothy Putnam; Maria Richwine as Sister Lorna.

EPISODE #15 (39) (FEBRUARY 25, 1987) "DEADLY COLLECTION"

DIRECTED BY: David Hemmings. WRITTEN BY: Nancy Ann Miller. STORY BY: James Schmerer.

Mike reluctantly teams up with rookie PI Scott Warren to find an extortionist who killed one of their mutual friends. The young PI makes fun of Mike's lack of technological skills.

CAST: Mickey Dolenz ("Monkees") as Scott Warren; Gloria Loring as Marian Collins; Edward Albert as Oliver Alden; Randy Murzynski as Randy; Robert Viharo as Kalber; Dawn Mangrum as Candace.

EPISODE #16 (40) (MARCH 4, 1987) "GREEN BLIZZARD"

DIRECTED BY: Thomas J. Wright. WRITTEN BY: Don Balluck.

Mike's bookie unknowingly pays him off with counterfeit money. Mike's search for the culprit leads him to a young graphics designer with a gambling problem.

CAST: Caryn Richman ("The New Gidget") as Stephanie Caldwell; Peter Scolari ("Newhart") as Rudy Shales; Peter Tomarken as Peter; Claude Akins ("The Misadventures of Sheriff Lobo")as Charlie Duryea, Mike's bookie; Stuart Pankin as Jenkins; Christopher Hewett ("Mr. Belvedere") as Wembley; Elizabeth Gorcy as Lisa Gant (Velda's temporary replacement).

EPISODE #17 (41) (MARCH 18, 1987) "THE LAST LAUGH"

DIRECTED BY: David Jackson. WRITTEN BY: Arthur Ginsburg.

Mike's search for the killer of a promising young comedienne leads him to Los Angeles and a quite remarkable walk on the beach at Malibu (rolled up long pants and rolled up long sleeve shirt, all done to "Surfing Safari"). The Face shows up on roller blades at Venice.

CAST: Arleen Sorkin as Tracy; Shelley Berman as Harry Saks; Christopher Norris as Cynthia; Pagrick Dollaghan as Safire; and Robert Walden as Gary Kurtz.

EPISODE #18 (42) (MARCH 25, 1987) "LADY KILLER"

DIRECTED BY: Paul Lynch. WRITTEN BY: Nancy Ann Miller and Edward Di Lorenzo. STORY BY: Edward Di Lorenzo. (Interlude: the April 11, 1987, edition of *TV Guide* ran a rerun of "Mike Gets Married" and announced that "The New Mike Hammer" would now be seen on Saturday at 8:00 P.M.)

Hammer protects a magazine editor Claire Morgan from a slasher.

CAST: Barbara Carrera as Claire Morgan; Joan Severance as Pauline Turner; Dr. Joyce Brothers as Herself; Jenilee Harrison as Maggie Williams; Charles Siebert as Charles; Dennis Cole as Kevin Landers.

EPISODE #19 (43) (APRIL 15, 1987) "MIKE GETS MARRIED"

DIRECTED BY: Paul Braverman. WRITTEN BY: Paul Bentley Diamond.

Mike gets a call from INS saying they are holding a woman who claims to be Mrs. Mike Hammer. She's not his wife, of course, but Mike goes through a sham marriage to keep her in the country until he figures out what's going on. The Face observes the ceremony performed by DA Barrington.

CAST: Barbara Stock as Marie; Greg Evigan as Paul Linnett; Roxie Roker as Esther; Tim Choate as Spooner.

EPISODE #20 (44) (APRIL 29, 1987) "A BLINDING FEAR"

DIRECTED BY: Stacy Keach. WRITTEN BY: Stephen Lord. STORY BY: Jay Bernstein.

Mike doesn't want anything to do with a kidnapped dog case until he meets the dog's owner, Jennifer, the young blind daughter of millionaire A. Walter Decker. At the braille institute The Face is in the audience. But soon the girl herself is kidnapped by a mysterious woman.

CAST: Ken Kercheval as A. Walter Decker; Michael Ansara as Sandor Kraken; Heather Thomas ("Fall Guy") as Andre; Ian Abercrombie as Jennifer; Persis Khambatta as the mysterious woman; Duke Stroud (Don Stroud's son) as one of Kraken's men.

EPISODE #21 (45) (MAY 6, 1987) "GREEN LIPSTICK"

DIRECTED BY: Ted Lange. WRITTEN BY: Gregory S. Dinallo.

Exploring nefarious dealings in the music business, Mike meets his daughter Jamie Jynx, the result of his romance with mom, Marcy Markham. She's a singer like her mom; her band is "Snowblind.")

CAST: Emma Samms as Jamie Jynx; Vanity as Holly.

EPISODE #22 (46) (MAY 13, 1987) "A FACE IN THE NIGHT"

DIRECTED BY: Jay Bernstein. WRITTEN BY: E. Nick Alexander.

Aussie PI Harry Quayle is in New York City trying to locate best-selling novelist Frederick Flynn, who writes thrillers about Nick Steele, a hard-boiled PI. Harry shows him a picture of Mike and The Face who we learn works for Frederick Flynn. (This episode may also be known as "Pulses in a Ripple Tank," which might have been a working title stressing a key scene.)

CAST: Mary Frann ("Newhart") as Harriet ("Harry") Quayle; Donna Denton as The Face (right in the ad); Jay Bernstein as the mysterious Mr. Milo who sports a deadly cane.

17. "Mickey Spillane's Mike Hammer: 'Murder Takes All'" (1989)

Keach as Hammer with Don Stroud as Pat Chambers. Stroud made a fine Chambers, believable both as friend and cop, and is the actor most identified with the role.

The last regular season episode of "The New Mike Hammer" was broadcast in the summer of 1987. In September, 1987, the series aired in rerun on Saturday nights on the USA Network. Its success in that time slot led to one last Stacy Keach appearance as Mike Hammer on CBS-TV. Possibly producer Bernstein viewed this as yet another backdoor pilot for Hammer, but more likely he hoped to initiate an occasional Made-for-TV movie, in the way a number of departed series ("Murder She Wrote," "Gunsmoke," "Rockford Files") have enjoyed a telefilm afterlife.

"Murder Takes All"—working title: "Madonna in Red"—aired May 21, 1989.

A hood named Johnny Roman wants Mike to go to Las Vegas to get some dirt on his girlfriend in a palimony suit. Mike doesn't want to go, is abducted and drugged, waking up in a small prop plane over the desert near Vegas. He's told to hold onto the rip cord and pushed out of the plane. Typical of the telefilm's spoofy approach, Hammer lands in the middle of the street near the Horseshoe Casino on the Vegas strip.

Considering Las Vegas the "decadent land of Oz," Hammer walks down to the Hilton where Johnny Roman's name is on the marquee for his "Heart-A-Thon." Mike he notices he's got a key to Room 1639. But it's soon obvious he's been shanghaied to take the blame for Roman's sudden on-stage death. He's detained by head of hotel security Leora van Treas (Michelle Phillips—appearing in the first and the last telefilm).

Helen Durant (Lynda Carter, "Wonder Woman") bails Mike out; she's looking for Roman's diary. Johnny got her pregnant when she was a young chorus girl. Amy, her daughter, was raised by Helen's rich husband.

Hunting for the diary, Mike chases a bad guy from a chorus girl's dressing room to the catwalks over the casino. In the fight, they fall through to the gambling tables. As Mike looks up The Face smiles down at him. Why is the Face routine being continued after its conclusion in the final episode? And why is actress Donna Denton unbilled when her identity was revealed previously?

Looking for clues, Mike finds Amy Durant and Brad Peters (a pre-stardom Jim Carrey} also looking for clues. Brad keeps saying he's an accountant. Someone named William Bundy is involved. Mike finds a key in the chorus girl's wardrobe. A key to what?

Brad sets up Mike for a solo trip to the desert, then when Mike returns they go to see Bundy. He's dead, of course.

Helen gives Mike a suitcase of money to pay for the return of the diary. The switch will be made at Hoover Dam. Waiting is Leora. Riflemen from the Durant clinic on the catwalks shoot Leora. Mike kills them all but he still doesn't know who set it up. Six people are dead because of the diary. But the real story is that Carl Durant and Johnny Roman were stealing money from the foundation.

Afraid, Helen wants Mike to sleep in her cabin on her boat on Lake Mead. But Mike doesn't go there. In the morning when Carl and Brad arrive looking for Helen, and open her cabin door, the entire boat explodes. Mike jumps overboard and goes to confront the femme fatale responsible.

After dumping all the money into the telethon bin, Mike returns to Manhattan. Back at the Lite N Easy, he picks up a blonde who early in the proceedings had slipped away from him. Mike muses you don't have to go to Las Vegas to gamble. "In my line of work every day you're alive, you beat the odds. One thing for certain, this was my lucky night."

With Ray Danton back directing, "Murder Takes All" makes a disappointing conclusion to Keach's run as Hammer on CBS. He is fine in the role, as usual, but hampered by a confused, even incoherent script that propels the detective like a pinball, bumping from one bumper to another. The idea of a strong hero, and a detecting detective, gets lost. And Lynda Carter makes a pale replacement for Lauren Hutton in the previous, superior Danton-directed telefilm.

As an attempt to launch of series of Hammer telefilms, "Murder Takes All" is misjudged. In an attempt to provide glitz and production values, the Las Vegas setting—from Glitter Gulch to Hoover Dam—displaces Manhattan, that other important character in Mike Hammer's world. Speaking of important characters, Pat and Velda are walk-ons, Barrington doesn't even rate that, and the likes of Moochie and Ozzie the Answer don't have a chance. Yet Bernstein insists on bringing The Face back into play when that gimmick has been resolved and played out.

Nonetheless, seeing Keach as Hammer is always a pleasure. He carries this telefilm on his back, and to the degree that it works as watchable, entertaining TV, the credit is his.

"Mickey Spillane's Mike Hammer: 'Murder Takes All'" (1989)

Jay Bernstein Productions, Columbia Pictures Television and CPT Holdings Inc. • Running time: 92 minutes • Release date: May 21, 1989

WRITERS: Mark Edward Edens and Rudy Day; DIRECTOR: John Nicolella; PRODUCERS: Jay Bernstein, Peter Dunne and Jeffrey Morton; CINEMATOGRAPHER: Frank Beascoechea; MUSIC: Ron Ramin; CAST: Stacy Keach (Mike Hammer); Linda Carter (Helen Durant); Lindsay Bloom (Velda); Don Stroud (Captain Pat Chambers); Jim Carrey (Brad Peters); Stacy Galina (Amy Durant); Lyle Alzado (Reggie Diaz); Royce D. Applegate (Bundy); John Calvin (Carl Durant); Jessie Lawrence Ferguson (John McNiece); Edward Winter (Johnny Roman); Michelle Phillips (Leora Van Treas); Lee Benton (Jennie); James "Gypsy" Haake (Madame); Kelly Andrus (Prostitute #1); Michael Bower (Velda's Nephew); Jennifer Ciesar (Showgirl #1); Gene Freedman (Maintenance Man); Toni Aileen Hart (Wedding Counselor); Rosalia Hayakawa (Maid); Stephanie Lund (Nurse #1); Kelly Jerles (Barbara Leguire); Paul Petersen (Stanfield); Lauren Taylor (Showgirl #2); Joelle Waide (Prostitute #2); Lisa Wiley (Nurse #2); Denise Young (Woman in Lingerie)

18. "'Come Die with Me': A Mickey Spillane's Mike Hammer" Mystery (1994)

Pamela Anderson and Rob Estes make an unlikely Velda and Mike Hammer in the revisionist "Come Die with Me" (1994). Both actors might have fared better in a more traditional take on Spillane, and not this Miami-based travesty.

An awkwardly titled telefilm, "Come Die with Me: A Mickey Spillane's Mike Hammer Mystery," served as a backdoor pilot starring Rob Estes ("Silk Stalkings") and Playmate Pamela Anderson ("Baywatch") as Hammer and Velda. With Manhattan replaced by Miami Beach (though much of the filming took place in San Diego), and with the big band sounds associated with prior Hammer TV projects abandoned in favor of Latin salsa beats, "Come Die with Me" is without question the worst Mike Hammer film ever made. It makes "My Gun Is Quick" look like "Kiss Me Deadly." It makes the weakest episodes of both the McGavin and Keach series seem sublime. No surprise, then, that "Come Die with Me"—airing December 6, 1994, as a CBS Tuesday night movie—was not picked up for development as a new series.

With Jay Bernstein again on the producing end, the telefilm is an attempt to update and reinvent Hammer for a new, younger generation of viewers, with some heavy-handed nods to the Keach version and only the vaguest hints of the project's Spillane roots. From the prior Bernstein series come a new army of so-called Hammerettes, an embarrassing array of bosomy babes who find Estes irresistible—one cleavage-sporting cutie with a stalled car wants a "jump" from him, a door-to-door milkmaid is collecting for "the milk fund," and on and on. These sexist embarrassments cripple the effort to present a hipper, younger Hammer, though Estes is pleasant male eye candy and Pamela Anderson is an appropriately larger-than-life Velda. Further, the Miami Beach setting is, yes, milked for T & A, with bikini girls everywhere, and Velda sporting sometimes ridiculously inappropriate office attire.

"You know a lot of people think it's glamorous being a Miami private eye," Hammer's voiceover tells us, "but actually the work can be pretty darn sleazy. That's fine with me. Sleaze is my meat." American culture has gone from disapproval by federal agents in "Kiss Me Deadly" of Hammer's divorce work to smirky celebration of it in this telefilm—"It's Hammer Time," the CBS ads proclaimed. Not really.

Only Bernstein's holding the rights to the famous Hammer name justifies using that name for a private eye telefilm that so rarely has anything to do with its source material.

A tiny nod to the retro nature of the Keach series is seen in young Estes' proclaimed love for the Rat Pack era, echoed in the title and a weak Sinatra sound-alike rendition of "Come Fly With Me." We also learn that Mike Hammer became a P.I. because of the Frank Sinatra movie, "Tony Rome"—the notion that the most famous tough detective in literature became a P.I. because of a movie based on a middling Spillane imitation is the stuff of madness.

The Sinatra motif gets scant attention, however, while a pointless Kent Williams cameo as a beach tipster called "Jugs"[!] reminds us overtly of how much better the Keach version was.

As for Spillane's version, we do have a Velda—who has an off-camera "deadbeat husband," though she clearly views Mike as her guy—and even Pat Chambers, this time a sergeant of "Robbery/Homicide," and oh yes: a woman. "Old Army buddy" Pat is an apparent lesbian in an uncomfortably over-played performance from the usually much better Darlanne Fluegel. In the meantime, Velda and Hammer constantly bicker in a sexually-loaded, road company "Moonlighting" sort of way.

No hat for this Hammer, of course, much less trenchcoat, not in Miami, though he carries an automatic ("Betsy" again, in another minor nod to Keach), drinks beer, and subjects us to dismal, jokey voiceover that avoids any hint of *noir* poetry ("Ever try to get barf smell out of your car?"). The new Hammer has a catch-phrase, replacing the Keach, "I'll make a note," with "I do this for a living." The private eye is so proud of this witticism that he posts it on Miami Beach buses, with a photo showing him surrounded by Hammerettes. Indeed this Hammer likes the ladies, and they like him, and he's up to the challenge of fisticuffs, on the rare occasion the script gives him the opportunity. Late in the proceedings, he and Pat do a very muted version of the "let the law take care of it, don't go out on a vendetta" song-and-dance.

With nobody to avenge except his own hurt feelings, this Hammer has almost no relationship to Spillane's or even Keach's. The telefilm is primarily a comedy, and an extraordinarily dumb one, with limited action—thirty minutes in, a routine car chase comes along, complete with fruit stand mishap. A fist fight, brief though it is, finally shows up 41 minutes into the 90-minute proceedings, and 51 minutes in, we finally get a murder ... though the latter is played for laughs, with federal agents tasering Hammer. For reasons unknown, characters are constantly eating, with the butch Pat Chambers chomping on apples.

The telefilm manages to get worse after it turns into a semblance of a crime story in its final half hour, when Hammer—fleeing from two corrupt uniformed cops—gets accidentally entered into a Spring Break dance contest being judged by Dr. Joyce Brothers, who treats us to a sexy little dance. For those who have not been struck blind by this display, the only legitimate Spillane sequence is up ahead ... but it seems jarringly out of place in these farcical proceedings.

Clumsily set up in dialogue by a mechanic pal of Mike's, the beaten-up car the detective's driving is known by the audience to have a driver side air bag. With the bad girl in back holding a gun on him, Mike hits the gas and crashes, with the air bag inflating to save him, sending the bad girl crashing through the windshield in a bloody mess of shattered glass. "Rest in pieces," the suddenly tough Hammer says.

The air bag ending was Spillane's sole contribution to the telefilm. The writer prided himself on coming up with shocking endings. He turned it over to Bernstein, who utilized it as a grim conclusion to an otherwise Spillane-free piece of fluff.

It's night time in Miami. A hood in a panama hat is lighting a cigarette and following Hammer, who is looking for a guy at a crap game at the Don't Come Inn in Little Havana. Mike says in voiceover: "But did I mention that the crap game is on the third floor? My name is Mike Hammer and I do this for a living. Let me start over from the beginning." Mike is thrown out of a window headed toward the street. His open-mouthed scream fills the screen.

Voluptuous women in bikinis litter the beachfront. This incarnation of Mike Hammer is taking photos (through his office window) of a long-haired blonde applying suntan lotion while she lounges atop a small yacht at the dock. Mike's voiceover states that he had no idea that the woman he would want to stay with forever was about to walk through his office door.

Pamela Anderson's Velda, dressed in a double-breasted grey business suit, pulls some papers from a filing cabinet. Says Mike, "No, that's not her. That's just Velda. She's my secretary." (This is likely the moment that Mickey Spillane shut off the TV.) Velda has a business degree from the University of Miami and speaks three languages. She also wears glasses, yet for some reason still looks like a bimbo.

Velda tells Mike that his last client and his wife are getting back together and suing Mike. She scolds him that all private eyes don't have to be so sleazy. Mike tells her that people who use private eyes are creeps and they're looking for someone creepy to get creepy things done. He's nattily dressed in a grey business suit, subdued grey print tie and severely starched white shirt. His suit is a slightly darker shade than Velda's; hers is just cut way above the knee. Oh, and he's reading the Sunday Comics page. On his wall is an almost life-sized painting of a classic car.

The client who walks in is a striking young brunette, dressed demurely in a lavender print dress. Her unlikely name is Trinity Sinclair. Velda notices that Mike finds Trinity attractive and elbows him as he appears to forget to introduce her. Mike acts nervous and (ludicrously) offers his client a cigar ("I don't smoke," she says).

Miss Sinclair is looking for her dad, Felix, who has been missing for fourteen years, even though he's been sending her money from Miami for the last five. She gives Mike a photograph that he examines as thoroughly as he has examined her. She came to see him having seen his cheesy ad on the side of a bus. Trinity relates that her mom and dad used to fight. Velda and Mike speak at the same time—Velda: "Money"; Mike: "Sex."

Mike turns Trinity down because the trail is too old. She walks away but comes back with $1000 in cash. He takes part of it and says if he's not successful, he'll give her the rest of her money back. Trinity hugs him in gratitude; Velda makes a face.

Since Trinity's dad liked to bet on the ponies, Mike and Trinity head to the track. Mike randomly picks an older teller (Bert Remsen) at one of the betting windows to show the photograph. After some heavy-handed comedy, the old guy says he recognizes Felix as a bettor who would show up the last Friday of the month and put $800 on the eighth horse in the eighth race.

At the racetrack office, Mike makes a few more groaner jokes and behaves in fashion quite unlike Spillane's Hammer or indeed any Hammer of the previous screen incarnations. Trinity gets all excited when the manager identifies Felix as Donald Acuff.

Back at his office, the door says "Mike Hammer Private Eye." The office number is 1842 and the décor is pastel. Trinity asks Hammer if there's anything between him and Velda. He tells her no; Velda is married ("unhappily of course"). Mike's next-door neighbor Lily says hello and says she is planting some bulbs. She's blonde, bosomy, in a low-cut top.

Mike and Trinity drive to the beach in his classic convertible. Trinity jumps out to frolic along the water's edge. She doesn't want "such a perfect day" to end, so they go the Cool Caribbe for drinks and dancing. They talk about Trinity's senior prom—Mike says he missed his—and that she's never had a drink before, as her character descends deeper and deeper into an unbelievable naivete. He steals a look down her cleavage and she places her hand on the inside of his thigh. In the parking lot they start kissing in the front seat of his convertible. He strokes her leg, she starts moaning, but soon she gets sick and throws up in his classic car.

The next day, Mike is trying to get the barf smell out of his convertible. Another Hammerette, a pig-tailed blonde in a black polka-dot bikini, asks for a donation for Florida Milk Relief. He says put him down for $50. He drops off Trinity's vomit-stained clothes at a specialty cleaners—"We like it DIRTY"—run by Hammerettes in yellow cut-off tees.

Checking up on Felix Sinclair, Mike drops in on his old Army buddy, Pat Chambers of the Miami Police Department, a very butch female. At the police range, Mike and Pat participate in a shooting match for imaginary money. Pat agrees to do some research on Felix for her friend.

Velda, displaying increasing jealousy about Trinity, has a line on a Donald Acuff, who turns out to be a black guy who chases Hammer in an unfunny, racist sequence. Mike spends the night with his client.

Mike is taking Trinity back to her hotel when he notices they are being followed by a

Jeep driven by a guy with a platinum flattop haircut. Mike loses the tail but stops after running over a fruit stand. The police give him a ticket for reckless driving. Mike gets Pat to drive Trinity back to her hotel. The man in the Jeep follows.

Mike rides really high in the seat of his loaner car, a tiny yellow convertible. Outside his office, a woman in a red-polka dot halter top needs "a jump" (for her stalled car). The glass in the office's front door is broken. As Mike enters, Velda slugs him by mistake.

Mike follows a lead about illegal gambling operations on the beach. A snitch named Jugs directs him to where we started this journey—the Don't Come Inn. Mike walks up the stairs looking for gambling action. Mike spots Felix, who has dyed his hair blonde. Felix beats up on Hammer, and throws him out the third floor window onto the street. ("This is where I came out and you came in.")

Mike wakes up in the Palm City Hospital. Velda is complaining that the case has cost them $6,000 and the girl only gave them $300. Velda doesn't trust Trinity, who has checked out of her hotel. Trinity comes in and, when Mike seems to believe Velda, Trinity walks out, mad. Mike in his hospital gown chases her out of the hospital, catches her, flashes his bare behind, and tells her he loves her. They head to the racetrack because it's the last Friday of month, when Felix does his gambling. The old man behind the tote tells Mike that Felix has already been there placing his bet, but as they leave, Felix walks in. And so does Flattop.

Spotting Acuff, Mike gives chase but finds him dead in a car, shot by Mike's missing .45, which disappeared after his tryst with Trinity. FBI agents taser him, then bring him around. Hammer wakes to see Trinity being held by Flattop in the fleeing Jeep. When the FBI doesn't believe his story, Mike breaks away but Pat pulls a gun on him and says she'll go for head shot. Mike pretends to give up, but knocks her out and takes off.

Hammer stops at Nathan's Tailor-made shop for help getting his handcuffs removed. Nathan, an Asian, asks if anyone knows that Hammer has come there. Mike says, "Nobody." The phone rings, Nathan picks it up, hands it to Mike and says, "It's Nobody." Or in this case, Velda.

Pat also knows Mike well enough to head right to Nathan's. Mike figures out that the bad guys broke into his office to plant something, not steal something. Mike asks for three days to work it out; Pat gives him two.

Velda cleans windows at the office to get in on the pointless T & A. Then Hammer mechanic pal Luis has a "discreet, new set of wheels" for Mike—dull green, tag number JKF P22. Luis is reminiscent of the mechanic in "Kiss Me Deadly," a nice comic character that illustrates what the telefilm was aiming for.

Mike chases a lead to Daytona where a blonde Hammerette in a bikini on roller skates tells him his ice cream cone is "dripping." How is this humor? Without his .45, Mike needs to buy a gun. Soon he's set up with a middle-man who drives him to a meet where hoods immediately put a sack over his head and ask: "Why is a Miami private eye trying to hire a button man in Daytona?"

The leader, a man with a Fu Manchu mustache, thinks Hammer is a funny name, and calls him "Mr. Screw." Again, how is this humor? The hood also thinks it would be a good idea to use a blow torch on Mike to find out what he's really after. Suddenly we have a tough scene in this fallen soufflé. Mike tells the hoods he's the guy they framed for Acuff's murder, the snitch who ratted out Petrini to the controlling mob hierarchy called the Trinity. This changes their entire attitude. They say Acuff is actually Gimpy Margarita—perhaps the dumbest name ever concocted by a screenwriter. The hoods let Hammer go because they don't like the Trinity mob.

In a transition T & A scene, Mike is at an outdoor bar, reading the *Daytona Herald*. He places the cold drink between his legs. A redheaded waitress says, "Do you want me to hold that for you?" She has on a low-cut halter top and leans over the table suggestively. This is an excellent example of how desperate young actresses in Hollywood are for work.

Inside the paper is an obituary for "Michael Angelo Margarita, past local crime figure." He was part of the Trinity crime organization and was called Gimpy because he lost two toes in Vietnam. He was fifty-six and survived by his mother Angelina. At her nursing home, Angelina tells Mike that the girl in his client's photograph was her granddaughter, killed by a letter bomb meant for Gimpy, who was skimming money from the mob. That's why Gimpy decided to testify for the feds.

But baby brother, Teddy Trinity (twelve in the photograph), is still alive: "That's the little bastard right there." The kid is now twenty-six.

Pat gives Mike a lead to Teddy's former juvenile parole officer who tells Mike that Teddy married his daughter. But not the way you think: "He's a priest." At his church, Father Trinity has a Trojan jacket over his raiment and agrees to hear Mike's "confession." Mike tells him about a girl he was in love with but found out she was a liar. Trying to pull his chain, Mike tells the priest that he thinks there are times when violence is justified.

"When you talk to her," he says to the attentive priest, "tell her Mike Hammer says hi." He slips a business card through the hole in the confessional. As Mike waits outside the church, he sees the priest talking to two Daytona policemen. They are Trinity and Flattop. The very interesting notion that a priest would hire hitmen is explored not at all.

Two federal agents are following a skimpily clad Velda at the marina. One takes pictures but loses his balance. Then she walks down the dock holding a pizza box on her right hip.

Back in the honeymoon suite at Mike's hotel (the only room available, of course), Mike is setting up a camera to get the two cops on tape admitting they set him up. The corrupt cops think they have him at their mercy. The woman who called herself Trinity says, "I haven't killed anyone all day." Flattop does a lot of scowling.

Mike tries to get them to talk. He mentions the money the priest paid them to kill Acuff. Mike pretends that he'll take money to leave. The girl tells Flattop to wait in the hall. She says, "I killed the guy. I gotta get paid. I'll give you half. Vince's half."

Mike senses the worst as she goes out on the balcony that overlooks the pool far below. Mike takes one look at Vince/Flattop coming in, then runs for the balcony and jumps. As Mike pulls himself from the pool, he climbs over yet another brunette in a bikini ("You're getting me all wet").

Mike runs to the beach. There he strips off his wet pants and three lovelies start applauding. Someone grabs Mike and paints the number 8 on his chest. They believe he's a contestant in a beach dance competition. Dr. Joyce Brothers is one of the judges: "Alright everybody. Let's party." Among many bikinis, Mike is dancing with a redhead in a white bikini. The evil cops are watching, waiting for their chance.

Mike wins the dance contest, for no good reason, and his prize is a trip to Cozumel. Mike body-surfs into the crowd to get away from the cops. Flattop tries to hit Mike with a night stick; Mike uses a boogie board to ward off the blows. Mike knocks out Flattop, borrows a skateboard and heads away. It has come to this: Mike Hammer on a skateboard.

After dealing with the bad guys, Hammer is still down all the money for the hotel, the milk fund pledge, repairs on his convertible, and the car he wrecked that was owned by the feds; but at least he has the free trip to Cozumel. After Velda leaves for a dental appointment,

Mike wonders to himself if she's wearing his new smoking jacket. Apparently, she is. Finally, how is this humor?

As "V" drives away, Mike sees his ad on the side of a bus: MIKE HAMMER—I DO THIS FOR A LIVING—PRIVATE EYE 555-9696 with himself pictured with Hammerettes. As he speeds off in his repaired convertible, we see his prestige license plate: Florida 1 HAMMER Dade.

And he and his car drive into the busted pilot sunset, where they so richly belong.

"Come Die with Me" (1994)

CBS Entertainment Production, Caroline Film Productions and Jay Bernstein Productions • Running time: 94 minutes • Release date: December 6, 1994

WRITER: John Lau; DIRECTOR: Armand Mastroianni; PRODUCERS: Jon C. Andersen (as Jon Andersen), Jay Bernstein and Jeffrey Morton; CINEMATOGRAPHER: James R. Bagdonas (as James Bagdonas); MUSIC: Ron Ramin; CAST: Rob Estes (Mike Hammer); Pamela Anderson (Velda); Randi Ingerman (Trinity); James Hong (Nathan); Geoff Meed (Schlitz); Joyce Brothers as Dr. Joyce Brothers (herself); Darlanne Fluegel (Pat Chambers); Brian Brophy (Agent Chutuk); Mark S. Porro (Father Trini); Julian Reyes (Luis); T.J. Castronovo as T.J. Castronova (Probation Officer); Jason Kristofer (Not So Young); Mick Rossi (Guns Are Us); Greg Gault (Gimpy Margarita); Deprise Brescia (Angela); Kim Delgado (Agent Hotz); Tony Jefferson (Donald Acuff); Coe Lewis (The DJ); Dennis Lau (Doughnut Man); Thomas J. Hageboeck as T.J. Hageboeck (Motor Cop); McLendon Winbush, Sr. (The Greeter); Elizabeth Armijo (Pretty Clerk); Danielle Raciti (Rollerblader); Christopher Canole (The Sheik); Bob Tedde (Rockola); Marty Eldridge (Rockola); Mark DeCerbo (Rockola); Doug Booth (Rockola)

19: "Tomorrow I Die" ("Fallen Angels," 1995)

Actor Bill Pullman portrays a mysterious drifter whose aw-shucks manner conceals something deadly in "Tomorrow I Die" (1995), adapted from the Spillane novella of the same name.

The two-season Showtime neo-*noir* anthology series, "Fallen Angels," based its episodes upon stories written by well-known authors of hardboiled fiction. Mickey Spillane was an obvious choice, and the series lent its tight thirty-minute format to an adaptation of a Spillane novella first published in *Cavalier* (February, 1956), and later the title story of the Spillane collection, *Tomorrow I Die* (1984, edited by co-author Collins).

This story is Spillane's variation on Robert Sherwood's hostage classic, "The Petrified Forest," and is a tense, taut tale in its own right with the customary Spillane surprise ending. The adaptation, however, adds one extra twist that brings a non-characteristic nihilism to the proceedings, turning one of the most faithful Spillane-on-screen adaptations into a story at odds with the writer's theme of rugged heroism.

The Stephen Katz screenplay is otherwise remarkably true to Spillane's novella, with Bill Pullman's nameless hero (who may or may not be washed-up actor "Rich Thurber") delivering a voiceover that frequently uses Spillane's own words, a relative oddity in adaptations of the writer's work. Director John Dahl was, for a time, a film director closely associated with neo-*noir*, celebrated for "Kill Me Again" (1989), "Red Rock West" (1993), and particularly "The Last Seduction" (1994). In recent years he has become a top director of television, with series credits including "Dexter," "Justified," and "True Blood." Directing scenes that involve multiple actors in small spaces is extremely difficult, but Dahl manages it well, with interesting camera angles and lighting choices that range from candy-neon in a '50s diner to a shadow-drenched miner's shack.

The cast assembled for this half-hour episode rivals any of the Spillane feature films. Joining Bill Pullman are Heather Graham ("Boogie Nights"), Dan Hedaya ("Mullholland Drive"), Kim Coates ("Blackhawk Down"), Dean Norris ("Starship Troopers"), and Jack Nance ("Twin Peaks"). Particularly good is Robert Altman regular Bert Remsen, as the old miner who takes one look at Pullman's "Thurber" and knows the robber/kidnappers are in trouble. Remsen had just appeared in "Come Die with Me" as a racetrack betting window clerk, hamming it up in a very unfunny and unbelievable role. Here, however, he is fine. Take Spillane seriously and actors will perform well.

The tension is established early on with the disturbing killing of a waitress (Grace Zabriskie, also of "Twin Peaks") and kept taut throughout. Spillane's plot and much of his dialogue is retained, with only the appearance of the small-town's mayor (who "Thurber" is mistaken for by the bad guys) being omitted.

A case can be made that this is the finest television production Spillane ever received. But the troubling final twist—in which Thurber switches from tough-guy savior to homicidal sociopath—is so at odds with Spillane's ethos that the end result is a kind of elegant betrayal.

"Tomorrow I Die" is episode five of the anthology's second season, first airing November 5, 1995. The credits open with a stylish piano melody panning into a train station. It's all in black-and-white, of course. The melody changes into the obligatory moody sax of film *noir*, with a theme that shamelessly borrows from John Barry's "Body Heat" score.

Introductory images reveal an attractive woman in bra and panties attaching her garter belt, putting on her lipstick, and preparing her purse, including slipping in a .38. Then images follow of smoke, handcuffs, a man walking down presumably mean streets, and a sultry kiss, as narrator Miguel Ferrer's warm baritone leads us in: "Rich Thurber is just another guy who stops in a bar for a cool beer on a hot day. Or is he? When gangsters fleeing a bank robbery take the patrons hostage, Thurber's true nature is revealed in Mickey Spillane's 'Tomorrow I Die.'"

As the credits roll, the world is in full color now, a Rock-Ola Rocket jukebox playing a country song, "Breakin' the Rules" by Hank Thompson.

When his cross-country bus makes a brief refueling stop, a stranger in a straw hat (Pullman) enters a small-town bar looking for a cold beer and quickly downs it. The barmaid (Zabriskie) tells him to take it easy, commenting that he looks familiar. Clarksdale's town sheriff (Nance) also says the stranger looks familiar. Carol (Graham), the sheriff's lovely daughter, leans suggestively at the juke box. She sashays over to the bar, stops near the stranger, her tan slacks just a little too tight. She tells the others that the stranger is Rich Thurber, "a couple of years back, one of Hollywood's hottest up-and-coming." The sheriff says, "Well, how come *I* know you, son? I don't go to the pictures." The daughter tells her father that Rich—star of "Dangerous Deception," "The Wrong Side of the Law" and "Between Two Worlds"—was "on all the magazine covers."

"Rich Thurber" (as we'll call him) has been behaving in an "aw shucks" manner, making harmless open-arm movements that highlight his cocked-back straw hat, light suit and loosened collar, from which a printed tie shows off random swirls.

The sheriff's daughter (think "farmer's daughter") teases Thurber: "You used to give me the kind of itch a small-town girl doesn't know how to scratch." He looks at her and replies, "Is that right?"

Four hoods come in, one dragging Thurber out of the dingy restroom where multiple beers have sent him. They've just robbed the bank. They mistake Thurber for Mayor Armbruster, whose poster in the bar shows him with a straw boater. With the mayor and the sheriff as hostages, the hoods figure, that should delay the search for the hoods. Why should the hostages cooperate, when their captors admit they will be killed? Top dog Mr. Auger (Hedaya) says, "You'd be amazed at what a person will do for just one more hour of life." They give the waitress a glass of Tabasco-spiked tomato juice to drink, telling her that she won't be killed until she finishes it. But when she chokes on it, the punk who likes to be called Trigger (Coates) shoots her. Spillane describes him as "crazy as a loon."

They drive out into the desert in two cars with Thurber in the lead. Rich's driving is so deliberately bad that a dust cloud is thrown up and the second car goes down an embankment, killing Leo the driver. Carol and another hood are thrown, but the money is in the car that's now down the hill—the only car in Hollywood history that hasn't burst into flame after such a ride. Now there are only three hoods, and they must wait until daylight to get the money back. The sheriff directs them to a prospector's shack to wait it out.

The old man's name is Tillson (Remsen). He sizes up the hoods immediately and also Thurber. He doesn't know him, but he knows the type. Mr. Auger tells them that in the morning, Carol and "Mr. Mayor" will go after the money. If the couple does not return by sunset, the hoods will kill her father.

In Tillson's old truck—with bug eyes and tooth-like slats down the front—Thurber and Carol set out to retrieve the loot (or as Rich calls it "the cabbage"). Carol wants him to get the money but, instead of returning it, go for help to rescue the others. He tells her that he'd thought about killing her and just leaving with all the money ($750,000). But he's decided against that, saying, "I'm doing it for you." She gives him a knowing smile. She calls him a hero and says she knows what he is. But in voiceover, Thurber says he's sure "she didn't."

They find the car and dead hood covered with "pictures of dead presidents." Carol wants Thurber to do "reckless things," kisses him "so hard he saw stars." He turns her around facing the truck: "For the next half hour it was only me. A hero, she had said. And what I did to her wasn't going to earn me any medals." This is a departure from Spillane, who indicates that a lusty love vibe exists between the two, but they don't perform James M. Cain-like sex at the scene of an auto accident.

On the way back to the shack, a shaken Carol wants to know what kind of actor he is. She doesn't think that the leading man of "Dangerous Deceptions" would have done the things "you just did to me." Her eyes do not show warmth and anticipation anymore. They are hardened and hurt. Rich stops the truck before they arrive and hides the money, filling the bank bags with leaves.

"A little insurance," he says. He doesn't exactly have a plan, but he wants to keep dealing.

Inside the shack, the sheriff wants to know why the "fool" didn't take his daughter away to safety. Rich allows Carol and himself to be searched (Trigger gives him a light frisk, anxious to get his hands all over Carol) before he goads shotgun-wielding Allen (Norris), the smart second-in-command, into making a move. Rich kicks him in the groin. When everyone gets all excited, Thurber points out that they really don't know where the money is—all they have are two bags of leaves. Allen confronts Mr. Auger. When Mr. Auger calls him a "dumb hood," Allen blows Auger's head off. Francis, who much prefers the nickname Trigger, responds by shooting Allen. That leaves only crazy-as-a-loon Trigger/Francis alive.

Trigger holds a gun on them as they sit at Tillson's table. The hood picks up Rich's straw boater from the floor and puts it on. He's figured out that Rich is not exactly what he's pretending to be—certainly not a hick mayor. Rich says, "It's too bad you won't live long enough to know for sure. I've got a trick or two up my sleeve."

Rich goads the hood, calling him "crazy," and referring to him as "Francis."

Mr. Tillson asks Thurber, "Aren't you going to warn the poor slob?" Trigger replies, "I just warned him." Tillson shoots back, "I ain't talking to you." He looks at Rich, "Tell them what you are."

Rich looks at Carol and says, "I'll see you in the next life." Trigger points his revolver directly at him. Rich thinks: "I could tell from the stupid grin on his face he didn't have a clue." When Trigger smiles and looks away at Carol, Rich ejects a sleeve gun into his left hand and shoots him.

Tillson says, "I knew it. I seen it right off. I knew it all along."

In voiceover Rich tells us, "They'd all seen it. But what I'd seen was an opportunity to be myself again." At this point Rich ejects another sleeve gun into his right hand. "What they'd seen if they had only known it, was that I was a killer, too."

This, more or less, is where Spillane ends. The screenwriter and director have another twist up their sleeve, painting him as a very bad man, capable not just of robbery but murder.

Spillane's reaction to the adaptation was generally positive. He called it a good production, but thought the extended, negative ending ruined the story. In truth, it plays chillingly well. But that choice by director Dahl and screenwriter Katz relegates this fine production from definitive Spillane adaptation to interesting footnote.

"Tomorrow I Die" ("Fallen Angels," 1995)

Mirage Enterprises, Propaganda Films and Showtime Networks • Running time: 30 minutes • Release date: November 5, 1995

WRITER: Steven Katz; DIRECTOR: John Dahl; PRODUCER: Sydney Pollack; MUSIC: Peter Bernstein. CAST: Kim Coates (Trigger); Heather Graham (Carol Whalen); Dan Hedaya (Auger); Jack Nance (Sheriff); Dean Norris (Allen); Bill Pullman (Rich Thurber); Bert Remsen (Old Man)

20. "Mickey Spillane's Mike Hammer, Private Eye" (1997–98)

The definitive small-screen Mike Hammer of the mid–1980s returned for a late '90s revival, further cementing Spillane's private eye as the signature role of film and Broadway star Stacy Keach.

In 1997, three years after the abysmal "Come Die with Me," Jay Bernstein abandoned the notion of rebooting Hammer and enlisted Stacy Keach to return as the real Mike Hammer in a lower-budgeted version of the series, renamed (yet again), "Mickey Spillane's Mike Hammer Private Eye." Twenty-six episodes were shot and appeared in syndication, usually at odd hours and without much fanfare.

Again, the famously raven-haired Velda is portrayed as a blonde; whether Lindsay Bloom was unavailable or considered too old for that part is unknown. The new Velda, Shannon Whirry, remains best-known for appearing in R-rated erotic features, and indeed she represents the most overt return of the "Hammerette" type to this surprisingly downbeat series.

The age difference between Hammer and Velda results in Keach and Whirry moving from brother-and-sister relationship into father-and-daughter, unlike that in any Hammer iteration prior. Whirry's Velda even enjoys a brief romance with Hammer's non–Spillane-created young associate, Nick Farrell, played by Shane Conrad, a hunky young actor brought in for painfully obvious demographic concerns.

The revival series suffers by comparison with the production values of previous Bernstein efforts (even "Come Die with Me") due to its lack of quality sets, lower-tier guest stars, and an insistence on utilizing the most mundane plots and unbelievable action. The series does have one considerable attribute, and that is the return of Keach to a part he wears as easily as his rumpled trenchcoat.

More than ever, the assured Keach carries the series on his shoulders, with humor and panache, oddly benefiting from a more *noir*-ish tone due to shadow-filled cinematography designed (as was the case with Hollywood's original films *noir*) to disguise the paucity of under-dressed sets.

Episode one ("Prodigal Son") opens with stylistic *noir* flair and an easy jazz score. Mike is walking down a familiar mean street, amid almost illegible graffiti and the haze of too much cigarette smoke. "People don't change," he tells us in voiceover. "When I first entered this business twenty years ago, heroin was hip." He's questioning a junkie, heating up a hit, about a missing young man. A cop friend, Chic Farrell, has a son who was "lost to drugs," but when Hammer finds the son he's "lost forever."

Chic tells Mike the guys are on the third floor. Mike heads that way; a hood jumps him in the hallway. After he knocks the hood out, Mike muses, "When I was younger it was the Russians are coming. Today it's the Russians are here." It's a pop-culture reference to an old film that only the Baby Boomers in the audience will recognize.

The father confronts two Russian mobsters blaming them for his son's death, and winds up dead.

All this happens before the opening credits, which alternate between straight and comic, in the manner of the 1980's series.

Mike is at a bar where fellow cops are having a sendoff for their fallen friend, Captain Gale Farrell, Sr. Farrell's other son Nick seems lost at the affair. Mike tries to make him feel better by saying that his father talked about him all the time. "That's a lie," Nick says, and walks away.

But soon Nick joins Hammer in the search for his dad's killer and ends up on Hammer's team. Hammer's voiceover tells us, "My anger had focus. I wanted to find a drug dealer and a cop killer. And introduce him to Hammer justice." In the background are glimpsed the Twin Towers of the World Trade Center.

At the police station Mike is working with Skip Gleason (Peter Jason), the surrogate

Pat Chambers of the series. While Skip is distracted talking with the department's Russian expert, Mike snags a picture of a hooker seen at Farrell's killing. Nick comes in at Skip's request but displays a bad attitude.

Back in his office, dinosaur Mike needs Velda's help with pulling up a file on the computer. She puts out his cigarette in an ash tray, continuing her character's disapproval of the habit dating to Lindsay Bloom days. Velda's dressed in a long-sleeved lavender sweater hugging her curves, a very short dark skirt, and a black scarf around her neck that drapes between her cleavage. She has shoulder length brownish-blonde hair and a pleasant voice.

She finds what Mike needs in a file from the hall of records: Beagle Properties. Mike tells her, "Sweetheart, I love you," and kisses her above her left eye near her hair. She responds, "Stand in line." Which means what? Attractive as Whirry is, her relationship with her boss is a faint shadow of Roberts and Bloom.

Mike goes to Beagle Properties but gets very little information, his approach rude enough to prompt the woman there to call security. Eddie, the security chief, turns out to be an old friend of Mike's, telling the woman, "He's a hell of a guy." As Mike leaves, he see a new "Face," a gorgeous redhead this time, in an elevator that closes on him. Again, why is this gimmick, resolved in the last regular CBS episode, being revived? For some viewers, it may serve as a nice link to the earlier, better series.

Hammer goes to see Itchy, a Russian bigwig who gives the PI the name of a guy "who owns the drug trade," so-well known that Mike knows it already. So why did we bother with this scene, other than to kill a few script pages?

At the Hotel Deluxe, Mike rescues the Russian hooker, takes her to his office, and tries to get some answers. She explains that she was on a "snow ride" and really doesn't know anything. She fingers her pimp Struebben, who Mikes calls "Fur Boy." He calls Skip to take the black pimp to the 35th precinct house to get some answers. At first, it's a no-go until Mike and Skip put a big white guy into the holding cell with Fur Boy. Mike calls him Fur Boy's new boy friend and wants to know if Skip can have a marriage performed. This is not the Keach Hammer at his best, substituting homophobic, racist humor for genuine toughness.

Fur Boy gives them a location in Brooklyn. But police Russian expert Gorby is raiding an Italian mob who sell pure "china white" heroin, and lots of lead flies. Gorby is killed, but Nick Farrell comes in with a weapon saying he tried to stop it. Skip arrests him, of course.

At the 35th precinct, a bad day gets worse as "human ulcer" Deputy Mayor Barry Lawrence comes in, played by Kent Williams, doing his Barrington character under a revised name, perhaps to avoid royalties to whatever TV writer thought the original character up. The Deputy Mayor releases Nick, but gets mad at both Hammer and Skip for messing up a "front page" story.

Mike encounters Maya Ricci, the attractive yoga teacher who has a studio next door. She tells Mike that her dog is missing, and seems to think of the animal as a human being. Maya is a new recurring character who will provide delightful little interludes, Old School PI confronted with New Age earth mother. Portrayed by Keach's wife, Malgosia Tomassi, Maya wears long blonde pigtails braided from the top of her head. Mike considers her sweet, "but a little crazy. Unlike my next visitor."

That next visitor turns out to be Nick, who tells Mike that he took the fall for his older brother's drug arrest. He was a juvenile and his brother would have done time. Nick becomes Hammer's client, but of course he can't pay. Mike's décor includes a dart board and several cases of Southern Comfort stacked against a wall.

The Italian mobster calls from the beach telling Mike that someone set up the police raid, planting drugs and guns there for the police.

When Mike gets to the office, a bizarre scene ensues with Fur Boy and a brunette hooker who turns crazy when it appears the pimp is going to reveal the source of the bad H to Mike. She fires about twenty shots, one wounding Fur Boy. Nick comes in the back way and shoots the gun-crazy woman. Before he dies, Fur Boy gives Mike a clue to the Russian mob—the art gallery. The crazy woman, not dead, rises up to shoot Mike, and Nick shoots her some more. Lots of bullets, no reloading. Then Mike notices a hood in the skylight and shoots him. The hood falls through to the floor and Velda screams. Illogical but action-packed.

Following Mike's confrontation with the killer, Nick comes to see Mike and Velda. Mike says he could use another pair of hands around his office. They have a drink to seal the deal. His first case: find Maya's missing dog.

The series continues along in the same fashion, entertaining in a non-demanding way, well-suited to late-night channel surfing, with the comforting presence of iconic Keach, who sometimes noodles at the piano in Lou's, the bar replacing the Lite N Easy, heretically featuring Budweiser and Bud Light.

Pat Chambers never appears. In the early 1990s, Don Stroud was injured playing Good Samaritan to a man being attacked by a mugger—the courageous Stroud was stabbed numerous times and lost the sight of one eye. This tragic incident has been used as an excuse for his non-participation in the Hammer series, but the issue was more likely money, as Stroud remained active through the 1990s and is still acting.

A pair of two-part episodes became "movies" for release on DVD. "Songbird" refers to Lila B (played by Moira Walley), a gifted jazz songstress with a good taste in music and bad taste in men. She's singing with Des Long (Jack Sheldon) and his All Stars at Lou's, her opening number a lovely slow rendition of "You Made Me Love You." Her latest ill-chosen lover is Johnny Dive (Frank Stallone), who rats on his boss Vito. Vito knows that he can locate Johnny through Lila B. In a typically careening plot, one of the All Stars is a murder victim, prompting Mike to sit in as keyboard man—he plays "Harlem Nocturne." The New Face is there as a cigarette girl.

The musical content and theme of the two-parter reflect Keach's love for both the Great American Songbook and jazz, and this elevates "Songbird" into a decent slice of neo-*noir*. Hammer in his voiceover even quotes the great Frank Loesser: "My time of day is the dark time. Give me the wee small hours of the morning. You can keep the rest."

Less moody but interestingly quirky is "A New Leaf," in which Mike under a cancer threat tries to break his three-pack a day addiction. Velda, of course, has been trying to get him to quit since the early 1980s. Artie Chilton, a tobacco company scientist, has developed a strain of nicotine 3.5 times more addictive than regular cigarettes. He comes to Mike for protection and is killed before the opening credits. A winded Mike is soon getting scared by a lovely doctor reading his x-rays.

Mike questions an executive at Minute-Man ad agency about Artie. The company logo is a cartoon rabbit smoking a cigarette in the Joe Camel manner. Before he's done, Mike will be hired as the new Minute Man spokesman (perhaps in a satiric nod to Spillane's Lite Beer ads) and will visit tobacco magnate, "the General," at his plantation-type home down south.

Every character Hammer encounters is a Southern Gothic caricature, sometimes mildly amusing, sometimes just bizarre. For instance, the General has some troops who periodically march through the scenes. In one, the New Face is right in the middle of the formation.

"A New Leaf" has other odd aspects. Nick and Velda become an item, for a while, an indication of how far the series has drifted from Spillane. If the creative juices are flowing in the satire on ad agencies, they are dried up elsewhere, as demonstrated by the copping of the famous "crop duster" scene from "North by Northwest." Unlike Cary Grant, Mike Hammer shoots down the plane; but when the fireball roars, Hammer says, "So much for the friendly skies." So much for witty dialogue.

For reasons too trite to describe, Pat Chambers stand-in "Skip" and Barrington stand-in "Barry" wind up shoveling dirt alongside the highway. Hammer gets them released, and they trick him into giving them an expensive meal.

At Lou's, Mike's feeling pretty good about himself. He lights up a cigarette and starts coughing. The scene ends with his putting out the cigarette. Hammer quits cigarettes just as the series quits him.

The best that can be said for the syndicated "Mike Hammer, Private Eye" is that Keach maintains his dignity and the integrity of the character, and that it is a passable time-waster.

In three series and four telefilms, Stacy Keach delineated the definitive latter-day Mike Hammer. Oddly, all those series and TV movies add up to roughly the same amount of screen time as the two-season Darren McGavin series. Good as McGavin and his series are, the Keach version—for all its ups and downs—is the television Mike Hammer that made the greatest impact.

"Mickey Spillane's Mike Hammer, Private Eye" (1997-98)

Season 1

Episode #1 "Prodigal Son"

Directed by: Allen Barton. Written by: no writing credit.

After friend Captain Gale ("Chick") Farrell, Sr. is killed investigating the death of his son, Mike follows the leads to Russian mobsters. He wants to introduce them to "Hammer justice."

Cast: Kent Williams (Guest star); William Lucking; Ric Mancini; Peter Jason.

Episode #2 "Beat Street"

Directed by: Rex Piano. Written by: Chris Baena.

Patrick Dean, a suspected polluter, hires Mike to clear his name, but the reporter who wrote an expose on the accused is found dead, making Dean a murder suspect.

Cast: Tracy Scoggins; Peter Allas; Mark Arnott.

Episode #3 "www.murder"

Directed by: Rex Piano. Written by: Chris Baena.

Mike is hired to look into the disappearance of a girl who may have been killed in a "snuff film" shown on the internet.

Cast: Lillian Adams; Debra Christofferson; Jason Schombing.

Episode #4 "Hoop Nightmares"

Directed by: Rex Piano. Written by: George Melrod.

When a basketball player's sports agent is murdered just before he becomes the number one pick in the draft, he turns to Mike to prove his innocence.

Cast: Joe Bays; Mongo Brownlee.

EPISODE #5 "FALSE TRUTHS"

DIRECTED BY: Wayne Ewing. WRITTEN BY: Chris Baena

Mike flies to tinsel town to help an actress accused of murdering her lover and producer.

CAST: Ed Wasser; Barry Jenner.

EPISODE #6 "HALLOWEEN"

DIRECTED BY: Jonathan Winfrey. WRITTEN BY: John Henry Reed.

Someone is targeting Hammer's friends in the style of a cult killer that Mike put in jail.

CAST: Joe Bays; Paul Kersey.

EPISODE #7 "SINS OF THE FATHER"

DIRECTED BY: Greydon Clark. WRITTEN BY: George Melrod.

The murder of a priest puts Hammer on the trail of a serial killer murdering prostitutes.

CAST: Jack Betts; John Cassini; Steven Culp.

EPISODE #8 "BODY COUNT"

DIRECTED BY: Jim Lemmo. WRITTEN BY: Jake Kalleen.

After a surgery patient's body emits toxic gasses, killing him and three members of a surgical team, his daughter hires Mike to solve the crime.

CAST: George Murdock; Caroline Williams.

EPISODE #9 "A PENNY SAVED"

DIRECTED BY: Wayne Ewing. WRITTEN BY: Zoltar Suma.

When a simple-minded janitor all but frames himself for the murder of a stockbroker, he asks Mike to prove his innocence.

CAST: Robert Katims; David St. James.

EPISODE #10 "THE LIFE YOU SAVE"

DIRECTED BY: Wayne Ewing. WRITTEN BY: Chris Baena.

After witnessing suspicious behavior between a cop and a mobster, Mike saves the cop's life and the mobster is arrested. Then on his birthday, Mike gets a call saying he has twenty-four hours to live.

CAST: Greg Proops; Saul Stein.

EPISODE #11 "THE LONG ROAD TO NOWHERE"

DIRECTED BY: Jonathan Winfrey. WRITTEN BY: Brian Oppenheimer.

When a mystery writer hires Mike to help him with an ending to his latest book, he is murdered, but his book holds the key to his killer.

CAST: Robert Rusler.

EPISODE #12 "THE ART OF MURDER"

DIRECTED BY: Rex Piano. WRITTEN BY: George Melrod.

The artist Velda is seeing is murdered. Mike investigates.

CAST: Peter Allas, Michael Fairman; Sven Ole Thorsen.

EPISODE #13 "COUNTDOWN TO MURDER"

DIRECTED BY: William Lucking. WRITTEN BY: Peter McGovern and Michael O'Connell.

When Mike's old flame is accused of murdering her ex-husband and co-star right before their Broadway play opens, Mike tries to clear her name.

CAST: Robyn Peterson; Brian Reddy.

EPISODE #14 "THE CUTTING EDGE"

DIRECTED BY: Wayne Ewing. WRITTEN BY: Richard Johnson.

Mike becomes a convict's alibi when a cutting-edge computer chip is stolen by a masked murderer with the same modus operandi and even the same limp.

CAST: Gregg Daniel; Michael Wiseman.

EPISODE #15 "DEAD MEN TALK"

DIRECTED BY: Rex Piano. WRITTEN BY: Jason Hughes.

A friend of Mike's who is believed dead turns up and asks Mike to find out who was behind the attempt on his life and the deaths of two others, who were less lucky.

CAST: Ryan Cutrona; Shelley Malil.

EPISODE #16 "A CANDIDATE FOR MURDER (ONE HAPPY GUMSHOE)"

DIRECTED BY: Jonathan Winfrey. WRITTEN BY: Chris Baena.

Barry Lawrence is running for district attorney and he becomes Mike's main suspect when his mistress is murdered.

CAST: Suzanne Krull; Caroline Williams.

EPISODE #17 "DUMP THE CREEP"

DIRECTED BY: Dimitri Logothetis. WRITTEN BY: Pete McGovern and Michael O'Connell.

After Mike berates a radio host on the air for telling Mike's girlfriend to dump him, he becomes a suspect when the host is murdered.

CAST: Gregg Daniel; Greg Grunberg.

EPISODE #18 "BIG BROTHER'S SECRET"

DIRECTED BY: Rex Piano. WRITTEN BY: Raul Panadero.

The murder of an investigative reporter who was a friend of Mike's leads the private eye to stolen satellite photos.

CAST: Signy Coleman; Gregg Daniel.

EPISODE #19 "LUCKY IN LOVE"

DIRECTED BY: Rex Piano. WRITTEN BY: George Melrod.

When a gambling buddy of Mike's is murdered, he is asked to help out with his friend's race horse.

CAST: Shelley Malil; Mickey Rooney.

EPISODE #20 "THE MAYA CONNECTION"

DIRECTED BY: Dimitri Logothetis. WRITTEN BY: L. L. Thomaso.

When Maya Ricci's lover comes to town, he draws Maya and Mike into a web of espionage and assassination.

CAST: Maxwell Caulfield; Gregg Daniel.

EPISODE #21/22 "SONGBIRD, PART 1"/"SONGBIRD PART 2"

DIRECTED BY: Jonathan Winfrey. WRITTEN BY: Peter McGovern and Michael O'Connell.

Lila B. Is a singer who is romantically involved with mobster Johnny Dive. When she becomes a murder suspect, Mike is called in to help. In this episode Shannon Whirry sings "Danny Boy" and Stacy Keach plays "Harlem Nocturne" on the piano.

CAST: Moira Walley as Lila B.; Jack Sheldon as Des Long; Frank Stallone as Johnny Dive; Matt Gallina.

EPISODE #23 "CHOP SHOP"

DIRECTED BY: Rex Piano. WRITTEN BY: Brian Oppenheimer.

Mike goes to Texas to attend a friend's wedding, but discovers that human organ thieves have kidnapped the bride.

CAST: David Doty; Tommy Rosales.

EPISODE #24 "GONE FISHIN'"

DIRECTED BY: William Lucking. WRITTEN BY: Peter McGovern & Michael O'Connell

Mike and Skip are trapped in a bar by bank robbers, and they left their guns at home because they were going fishing.

CAST: Burt Bulos; Whip Hubley.

EPISODE #25/26 "A NEW LEAF, PART 1"/" A NEW LEAF PART 2"

DIRECTED BY: Jonathan Winfrey. WRITTEN BY: Jennifer Boller.

Mike investigates the death of a tobacco company scientist and the murder of a member of the family that owns the tobacco company.

CAST: Jack Riley as Puff Puff the Bunny; Whip Hubley, Aloma Wright.

APPENDICES

A. The Hammer (Film) Code

Including telefilms, Mike Hammer has appeared in thirteen feature-length movies. About half of these are available on home video, and the rest appear at least occasionally on cable television. "I, the Jury" (1953) is perhaps the hardest to see, although the under-rated film has received occasional revival screenings—sometimes in its original 3-D.

In the novels, Hammer's operational code remains consistent throughout his lengthy career. His code in the feature films varies somewhat depending on the individual screenwriter and director, and their sympathy with (or antipathy toward) the Hammer character. Spillane's use of personal pronouns in his titles represents a recurring motif: "I," "Me," and "Mine" appear in over half of the titles. Spillane once remarked with amusement that he had to change his way of titling his books because he ran out of pronouns. He was only half-kidding. Nonetheless, those pronouns indicate the major difference between prose and film presentations of Hammer—only in the novels does the close identification of reader/viewer and character take hold. That limitation has limited the success of adapting Spillane and Hammer to the screen, although certainly few authors (or writers, to give Spillane his preference) can point to a better film adaptation of their work than "Kiss Me Deadly." Spillane's decades-long dislike of the film, and the filmmakers' intrinsic dislike of Spillane's character, makes an ironic point of interest, yet ultimately moot: their tumultuous collaboration has become an acknowledged classic.

Robert Aldrich and A.I. Bezzerides notwithstanding, Mike Hammer on film remains at heart consistent with that of the novels. Virtually all of the screen Hammers—even Ralph Meeker and Rob Estes—have an enhanced sense of duty and friendship, and very much distrust the motives of society and its ability to deliver effective justice. And, yes, revenge is a staple in the screen Hammer's world, particularly with regard to retribution for the death of a friend.

The 1950s saw much criticism of Hammer (and Spillane) for sex and sadism, castigating the writer for even creating such a character, when all he did was fashion genre entertainment that reflected changes in post-World War II society. Initially, the films could not present the unadulterated sex and violence of Spillane's pages, as a comparison of the 1953 version of "I, the Jury" with the 1982 version demonstrates.

The original film could only suggest Charlotte Manning's confrontational striptease, while by the time of the 1982 remake, Mike had already slept with Charlotte before the movie's climactic scene. The nudity of the remake was a welcome return to the novel's original intention, but hardly as surprising or shocking as it would have been in 1953. Mike's take on this striptease is the key characterization factor. His motivation and response remain the same. He is still the avenger, impervious to sexual bribery, the deliverer of (rough) justice. Mike protects the innocent, sometimes with a quick and vicious response, sometimes with methodical stalking.

Many fans of mystery and detective films are familiar with Raymond Chandler's famous essay, "The Simple Art of Murder" (1950), outlining his perfect code for the private detective: "Down these mean streets a man must go who is not himself mean, who is neither tarnished nor afraid....He is the hero....He must be a complete man and a common man and yet an unusual man. He must be a man of honor....He must be the best man in his world and a good enough man for any world....He is neither a eunuch nor a satyr."

Chandler's key word describing his detective Philip Marlowe is "hero." Few critics would describe Mike Hammer as a hero by the Chandler definition, yet both Marlowe and Hammer on screen can be accurately defined by that word.

Compare Humphrey Bogart's portrayal of Marlowe in "The Big Sleep" (1941) and Dick Powell's screen version of Marlowe in "Murder, My Sweet" (1945) with Ralph Meeker's Mike Hammer in "Kiss Me Deadly" and Spillane himself in "The Girl Hunters." The Marlowe/Hammer difference is striking only because the directors and writers of Hammer on film do not flinch in their portrayal of Chandler's mean streets. The film world of Bogart and Powell is romanticized toughness, soft-focus mayhem; the film world of Meeker and Spillane is a more realistic melodrama, gritty, hard-edged—where the streets are not just called mean, they actually are.

The film Hammer is an amalgam of two character types: the hero and the revenger. The film Marlowe is also a hero/revenger, a point film critics often gloss over. Hammer and Marlowe exhibit both sides of the classic hero/avenger, as most clearly defined by Shakespeare's tormented heroes.

Take Robert Mitchum's contemporized Marlowe in the 1978 UK remake of "The Big Sleep." This film shows the grit of the PI world and also the darkness—both of the soul and time of day. Aldrich's "Kiss Me Deadly" and the Spillane starring/produced "The Girl Hunters" have that same darkness, just displayed years earlier.

If the Hammer film code is much the same as the novels, any shades of difference reflect the agenda of the director and screenwriter—which is not necessarily a bad thing, as adaptation of a novel is obviously an interpretive art. Still, no matter how hard Robert Aldrich and A. I. Bezzerides try to make us dislike their Mike Hammer, the audience still admires a man who can rise up when something evil enters his world, and respond in harsh kind.

Spillane created Hammer to be a hero who fought the villain by co-opting the villain's means. In a world without moral absolutism, such simplicity retains a timeless appeal. Now if there could only be a clear-headed film version of *One Lonely Night*, the greatest Mike Hammer film of all might yet be made.

B. "'The Girl Hunt' Ballet" ("The Band Wagon," 1953)

In the 1950s, many Mike Hammer parodies and satirical references were seen in print and on film.

Appropriately enough, a number appeared in comic books, that field where young Mickey Spillane had toiled. Notable among them is "My Gun Is the Jury," the lead-off story in *Panic* #1 (March 1954), EC Comics' own imitation of their successful *Mad*, a Jack Davis-drawn parody the "socko" ending of which reveals the Hammer character to be a transvestite (a story that was among the comic books that caught a Senate Committee's disgusted attention). At least as memorable is Walt Kelly's "Mucky Spleen: The Bloody Drip," which appeared in the compilation *Uncle Pogo So-So Stories* (1953).

On film, the best and most high-profile Spillane parody is undoubtedly the "Girl Hunt" ballet in Vincente Minnelli's MGM musical "The Band Wagon" (1953).

A playbill reads "The Band Wagon," Stratton Theatre, the show-within-the-show of this Fred Astaire musical. The ballet is spelled out in detail—Scene 6: "GIRL HUNT: A Murder Mystery in Jazz." The cast list is:

Rod Riley...Tony Hunter (Fred Astaire)
The Blond/The Brunette...Gabrielle Gerard (Cyd Charisse)

It's a "Rod Riley" thriller by "Mickey Starr" and acted out in an imaginative, loving parody, with Fred Astaire certainly the most offbeat Mike Hammer casting choice of all and Cyd Charisse as the embodiment of every Spillane woman—good *and* bad. What a Velda she would have made. What a Charlotte....

The sequence opens with an orchestral fanfare that includes sirens and moving spotlights on the curtain, which displays mock-ups of Spillane-style paperback covers. The titles include "Girl Hunt," "Dames Kill Me," "Kill Me Cutie," and "Stab Me Sugar." "Girl Hunt" is larger than the rest, and centered, with one cover largely obscured thanks to a banner that reads "Rod Riley."

These imitation Spillane paperback covers have a dash of *Spicy Detective* thrown in. A banner across the top of "Girl Hunt" reads: "She Had to Die!" At the bottom another banner reads: "Ralph Hardley, Publisher." The cover resembles "I, the Jury," with the fedora-sporting PI holding a .45 in hand. He's facing a beautiful woman who wears a pale lavender outfit.

The woman on the cover of "Dames Kill Me" has on a green dress disarrayed to show her bra and a lot of leg. The two covers on the right depict women menaced by knife-wielding men. "Stab Me Sugar" shows one of the women holding a sheet over her nude body. If only the actual film of "I, the Jury" had been so bold.

Machine-gun fire splits the curtain down the middle and Fred Astaire as Rod Riley begins a Hammer-like voiceover. This murder mystery in jazz is a twelve-minute long ballet. Astaire is dressed in a light lavender suit with a navy shirt and an off-white tie. He sports an off-white fedora with a navy band and is wearing a ring on his right pinkie finger.

Cyd Charise is all of the deadly women in the life of Fred Astaire's Rod Riley, an affectionate tribute to Mickey Spillane and Mike Hammer. If Astaire seems an unlikely Hammer, he is perfect here, and what a Velda Cyd Charise would have made.

The sequence opens with Rod's soliloquy: "The city was asleep. The joints were closed. And the rats. The killers were in their holes. I hate killers. My name is Rod Riley. I'm a detective." He lights up a cigarette and continues, "I had just finished up a tough case and was ready to hit the sack."

Suddenly a long-haired blonde in a light yellow dress dances her way into the scene. Rod shares his cigarette with her. "I can smell trouble a mile off. And this poor kid was in trouble. Big trouble. Scared as a turkey in November."

A hood wearing a trench coat enters, menacing them. He picks up a bottle that suddenly explodes, evaporating him. "There was nothing left of the guy. Nothing at all. Except a rag, a bone and a hank of hair." Literally.

Some hoods enter and take away a green gem. Rod "plays a hunch" and goes to a fancy ladies shop. He enters by the green door. Three young ladies—a blonde, a brunette and a redhead—are modeling gowns. The green gem is on display. The music shifts and Cyd Charisse enters as a brunette wearing a form-fitting dark green gown. "She came at me in sections. More curves than a scenic railway. She was bad. She was dangerous. She was selling hard, but I wasn't buying." She dances her way into a dressing room. There Riley finds a bolt of cloth that matches the rag the hood left.

Hidden among the hat dummies and miscellaneous dummy body parts, a hood in a black fedora jumps up to confront Riley. Two others join in, one hitting a dummy's head with a mallet. The sinister "Mr. Big" enters, dressed all in black wearing a hat and sporting a cane.

Riley chases Mr. Big down to the subway at Times Square and 42nd. The blonde slides in, this time dressed in diaphanous light blue. They dance seductively while in the background hoods shoot guns and slug it out. Soon bodies are all piled up behind them. As another hood explodes in a cloud of smoke, the blonde dances away and runs down the stairs.

Following up on "a long shot," Riley climbs a steep orange stairway to a bathroom where the blonde is taking a bubble bath. She has on a mask similar to those in Greek drama and is wearing the green ring on her left hand. Riley says, "I was beginning to see daylight." Two hoods knock him out and take the ring. "These hoods were smart, but they made on big mistake. They got me mad."

Riley then enters Dem Bones Café, where a sexy girl skeleton sports a blonde wig. The skeleton's hips move seductively. He enters through another green door. Everyone inside is dancing to the jazzy score, taking exaggerated steps to the off-beats. All the hoods are dressed in black. Riley enters in a light suit and hat, immediately standing out. A big choreographed fight ensues. At the bar, the brunette sits completely covered to her pretty neck. She steps out, revealing a low-cut, skin-tight red dress and dances his way. Riley is entranced and puts his .38 back in his shoulder rig. The red dress is split to the waist, revealing long shapely legs.

"Suddenly all the pieces fitted together," Rod tells us. "I knew how the crime had been done. The high note on the trumpet had shattered the glass, the glass with the nitroglycerin." He slides the glass down the bar, exploding it. "Now I knew who the killer was and it didn't matter anymore. Killers have to die."

Mr. Big shoots once at him and Riley replies with four shots. The killer falls into Riley's arms, revealed as the blonde, still dressed in the light blue outfit underneath the trench coat. Riley takes the green ring from her right hand. She gives him a kiss before falling back dead.

The ballet closes as it began with Riley in soliloquy in front of a city streets background. "Another page in the casebook of Rod Riley was finished. The city was asleep. The joints were closed. The rats, the hoods and the killers were in their holes. I felt good, but something was missing."

He stops full screen and muses as the black-gloved hand of the woman in the red dress reaches in with a light for his cigarette: "She was bad. She was dangerous. I wouldn't trust her any further than I could throw her. But she was my kind of woman." Arm-in-arm, they exit stage left. The curtain closes and they reemerge to great applause.

Liza Minnelli and Michael Feinstein provide some valuable insights in their commentary (included on a DVD edition released in 2005) on scene 27: GIRL HUNT. Liza mistakenly credits the murder mystery inspiration to Raymond Chandler, but Feinstein quickly corrects her to Mickey Spillane. They reveal that the inspiration for the ballet was the 1952 *Life* magazine article on Spillane. She also notes that the redhead in the fashion show is Julie Newmar. Feinstein points out that the orange staircase was based on a *Look* magazine cover.

The dialogue is a dead-on affectionate pastiche of Spillane: treating the city as a living character, the dream sequences, the musing about dangerous women, the obvious clues, the lust for revenge, and the feeling of good winning over evil. It works so well as a musical, it's no wonder Spillane was approached to do a Broadway show called "Oh, Mike!"

Unlike so many of the parodies, this one is loving, and the filmmakers recognize the poetry of the *noir* detective yarn, and specifically the Spillane variety. Mike Hammer's creator mentioned to the authors that his favorite films were not detective thrillers, but Fred Astaire musicals. So it's no surprise he returned the tribute by naming his comeback Hammer novel *The Girl Hunters.*

C. Who's Who of Spillane on Film

WESLEY ADDY (1913–1996) played Pat Murphy (Chambers, renamed by Bezzerides and Aldrich) in "Kiss Me Deadly" (1955). His layered performance in this role likely drew upon his stage experience as a Shakespearean actor. Indeed, his Horatio opposite Maurice Evans' Hamlet on "Hallmark Hall of Fame" (1953) helped set a high standard for TV productions of the Bard. This accomplished, distinctive performer appeared in numerous other pictures for Aldrich, including "The Big Knife" (1955), "What Ever Happened to Baby Jane?" (1962), "Hush...Hush, Sweet Charlotte" (1964), and "The Grissom Gang" (1971), Aldrich's period-piece adaptation of another controversial private-eye yarn, James Hadley Chase's much pilloried *No Orchids for Miss Blandish* (1939).

JOHN ALTON (1901–1996), the celebrated cinematographer of "I, the Jury," was born in Hungary. He won the Academy Award in 1951 for "An American in Paris." A stylish innovator, he practiced his magic with unconventional camera angles and lighting that worked particularly well in such film *noirs* as "He Walked by Night" (1948), "Raw Deal" (1948), and Joseph H. Lewis's "The Big Combo" (1955). He outlined his theories in the landmark work, *Painting With Light* (1949).

Jay Bernstein, Mickey Spillane, and Stacy Keach (left to right) sporting fedoras at Spillane's 80th birthday party in Murrells Inlet, South Carolina, March 9, 1998. Photograph by Jane Spillane.

ARMAND ASSANTE (October 4, 1949–) played Mike Hammer in a disarmingly offhand manner in the 1982 Larry Cohen rewrite of "I, the Jury." His was a compelling performance with verve and physicality, with a crisp delivery of comedic voiceovers. He has appeared in over one hundred movie and TV productions, playing Goldie Hawn's boyfriend in "Private Benjamin" (1980), Cesar Castillo in "The Mambo Kings" (1992), and John Gotti in "Gotti" (1996). He has appeared on the television series "NCIS" (2007) and "Chuck" (2010).

WHITNEY BLAKE (1926–2002) played femme fatale Nancy Williams in "My Gun Is Quick" (1957). She is best remembered for the role of Mrs. Baxter on the "Hazel" TV series (1961–65). She appeared frequently on 1950s-1970s television, including such series as "M Squad" (1958), "Richard Diamond, Private Detective" (1959), "77 Sunset Strip" (1960), "Tightrope" (1960), and "Ironside" (1975). Her daughter is actress Meredith Baxter-Birney.

LINDSAY BLOOM (August 28, 1952–) portrayed Velda more times than any other actress during her stint with the various Stacy Keach telefilms and series, 1984–1989. Voluptuously attractive, Bloom gave the role warmth and humanity, retaining a sex appeal though relegated to a wholesome, sisterly version of Hammer's secretary. During the 1970s, she appeared in several sexy comedy/action pictures tailored for the drive-in crowd, such as "Six-Pack Annie" (1975), "Cover Girl Models" (1975), and "H.O.T.S." (1979).

ROBERT BRAY (1917–1983) portrayed Mike Hammer in "My Gun Is Quick" (1957), the least commercially and artistically successful of the theatrical Hammer films. Just as Biff Elliot was a World War II veteran, Bray was a Marine Master Sergeant who saw action in the South Pacific. His best-known role was that of Ranger Corey Stuart on the "Lassie" TV series in the mid- 1960s. The action took place in a national forest, familiar territory for Bray, who was born in Kalispell, Montana.

BART BURNS (1918–2007) portrayed Captain Pat Chambers in the 1958–59 TV series, seen in many but not all of the episodes. He had already appeared in over two dozen TV shows. Burns also had a distinguished record in World War II. He was a Marine captain who won a Silver Star on Iwo Jima when he helped a tank navigate a minefield. He was born George Burns, but changed his name to avoid confusion with the famous comedian. He had a long, distinguished career in TV on such shows as "The F.B.I." (1966), "Kojak" (1973), "Police Story"(1975), and "Lou Grant" (1981). He made occasional movie appearances, notably "Seven Days in May" (1964).

BARBARA CARRERA (1945–) was the second actress to play Spillane's signature femme fatale, Charlotte Manning, and the first to disrobe as the role famously calls for. A Nicaraguan-born former model, she joins Shirley Eaton on the very short list of actresses who appeared opposite both Mike Hammer (Armand Assante in "I, the Jury," 1982) and James Bond (Sean Connery in "Never Say Never Again," 1983).

PEGGIE CASTLE (1927–1973) was the first actress to portray the duplicitous Charlotte Manning. Tall, blonde, curvaceous, she exuded both intelligence and sexuality on screen, making her an excellent choice for the role. She also played a seeming femme fatale as Venus in the Spillane film "The Long Wait" (1954). She appeared in numerous B

Barbara Carrera as Charlotte in "I, the Jury" (1982).

movies and a remarkable number of TV episodes from the middle 1950s to the early 1960s, with a regular role as Lily Merrill on "Lawman" (1962). She even turns up in one episode of the McGavin "Mike Hammer" TV series in 1959 ("The Big Drop"). Poor health due to alcoholism contributed to her tragically early death at 45.

REBECCA CHANEY *See* THE FACE.

MAXINE COOPER (1924–2009) is perhaps the most memorable big-screen Velda (in "Kiss Me Deadly," 1955). She trained at the Pasadena Playhouse and was with the USO in 1946, entertaining the troops in Europe. She remained in Europe for over five years, appearing on stage and in BBC productions. Richard Aldrich cast her as Velda after seeing her perform as Anitra in "Peer Gynt." Her dark, unusual beauty and distinctive ethereal delivery made her perfect for Aldrich's version of Hammer's partner/secretary. After her marriage, she became a noted leftist activist, helping organize Hollywood groups to march with Martin Luther King, Jr. in Montgomery, Alabama in the 1960s.

DONNA DENTON *See* THE FACE.

FRANK DE VOL (1911–1999) is remembered for four Academy Award film score nominations, including "Cat Ballou" (1965), as well as TV series theme music, including "The Love Boat" and "My Three Sons," a hit single in 1961, and mood music, marketed as "Music by De Vol." He was also a skilled comic actor, memorably portraying sad-sack band leader Happy Kyne on "Fernwood 2-Night"/"America 2-night."

PAMELA DUNCAN (1924–2005) played Velda in "My Gun Is Quick" (1957). A voluptuous, exotic brunette, Duncan is known for her appearances in two of Roger Corman's cult science-fiction movies, "Attack of the Crab Monsters" (1957) and "The Undead" (1957). She appeared on numerous TV series of the 1950s and '60s, including "Gang Busters," "Cowboy G-Men, "The Adventures of Wild Bill Hickok," "Mr. And Mrs. North," "Dragnet," and "Perry Mason."

BLAKE EDWARDS (1922–2010) wrote and directed (for Victor Saville) the unsold Brian Keith-starring "Mike Hammer" TV pilot in 1954. He found small-screen success with his Hammer-influenced "Peter Gunn" (1959) and went on to great Hollywood success with such movies as "Breakfast at Tiffany's" (1961) and the Pink Panther series. He began his career as an actor but turned to radio script-writing in the mid-1940s, including two Dick Powell shows: "Rogue's Gallery" and "Richard Diamond, Private Detective." Both revealed the light touch Edwards brought to the hard-boiled PI.

SHIRLEY EATON (January 12, 1937–) became a film icon as the golden Bond girl of "Goldfinger" (1964). Shortly before, she had played Laura Knapp in "The Girl Hunters" (1963). Like Peggie Castle, she brought both intelligence and sex appeal to her femme fatale role, spending much of her screen time in a series of skimpy bikinis. Eaton began her career in British comedies such as the "Carry On" and "Doctor" series. She appeared in an updated remake of Agatha Christie's classic "Ten Little Indians" (1965), and enjoyed considerable Hollywood success in the later 1960s, retiring after playing Sax Rohmer's female Fu Manchu, Sumuru, in several low-budget foreign quickies. Her autobiography, *Golden Girl* (2000) includes a Spillane preface.

Pamela Duncan as Velda in "My Gun Is Quick," (1957).

BIFF ELLIOT (July 26, 1923–) was the first actor to portray Mike Hammer on screen. He was born "Leon" in Lynn, Massachusetts, but his brothers called him "Bith," which later became Biff when the young man took up boxing. This led to competing in the Golden Gloves, Elliot's slim physique leading his opponents to misjudge his toughness. Soon he won the North Maine championship, advancing to the New England regional championships, and would have been on his way to New York when his mother stopped it. Instead, he went to the University of Maine where he played on the freshman football team. From college he entered the army in 1943, assigned to North Africa as an infantryman in the 34th division. In Milan where, as part of a reconnaissance patrol, he saw the Italian partisans take out their revenge on il Duce. After the war, he returned to college, took many courses, and eventually decided to become a writer. This proved unsuccessful, so he tried his luck as an actor, having studied drama in college. After a year of knocking on doors, he finally got a break and appeared in the first of numerous TV shows, on "Lights Out" in 1951.

He got his big screen break when I. H. Prinzmetal, a noted Hollywood attorney, saw his appearance on a televised episode of "The Doctor" entitled "A Letter from a Soldier." Prinzmetal called producer Victor Saville and recommended testing Biff for the role of Mike Hammer in the forthcoming "I, the Jury." Elliot spent an entire night before his test re-reading the novel and other Spillane books. He did one scene with Preston Foster (who would play Pat Chambers) and landed the role. Stardom eluded Elliot, but the actor enjoyed a long and successful career, including appearances in such films as "The Enemy Below" (1957), "Pork Chop Hill" (1959), "PT-109" (1963), and "Save the Tiger" (1973). His many TV appearances included "Meet McGraw," "Perry Mason" and "Star Trek." Later in life he became a popular sportscaster in Los Angeles.

HARRY ESSEX (1910–1997), the screenwriter and director of "I, the Jury," had a career that lasted over fifty years. He worked (uncredited) on the Jack Webb big-screen production of "Dragnet" (1954) and several notable docu-*noirs*, including "He Walked By Night" (1948) and "Kansas City Confidential" (1952). He is perhaps best remembered for "Creature from the Black Lagoon" (1954), but also wrote such major films as "The Sons of Katie Elder" (1965) and Robert Aldrich's "What Ever Happened to Baby Jane" (1962). In the 1960s, he contributed scripts to "77 Sunset Strip" and "The Untouchables."

THE FACE (ca. 1985–) is the lovely mystery woman Mike Hammer kept encountering all around New York City in the various Stacy Keach series. On the CBS-TV series, she is portrayed by Donna Denton, who appeared in several of the sword-and-sorcery "Gor" films.

In the syndicated series, the Face (a different character?) was portrayed by Rebecca Chaney (sometimes spelled Rebekah Chaney), who later appeared in the comedy, "Cougars Inc." (2011) and other B-movies. She was born August 12, 1978 in the hallway of a Hilton Hotel on the Texas state line.

PRESTON FOSTER (1900–1970) was a rugged leading man of 1930s movies who evolved into a respected character actor. Perhaps his most famous appearance was in John Ford's Academy Award-winning, "The Informer" (1935). After a lengthy movie career, Foster guest-starred on TV series, including "Waterfront" (1954), "Gunslinger" (1961) and "77 Sunset Strip" (1964). His turn as Pat Chambers in the 1953 "I, the Jury" is a fatherly take unseen elsewhere.

HY GARDNER (1908–1989), longtime columnist for *The New York Herald Tribune*, played himself (poorly) in "The Girl Hunters" (1963). He became a close friend of Spillane's after they first met in the 1950s; they corresponded for many years. Gardner was a panelist on the first version of the TV show, "To Tell the Truth," published several humorous books, and had his own TV interview show from 1954 to 1963. When the *Tribune* folded in 1966, Hy and wife Marilyn (nee Boshnick and his former secretary) moved to Miami, where the TV and radio shows were continued.

TAY GARNETT (1894–1977) was a naval aviator in World War I. The jewel of his Hollywood directing years is the James M. Cain adaptation, "The Postman Always Rings Twice." By the 1960s, Garnett had moved to television, working on such shows as "The Untouchables" (1959–60), "Naked City" (1960–61), "Rawhide" (1962), "Bonanza" (1964–65), and "Death Valley Days" (1964–66). His work on "The Delta Factor" (1970) marked the end of his career. Garnett was credited as both director and writer, but was in failing health and the movie is certainly not his best work.

STACY KEACH (June 2, 1941–) played the role of Mike Hammer on screen longer than any other actor, from 1983 to 1998, with the same energy, commitment and skill he brings to Hemingway or King Lear. His Hammer appeared in four TV movies, two different incarnations of the CBS-TV series, and in a slightly revisionist syndicated series of 1997–98. Keach is an actor of great accomplishment, capable of the high drama of Shakespeare and the low sitcom likes of "Titus" and "Two and a Half Men." His long list of film credits include "Fat City" (1972), "The Long Riders" (1980), and "American History X" (1998). He brought a presence to the role of Hammer, equaled only by fellow stage actor Ralph Meeker and Mickey Spillane himself.

LAURENE LANDON (March 17, 1957–) made a blonde Viking of Velda in the 1982 "I, the Jury" remake. Possessing a high-energy personality combined with raw sex appeal, she appeared as Hammer's secretary/partner shortly after completing the underrated Robert Aldrich film about lady wrestlers, "...All the Marbles" (1981), with Peter Falk.

ERNEST LASZLO (1898–1984) was born in Hungary and became a frequent collaborator with directors Robert Aldrich and Stanley Kramer. His cinematography appeared in more than sixty films, including "Judgement at Nuremberg" (1961), "It's a Mad, Mad, Mad, Mad World"(1963), "Fantastic Voyage" (1966), and "Airport" (1970), all nominated for the Academy Award. He won that award in 1965 for "Ship of Fools."

CLORIS LEACHMAN (April 30, 1926–), now a Hollywood icon, was introduced in "Kiss Me Deadly." Her career has been long and varied. The Iowa-born Leachman was Miss Chicago in the 1946 Miss America competition and made her first big Hollywood success as the mom on the "Lassie" TV show, a far cry from Mickey Spillane. The winner of nine Emmy awards, more than any other actress, she is well-remembered as Phyllis Lindstrom on "The Mary Tyler Moore Show." Her best-loved film role is undoubtedly Frau Blucher in Mel Brooks' "Young Frankenstein" (1975), but she has been lauded for dramatic roles on film and stage, and at this writing remains active. For film *noir* enthusiasts, her first appearance remains her most memorable, as the ill-fated Christina.

DARREN McGAVIN (1922–2006) played Mike Hammer in the 1958–59 30-minute syndicated TV series "Mickey Spillane's Mike Hammer." McGavin's early film career included selling dope to Frank Sinatra in "Man With the Golden Arm" (1955) and replacing Dean Martin as Jerry Lewis's straight man in "The Delicate Delinquent" (1957). His Hammer was a wise-cracking, nimble guy whose affability could turn a nasty corner, with the beatings he dishes out (and occasionally takes) suitably Spillane rugged. Toning down the toughness, McGavin brought a similar approach to another private eye series, the short-lived but much-admired "The Outsider" (1969), and Old School reporter Carl Kolchak in "Kolchak: The Night Stalker" (1974), the cult success of which led to decades-later guest appearances on TV's "The X-Files." He became a popular-culture icon not as a private eye or vampire chaser, however, but as the beleaguered father in the classic Jean Shepherd film, "A Christmas Story" (1983), making him the only Mike Hammer actor to rate a Christmas-tree ornament. His long, prolific career included over two-hundred productions in television and film.

RALPH MEEKER (1920–1988) may be best remembered for his role as Mike Hammer in "Kiss Me Deadly," but he was also an award-winning stage performer. He received the New York Critic's Circle Award in 1954 for his performance in William Inge's "Picnic." For a short time, he was a hot actor in Hollywood. In 1957 alone, he appeared memorably in Stanley Kubrick's classic anti-war film, "Paths of Glory," Sam Fuller's "Run of the Arrow," and (as the Hammer-sound-alike "Mike Valla") opposite Jane Russell in the sexy comedy, "The Fuzzy Pink Nightgown." His sullen, smirky screen presence, however, fated him to secondary roles, often bad guys (Anthony Mann's "The Naked Spur," 1953) and by the early '60s he was working primarily in television. In the wildly successful 1972 TV movie "The Night Stalker" (that spawned the later series), Meeker has a secondary role to Darren McGavin's lead, the two Hammers sharing the screen in several scenes.

LEE MEREDITH (October 27, 1947–) played Marty at the Lite N Easy bar that Stacy Keach's Mike Hammer so often frequented; however, she appears only in the first two telefilms, not making the transition to the series itself. She is a statuesque buxom blonde with a great sense of humor and a warm screen presence, famous as "Ulla," object of Zero Mostel's lust in the classic comedy, "The Producers" (1968). She also appeared with George Burns and Walter Matthau in "The Sunshine Boys" (1975). She made an indelible mark as "the Doll" who accompanied Mickey Spillane in numerous Miller Lite Beer commercials in the 1970s-1980s, the only female member of the Lite Beer All-Stars.

STAN PURDY (1926–2010) wrote and conducted the jazz music for "Mickey Spillane's Mike Hammer Story" LP, which was also released in variant 45 rpm mini-albums. A radio-style play starring Spillane as Hammer, with Bettye Ackerman as a mystery woman, is one side of the LP, and a Hammer suite of jazz compositions is on the other. Material from the album was used in the Spillane-starring film "Ring of Fear" (1954), with "The Mike Hammer Theme" and "Velda" specifically credited. In the late 1950s, Purdy left a successful career conducting and composing for top jazz and dance bands to become an educator, initially on the high school and then college level.

ANTHONY QUINN (1915–2001), initially a Hollywood second-string Latin lover, used his charismatic, physically imposing presence to rise to major stardom. As Johnny McBride in "The Long Wait" (1954), he starred in the only non-Mike Hammer Spillane vehicle produced by Victor Saville. He appeared in many successful movies during his long film career, including "Zorba the Greek" (1974), "The Guns of Navarone" (1961), and "The Magus" (1968). He was the first Mexican-American to win an Academy Award—best supporting actor as Marlon Brando's brother in Elia Kazan's "Viva Zapata!" (1952). He won again for his performance as Paul Gauguin in Vincente Minnelli's "Lust for Life" (1956).

GABY RODGERS (March 29, 1928–) became a film *noir* icon thanks to one role: the false Lily Carver in "Kiss Me Deadly." She appeared in only one other movie—"The Big Break" (1953)—but was a staple of 1950s and early 1960s TV, appearing on numerous anthology shows, including "The United States Steel Hour," "Goodyear Playhouse" and "Studio One." In a 2002 interview with Wes Clark, she claimed director Robert Aldrich wanted her to play the part of Carver as a lesbian, but the only vague indications of that are her short hair and the distinctive black suit with its wide white lapels. She also recalled that she spoke to Spillane "about her character, but it didn't help." Rather remarkably, she is a "German who grew up in Holland and played with Anne Frank as a girl."

TANYA ROBERTS (October 15, 1955–) made a memorable Velda in the CBS-TV movie "Murder Me, Murder You" (April 9, 1983). For many viewers, she is *the* Velda. Blessed with the dark beauty and physical grace described by Spillane in the Hammer novels, Roberts was impressive in this, her only appearance as Velda. Her big break on TV came when she was added to the cast of "Charlie's Angels" in 1980. She used that experience to begin her movie career and appeared in the Mike Hammer TV movie between big screen projects. Reportedly she turned down continuing her role of Velda to appear in "Sheena: Queen of the Jungle"(1984), a movie that unfortunately was not well-received. Like Shirley Eaton, Roberts went on to be a Bond Girl ("View to a Kill," 1985). By the early 1990s, she was appearing in low-budget erotic thrillers such as "Night Eyes" (1990) and "Inner Sanctum" (1991), mostly seen on cable TV. She made a nice comeback later that decade with a recurring role on "That '70s Show."

VICTOR SAVILLE (1895–1979) was the respected British director and producer who bought the rights to four of Mickey Spillane's most successful novels at the height of their commercial success. Respected for his work both in Great Britain ("Evergreen," 1934) and at MGM in Hollywood ("Goodbye, Mr. Chips"), Saville made an unlikely fit with Spillane's source material, and later admitted he was "slumming" for commercial success. Spillane long contended the Saville bought the rights only to help finance the producer's more ambitious Biblical picture, "The Silver Chalice" (1954), marking the screen debut of Paul Newman, who once apologized for the notorious flop in a famous Hollywood trade-paper ad. Lesser Samuels, screenwriter of "The Silver Chalice," also wrote the script for "The Long Wait" that same year. "The Long Wait" is better.

Producer Victor Saville supervises as a (momentarily) happy Mickey Spillane signs a four-picture deal (1953).

MARGARET SHERIDAN (1926–1982) was the first actress to portray Velda, and one of the best, striking, dark-haired, with cool beauty to match her cool intelligence. Discovered by Howard Hawks while still in college, she was the famous director's pick to co-star with John Wayne in "Red River," turning down the role because she was pregnant. She later gave a memorable performance for producer Hawks opposite Kenneth Tobey in "The Thing from Another World" (1951).

JACK STANG (1923–1996), a tough ex-Marine who served in Guadalcanal in World War II, was a policeman buddy of Mickey Spillane's in Newburgh, New York. He became the physical prototype for Mike Hammer, posing for the "Mickey Spillane's Mike Hammer Story" LP. Spillane pushed him hard for the Hammer role before and after "I, the Jury," even making a short test film that received considerable publicity. Later, Stang portrayed himself in "Ring of Fear" (Spillane misremembered Jack as playing "an unnamed Mike Hammer"). The sometime actor's rugged screen presence got him work on Broderick Crawford's TV series "Highway Patrol," but ultimately Stang decided to leave Hollywood and return to his family in New York.

DON STROUD (September 1, 1943–) grew up in Hawaii, where, at one time, he was ranked fourth in the world surfing community. He began his acting career at the age of eighteen as Troy Donahue's stunt double on ABC-TV's "Hawaiian Eye" (1959). He moved to Hollywood to get into the business, usually playing bad guys and character roles, appearing in the Clint Eastwood films "Coogan's Bluff" (1968) and "Joe Kidd" (1972), and assorted action films. He portrayed Pat Chambers in the Hammer series from 1983–1989, with a light touch that off-set his considerable physical presence, displaying an easygoing affability, making a perfect foil for Stacy Keach's TV Hammer. For many, Stroud is the definitive Chambers.

MALGOSIA TOMASSI is an actress and interior designer born in Warsaw, Poland. Tomassi met Stacy Keach on the set of "The Return of Mike Hammer" in which she was playing the role of a nun. In the 1997–1998 syndicated version of the series, she portrayed yoga instructor Maya Ricci, whose office was near Hammer's. She also played the role in the three-volume full-cast audio series, "The New Adventures of Mike Hammer." She married Keach in 1986; they have two children, Karolina and Shannon.

Jack Stang as Mike Hammer appearing with Bettye Ackerman as a femme fatale in the lost Mike Hammer test film, written and directed by Spillane in 1953.

FRANZ WAXMAN (1906–1967), one of the greatest film composers, was born in the part of Prussia that became Poland. His first American movie score was for James Whale's "Bride of Frankenstein" (1935). He worked often for Alfred Hitchcock, including such classics as "Rebecca" (1940) and "Rear Window" (1954), and won Academy Awards for "Sunset Boulevard" (1950) and "A Place in the Sun" (1951). He was also nominated for best music for "The Silver Chalice" (1954), the film Victor Saville reputedly made with the proceeds from his first several Spillane films.

SHANNON WHIRRY (November 7, 1964–) played Velda in the syndicated "Mike Hammer, Private Eye" (1997–98). Strikingly beautiful, buxom, with blonde-brown hair (not brunette as per Spillane's Velda), she displayed a feisty on-screen persona as Hammer's secretary. She became something of B-movie icon in the 1990s, playing numerous roles in such erotic thrillers as "Animal Instincts" (1992) and "Body of Influence," but later appeared in more mainstream fare, mostly notably as Robert Oppenheimer's wife in the BBC production "Nuclear Secrets" (2007).

KENT WILLIAMS (December 27, 1950–) portrayed D. A Barrington for the CBS-TV Hammer and the similar D. A. Barry Lawrence for the syndicated series. Born in Manhattan, Williams is the son of a big band leader and a former June Taylor dancer. Williams is a top voice actor for animated films and video games, notably "Dragon Ball Z," from 1989 through the present.

D. Stars of the Hammer Film Universe

Mike Hammer Biff Elliott, "I, the Jury" (1953). Brian Keith, Mike Hammer TV pilot (1954). Ralph Meeker, "Kiss Me Deadly" (1955). Robert Bray, "My Gun Is Quick" (1957). Darren McGavin, "Mickey Spillane's Mike Hammer" TV series (1958–59) 78 episodes. Mickey Spillane, "The Girl Hunters" (1963). Kevin Dobson, "Margin for Murder" CBS TV movie (10-15-1981). Armand Assante, "I, the Jury" (1982). Stacy Keach, "Murder Me, Murder You" CBS TV movie (4-9-1983); "More Than Murder" CBS TV movie (1-26-84); "Mickey Spillane's Mike Hammer" CBS TV series (1984–85) (24 episodes); "Return of Mickey Spillane's Mike Hammer" CBS TV movie (4-18-1986); "The New Mike Hammer" CBS TV series (1986–1987) (22 episodes); "Murder Takes All" CBS TV movie (5-21-1989). Rob Estes, "Come Die with Me" CBS TV movie pilot (12-6-1994). Stacy Keach, "Songbird" syndicated TV movie (1997); "A New Leaf" syndicated TV movie (1997); "Mike Hammer Private Eye" syndicated TV series (1997) (26 episodes).

Velda (Velda Sterling) Margaret Sheridan,"I, the Jury" (1953); does not appear, Mike Hammer TV pilot (1954). (Velda Wickman) Maxine Cooper,"Kiss Me Deadly" (1955). Pamela Duncan, "My Gun Is Quick" (1957); never appears, mentioned in pilot episode, "Mickey Spillane's Mike Hammer" TV series (1958–59) 78 episodes; never appears, "The Girl Hunters" (1963). Cindy Pickett, "Margin for Murder" CBS TV movie (10-15-1981). Laurene Landon, "I, the Jury" (1982). Tanya Roberts, "Murder Me, Murder You" CBS TV movie (4-9-1983). Lindsay Bloom, "More Than Murder" CBS TV movie (1-26-84); "Mickey Spillane's Mike Hammer" CBS TV series (1984–85) (24 episodes); "Return of Mickey Spillane's Mike Hammer" CBS TV movie (4-18-1986); "The New Mike Hammer" CBS TV series (1986–1987) (22 episodes); "Murder Takes All" CBS TV movie (5-21-1989). Pamela Anderson, "Come Die with Me" CBS TV movie pilot (12-6-1994). Shannon Whirry, "Songbird" syndicated TV movie (1997); "A New Leaf" syndicated TV movie (1997); "Mike Hammer Private Eye" syndicated TV series (1997) (26 episodes).

Pat Chambers Preston Foster, "I, the Jury" (1953). Robert Bice, Mike Hammer TV pilot (1954). (Pat Murphy), Wesley Addy, "Kiss Me Deadly" (1955). Booth Coleman, "My Gun Is Quick" (1957). Bart Burns, "Mickey Spillane's Mike Hammer" TV series (1958–59) 78 episodes. Scott Peters, "The Girl Hunters" (1963). Charles Hallahan, "Margin for Murder" CBS TV movie (10-15-1981). Paul Sorvino, "I, the Jury" (1982). Don Stroud, "Murder Me, Murder You" CBS TV movie (4-9-1983); "More Than Murder" CBS TV movie (1-26-84); "Mickey Spillane's Mike Hammer" CBS TV series (1984–85) (24 episodes); "Return of Mickey Spillane's Mike Hammer" CBS TV movie (4-18-1986); "The New Mike Hammer" CBS TV series (1986–1987) (22 episodes); "Murder Takes All" CBS TV movie (5-21-1989). Darlanne Fluegel, "Come Die with Me" CBS TV movie pilot (12-6-1994); "Songbird" syndicated TV movie (1997); "A New Leaf" syndicated TV movie (1997); "Mike Hammer Private Eye" syndicated TV series (1997) (26 episodes).

The Women Charlotte Manning, Peggie Castle; Esther Bellamy, Tani Seitz; Mary Bellamy, Dran Seitz; "I, the Jury" (1953). Janice Graham, Virginia Lee; Barbara, Carol Brewster; Mike Hammer TV pilot (1954). Christina,Cloris Leachman; Lily Carver, Gaby Rodgers; Michael Friday, Marion Carr; "Kiss Me Deadly" (1955). Nancy Williams, Whitney Blake; Dione, Patricia Donohue; Red, Jan Chaney; "My Gun Is Quick" (1957). See chapter 10, "Mickey Spillane's Mike Hammer" TV series (1958–59) 78 episodes. Laura Knapp, Shirley Eaton; Nurse, Kim Tracy; "The Girl Hunters" (1963). Daisy,Donna Dixon,"Margin for Murder" CBS TV movie (10-15-1981). Charlotte Bennett,Barbara Carrera,"I, the Jury" (1982). Paula Corey, Delta Burke; Chris Jameson, Michelle Phillips; Michelle Jameson, Lisa Blount; Marty, Lee Meredith;"Murder Me, Murder You" CBS TV movie (4-9-1983). Sandy, Lynn-Holley Johnson; Eve Warwick, Robyn Douglass; Marty, Lee Meredith; "More Than Murder" CBS TV movie (1-26-84). See chapter 14, "Mickey Spillane's Mike Hammer" CBS TV series (1984–85) (24 episodes). Joanna Lake, Lauren Hutton; Jenny, Lee Benton; Nun, Malgosia Tomassi; "Return of Mickey Spillane's Mike Hammer" CBS TV movie (4-18-1986). See chapter 16,"The New Mike Hammer" CBS TV series (1986–1987) (22 episodes). Helen Durant, Lynda Carter; Amy Durant, Stacy Golina; Leora van Treas, Michelle Phillips; Jenny, Lee Benton; "Murder Takes All" CBS TV movie (5-21-1989). Trinity, Randi Ingrian; Agent Hotz, Kim Delgado; "Come Die with Me" CBS TV movie pilot (12-6-1994). See chapter 20, "Songbird" syndicated TV movie (1997). See chapter 20, A New Leaf" syndicated TV movie (1997). See chapter 20, "Mike Hammer Private Eye" syndicated TV series (1997) (26 episodes).

The Writers Harry Essex, "I, the Jury" (1953). Blake Edwards, Mike Hammer TV pilot (1954). A. I. Bezzerides, "Kiss Me Deadly" (1955). Richard Collins and Richard Powell, "My Gun Is Quick" (1957). See chapter 11, "Mickey Spillane's Mike Hammer" TV series (1958–59) 78 episodes. Mickey Spillane, Roy Rowland and Robert Fellows, "The Girl Hunters" (1963). Calvin Clements, Jr., "Margin for Murder" CBS TV movie (10-15-1981). Larry Cohen, "I, the Jury" (1982). Calvin Clements, Jr.,"Murder Me, Murder You" CBS TV movie (4-9-1983). Bill Stratton and Stephen Downing,"More Than Murder" CBS TV movie (1-26-84). See chapter 14, "Mickey Spillane's Mike Hammer" CBS TV series (1984–85) (24 episodes). Larry Brody, Janis Handler and James M. Miller,"Return of Mickey Spillane's Mike Hammer" CBS TV movie (4-18-1986). See chapter 16, "The New Mike Hammer" CBS TV series (1986–1987) (22 episodes). Mark Edward Edens,"Murder Takes All" CBS TV movie (5-21-1989). John Lau, "Come Die with Me" CBS TV movie pilot (12-6-1994). Peter McGovern and Michael O'Connell,"Songbird" syndicated TV movie (1997). Jennifer Boller, "A New Leaf" syndicated TV movie (1997). See chapter 20, "Mike Hammer Private Eye" syndicated TV series (1997) (26 episodes).

The Directors Harry Essex, "I, the Jury" (1953). Blake Edwards, Mike Hammer TV pilot (1954). Robert Aldrich, "Kiss Me Deadly" (1955). George A. White and Phil Victor (Victor Saville). "My Gun Is Quick" (1957). See chapter 10, "Mickey Spillane's Mike Hammer" TV series (1958–59) 78 episodes. Roy Rowland, "The Girl Hunters" (1963). Daniel Heller, "Margin for Murder" CBS TV movie (10-15-1981). Richard Heffron, "I, the Jury" (1982). Gary Nelson, "Murder Me, Murder You" CBS TV movie (4-9-1983). Gary Nelson, "More Than Murder" CBS TV movie (1-26-84). See chapter 14, "Mickey Spillane's Mike Hammer" CBS TV series (1984–85) (24 episodes). Ray Danton, "Return of Mickey Spillane's Mike Hammer" CBS TV movie (4-18-1986). See chapter 16, "The New Mike Hammer" CBS TV series (1986–1987) (22 episodes). Ray Danton, "Murder Takes All" CBS TV movie (5-21-1989). Armand Mastroianni, "Come Die with Me" CBS TV movie pilot (12-6-1994). Jonathan Winfrey, "Songbird" syndicated TV movie (1997). Jonathan Winfrey, "A New Leaf" syndicated TV movie (1997). See chapter 21, "Mike Hammer Private Eye" syndicated TV series (1997) (26 episodes).

E. Mickey Spillane in His Own Words

Mickey Spillane interviewed by Max Allan Collins at Spillane's oceanfront home in Murrells Inlet, South Carolina, in November 1997. The interview was conducted for the documentary *Mike Hammer's Mickey Spillane* (1999).

MAX ALLAN COLLINS: Mickey, you've had a wide-ranging career, and though you're obviously most famous for your bestselling novels, what I'd like to explore today are the movies, the commercials, and all the various MIKE HAMMER licensing. But first, you don't consider yourself an "author," do you?

MICKEY SPILLANE: I am not an author. I am a writer. Now the difference is that an author would be Eisenhower. Would be, Churchill. They wrote their memoirs and all this. They write one thing. This is part of history more or less. But a writer is on a day-to-day job. All the time he's writing, this is a job for him, he's making money to keep the smoke comin' out the chimney.

MAC: When did you start writing?

SPILLANE: I started writing when I was in junior high school in Elizabeth, New Jersey. This was at the time of the Depression, when they started Prohibition and all. Now kids get to know things. We're crawling under garages, we knew were all the bootleggers hid their stuff. And I was writing stories about bootlegging for the *Elizabeth Daily Journal.* Man, it was somethin'. But that's when I got the idea of being printed. It's nice seein' yourself in print. Then I found out you could write for money—people would pay you for these things! And I started writing stuff for like *Liberty Magazine, Saturday Evening Post.* Never used my own name. 'Cause they used house names.

MAC: When you went to college in Kansas at Fort Hays, I understand you were making more money writing than the dean of the college was earning.

SPILLANE: 'Cause everything I turned in as a report for English. I was taking writing courses for Pete's Sake. I was selling, I was turning in my carbon copies what I'd already sold in New York.

MAC: So you dropped out of college and went back to New York and the writing game.

SPILLANE: Yeah, I started with slicks, then I worked my way down to the pulps, then I worked my way down to the comic books. Now you're going downhill in class. But you're goin' up in money. And I made a lot more money out of comic books than I ever did out of slick magazines.

MAC: You were kind of a pioneer in the comics field.

SPILLANE: I was in the first group of writers, when we first started comics. I was working for Funnies Inc. We used to work at all hours. We each had a place in New York and the artists were over there and the writers were over here and we're bangin' stuff out. Stan Lee was the guy, he could write on three typewriters at once, you know. And Jack Kirby was drawing Captain America, Human Torch.

MAC: Those are some of the features you worked on as a writer yourself, aren't they?

SPILLANE: Oh yeah, Sub-mariner, the Human Torch, Blue Bolt, Captain America, oh—a whole kit and kaboodle of 'em. We did those things with Classic Comics, too. When Classic Comics first come out—when you would take a book like *Count of Monte Cristo.* Now I wrote that one and Kirby drew it.

MAC: The postal regulations for comics required a minimum of two pages of prose. Short stories with your byline appear in lots of Golden Age "Marvel" comics.

SPILLANE: You got $25 a shot for two pages of these things. And these

Mickey Spillane and his typewriter, circa 1954.

things would take up to a half hour to write, you know. But at that time, $25 was a lot of money. You could write four a day and you're getting $100 a day when a hard-workin' man out there is making $35 a week.

MAC: I know you left the comic book field in '42 to enlist; you were a flight instructor during World War Two. Paperbacks got started in those years, really, didn't they? Reprints handed out to servicemen?

SPILLANE: When I was in the army, I saw the initial attempt of getting reprints into paperback on the market. And all I could think of was, after the war, they're going to be putting out original paperbacks. This is the new concept coming up, something brand new and different.

MAC: But after the war, you went back into comic books.

SPILLANE: Yes, but I recognized what was the new market was—paperback books. That's why I wrote *I, the Jury*. But the main reason it got me there was I had to get out of New York City. I couldn't stand that place any more. I wanted to live out in the country up in Newburgh, New York, and I needed $1,000 and at that time you only gave $250 to a writer to write a mystery story. I needed $1,000. So I wrote *I, the Jury*—I got my thousand.

MAC: When *I, the Jury* was published in hardcover, it didn't sell particularly well, but when the paperback came out, it was an instant smash. Did all this fame and money change your lifestyle much?

SPILLANE: Naw, we lived in Newburgh, New York, in the cement-block house I built. We were out in the country. You go around in dungarees—you shovel snow in the winter time. Now, I came up with some of the great editors in publishing. The big one to me was Victor Weybright. I brought up *One Lonely Night* to him, in a paper bag. I had a pair of dungarees on and T-shirt, just came out of Newburgh—hot summer day. And I brought my manuscript into him in that brown paper bag—I had been carryin' this thing under the seat of my car for the last week. Kickin' it back every time it came out. I gave it to him, he calls the bank across the street, gets two security guards to come up with guns. They took this thing down with their hands on the guns, to cross the street to put it in the bank safety deposit box. And I said—I don't dare tell him I had it under the seat of my car for a week kickin' it around. But I stayed in Newburgh as much as possible—I didn't get involved with Hollywood or the New York bunch unless it was business and necessary.

MAC: What do you think it was about your character Mike Hammer that connected so well with the public?

SPILLANE: When the war was over, people were used to violence. You know I was in the military—I knew what they were thinking, I knew what they were eatin' and dreamin'. That's why I didn't make Mike a pilot like I was. I made him come out of the trenches where most of the people were. And they knew what a person's mind could do to them when they came back and a .45 was the gun that they used, you know.

MAC: Do you think there was a loss of innocence after the war, that made readers connect to your overtly violent, sexual material?

SPILLANE: Sex and violence are punctuation marks in a story. The whole thing isn't written about sex and violence. There's a story involved.

MAC: Even so, you took a lot of heat for sex and violence.

SPILLANE: I have gotten the worst reviews in the world. Nobody has ever gotten them as bad as me. And they would say this man writes the most trivial garbage in the world, it's terrible, it's infused with sex and violence and don't ever read this stuff. So we made this big ad out of the bad reviews, quoting from them. Then underneath we'd have a line like, this book sold six million copies. The top of the ad said, Mickey Spillane says about his new book, "I hope this one gets lousy reviews." I wrote for entertainment, I wasn't trying to educate anybody.

MAC: You were one of the first celebrity writers in America, certainly one of the first writers to become a pop culture figure. You did lots of early '50s TV—"Milton Berle," "Steve Allen," and other shows.

SPILLANE: Oh, once I was doin' a Christmas TV show and the famous old actor (Basil Rathbone) who was going to recite "The Night Before Christmas" was sittin' on a bar stool in front of a big crowd. In back of him there was a big movie screen they were going to show slides of each section of "The Night Before Christmas." Now I had just finished one TV show and the guy who was going to do this was a very famous actor and he was down there and he was drunk as a skunk. I went upstairs and I told the director, "Hey you know, how are you goin' to do this show, the guy's down there drunk." He went down there he comes back, "Oh what are we going to do?" I said, "Tell you what, I'll do it for you if you want me to." He says, "Would you?" I says, "You got nobody else to do this." He says, "Could you do it?" I said, "Sure I'll do it for you." So I went out and in the meantime, this director's lookin' for a script for me and the show starts. And I have a bar stool out there and in the sponsor's booth, in the back there, they had glass across there, I could see the screen reflecting up there so I could time it in perfectly. So we started off and I said "The night before Christmas and all through...." In the meantime this poor director's goin' nuts. The script comes out, the guy, they threw it down to across my feet, and I kicked it back. And the guy come out and he threw it again and I kicked it back. In the meantime I'm goin' on with it. Now the audience, imagine the people seein' this, they're laughin' like a son-of-a-gun. But the at-home audience never saw that foot go like that. So I finished and I said "To all a good night." It was a fantastic show. And I looked at the director, he's dripping sweat. He didn't know I knew "The Night Before Christmas."

MAC: By 1952 you'd written seven novels, six of them Mike Hammers, and they were already the seven bestselling mysteries written up to that time. So I guess it was inevitable that Hollywood would come knocking; they even spoofed you and Mike Hammer in "The Band Wagon," with Fred Astaire as Hammer.

SPILLANE: Victor Saville was the producer on "Goodbye, Mr. Chips," a great picture. I thought, this is my early concept of Hollywood, I would think that Hollywood would think enough of a book that sold a lot of copies that they would make a good picture out of it. Now all Saville wanted to do was buy my name and my character and he made four movies. 'Cause he wanted to make a big picture fast called "The Silver Chalice." It fell on its face and it couldn't have happened to a nicer guy. Because Saville loused up those pictures so badly just to make money, now I suddenly saw the greed in these Hollywood characters. That's why I'm very careful when I deal with Hollywood. I don't like it unless I can deal with somebody I know well.

MAC: First of the Saville pictures was "I, the Jury," shot in 3-D. It's a terrific looking picture, with cinematography by John Alton, who's a legendary film *noir* figure.

SPILLANE: They shot it in 3-D, but it didn't stay that way long because, not enough theaters had 3-D equipment. That thing never went. It was too expensive to put in two separate projectors and, you know, the glasses and all that sort of thing.

MAC: You were unhappy with the actor selected to play Mike Hammer.

SPILLANE: Biff Elliott. And, poor Biff lost his career because of it. First of all they surrounded him by big guys—Biff was my size. He had a Boston accent and he was left-handed. And he did these silly things like pickin' up a perfect bullet and identifying it, "Ahh, a 38!" That was supposed to be smashed into a wall, it shoulda looked like a quarter. But Biff was a good actor. Just miscast. He won a lot of awards in New York for live television shows. But this isn't live TV. This is movies that you're gettin' involved with. And if you come out of New York and you're not used to that and you're a novice out there in Hollywood, they walk all over you.

MAC: Is it true you walked out of the premiere, and never saw the picture in full till years later on TV?

SPILLANE: Yeah, I walked out. I just couldn't take it anymore. When I saw Biff get hit on the head with the coat hanger, and get knocked out, I said, this isn't Mike Hammer. They gave Darren McGavin, when he played Mike Hammer, they gave him a .38 and I said, "Why didn't you use a .45?" He says, "They said my hand was too small." You go in the army, you don't say, well, my hand's too small for a 45. You shoot that gun! The .45 has something nasty about it. Do you know why the .45 was put in production? They had to have a gun that would stop you and flip you over backwards if you got hit.

MAC: Biff Eliot was signed for a long-term contract, but when the public didn't take to him, Saville sort of punted. He didn't choose another Mike Hammer for the second picture; instead, he did the one non-Hammer you'd written up till then, "The Long Wait."

SPILLANE: That was better. Anthony Quinn was good in that show, he was a good character for the part of Johnny McBride. But the guy who wrote it (Lesser Samuels), never read the book. It was pretty badly done in that respect because the story line was screwed up. Tony Quinn's a nice man, and a great actor, and after he shot the picture, he read the book, and he remembers what they had in the script. He says to me, "That wasn't the story at all!" Which was true.

MAC: This is about the time you decided to finance your own screen test for your friend Jack Stang, who you had wanted to play Hammer all along. In fact he plays a small role as a pool-hall tough in "I, the Jury."

SPILLANE: Jack just died last year. This guy looked like he could be Mike Hammer. You look at this fellow, you could say he was a peace-lovin' guy, but don't tangle with him. He was one of the group of marines that went onto a Pacific island and they went in with one hundred-and-twenty guys and there were four left when they came out. Jack was one of the four. And he was a tough man, physically, mentally and able to accomplish anything he wanted to do. And I always wanted this guy to be in the movie to play the part. But unfortunately, he never was able to handle certain types of scenes. He wasn't an actor, he was a cop. Acting isn't in a cop's job unless he's doing an interrogation or something like that, then he can act.

MAC: Where was Stang a cop?

SPILLANE: Newburgh, New York. And later, when he was with me, we were workin'—I'm not going to tell you about this 'cause it's kind of restricted still. That I save for my biography which I'm never going to write anyway.

MAC: You used Stang's picture on the cover of your "Mickey Spillane's Mike Hammer" LP (featuring a radio-show-like story by Spillane); but *you* played Hammer. The "Mike Hammer screen test" got written up in several men's magazines, but Saville rejected Stang, and the short film is lost, isn't it?

SPILLANE: Oh yeah, yeah. This was one of Saville's ways of keeping me away from the set. He had a crew come over. We shot a really good little test, which got buried someplace. I wish I could get that back. But, it's one of the things that Hollywood does to you. They go all out to give people a screen test, when they already know they're not going to be using 'em—it's all because this guy's got his eye on that girl over there, or that guy wants somethin' from over here, see. That was a creepy situation in those days. It's not too nice now, believe me.

MAC: You directed this yourself?

SPILLANE: Yeah, it come out great too. I'll tell you who was in it. Jonathan Winters played a hobo. Bettye Ackerman was in it; she was the nurse on "Ben Casey." We had good people on that thing. Who later became big stars.

MAC: Saville wasn't interested in Stang, but your test film attracted John Wayne's attention. Both you and Stang were hired to appear in a Batjac production, "Ring of Fear." You played yourself and Stang was clearly Hammer.

SPILLANE: Yeah, Jack Stang played the part of Mike Hammer and was never identified. 'Cause in the picture they say, "Is that him?" I say, "That's him." Jack threw his own last line in when the killer gets destroyed: "Couldn't have happened to a nicer guy." They left it in, so I was glad Jack had somethin' to do with that. Poor Jack, though, he couldn't remember a line, he went crazy tryin' to remember lines.

MAC: "Ring of Fear" is an unusual picture; it's a mix of actors like Pat O'Brien and Sean McClory from the John Ford stock company, and celebrities like yourself and Clyde Beatty. It's also rumored that you heavily doctored the script.

SPILLANE: What happened was, Batjac had the Clyde Beatty Circus under contract. Duke had put money into this. And they had to do this picture or Duke was going to lose all his money. So when they came to me after they saw the first cut of the shoot, it was aw, geez, it was terrible. Now I was already back in Newburgh, New York. They called me up I think it was on a Wednesday, or a Tuesday. They said, "Can you get out here?" I says, "Sure, sure be glad to." I knew everything, I knew exactly where the problems were, I saved all the paper, I knew where all the out-takes were. A lot of out-takes are great to use. I started to work on Friday, I worked all day Friday, all day Saturday. Now Sunday I'm workin' down there and I'm staying up at the Beverly Hills Hotel, the beautiful place. And anyway, in comes Andy McLaglen, who's a big director now. And he came in and he says, "How are you doin'?" I'm sittin' there havin' a cold beer 'cause I was thirsty and I said, "I'm all done." Now he thought I meant I was all done for the day, 'cause it was like twelve o'clock and figured I was goin' to take a half a day off, that's okay. He says, "Oh, that's nice." I says, "Well, I think maybe I better go home." He says, "Well, what do you mean?" I says, "Well, I'm done." He says, "What do you mean you're done?" I said, "I'm done with the script." He says, "What? Let me see that."....And in the meantime, they have to get the Clyde Beatty show back together, I went back to Newburgh. I didn't want to stick around Hollywood. And I had the best accommodations and that beautiful hotel, where the Polo Lounge is and all that sort of stuff.

Behind the scenes on "Ring of Fear": (left to right) Sean McClory, Pat O'Brien, unknown (back to camera), Clyde Beatty, Jack Stang, Mickey Spillane.

And I went back to Newburgh. Now they get all set and they go to look for me and they can't find me. They called every boarding house, every hospital, every saloon. And finally Bob says, "Let's try Newburgh." And I was in Newburgh. They says, "What you doin' there?" I says, "What am I going to do in Hollywood?" He says, "Get out here!" So I come out and we started the picture again and the picture was a success. Now they didn't know what to do about that, 'cause they didn't pay me for (writing) it, I wouldn't take any money for it.

MAC: And that's when John Wayne stepped in.

SPILLANE: That's where I got my lovely old car, now 41 years old. It's a '56 Jaguar. It was given to me by John Wayne. Actually what it is, is a Hollywood thank-you card. Duke he didn't know what to give me, and I didn't take any money for doin' the rewrite. So, he knew I liked cars—at that time I was a hot-rodder and I used to look at these lovely cars out there in Hollywood but I never thought of owning one—and here I am up in Newburgh, New York on a wintry day, I open up the front door and there out in front of the house is this car sittin' there and it had a big red ribbon wrapped around it with a card that said, "Thanks, Duke."

MAC: You and John Wayne were good friends.

SPILLANE: Yeah, we were friends, yeah. He was a nice, he was a very nice man. He was nice to people. He didn't do nasty things. He liked to see a picture put together, make a success of it and you earn your income. We're in a business. You know, show business has two words to it and the biggest word is business. That show stuff stinks. It's part of the business, that's what it is.

MAC: You also occasionally would do little doctoring of scripts for him wouldn't you?

SPILLANE: Oh, yeah, yeah. I've done a lot of that kind of thing. But I don't like that. I don't like to write on somebody else's work. Now, sometimes if they say, "What's wrong with this?" And you can show them what is wrong in a sequence, like when Duke's producer Bob Fellows took me to see a screening of one of Wild Bill Wellman's pictures. Bill had two things out of position. And nobody could figure it out. And Bob Fellows says "Bill, I got a guy here...." Now Bill's on the stage, we're up in the dark in the balcony. Bob says, "I got a guy here who knows what's wrong with your picture." And Bill, suddenly his mood changed, 'cause Bob was his friend, "Yeah, Bob, what, what?" Bob says tell him, so I tell him, he says "Who does the son of a gun think he is?" And Bob says, "He's Mickey Spillane." And Bill says, "Doggoneit! He's exactly right." They re-edited the picture and it was fine. I forget what picture it was. But it worked out.

MAC: You got friendly with Clyde Beatty on "Ring of Fear," didn't you? And ended up traveling as a circus performer?

SPILLANE: I got to be a real circus buff. And every year I'd go out with the Ringling Circus or Clyde Beatty. And it was fun knowing these people. It's just another world by itself. The circus is a world outside of this world. They go from one place to another, they know each other, they inter-marry, they can do each other's acts.

MAC: Your specialty was getting shot out of a cannon.

SPILLANE: What you're doing—you're sittin' on a thing like a bicycle seat in there—it's compressed air that throws you out—shooom! And there's no impact to it. Now the boom that goes with it, it's all the eye wash.

MAC: The next Saville-produced picture, "Kiss Me Deadly," has come to be highly regarded. I think you know we disagree on this; I think it's a great movie. But you don't think much of it, right?

SPILLANE: Aldrich made that picture, and he's another one, he didn't care about who wrote it or how many sales it had. And he completely rewrote the whole story line and I saw it the other night—they went and they found the missing ending on it, which was only about maybe 30 seconds long. Now I had seen that original ending when I first saw the movie, so I knew what was there. It's a big cult thing in France. Why it became that, I don't know.

MAC: Well, we agree that the final Saville production—"My Gun Is Quick"—is by far the worst Mike Hammer movie ever made.

SPILLANE: Oh, terrible. I felt sad for the actors who had to play in it—they got paid for it, but that's it. They got no recognition, nothing came out of it. The guy that played Hammer, Robert Bray—boy, he didn't ever hit big stardom, but you know, he was a competent actor. He was caught in the wrong vehicle. And I always thought that Saville would have the sense to do what was right and he never did.

MAC: Around the same time, you got involved with television. The pilot for the syndicated "Mickey Spillane's Mike Hammer" series starred Brian Keith.

SPILLANE: Yeah, Brian Keith did it. He was good in it, too. I don't know what happened there, because I wasn't on top of that production. I don't know why he wasn't chosen. He was young at that time, very young. Of course he's dead now. Then Darren McGavin got it. He played it with humor. Some guys have that ability and he has that ability. So it was a different concept. But for TV, it was a good concept. I wouldn't write that. But for half-hour TV in black and white, it came across. We did the show for two years and Darren wanted to do "Riverboat" on network TV, and he gave up our syndicated show. And they stopped doing "Mike Hammer" then.

MAC: You did have some complaints about that version of "Mike Hammer," though.

SPILLANE: Oh, they always gave McGavin these little revolvers. Well, that's silly because a .45 is so tight with Mike Hammer. That's *the* gun. It's like giving Robin Hood a slingshot instead of a bow and arrow.

MAC: Shortly after this, you played Hammer yourself. It was producer Bob Fellows, from "Ring of Fear" again, so Fellows must have shared my view that you were the one who came across like Mike Hammer in that film, not Stang. Anyway, how was it that you came to write and star in a Mike Hammer movie?

SPILLANE: They asked me to. It wasn't my idea. Of course, I said certainly, you know. It was fun to do. I knew the words because I had written the script. And I was in charge of casting. So I looked very tall because I wouldn't hire anybody that wasn't any bigger than that. So I could swagger through the picture. I was the same size as my leading lady, practically. I was a little bit bigger than she was. But we made the picture, had a good time making it. We had a happy set. That was good about this. We were right next to Burton and Liz Taylor, they were makin' the picture "The VIPs."

MAC: How much of the picture was shot in America, and how much in England?

SPILLANE: We shot all of the establishing shots in New York. Shots where we're going in and out of, like the Blue Ribbon Restaurant, but the actual stuff, the big stuff the dialogue and all we shot over in England.

MAC: I've always wondered why the feature's credits call "The Girl Hunters" a 'Colorama' production, when it's in black and white.

SPILLANE: We ran out of money had to make it in black and white. And, so we couldn't do it in color, and James Bond was coming with "Dr. No" at that time. And we were in competition with all this money that was goin' into the "Dr. No" picture. I licensed rights to some novellas I wrote to my English publishers so they could make books out of 'em. 'Cause we got stranded over there by Hollywood. They wouldn't pay their bills and I had to pay their bills for them.

MAC: Who was your director on the picture?

SPILLANE: Roy Rowland. I don't know where he is now. I said, "Why do you guys gotta interrupt us with this tea time business?" They said, "Oh, sir that's in our contract, we always have our tea time, you know." I says, "Why don't you have tea time all day? You know you don't have to do it at two, ten and three." "Oh, all day, sir?" "Yeah. We'll have tea carts here and you can have all day long and all the cookies you can eat." So we brought the tea in. And man all the pastries they could eat—they had a ball!

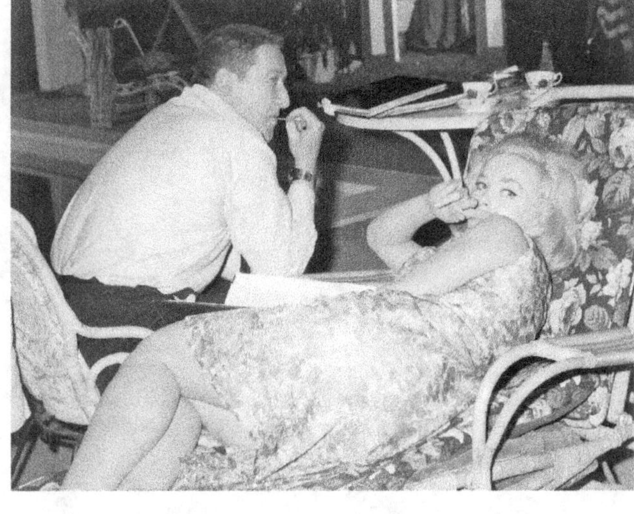

On set with Shirley Eaton on "The Girl Hunters" (1963).

MAC: Why was that an English picture?

SPILLANE: It wasn't an English picture, it was a cooperative picture. But the English government had a funny set-up there; if you're using so many English actors shooting on English soil, the government puts money into the picture. And it was one of those co-op things. We were using a lot of Canadians because they had American accents.

MAC: How did you get along with Shirley Eaton?

SPILLANE: Great! Shirley was this beautiful blonde, my leading lady. Now this one scene is set so that here is Shirley and I on that couch, and the camera's way in the back and all the crew is behind the camera. We start to shoot, and we go through as we're getting together on the couch and things started to happen. The camera comes forward and forward and forward and finally gets right on top of it and fades out because it's so close we go out of focus. So anyway, I'm an amateur, I'm not a professional actor and I'm on the couch and boy, there's no world out there, just Shirley and me and I forget everything, and there's not a sound, the camera's comin' closer and closer. Now when you say "Cut" on a set, there's instant pandemonium. And everybody gets up, rushes, runnin' around. So the camera comes out, goes out of focus, the director says, "Cut!" And nobody moved. He says "Cut!," and nobody moves. And this little voice way in the background says, "Throw cold water on 'em!"

MAC: You wrote the script to "The Girl Hunters," and stayed very faithful to the novel; but you added a famous scene involving a tough guy with an ice pick in a bar.

SPILLANE: That was based on something that really happened. I was tellin' Roy Rowland, the director, about this, and he said, "We gotta have that in the movie." I said, "But it's not in the book..." He said, "I don't care, I gotta have that scene." So we put it in the picture.

MAC: What's the true story behind that scene, then?

SPILLANE: Well, I had to meet a guy on 8th Avenue in New York City. This is a tough area. You get all the prostitutes and rough stuff down that way. And I had to meet this guy, he's a reporter, I was gonna meet him in a saloon. And he'd picked out the place. Now I went in there, I had my Mike Hammer clothes on—you know the black suit and the hat and all that stuff. I didn't have a gun on me. I used to have a gun on me, but I didn't have one this time. But in my pocket I had a clip of .45s. The gun was in the car that I

On set with Lloyd Nolan on "The Girl Hunters."

had parked. So I went in there and I got right on the end of the bar and ordered a beer. And the bartender looked at me very funny. And I looked at the guys in the bar and boy they started doin' these things they do in the movies, somebody comes in, there's going to be a shoot-out everybody starts moving chairs over—and there's one guy at the bar there and he was a Spanish-lookin' guy, and he had a funny look on him. And I looked at his hands he's got an ice pick. Now this time goes on a little bit and everything got very quiet. And the bartender moved away from me. And the guy's there and he sticks the ice pick in the bar and he pulls it back and the handle comes off and the pick stays in the bar. Now I know about this trick, what they do, they can stick you with that ice pick, meanwhile their prints are still on there and in the meantime you die of loss of blood, internal bleeding is what you die of. And the doctors don't even know you're stuck. So he's talkin' to me now and we could see that something's goin' on down there and this guy is, now I know, the next thing is he's going to approach me. And he's gonna either rob me, he's gonna stick me, or something, I don't know what is goin' on. You gotta come out of this thing lookin' like you knew exactly what you're doin'. In the meantime my heart's going boom boom boom boom boom. So I'm fairly calm, I don't want my hand to shake like this. This is a deadly situation. These guys are down there all lookin' at what's happenin'. So, I reach in my side pocket and say, "I just happen to have somethin' here to show you," I had this .45 clip in my pocket. So I reached out and put it on the table top, or the bar top like that, and I flipped that top bullet out with my thumb. Now that's a spring-loaded clip. And it went PING. And I had practiced something like this, this is fun time at home, you know, seeing how it worked. But this one worked perfectly. The bullet shot down about ten feet the bar and stopped right in front of that guy. Now the sound it made running along the bar was *zzzzzzzzzzz*. It stopped right there, just like I had a wire on it. And he's lookin' at that, and everybody saw the bullet go down there, everybody heard that. And I could see this guy lookin' at that. Now I have to top this off. I can't just let him look at it. I had to say something so terrible, I scared the dickens out of myself. I looked down there and he looked up at me and I said, "Eat it." Now all these guys could think of was anybody who would have a clip in his hand had to have a gun that's got another clip in it. And anybody who would do a thing like that, will kill ya. And I'm thinkin' to myself, geesh, what kind of situation am I in, I can't...I feel like my feet are tied up in that barstool, I can't get to that door that fast, before I could even think my way out of this thing, the guy picked the thing up and looked at it—and swallowed the damn bullet. And then he ran out the door. And I see all of these heads lookin' this way. They didn't know what to do. So I finished my beer, put my clip in my pocket and looked around and I went out, I got outside and I said, "Am I nuts?" I went out of my head. I'll never do that again, and I never have. Wild.

On set with Shirley Eaton on "The Girl Hunters."

MAC: You made another feature, a few years later (1970), "The Delta Factor," but didn't star in it.

SPILLANE: Christopher George, the guy who played the lead in that picture, is dead now. He played the "Desert Rat" in television and was from North Myrtle Beach (near Spillane's home in South Carolina). I knew him as a little kid when he first came up and asked for my autograph. It was strange. You know, he finally grew up and he became a hero in the picture and I felt like an old man. But it was a fun picture to do. It was not a Mike Hammer picture. But it was interesting to do, you know. I like to work and I like to get involved with these things. Sometimes, whatever you do, when you're making movies, something always comes in that's a major source of annoyance to you unless you put your own money in, get your own set, you own the whole production, then you can direct it and you can do what you want to do with it. But this picture again had problems, they all have problems.

MAC: The director was Tay Garnett?

SPILLANE: Tay's dead now, he used to direct the "Bonanza" series and Tay was good, but he was an old guy. He used to write the captions in silent picture days. And he never was quite up to the type of picture-making that we're making today. He was great at westerns. But this wasn't a western.

MAC: I heard you were involved in the editing of that picture.

SPILLANE: The first cut was so bad...unfortunately they did a terrible thing. They kicked me off the set for tellin' 'em that. Now I forgot that I was chairman of the board, and I could've come back and fired everybody on the spot. I didn't think that. The director's cut was such a terrible thing, I stood up and I said "Tay, I want to tell you somethin'." And I just let him have it. I couldn't stand the incompetency that age brought on. When I get too old to write, I'm gonna quit. If I can't handle the job, I'm gonna quit. This guy shoulda quit a long time ago. I did a lot of re-editing. I mean we tore out spots in there that they had going—they'd walk forever in that thing. I took out most of the walks and got 'em where they were goin'. And we had to do these things to make any sense out of the picture.

MAC: You got back in front of the camera again yourself, a few years later, didn't you? For the Miller Lite commercials?

SPILLANE: We took Lite beer from Miller, took it from a beer that wasn't in existence and made the second highest selling beer in the world. It was the first of all of the light beer sales that beat everybody out. And today, I don't go anyplace, in an airport, people see me, they'll yell at me, "Hey Mick, where's the Doll?" Now she gets the same thing. They'll say to her, "Hey, where's Mick?"

MAC: And 'the Doll,' of course was–

SPILLANE: That was Lee Meredith. She played the sexy blonde in "The Producers."

MAC: The rest of the Miller campaign centered on ex-athletes. What was a writer doing in there?

SPILLANE: I was the only one satirizing my character. I played Mike Hammer with a beautiful blonde, and she is exactly my size, we're both 5' 8". But we made her wear high heels. So she was always bigger than me. We did these things out of joy and the public got a sense of satisfaction watching these things. They were like mini-movies.

MAC: You and Lee went out on the promo circuit for Miller, too.

SPILLANE: We didn't know if we were going to talk to a group of doctors and lawyers, or to a bunch of little old ladies. And boy if you talk to little old ladies, they got they, whooo, these are wild people. They are very sensual-minded, believe me.

MAC: Any particularly memorable moments from those years?

SPILLANE: Hundreds. Once we were in a bowling alley where Dick Butkus and Bubba Smith had a scene together. Now they have these black bowling balls. And in the commercial, Butkus picks up the ball and he looks at it and he says, "Gee, Bubba, this ball got no holes in it." And Bubba shoves his fingers in and says, "There are now." Now how they did that, over the holes of the ball where your fingers go, they covered it with black tape so the audience couldn't see that. So they made about a dozen attempts to get everything goin', finally Billie Martin says, "Roll that ball down here." So he takes the tape off and puts it on the other side. And now Butkus says "Gee, Bubba, this ball has no holes in it." And Bubba jams his fingers in and says, "OOWWW!" Boy, round and round after Billie Martin they went—they couldn't catch him.

MAC: Any stories about Lee Meredith?

SPILLANE: Oh, yeah! We had these red jackets on, they were manager jackets, our logos over here and our numbers on us and all—and we were able to keep these clothes. I called the Doll the next day, I said, "Have you worn your jacket out yet?" "I was walkin' down Hollywood Boulevard in my jacket," she says. "You ought to hear what those were saying to me!" Now if you can picture this big beautiful blonde walkin' down Hollywood Boulevard in a bright red jacket with the Miller logo on the back that said, "Tastes Great." I said, don't ever wear that out like that, jeez. 'Cause, if it said "less filling," it would've been just as bad with the way she was built. She was built so she needed to have a license plate on her to walk down the street.

MAC: What made you trade in writing for being a commercial pitchman for such a long period of time?

SPILLANE: People don't understand somethin'. I have a job to do. My job is to keep earning and pay my taxes. I don't want to go out and dig ditches every day of the week, you know. When it comes to writing, I get tired of doing one thing, and now I'm at the point where I can start enjoyin' tappin' the keys again, you know.

MAC: Larry Cohen bought rights from the Saville estate to do the early '80s "I, the Jury" remake. You didn't have anything to do with that, right?

SPILLANE: That's right.

MAC: That picture, which starred Armand Assante, was not to your liking, in particular?

SPILLANE: No, he didn't fit the character at all. Armand is a great actor. But he's a very short guy. He did not fit the things that we had. On top of which, they wanted to throw a lot of sex into this picture, which was not what I had in the book. And, as usual, they went out and did it their way. It wasn't a successful picture. Unless they stick to the original type of story, it's going to be a failure.

MAC: Around the same time you began a long-lasting, personally and financially rewarding association with television producer Jay Bernstein. How did that come about?

SPILLANE: I was sittin' on an airplane on a coast-to-coast flight and was about to go to sleep and Jay walked in and he said, "She walked toward me, her hips waving a happy hello." And I says to myself, oh, gee, I got another fan, he's gonna sit down here, and talk to me all night when all I want to do is sleep. Now I've heard of Jay Bernstein, but, you know, I didn't really didn't connect this guy with that, and Jay Bernstein was a star-maker, big star-maker at that time. And before we got into New York, I had sold him the rights to Mike Hammer for one dollar. And we've been together for twenty years. And we've been through motion pictures, three TV shows, we were doin' real well. We're very honest with each other, we don't mess around. He says, I give him fits 'cause I won't fight with him. He's used to people, "I demand this, I demand that." I don't demand anything from Jay. He always does right by me and I do right by him, and it's a good medium to be in when

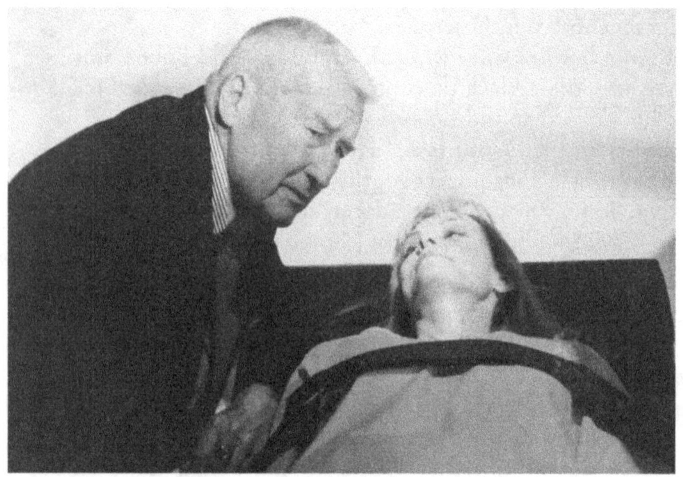

Mickey Spillane (as Ekhardt) with Patty McCormack (Mrs. Sterling) in "Mommy 2: Mommy's Day" (1997).

you are in a happy association. I think it's stupid when people steal from each other. How can you be partners with somebody who's going to steal from you, you know.

MAC: Stacy Keach is now almost as identified with Mike Hammer as you are.

SPILLANE: He's a well-adjusted actor. I think he went to Yale, you know, he went to all the schools. He does a lot of plays. He did big stuff like the "North and South" and, these big TV shows. But his big thing is Mike Hammer. Everybody knows Stacy Keach is Mike Hammer. So, who cares, as long as you got somethin' goin' for you that's good, viable and making money. So, Stacy came back as Mike Hammer in this new show, and everybody's very happy. They like Stacy. Apparently in this new show, it's not network, it's syndicated. It's on at a different hour. And they said, now they can go do things that couldn't do with the network version, make it rougher. The show is better now than it ever was. We've only seen two, so far—a week ago and then last night, and they are better. And they're making it on a much lower budget for some reason, but it's doin' well. Stacy's characterization is exactly right for this time and his age.

MAC: Let's come back, full circle, to comics. You wrote a Mike Hammer comic strip in the early '50s, but it didn't last long.

SPILLANE: We were the only comic strip that ever got kicked out because we got too sexy. But it was fun to do for a while. I had my friends do the artistry, Ed Robbins was doin' the art work, George Wilson did the lettering, I was doing the writing, with Joe Gill there helpin' me out.

MAC: Of course, Mike Hammer began as a comic book property, and in the last several years, you and I revived him for Big Entertainment.

SPILLANE: "Mike Danger" was the original prototype of Mike Hammer. And we had a good, happy three-year run with Big Entertainment.

MAC: You also helped me out with my two independent features ("Mommy," 1995, and "Mommy's Day," 1997). You played Patty McCormack's lawyer.

SPILLANE: I am not an actor, that's not my lifestyle. It's not my way of makin' a buck. But this was a nice time to do a nice little part...of course I didn't have a big role in it, you know.

MAC: You've taken a lot of hits over the years; no writer as successful as you are as ever taken such critical abuse. How were able to shrug off such vicious criticism?

SPILLANE: The public is the one that decides it all. Critics don't decide anything. Publishers don't decide. The public is the one who decides everything. If they don't buy the product, it fails. If they buy it, it goes. If all the people—to me, if a writer sells a lot of copies, he's good. I don't care if I don't read 'em. I know there are real writers on the market that I don't particularly like because I don't like the style of stuff that they do. But they sell a lot of books. So they're good at what they're doing.

MAC: I know you're a very religious man. Some people find your conservative beliefs to be at odds with what you're writing.

SPILLANE: I'm one of Jehovah's Witnesses, I don't write about that in a fiction story. I don't like to use street language. Anyway, my books were very moral. Mike Hammer had a black hat on, but you know, he did the right thing. It's just you were going against certain writing, accepted writing morals. I didn't care what they were sayin' at editorial offices. "You can't do it this way, you can't do it that way." Today, they have codes that they expect you to abide. I don't accept their codes. You got gender factors coming into it, you have to say certain things, go certain ways, you can't use certain words. They don't want you to use the word Negro, colored, they don't want anything that's identifiable. They don't want you talking about women in a certain way. I don't buy their attitudes. I don't like the way the world is at all today. Today's a mess.

MAC: You've brought Mike Hammer back, in the last several years, for *The Killing Man* (1989) and *Black Alley* (1996). And you keep threatening to write the "last" Mike Hammer novel. You're not going to kill Mike off, are you?

SPILLANE: No! He's my bread 'n' butter boy. I gotta keep that smoke comin' out that chimney.

Bibliography

Barnouw, Erik. *The Television Writer: Techniques and Practices.* New York: Hill and Wang, 1962. [Frank Kane teleplay notes]

Botham, Noel, and Tony Brenna. "Stiff Sentence for Drug Smuggling Turns Mike Hammer into Jelly." *National Enquirer*, December 25, 1984, p. 12.

Brooks, Tim, and Earle Marsh. *The Complete Directory to Prime Time Network and Cable TV Shows, 1946-Present.* New York: Ballantine, 1979.

Cameron, Gail. "The Soft Side of a Hard Egg." *Life*, September 8, 1961, pp. 127–130.

"Cheers for 'Murder Me, Murder You.'" *TV Guide*, May 28, 1983, p.23. ["best TV version of a Spillane thriller yet"]

Clemens, Matthew V. "Mickey Spillane the Myth," "Mickey Spillane alias Mike Hammer," and "Mickey Spillane The Dolls." *Femme Fatales* 7,7 (December 1998): 42–53, 60.

Collins, Max Allan. "Mickey Spillane." *St. James Guide to Crime and Mystery Writers.* Detroit: St. James Press, 1996. [Written in collaboration with James L. Traylor.]

_____. "Mickey Spillane in Hollywood." *Psychotronic Video* 28 (1998): 34—42.

_____. "Mickey Spillane: Lord of the Ring." *Videoscope* 60 (Fall 2006): 28.

_____. "Mickey Spillane's *Day of the Guns.*" In *1001 Midnights: The Aficionado's Guide to Mystery and Detective Fiction*, ed. Bill Pronzini and Marcia Muller. New York: Arbor House, 1986. [Written in collaboration with James L. Traylor.]

_____. "Mickey Spillane's Return to the Pulps." *The Thieftaker Journal Annual: Brass Knuckles and Back Alleys* 2,6 (1983): 10–13. [Written in collaboration with James L. Traylor.]

_____. "Mickey Spillane's Tiger Mann." *The Armchair Detective* 17,1 (Winter 1984): 74–79. [Written in collaboration with James L. Traylor.]

_____. *Mike Hammer's Mickey Spillane.* 1999 documentary included in the DVD boxed set "The Black Box: Shades of Neo-Noir," Troma, 2005.

_____. "The Real Hammer Film: Mickey Spillane's THE GIRL HUNTERS." *Video Watchdog* 62 (August 2000): 42—47.

_____. "This Is Mike Hammer." *Hardboiled* 2 (Fall 1985): 11–14.

_____, and James L. Traylor. *One Lonely Knight: Mickey Spillane's Mike Hammer.* Bowling Green, OH: Popular Press, 1984.

Crist, Judith. "1981 in Review: the 10 Best TV-Movies." *TV Guide*, January 2, 1982, pp. 4–6, 8.

_____. "The Return of Mickey Spillane's Mike Hammer." *TV Guide*, April 18, 1986, p. A6–A7.

_____."This Week's Movies: 'Mickey Spillane's Margin for Murder.'" *TV Guide*, October 16, 1981, pp. A-5, A-139.

Deeb, Gary. "'Hammer' kept alive for interim." *USA Today*, April 5, 1985, p. 4B.

Eaton, Shirley. *Golden Girl.* Foreword by Mickey Spillane. London: B. T. Batsford, 1999.

Elliot, Biff. http://www.biffelliot.com/.

Erasmus Hall High School. http://www.erasmushall.org/.

Everson, William K. *The Detective in Film.* Secaucus, NJ: The Citadel Press, 1972.

Forshaw, Barry. *Rough Guide to Crime Fiction.* London: Penguin, 2005.

Fort Hays State University. http://www.fhsu.edu/.

Francis, Paul. "How Stacy Keach's brother is standing by him: TV's Mike Hammer's on the 'inside' looking out." *Examiner*, February 19, 1985, p. 33.

_____. "Insider Grapevine: How Broad-Minded of 'Em." *TV Guide*, September 20, 1986, p. 17. [Nina Foch comment] Garnett, Tay, with Fredda Dudley Balling. *Light Your Torches and Pull Up Your Tights.* New York: Arlington House, 1973.

Gehr, Richard. "The Atomic Gun: Mickey Spillane." *Film Comment*, 20,5 (September-October, 1984): 38–39.
Gorman, Ed, Lee Server and Martin H. Greenberg, eds. *The Big Book of Noir*. New York: Carroll & Graf, 1998.
Green, Tom. "'Hammer' has just the right cocky tone." *USA Today*, January 26, 1984, p. 5D.
"Guess Who?" *TV Guide*, November 24, 1984, p. A-2. [Jay Bernstein's statement about "big-name" guests]
Halliwell, Leslie. *Halliwell's Filmgoer's Companion*. 6th ed. New York: Scribner's, 1977.
"Hammer in the Slammer." *TV Guide*, December 22, 1984 p. A-2. [Stacy Keach cocaine update]
Hoberman, J. "The Thriller of Tomorrow." Part of booklet included in the package of the Criterion DVD/Blu-Ray "Kiss Me Deadly," 2011.
Hunter, Evan. "Kiss Me, Dudley." In *The Comfortable Coffin*, ed. Richard S. Prather. Greenwich, CT: Gold Medal Books, No. K1297, n. d., pp. 162–168.
Internet Movie Database. http://www.imdb.com/.
"Jail turns Keach off on cocaine." *Atlanta Constitution*, March 16, 1985, p. 2.
Johnston, Richard W. "Death's Fair-haired Boy." *Life*, June 23, 1952, pp. 79–95. [The cover blurb reads: "Mickey Spillane: 13,000,000 books of sex and slaughter."]
Keach, Stacy. http://www.stacykeach.com/.
"Keach: Starving Artist." *TV Guide*, April 7, 1984, p. 25.
King, Bill. "Updating a tough guy: Stacy Keach shoots straight as the newest Mike Hammer." *Atlanta Constitution, TV WEEK*, February 26, 1984, pp. 4–5.
"Kiss Me Deadly." Criterion Blu-Ray DVD, 2011.
Latta, John. "Mike Hammer's Wife: We're Nearly Broke—But I'm Sticking with Him." *National Enquirer*, February 19, 1985, p. 35. [Jill and Stacy Keach]
Lavine, Elliott, and Bob Stephens. "Dark Voyage: A Passage through 25 years of film noir." *The Perfect Vision* 4,15 (Fall 1992): 120–132.
Library of Congress. http://www.loc.gov/.
MacKenzie, Robert. "Review: 'Mickey Spillane's Mike Hammer.'" *TV Guide*, March 30, 1984.
McGavin, Darren. "Interview." *Scarlet Street* 16, 1994. Quoted at http://www.darrenmcgavin.net/.
Maltin, Leonard. *Movie Guide*. New York: Plume, 2008. [Issued annually.]
Meyers, Richard. *TV Detectives*. San Diego: A. S. Barnes, 1979.
Murphy, Mark. "Sex, Sadism and Scripture." *True*, July 1952, p. 17+.
O'Connor, John J. "TV: Kevin Dobson as New Mike Hammer." *New York Times*, October 15, 1981, p. 24.
O'Hallaren, Bill. "She Was Willing to Dye for What She Believed In." *TV Guide*, September 6, 1986, pp. 34–37. [Lindsay Bloom]
Rough Guide to Cult Movies. London: Penguin, 2004.
Saville, Victor. *Evergreen: Victor Saville in His Own Words*. As told to Roy Moseley. Carbondale: Southern Illinois University Press, 2000.
Scheuer, Steven H. *TV Key Movie Reviews & Ratings*. New York: Bantam, 1961.
Shadoian, Jack. *Dreams and Dead Ends: The American Gangster/Crime Film*. Cambridge: MIT Press, 1977.
"The Shaving-Cream Caper." *TV Guide*, May 5, 1984, p. A-3. [cocaine found in Stacy Keach's luggage at London's Heathrow Airport]
Silver, Alain, and Elizabeth Ward. *Film Noir*. New York: Overlook Press, 1979.
Singer, Michael. "After Work, Stacy Keach Throws His Suits in a Corner." *TV Guide*, August 25, 1984, pp. 26–31.
Spillane, Mickey. "Writing Should Be fun." *Memories*, April/May 1990.
"Spillane's Dames." *Dare*, June 1954, pp. 46–47.
Traylor, James L. "Characternyms in Mickey Spillane's Mike Hammer." *The Armchair Detective* 16,3 (Summer 1983): 293–295.
_____. "The Great Detectives: Mickey Spillane's Mike Hammer." *The Strand Magazine* XXVI (October 2008): 65–66.
_____. "Mickey Spillane and Mike Hammer." *Clues* 5,2 (Fall/Winter 1984): 9–19. [Written in collaboration with John A. Traylor, M. D.]
_____. "Mickey Spillane: Interview." *Mystery Scene*, 23 (October/November 1989): 15–16.
_____. "The Violent World of Mike Hammer." *The Mystery FANcier* 7,6 (November/December 1983): 13–20.
Turner, Richard. "Keach Sentence Surprises CBS." *TV Guide*, January 12, 1985, p. A-1.
Turner Classic Movies Movie Database. http://www.tcm.com/.
TV Guide editors. *TV Guide: Guide to TV*. New York: Barnes & Noble, 2004.
"Waiting Game." *TV Guide*, April 19, 1986, p. 28. [Don Stroud and Lindsay Bloom await word of "Mike Hammer" renewal.]

Index

Numbers in ***bold italics*** indicate pages with photographs.

www.ingramcontent.com/pod-product-compliance
Lightning Source LLC
Chambersburg PA
CBHW081332090726
47907CB00011B/2454